Abou

Mark is a qualified solicitor who splits his time between protecting the rights of academics, writing thriller fiction and raising five mostly lovely children. He studied Archaeology and Ancient History at the University of Birmingham with a nod towards alternative theory, focusing on the relationship of the Giza complex to the stars; portolan maps; and the origins of civilisation and religion. It was within this flame the plots for his future novels were born. Mark's writing career extends back over a decade and his diverse portfolio includes three novels, a number of short stories and even a six-part sitcom. Long listed for the Amazon Breakthrough Novel Award, he is currently a featured author on the popular writing website Wattpad, garnering over 6,000 followers from all around the world and achieving well over one million reads of his first novel.

THE ATLANTIS DECEPTION

MARK H JACKSON

Unbound Digital

This edition first published in 2018

Unbound

6th Floor Mutual House, 70 Conduit Street, London W1S 2GF

www.unbound.com

ISBN (eBook): 9781912618231
ISBN (Paperback): 9781912618224

Design by Mecob

Illustrations by John Howse (XWWX)

Printed in Great Britain by Clays Ltd, Elcograf S.p.A.

Dear Reader,

The book you are holding came about in a rather different way to most others. It was funded directly by readers through a new website: Unbound.

Unbound is the creation of three writers. We started the company because we believed there had to be a better deal for both writers and readers. On the Unbound website, authors share the ideas for the books they want to write directly with readers. If enough of you support the book by pledging for it in advance, we produce a beautifully bound special subscribers' edition and distribute a regular edition and e-book wherever books are sold, in shops and online.

This new way of publishing is actually a very old idea (Samuel Johnson funded his dictionary this way). We're just using the internet to build each writer a network of patrons. Here, at the back of this book, you'll find the names of all the people who made it happen.

Publishing in this way means readers are no longer just passive consumers of the books they buy, and authors are free to write the books they really want. They get a much fairer return too – half the profits their books generate, rather than a tiny percentage of the cover price.

If you're not yet a subscriber, we hope that you'll want to join our publishing revolution and have your name listed in one of our books in the future. To get you started, here is a £5 discount on your first pledge. Just visit unbound.com, make your pledge and type ATLANTIS18 in the promo code box when you check out.

Thank you for your support,

Dan, Justin and John
Founders, Unbound

Super Patrons

Brian Allen
Phoebe Allman-Burt
Jason Ballinger
William Bonwitt
Hayden Bunday
Liam Carr
Lucy Chambers
April Chantler
Chris Chantler
RIS & UoP Colleagues
Kate Dance
Kirsten Duell
James Fisher
Steve Fleming
Sam Gardiner
James Golding
Mark Haley
Paul Harris
Boo Holmquest
Dan Hosey
Jenny Howse
Ciaran Howse
Chris Howse
Malcolm Howse
Brooke Howse
Tom Howse
Julian Hynd
Isabelle Jackson
Pauline Jackson
Victoria Jackson
Oliver Jackson
William Jackson

Mike James
Pauline Jeffs
Richard Johnston
Igor Kaplun
Jan Keeling
Dan Kieran
Amber King
Jules Kirby-Smith
Merv Langdale
Ewan Lawrie
Piers McEwan
Paul McInerney
John Mitchinson
George Newick
Gregory Olver
Inma Pérez Vázquez
Justin Pollard
Graham Pretty
Anthony Radcliff
Simon Reed
Zelda Rhiando
Richard Robinson
Richard Rutter
Kate Smith
Stuart Smith
Joy and Mike Swift
Mark Vent
Colin Waring
Craig Watkins
Luke Weston
Rachel Wright

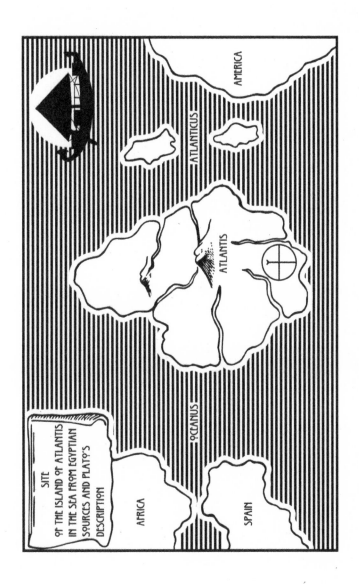

SITE OF THE ISLAND OF ATLANTIS IN THE SEA FROM EGYPTIAN SOURCES AND PLATO'S DESCRIPTION

AMERICA

ATLANTICUS

ATLANTIS

OCEANUS

AFRICA

SPAIN

Prologue

Lindow Moss Bog, December 43 CE

Teetering on the edge of unconsciousness, Caratacus squirmed as a pair of coarse hands pulled and tugged at his robes. Death was inevitable, yet still he managed a flicker of a smile. These men would never find what they sought.

He grimaced as a heavy hobnail sandal connected with his ribcage, the blow hard enough to flip him over and onto his back. He blinked and opened his eyes to find his chubby, chinless assailant peering down at him.

The Roman wrapped his pristine, cream-coloured sagum tighter around his chest to shut out the cold wind. He looked nothing like the brutish military commanders Caratacus typically dealt with. The man's regal air of arrogance and contempt for the soldiers around him made it clear he was a Roman of importance. It was an arrogance only men of unimaginable wealth and power could ever hope to wield with success, particularly amongst a group of Praetorian guards.

Caratacus sensed the Roman's gaze rake his naked body; the man's tight lips and beady eyes radiated a general air of cruelty which sent a chill coursing through the captured priest. His muscles twitched, tense in anticipation of what might follow. He broke eye contact and cleared his mind, attempting to relax. He wasn't far from death and rule dictated he must embrace the moment.

'You are a hard man to track down, Druid,' sneered the stranger. 'Or would you prefer I call you by your official title – Gatekeeper?' He paused, giving Caratacus time to digest the significance of this revelation. 'You seem calm for a man on his way to Pluto's realm. Do you not recognise me, priest?'

Caratacus puffed his cheeks and spat blood at the man's feet, regretting it as a wave of pain surged through his earthly body.

The Roman's eyes narrowed to slits. He stepped clear of the blood and raised a foot, mashing his muddy sandal deep into Caratacus' wounded shoulder. 'I am Claudius, Emperor of Rome, and conqueror of your pathetic island race.' Claudius hesitated before continuing, his eyes narrowing in hope of at least a flicker of recognition. 'Well? Have you nothing to say? It is not every day you chance upon a living god.'

Caratacus screwed up his eyes as another hobnail boot connected with his nether regions and a thick-fingered fist smashed into his jaw. 'Show respect, barbarian,' barked a Praetorian. An excruciating bolt of pain shot through him and he rolled back onto his side. He retched and coughed blood through his shattered jaw, wincing as he realised it was no longer attached to his skull. Between his legs he saw the soldier shrink away, fearful of his emperor's reaction. 'Sir, I'm not sure if he can speak.'

'Praetorian, your orders were to deliver this man unharmed. Is this unharmed, *stulte?*' The Praetorian shook his head and edged beyond the range of Claudius' sword. 'What good is he if he cannot speak?' Caratacus groaned as the heavyset emperor straddled his chest, barely registering the pain as Claudius slapped his cheek. He tried to resist, but the effort was futile. He gagged, choking on the blood coagulating in his throat. The light of the day faded to pinpricks. Death was close. Caratacus' heart stuttered as darkness enveloped him, beating its final beat as he surrendered himself to God.

'Where have you put it, Gatekeeper?' said Claudius. 'Tell me now or by Jupiter I swear I'll...'

The priest's head lolled, all life draining from his once-bright eyes. The Praetorians glanced at one another uneasily, each of them aware the Druid lay dead between their Emperor's thighs. Claudius cursed and shoved the body aside, watching with morbid interest as the battered body sank into a puddle of its own muddied blood. Killing the man was not part of the plan; well, at least not before he'd extracted a confession.

The Emperor thrust out a hand and one of his men pulled him to his feet. 'Cut his throat and bury him in the bog.' He clenched his fists. 'Then find his belongings. Find them, or I'll order you buried with him.'

Part One

The Lindow Man Bog Body, Cheshire

Chapter One

Jesus College, Cambridge

Dr John Hunter tipped back his head, gulping down water. He shuffled his feet and, with a flick of the wrist, swept sweat from his forehead. The Great Hall of Jesus College, Cambridge was in uproar and he couldn't understand why. Although he'd witnessed hundreds of speakers take to this podium, in no way was he prepared for the vitriol and incessant venom-laced heckling his every sentence instigated. He shook his head and gazed around the room. Even the Masters in the paintings lining the walls seemed to disapprove of his stance.

The lecture was not going quite as originally envisioned. When he announced the topic, he knew his theories would generate opposition, but nothing on this scale. Hunter scanned the room, recognising academics from institutions as widely spread as Edinburgh, Exeter, Stirling and Southampton. He thought of the bitter argument he'd fought out with his old supervisor, Professor Esmeralda Cleary. She'd ordered him to cancel, swearing he'd regret it should he disobey. Pride railroaded him into pressing ahead out of spite; a decision he was beginning to regret.

Cleary must have called in a few favours to assemble this kind of crowd, particularly one so hell-bent on disputing every word he dared utter. Usually academics reserved critique of this ferocity for periodicals: a domain where they could dissect and discredit theories in a measured and clinical fashion. In Hunter's mind, this face-to-face attack was both needless and disrespectful but, more than that, he felt betrayed by those he'd previously counted as friends as well as peers.

At last, as the louder cries of 'Rubbish!' and 'Nonsense!' died down, Hunter grasped the opportunity to press on with his material. 'As I was saying, Lindow Man was discovered with multiple wounds to the head; a fractured skull; broken jaw; snapped collarbone; and a slit throat.' He paused, turning to tap the gruesome picture lit up on the screen behind him. 'I assume the common consensus in the room is that this Iron Age man died as part of a ritual ceremony sometime around 50 CE. Perhaps sacrificed to appease a god for a bad crop, promote fertility or, given what was happening in the wider world, offered to the gods in exchange for protection against Roman invasion.'

A portly gentleman in the front row turned an odd shade of purple. 'And I suppose you're here to tell us we're all wrong.'

'To be frank, Dr Weadon, yes I am. Our profession has made it far too easy to tick the "ritual" box when we come across unexpected artefacts or scenarios in the course of our research. I bet if Jack the Ripper's dissected victims hadn't been discovered, archaeology would label him a high priest and his victims "ritual" sacrifices.'

With his effort to lighten the atmosphere falling on deaf ears, Hunter covered the uncomfortable silence by banging the lectern and slapping his pointer against the decaying man in the slide. 'I put it to you this man is a murder victim... The ritual argument is more than weak and warrants immediate re-examination. Common belief assumes Lindow Man to be a high-ranking priest or Druid. If true, then why did he struggle at the point of death? If a victim of sacrifice, why wasn't the kill clean? Compare him with a sacrificial bog body of a similar age.' Another bog body appeared on the screen. 'Manchester's Worsley Man was simply decapitated, his only other wound being behind the right ear, probably incurred while being knocked unconscious prior to death. This is not evident in Lindow Man. Indeed, if he were a member of the religious fraternity, why then wasn't he a willing participant? What could be more glorious for a priest than to be martyred? It is the ultimate selfless act, to give up one's life for the greater good and a higher cause.'

Hunter cleared his throat. 'But, and this is the crux of my theory, it is clear our Iron Age friend did not agree with this mantra. Instead of embracing death, all our evidence indicates he did everything in his power to evade it.' He pointed to the image of Lindow Man on the screen. 'Look at the V-shaped fracture on top of the skull. This wound can only have been inflicted by a glancing blow from something blunt; perhaps a rock thrown from distance or some kind of cosh.'

He tapped other parts of the body. 'Now combine this injury with a jawbone snapped in a fashion consistent with a punch and a shattered collarbone my forensics colleagues tell me was literally ground into the shoulder.' He turned back to his audience. 'What we have now is the makings of an alternative theory. Ladies and gentlemen, I submit there is no way this man can be a sacrifice. Lindow Man is a clear victim of torture and eventual murder.'

A few members of his audience booed and hissed. 'Forensics? Where do you think we are, Hunter, the Old Bailey or something?' someone barracked.

Hunter ignored the laughter and pressed on, refusing to be derailed again. 'I would go further and submit these wounds are consistent with those inflicted when someone is pursued. I believe Lindow Man was hunted down, murdered and buried in the bog. The question we should be asking is why?'

'Enough! Enough of this preposterous nonsense.'

Hunter's heart sank as Professor Cleary, immaculately dressed as always in a dark-brown tweed jacket and skirt, rose to her feet. 'I must object and question where your evidence has come from, Dr Hunter,' said the professor, addressing the room rather than Hunter. 'If indeed you have any evidence... Or is this another nail I should hammer into your already dubious credibility? Need I remind our distinguished guests of your scandalous foray into the Atlantis debate? Are we witnessing yet another of your fictional and unsubstantiated theories take form?' Turning back to the lectern she waggled a bony finger in Hunter's direction. 'We are a profession committed to dealing in evidence and proof, Dr Hunter, not idle speculation and guesswork.'

Hunter stammered incoherently, the right words refusing to materialise in his bone-dry mouth.

'How many more of these "lectures" are we going to endure,' continued Cleary, 'before you realise you are not, and never will be, the next Howard Carter? In fact, the way your career is progressing it won't be long before your name is only associated with that of a fraudster and a fantasist. Correct me if I'm wrong, but I'm told you set up this farcical lecture purely for the benefit of this country's sensationalist gutter press and of course for your own financial gain.' She waved a hand at a small man in the front row busily taking notes. 'No offence to you or your excellent publication, sir.'

The reporter grinned back, clearly enjoying the showmanship. 'None taken.'

'And so, Dr Hunter, do you deny you have made money from this absurd theory?'

Hunter stared down at his former mentor and drummed his fingers on the lectern, fighting hard to suppress the fury bubbling up inside him. 'Professor Cleary, I am not trying to discredit your work and indeed agree with many of your conclusions. I don't know what's going on here and question why you have gone to such great lengths to humiliate me so publicly. It's true I've spoken to the media, but only after they approached me. I am certain if you had something worthy of reporting they would probably speak to you as well.'

Cleary stared back at him in silence, her eyes narrowing just enough for Hunter to know his words had hit their mark.

'If you will not give me the courtesy of a reply,' said Hunter, 'at least give me the professional courtesy of listening to me speak.' He looked around the hall. 'That is why you are all here is it not?' Embarrassed laughter wafted about the room. Hunter waved his arm for silence, a silence which, this time, his audience granted.

'Thank you. Now, while I admit to a degree of speculation, the nature of the wounds supports my theory this man was hunted and captured. Whatever his pursuers were after they clearly didn't find it and resorted to torture. Unfortunately they were a little too enthusiastic in the task and killed our victim.'

'What makes you think this wasn't a straightforward mugging?' asked the reporter.

'It is possible, but then why would the killers bother to rough up their victim and prolong the chance of having witnesses appear? Surely a knife through the heart and a quick getaway would be preferable in those circumstances.'

'Assuming you are right, how do you know they didn't find what they were looking for and kill him afterwards?' said Cleary. 'Why all this cloak-and-dagger nonsense? What do you think he was hiding? The meaning of life? The keys to the kingdom of heaven?'

'This is perhaps where I can help you out,' boomed a voice from the back of the room. The man stood and made his way down the aisle towards the podium. 'My name is Hans Hoffmann.'

Hunter's eyelids flickered. He recognised the face from somewhere but could not place it. In this context, the long blond hair alongside the fitted, Armani-style cream suit looked very out of place amongst the drably attired academics. He flicked back his hair and shoved Hunter aside, grasping the microphone. 'Hello, Jesus. I am the owner of Hoffmann Developments.'

Hunter detected the hint of a German accent behind the façade of a British public school education. Hoffmann Developments rang a bell but again he couldn't quite place the context. Hoffmann winked at him and grinned, unveiling an expensive set of bright white-capped teeth. The smile... That was it; if memory served, Mr Hoffmann had recently executed a ridiculous publicity stunt on behalf of his company and parachuted into a garden party held within the grounds of Buckingham Palace. The feat had inadvertently or, as Hunter suspected, intentionally caused an enormous furore over the safety of the Queen and the competence of Palace security. Although Hoffmann possessed an invitation, the media still went into overdrive and the usual 'what if?' claptrap did the rounds for a good few days afterwards in the tabloids.

'I've acquired the rights to develop the Lindow Moss bog in the area where this Iron Age man was discovered.' Hoffmann smiled as a series of horrified gasps resonated around the room.

'But it's protected,' said Hunter. 'How did you get planning permission?'

'Don't be naive, Dr Hunter,' said Hoffmann.

'Balderdash,' said Cleary. 'The environmentalists would have been campaigning against you for months and I've heard nothing.' A murmur of agreement drifted about the room. 'Has this melodramatic drivel got anything to do with you, Hunter?'

'As much as I would love to discuss political ethics with you all I am here to deliver a much more exciting message,' said Hoffmann. He

7

thrust a hand in Hunter's direction. 'It is time to get down to business. Dr Hunter, I am here to offer you a job.'

A second gasp echoed about the auditorium.

'Your law requires the site must undergo a full excavation prior to the development phase,' said Hoffmann. 'You are the man I want in post to oversee the project.'

Hunter grasped the offered hand and leant against the lectern in a state of subdued shock. If Hoffmann was for real, he'd just presented Hunter with what might be the biggest dig of his career. Every archaeologist in the room would have killed for a chance like this.

'Plus,' Hoffmann continued, 'I want to give you the opportunity of proving your theory and discrediting that obnoxious woman standing over there.'

'Who are you to insult me? How dare you,' said Cleary, leaping to her feet. 'John, tell me you are not contemplating accepting this ridiculous offer? You do not have the pedigree.'

'Pedigree? How dare you, madam,' said Hunter, snapping out of his trance. 'Mr Hoffmann, I unequivocally accept your kind offer. Two thousand years ago a man was murdered on the Lindow Moss bog and I fully intend to find out why.'

Chapter Two

Hunter sucked in a deep breath in an attempt to reinvigorate his ine-briated mind. The billionaire had invited him out for dinner while the ink was still wet on their contract. Given the circumstances, it was an invitation he'd been compelled to accept. The meal started out civilly enough but, as more and more wine lubricated the evening, it soon dissolved into a drinking session at the Granta, a public house on the banks of the River Cam.

'Nice spot to knock back a pint or two wouldn't you say, Hunter?' said Hoffmann, nodding at the famous Mathematical Bridge and the beautiful mediaeval, red-brick buildings of Queens' College. 'Sitting here always used to make me feel I could achieve anything. Just knowing Sir Isaac Newton may have stood on this very spot to admire his bridge is just incredible.'

Hunter smiled. 'Sorry to burst your bubble, but Newton had noth-ing to do with the bridge. In fact, he died twenty-two years before the build date.'

'You're kidding? So who did build it?'

'A chap called James Essex in 1749. Don't worry, you aren't alone – many people still believe it was Newton. I'm not sure how the myth came about but it's funny how quickly it took hold. Now everyone, and not just the tourists, accepts it as fact.'

'I stand corrected, Dr Hunter,' said Hoffmann, taking a sip of his Spitfire bitter. 'On the subject of myths, I believe you've been a little guilty of chasing fables yourself.'

Hunter squirmed in his seat. Had he fallen for a ruse to get him talking about a topic he wished would just go away?

'You mentioned admiring the bridge in your past,' asked Hunter. 'Were you a student here?'

'Jesus College alumnus 1994. Like you, I came to study archaeology under the great Lord Renfrew of Kaimsthorn.'

'Are you serious – we took the same subject? And at the same col-lege?'

Hoffmann nodded. 'Which is another reason I know about your background in Atlantean lore.'

Hunter rolled his eyes. 'I take it you've read a few of my papers then?'

Hoffmann stroked his chin. 'I dabble in both current and alternative theory. So yes, your work has cropped up.'

Hunter licked the backs of his teeth and let out a defeated sigh, scanning the pub for anyone he knew. The subject of Atlantis was poison to the credibility of an academic and, given his antics earlier on in the evening, it was clear his credibility was on thin ice as it was. 'You're aware I gave up researching the topic a good three years ago?'

'Don't be so defensive, Dr Hunter, you have nothing to fear from me. I'm a believer. Lost civilisations, sunken kingdoms and buried treasure; we all know they're the real reasons students study archaeology. We all want to be Indiana Jones. Hard to imagine a stiff like Cleary feeling that way though.'

Hunter grinned. 'Careful, Hans, remember I'm one of those "stiffs" now.'

'Yes, but are you a stiff with an open mind or a stiff forced to sell out to save face?'

Hunter grimaced. 'Look, can we discuss this later? Perhaps somewhere a little less public. The label of Atlantean expert is not something I'm keen to promote any more. Right now I'd rather find out what you expect me to unearth in the bog. Are you expecting more bodies? Buried treasure? And while we're on the topic, how did you get your planning permission? I've had a quick look on my phone and there's no mention of it.'

'So many questions, Dr Hunter,' snorted Hoffmann. 'The short answer to the last one being I didn't. I made it up to generate some buzz in the papers. I need this news to go national.'

'Tell me you're joking,' said Hunter. He massaged his temples to stop his stress levels rising. 'Is the dig real? Please tell me the dig is real. My reputation is riding on this.'

'Don't worry, the dig is real enough. That's the one thing I do have permission for.'

A weight lifted from Hunter's shoulders. Not only was his job safe, but so was the site. 'Thank God. Okay, so why would you choose to court negative publicity?'

'Forget that for the moment. All will be revealed soon enough. Now, let me pour you another beer, and perhaps I can steer the conversation back in the direction of Atlantis…'

Hunter shook his head in defeat. 'Christ, you're like a dog with a bone.'

'I find it's the best way to get results.'

Hunter placed his glass on the table and began tracing a finger around its rim. 'For years I was obsessed with the city, obsessed to the point of stupidity. I read everything there was to read. I plotted maps, chartered boats, and probably spent as much time underwater as I did on land.'

'What do you mean, "to the point of stupidity"?'

'Obsession blinded my judgement; I wasn't thinking rationally. I made the error of trying to justify my theories by only using the evidence that fitted. I ignored anything that didn't.'

'Sounds like standard academic practice to me.'

Hunter snorted. 'True, but most theories don't usually get much further than the pages of some obscure periodical. My passion must have come through in a funding application and somehow managed to convince the university and the British Museum to co-fund an expedition to Thera.'

'In Greece?' asked Hoffmann.

'That's the one. I was convinced the Atlantis myth was borne out of the destruction of the Minoan civilisation by a supervolcano.'

'Not the best place to base a civilisation,' said Hoffmann.

'Definitely not. The eruption was four times the power of Krakatoa and twenty times more powerful than the eruption of Mount St Helens back in 1980.'

'Bloody hell.' Hoffmann grinned. 'So more than powerful enough to bury a civilisation in "one grievous day and night".'

'You've read Plato's dialogues?'

Hoffmann nodded. 'But of course. What would-be Atlantophile hasn't?' He paused. 'So what did you find on Thera?'

'Not what I hoped… I uncovered a previously unknown Minoan

settlement. A lucky break that justified the funding and probably saved my career.' Hunter sniffed, staring glassy eyed at the River Cam over the German's shoulder. 'As for Atlantis and its circular city of walls and moats… I guess it just wasn't meant to be.'

Reality dawned on Hunter as he dragged himself into semi-consciousness. He opened his eyes but instantly regretted it and snapped them shut. How could it be so bright? He lay for a few minutes with his arm crossed over his face and praying for death. But with the Grim Reaper seemingly busy elsewhere he slid to the floor and crawled on all fours to the kitchen. His head was pounding. He needed coffee and ideally through a drip.

As he passed the front door, he heard the letterbox open and snap shut with a crack that did his hangover no favours. He scowled at the unseen paperboy beyond his door and grabbed the local paper from his welcome mat. He scanned the headlines and rubbed his sleep-ridden eyes in disbelief as one particular story leapt out at him:

Germans Invade Cambridge College

The story had made the front page. He smiled and opened the paper to find the rest of the article. A picture of Hans Hoffmann, standing proudly in front of one of his developments, grinned out at him beside the text. Evidently the Hoffmann PR machine had wasted little time in publicising its involvement. He skimmed through the passage and winced as he reached the final line.

Prior to developing the site for housing, Hoffmann has offered to fund a full excavation in the hope of finding evidence to unmask an ancient killer.

'Bugger,' thought Hunter, 'That'll set a few metal detectors in motion.'

The phone rang. Hunter picked up the receiver.

'Hunter.'

'John, Hans Hoffmann here. Have you seen a copy of the article?'

'Yes, it's open in front of me now.'

'My plan to publicise our little excavation has unfortunately worked rather quicker than expected. Can you get yourself to the dig site ASAP?'

Chapter Three

Manchester

A broad, muscular man in his late thirties greeted Hunter with a cardboard sign at Manchester Piccadilly train station. The human buffalo thrust out a hand and introduced himself as Darren Frasier, Hans Hoffmann's personal bodyguard. Hunter took the hand but regretted it as his fingers were crushed in a vice-like grip. He threw his bags into a Hoffmann-branded Range Rover and flexed his fingers, pretending not to be in pain. This Darren fellow was certainly not someone to be taken lightly.

The journey to the dig site was a largely silent affair. Hunter used the time to review his notes while Darren absorbed himself in the build-up to an England football match on the radio. Forty minutes later the car pulled alongside a high, barbed-wire fence emblazoned with Hoffmann's corporate logo. Hunter swept his hair from his eyes and gazed through the fence in confusion. What the hell was happening? Beyond the fence, several uniformed police officers were mingling amongst Hoffmann's employees. They appeared to be conducting interviews.

'This is it, Dr Hunter,' said Darren. 'This is your dig site.'

Hunter slammed his door shut and stared up at the numerous CCTV cameras scattered about the gated entrance.

'This is a little over the top for a site still in the planning stages. What aren't you telling me? Why are the police here?'

Darren shuffled his feet and glossed over the question by raising an arm and hailing his boss. Hoffmann waved in their direction and excused himself from a conversation with a pair of police officers. He let the flap drop on the doorway of a large artefact tent which was doubling as the headquarters for an investigation. Confused by what was happening, Hunter decided simply to let the situation play out and followed in Darren's ample wake as he made a beeline for the property magnate. Hoffmann still hadn't told Hunter why he'd ordered him to the dig site at such short notice and he was keen to get answers.

'Mr Hoffmann, Dr Hunter as requested,' announced Darren.

Hoffmann shook his hand and grinned. 'I'll be with you in a minute, Hunter. Why don't you nip inside the tent and grab yourself a drink?'

Hunter nodded and, lifting the entrance flap aside, beckoned for Darren to follow. 'Come on, Darren. Don't hold back on me. What's going on? Why are the police here?'

Darren broke eye contact and looked at his feet. 'I should apologise, Dr Hunter. It's embarrassing but our current predicament is my fault.'

'Predicament? What predicament?'

'I was the guard on duty when it happened. Mr Hoffmann wanted his most experienced man on site but I failed him. The bastards slipped by me and contaminated our water supply with Rohypnol.'

'Rohypnol? The date-rape drug?'

'Indeed, it knocked my team out for hours. When I… Well, you can see for yourself.' Darren swept aside a flap at the rear of the tent and waved a hand at the scene beyond. Hunter took a deep breath and, fearing the worst, stepped back into the winter sunshine. His fears were well founded. Mounds of earth and a series of shallow pits covered the dig site, each of them no wider or deeper than a metre.

'Jesus, there's more than usual,' he whispered.

Darren looked puzzled. 'You know about these? So you know what they are?'

'The work of black-market treasure hunters I expect. They're the bane of my professional life. I'm guessing several local scavengers spotted the newspaper article and hightailed it to the site with metal detectors.' Hunter took another look at the pits and shook his head. 'Saying that, scavenger pits aren't usually as regularised as these.' Hunter balled his fists, cracking his knuckles in frustration. 'It's almost as if someone systematically dug a bunch of test pits right across the site.'

Darren nodded. 'Your analysis is correct. This was well planned and premeditated. Not only did the perpetrators disable the CCTV and drug my men, they must have coordinated the actions of at least two dozen labourers to dig this many holes in the time frame.'

'Yes…' said Hoffmann, arriving behind Darren and slapping a hand on his employee's shoulder. 'And this great lump let them get away with it. Darren, can you fetch us two mugs of the muck passed off as coffee round here? Dr Hunter and I need to have a little chat.' As his bodyguard moved out of earshot, Hoffmann kicked some of the stacked soil into a nearby pit and frowned. 'First impressions, Hunter?'

Hunter exhaled. 'Perplexing isn't it? I must admit in light of the media coverage I expected metal-detector damage.' He paused. 'But this… This uniformity is something else altogether.'

Hoffmann looked pleased. 'My thinking exactly. Whoever did this knew they weren't looking for a metal object… Well, not one picked up by a common detector anyway.' Hunter frowned, unsure how to take Hoffmann's last comment. 'Perhaps now you can understand the reasoning behind my theatrics last night in Cambridge. It was the only way I could learn more about the group I'm up against. It is unfortunate the results suggest they are a ruthless and well-backed outfit.'

'If your intention is to worry me, Mr Hoffmann, you're succeeding.' Hunter bent down and examined the empty pit. 'But assuming you're right, what do you think this group was after?'

Hoffmann motioned for Hunter to follow him and pointed to a makeshift car park beyond the excavation site. 'Would you be so kind as to accompany me to my car? There is something you need to see.'

With little other choice, Hunter shrugged and rose to his feet, zigzagging between the pits towards another blacked-out Range Rover.

'The police have no leads regarding motivation.'

'But you do, don't you?' said Hunter. 'What are you holding back and why?'

Hoffmann smiled. 'If I told them, they'd want to see it.'

Hunter stared at him in surprise. 'See what? How are you so sure this group didn't leave with their prize?'

'Why, my dear Hunter…' said Hoffmann, waving a remote key card at the car. 'Because I found it first.'

There was an audible clunk and the back doors of the Range Rover sprang open. Hunter peered inside in confusion. 'It's empty.'

Hoffmann clicked his remote again. 'Only to the untrained eye.'

A small motor whirred somewhere inside the car and a side panel slid away to reveal a small, stainless-steel attaché case. A vast biohazard warning label covered the lid, bordered on each side by a small, unobtrusive line of text:

Open With Care – Environmentally Controlled Contents Within.

Chapter Four

Monaco

Hunter spent most of the next day stepping in and out of various cars and aircraft on his way to Hoffmann's personal yacht. Named the Aurelian, the boat was moored just off the coast of Monaco and rumoured to more than hold its own amongst the other floating playthings of the world's elite. Although the delay was frustrating, Hunter knew the Aurelian would be the perfect location to examine the contents of the case without attracting unwanted attention. Crucially, Hoffmann had commissioned a small cleanroom to be installed on board the yacht; somewhere they could open the package with some degree of safety. For all they knew, the case might contain a strain of anthrax or maybe something worse.

With sunset approaching and on the final leg of his journey, Hunter gazed from the helicopter window and looked down onto one of Europe's most beautiful vistas. The famous Mont Des Mules rock was tinged orange in the glow of the evening sun and lit up by the hundreds of luxurious harbourside hotels staggered up its sides. Framed by the Alps on one side and the crystal-clear waters of the Mediterranean on the other, the lights of the various casinos and nightclubs were flickering on, ready and willing to extract the wealth from Europe's nouveau riche. A mile from shore he could see the Aurelian. It looked more like a small liner than a yacht. Hunter's stomach lurched, his body confirming the helicopter's descent towards the ring of blinking red lights illuminating the Aurelian's helipad.

Hoffmann hadn't been exaggerating. The Aurelian was a creature of both beauty and style with no expense spared. Hunter stepped down onto the helipad and caught his breath as he entered Hoffmann's opulent world of marble floors and mahogany panelled walls. The entertainment deck alone boasted two bars, a dining hall and there was even a well-stocked library housing an impressive selection of rare and antiquarian books. Hunter pulled a first edition copy of *Oliver Twist* from the shelf. Signed by Dickens himself, this book alone was worth thousands of pounds and Hoffmann had an entire library full of such volumes.

Hunter sat himself down on the edge of an oak reading desk and pulled a second volume from the shelf. It was a draft copy of *The Lost World* and included notes and annotations made by none other than Conan Doyle himself. He rolled his eyes in frustration as a gentle cough interrupted his reading. Hunter turned to find a scrawny young man in a white lab coat staring at him from the doorway. 'What now?'

'Mr Hoffmann is ready for you, Dr Hunter.'

Hunter's heart rate rose, his fatigue forgotten as a surge of adrenaline rushed through his veins.

'Please come with me to the sterilisation suite.'

Hunter followed the technician down a spiral staircase and found himself face to face with a large plastic tube, open on one side. The technician nodded at the cleanroom bunny suit hanging on the wall and Hunter lifted it down from its peg and pulled it on over his clothes. He winced in pain as the technician forced a close-fitting helmet onto his head. With a final thump it clipped into place and hissed as it sealed itself against his shoulders.

'How does that feel? Can you breathe?' asked the technician.

'It's a tad tight but it'll do the job,' said Hunter. 'Is Hans already inside?'

'Yes, sir. He's desperate to start.'

'Is the room operating within the agreed parameters?'

'Yes, sir. We've got two ULPAs running and the air pressure and humidity are set to replicate the conditions in the peat bog.'

'Great, then I guess it's time for my shower,' said Hunter. The technician nodded and ushered Hunter into the open tube. He pushed a large red button to the tube's left. It swished shut behind him, trapping him inside. Hunter turned to give the technician a thumbs up and almost lost his footing as a high-power antibacterial spray battered his body. He turned to avoid eye contact, his cheeks flushed with embarrassment as he waited for the opposite side of the tube to slide open.

The space was small for a cleanroom and Hunter looked up to see the two ULPAs, or ultra-low penetration air filters, whirring away above him. They were there to remove any internally generated contaminants as well as control the air pressure and humidity. Remarkably, they ensured the room would remain at a level over ten thousand times cleaner than a hospital operating theatre.

The attaché case lay on a table in the centre of the room and he could see Hoffmann standing over it. His benefactor shuffled his feet, looking pensive. Hunter guessed the German must have an idea what the case contained, but it was clear from his nervous fidgeting he didn't know for sure. The decontamination tube sealed behind him and Hoffmann raised a gloved hand to acknowledge Hunter's entrance. Hunter grinned and took a step towards him. But something made him stop. Hoffmann didn't seem to be looking at him but rather at something behind him. Mystified by the snub, he turned and his heart missed a beat as he realised a third person had entered the room. The tube hadn't shut at all, it had opened.

Even through such unflattering attire as a bunny suit, it was clear the new arrival was female. Hunter geared up for a charm offensive but held back as one of the room's many spotlights illuminated the face under the helmet. It was a face from his past and one he thought he'd never see again, let alone in this context.

'Inmaculada Pérez...' said Hunter, hissing her name through his teeth. 'I thought you were still in...'

'Brazil,' she interrupted. 'Hans, you didn't tell me Hunter was joining us on this project. I thought he was just your cover story. I guess this is the reason you shooed me out of here for ten minutes?'

Hoffmann winked at Hunter. 'I thought it would be a nice surprise for you both. A good opportunity to bring two old naval archaeologists back together.'

'I hope this is a joke? You seriously expect me to work with her? Not only did she rat me out and leave me for dead but she's my ex-fiancée for Christ's sake. Not that she ever returned the ring,' said Hunter, his right eye twitching as he spat the venom-coated words into his suit's microphone. 'She's a liability, Hans; she'll screw you over and sell you out to the highest bidder.'

'That's no way to talk about someone who's still technically your fiancée,' said Hoffmann.

Hunter bit into his quivering lip. 'And her name is dirt in academic circles. No one will take us seriously with her name on the papers.'

'Your career isn't exactly going from strength to strength either,' said Inma, her Hispanic accent still as thick as he remembered. 'I heard what happened at Jesus. Caused quite a stir didn't you?'

Hunter stared at her in disbelief, a series of conflicting feelings spinning in his gut. Elation at seeing his would-be wife again mixed with borderline hatred at her treatment of him. She'd left him to rot in a Rio prison for two months, selling him out for a few lousy Brazilian *real*. The night terrors were still all-too real, his dreams forcing his body to convulse as a steady flow of imagined water cascaded and beat against his cloth-covered face.

'ENOUGH,' snapped Hoffmann. 'I'm paying the two of you to work together. I suggest you put your differences aside and remember why you're both here. There is a find on the table in front of you and believe me it is a game-changer. Work together and you could literally change the world.'

Hunter held Inma's gaze. She tutted and pushed past him, turning the case and drumming her fingers against its sides. 'Do you really believe this is the find we've been searching for?'

Hunter shook his head. 'Fine, ignore me. How I ever had feelings for someone like you...'

'Stand down, Pérez. I want Hunter opening this thing. He's right about your reputation and I don't want to give anyone an easy in to debunk this find.' Inma stood her ground, refusing to budge until Hoffmann physically manoeuvred her aside.

'Come on, Inma, play the game or Mr Hoffmann will put you on the naughty step,' said Hunter, exaggerating his public school, English accent. He took his position in front of the case, his heart racing in anticipation. Could Hoffmann be right about this find? Could the case really contain a lost archaeological treasure? He centred himself and tried to regularise his breathing. A rush of stale air hissed from the seals as he flipped the locks.

'The moment of truth,' said Hoffmann.

'What are you waiting for, Hunter, an invitation from God?' said Inma. 'Just open the damn thing.'

Hunter dismissed the comment with a contemptuous flick of his wrist and, giving the case his full attention, he lifted the lid.

'A leather bag?' said Inma, her head blocking Hunter's view. 'It's just a leather bag.'

Hunter eased her away and stared at the case's contents in disbelief. 'What's with the negativity? This is incredible.' He picked up a soft-bristled brush and dislodged a section of dried mud still attached to the bag's exterior. 'It's hardly degraded at all,' said Hunter, 'and what about these patterns? I've never seen such detail in an artefact of this type. This was the work of an artisan at the very peak of his power.' He leant forward and dabbed the ornate set of geometrically perfect vines and tendrils. 'By the look of the edging they were originally sealed with gold.' He shook his head. 'This is definitely not British. What do you think, Inma? La Tène?'

'It could be. La Tène artistry certainly favours a continuous vegetal motif. Wouldn't that date it to between 500 and 300 BCE?'

'Yup. The De Navarro II phase. This would have been a prize possession for someone. Hell, this would have been a prize possession for a whole village.'

'Given the state of preservation it can't have seen much daylight during its phase of use,' said Inma. 'Implies a ceremonial function. I wonder what Lindow Man was doing with it on his person so far from any known settlements.'

'Come on guys, hurry it up; I've already seen this,' said Hoffmann.

'Patience, Hans,' said Hunter. 'A find of this significance must be recorded in accordance with recognised procedure. I may have missed out on logging the find in situ but that doesn't mean I will not do my job properly now. We need to take photographs, samples for carbon dating and, due to the presence of gold, I'd like an external opinion as to the possibility of the Treasure Act applying. At the very least we're legally obliged to lodge a report.'

'I told you it would be a mistake hiring him,' said Inma.

Hoffmann shook his head and passed Hunter a pair of rubber-coated tongs.

'Just get on with it,' said Hoffmann. 'We can do all that stuff later. As for photographs, you can take HD-quality stills from the video. Everything we are doing is being recorded.'

Hunter looked up and acknowledged the protruding lenses of various cameras built into the walls. He looked between Hoffmann and Inma. 'Can you promise me first publication rights?'

'You can have them,' said Inma. 'I'm over all that academic crap. Just acknowledge me in the paper and you can do what you want. I'm here to see results not point-score with the readers of *Current Archaeology*.'

Hunter looked at Hoffmann. The German shrugged. 'I can get someone else if you prefer. That Cleary woman seemed game.'

Hunter held up a hand in defeat and lowered the tongs. He ran their tips around the seams of the bag with an assured air of professional ease and found the opening. Millimetre by millimetre, he prised the bag apart. Something glinted in the light. Inma reacted first, leaning in front of him and blinding him with a spotlight before he could get a fix on what he'd uncovered.

'What can you see?' asked Hoffmann, elbowing Inma to one side.

'If you could give me a chance to examine it properly…' said Inma, pushing back.

'It's a carved cylinder,' said Hunter.

Hoffmann darted forward and, before Hunter could stop him, made a grab for the artefact.

'NO,' screamed Inma, but her warning came too late, the leather splitting and ripping in two like wet newspaper. Leaving the cylinder in place, Hoffmann retracted his arm and raised a hand in apology.

Hunter stared at the lab table open mouthed, his gaze flitting between Hoffmann, the cylinder and the bag. He felt numb. This could not be happening. Cleary was right, this wasn't archaeology; Hoffmann was just another of the cornucopia of grave robbers littering the subject's dark history. 'That bag – that bag was priceless,' he stuttered.

'Don't worry, I won't tell anyone you were involved,' said Hoffmann.

'I wasn't bloody well involved.'

'Hunter, just calm yourself down and take a look at this,' said Inma. She lifted the cylinder from the bag and placed it in his hands.

'Are you kidding? So now we're just ignoring every procedure under the sun? I'll be vilified for this. Not that I'd expect you to care but I've still got a career to carve.'

'Just look at it, you sanctimonious fool. You are holding your future in your hands. Surely you can't be so blind as to not recognise that.'

Hunter scowled but Inma was right. Maybe he could still salvage the situation. He looked at the object in his hands and his heart fluttered. The bag was exceptional on its own; if presented in combination with this cylinder the archaeological community would need defibrillators to resuscitate its membership. He tilted the artefact and raised it to the spotlight. It was a rich, golden-bronze colour and glittered with the grace and refined beauty of a precious metal.

'What do you think it's made from? Worked granite?'

'There's no grain,' said Inma. 'It has the lustre of gold but the weight isn't right. Could it be pyrite? Might even be a worked meteorite.' She stroked its smooth, blemish-free surface. 'It definitely isn't indigenous to Britain.'

Hunter nodded and pursed his lips. 'Possible Roman import but no idea where it originated. Africa maybe.'

Hoffmann took it from Hunter and traced a gloved finger across its length, a childlike grin etched on his face. 'It's flawless.' He turned it over in his hands and gently shook it. 'Do you think it's solid or hollow? I can't see any joints.'

'Don't shake it you bloody... nice man paying my salary,' said Inma, grabbing it from Hoffmann and handing it back to Hunter.

'If it's hollow, whatever is inside should be well preserved. It looks airtight.' Hunter returned it to the light and examined the cylinder's flat end pieces. He grunted in triumph and placed the artefact under a magnifying glass to reveal a faint indented symbol. 'Two circles, one stamped within the other.'

'What do you think it means?' said Hoffmann.

Hunter shrugged. 'A fertility symbol perhaps?'

'A circle within a circle,' said Inma. 'I'm no symbologist but I know that one. It's an early expression of the divine or god, man being represented by the central circle with an all-encompassing deity surrounding him. The Freemasons still use it today. The central circle denotes the individual brother and the outer his duty to God and to his fellow man.'

Hunter ran a finger over the symbol and felt a little movement as the inner circle gave way under the pressure of his touch. Then, with an audible click, the top inch of the cylinder rose and came away in his hand. 'Bingo…' he whispered.

Hunter's hands shook with frenzied anticipation, his breath quickening at the endless possibilities of the cylinder's contents. This was his drug of choice – the allure of bearing witness to the work of men whose bones were nothing but dust was intoxicating. He tilted the tube, the silence in the room palpable. Three sheets of rolled papyrus slid from the cylinder's recesses, opening on contact with the sterile lab table. Hunter glanced at his slack-jawed companions. Each sheet was stamped with the same circular symbol as the container and stained to match its colour. Hunter peered into the tube, reaching inside to check it was empty. It wasn't. There was something hard and round trapped against the base. He dislodged it with a fingertip and his hand closed around some kind of coin-like object.

Inma pulled the cylinder from Hunter's grasp, flipping it over and shining a torch into its now-empty interior. 'Is that it? Three bits of paper. That's the treasure of Lindow II.'

Chapter Five

The rain lashed against Hunter's porthole and he could just about hear the wind howling through the mast rigging high above his head. He tapped the reinforced glass, impressed at the minimal impact the storm was having on the giant yacht. Built to withstand the roughest of seas, the Aurelian was absorbing Mother Nature's wrath with serene indifference. Hunter sighed and let his body fall backwards onto his bunk. He grabbed one of the satin pillows and buried his head, muffling a frustrated yell. It was the guttural yelp of a man running short of ideas.

Hunter threw the pillow aside and plucked the photocopies from the bedside table and shuffled through them for the umpteenth time. The three papyrus sheets stared up at him, inscribed as they were with crude representations of Europe, the Americas, and finally the whole world. Although excellent examples, maps of this type could be traced back to a period six hundred years before Lindow Man's death. Hunter's focus had therefore shifted from the artefacts themselves and onto the more unusual aspects of cartography the three maps exhibited.

He glanced at his notepad, bulging with a variety of unanswered questions. However, it was the use of the double-circle symbol that bothered him most. There were forty dotted over the maps and, try as he might, he couldn't find any kind of pattern. Why did the cartographer plot them? Some were more obvious than others: the symbol above the Giza Pyramids, for example, but in the main their positioning just looked random. To make things more confusing, a series of hieroglyphic numbers accompanied each symbol. It was possible they could be coordinates, but Hunter dismissed the notion since none of them bore any relationship to their modern counterparts.

On the plus side, their presence did offer a clue as to where the maps originated. The Britons were still using runes during the Iron Age and, given the distance, he doubted many of the indigenous residents would have even heard of Egypt, let alone visited. In all probability the artefacts were imported but, if true, how on Earth did they end up in the Manchester area and why? Surely maps of the world were next to useless for a people whose concept of the world extended no further than thirty or so miles around their village.

Exhausted by his efforts, Hunter rubbed his tired eyes and turned onto his stomach, letting the maps slide onto the cabin floor. He flinched as something prodded him in the hip. *Lindow Man's coin!* He bit his lip at the reminder of his unprofessionalism earlier in the evening. Inma's attitude had annoyed him throughout the cleanroom process and pulling the cylinder from his hand proved the final straw. Anger had clouded his judgement and he'd pocketed the coin in spite. Now his emotions were back in check he knew he should return the artefact to Hoffmann for logging.

He pulled the coin free of his pocket and spun it in the air. It was an innocuous object: a bland, two-inch disc with a cutaway at its centre. It reminded him of a thick two-pound coin with its centre pushed out. He scratched it with a fingernail and examined the surface for any damage. The lack of any marks confirmed it wasn't soft and he discounted pyrite. He couldn't be sure without seeing them side by side but it looked to be made from the same material as the cylinder.

Hunter frowned and traced the nine short lines engraved into the coin's surface. The thickest ran from top to bottom, split in two by the gap in the middle; the remainder clustered to one side to form an arrowhead shape with the coin's centre as its tip. Hunter flipped it in his fingers, hoping it would somehow develop the power of speech and reveal its significance. It did not.

A loud rapping on his door interrupted his train of thought, making him jump. His head jerked towards the sound and he watched open mouthed as Inma pushed her way into his cabin.

Hunter shoved the coin under his pillow and grabbed a shirt, pulling it over his head. 'Christ, Inma, you could at least wait for me to answer.'

She grinned down at him. 'Oh come on, it's nothing I haven't seen before – and this is important.'

Hunter pushed himself upright and, moving into the bathroom, splashed water on his face. 'Important? I take it you're here to explain why you left the alleged love of your life to die for the sake of a job? Come on, surprise me.'

'Can we do this later? I've just made a breakthrough.'

'A breakthrough with what? Have you admitted what a bitch you are to a shrink?'

'These maps are Egyptian right?' said Inma, apparently determined not to take the bait and engage in a fight.

'Okay, I'll bite. Yes, the hieroglyphics indicate a link to Egypt. Genius analysis, Dr Pérez.'

'But how much do you actually know about them?'

'I'm guessing not as much as you.' Hunter scowled and lay back on the bed. 'Look, have you got anything useful to say or have you just come here to point-score?'

'Fine. What's your experience with Egyptian cartography? Have you ever found any maps before today?'

Hunter scratched his head, trying to remember the outcomes of the few excavations he'd been a part of along the course of the Nile. 'You know, I don't think I have. Weren't most of them destroyed by Caesar when he burnt down the Great Library at Alexandria?'

'What if I told you the oldest known Egyptian map is currently the Turin Papyrus Map?' said Inma.

'Doesn't ring a bell.'

'Dated 2500 BCE...'

Hunter frowned. 'Go on.'

'The results of the carbon dating have just come in,' continued Inma. 'And we've got a raw date of 8100 BP.'

Hunter's jaw dropped. 'No way! You must have made a mistake. Eight thousand one hundred years? Did you say BP? What's the deviation?'

Inma looked at the notes in her hand. 'Yes, BP as in before present, so the data is raw rather than calibrated. They've defined present as AD 1950 and the deviation in this case is plus or minus two hundred years.'

Hunter rolled his eyes. 'Thank you for archaeology 101 but I'm not a grad student any more. I just misheard you.' He held out a hand for a copy of the results. 'The turnaround time is impressive. Did they go to Monaco's Atomic Energy Agency in the end? How many tests did they run? It can't have been many.'

'They did and they ran five,' said Inma. 'And before you ask, the results were consistent.'

Hunter glanced at the photocopies scattered about the cabin floor and felt for a wall, feeling a little light headed. 'Lindow Man dates to approximately 50 AD which means…'

'These maps predate him by at least six thousand years,' said Inma. 'Christ, they're almost four thousand years older than anything else we've got on record. And get this – they predate the first known world map by five and a half thousand years.'

Hunter swallowed hard. This was a lot to take in so late at night. 'Does Hoffmann know?'

'He's not here.'

'He's not here? What is more important than this?'

'He flew back to Germany for a meeting or something.'

'Really? He won't be happy to miss out on this.'

'He's missed more than just this,' said Inma.

Hunter frowned. 'There's more?'

'The Portolanic flaw.'

'The Portolanic flaw?' repeated Hunter. 'The failure to take the curvature of the Earth into account?' It was a mistake often made by the early mapmakers and linked to their failure to comprehend the Earth was not flat. The practice resulted in a huge degree of inaccuracy within early cartography, particularly in the creation of world maps.

'There's no other way to tell you this.' She took a deep breath. 'These maps don't have it.'

Hunter bit into his lip. 'Are you saying they're accurate?'

Chapter Six

Hunter paced the library searching for inspiration, his hands clasped behind his head. Should he call Hoffmann or leave him to complete whatever task dragged him from the yacht? It must be important or why go? Perhaps he should let the chips of fate lie where they'd fallen. He dropped his phone on the sofa, justifying the decision to leave Hoffmann in the dark to deal with a more pressing matter. He knew of only one source with an active portfolio in ancient cartography and this particular source would not react well to the presence of his benefactor: Professor Cleary. He'd fired off an email requesting advice from her but the sceptic in him wasn't hopeful.

The situation didn't feel real, as though it were happening to someone else while his consciousness floated somewhere above his body, numb to the implications and merely observing the spectacle. Inma's revelations darted in and out of his head. Could this really be the proof he'd been waiting for all these years? He'd been subjected to so much criticism during his career, his previously unwavering belief had almost been stripped bare. His mind was now conditioned to debunk anything even marginally outside the academic comfort zone within which his peers operated.

The screen of the phone lit up. It was Cleary. He took a deep breath. Could the feisty old bird forgive him for the outburst the other night? He held the breath and unlocked the screen. The message was positive. Thank God. Whatever Cleary's current opinion of him after their encounter at Jesus, the carrot of viewing maps predating perceived civilisation must have been enough to offset it.

The library door swung open and Inma burst into the room, making him jump. 'What is it with you? I came in here for some peace.'

'I wanted you to know I've spoken with Hans and he wants to fly us all back to the UK early tomorrow morning.'

Hunter closed his eyes in mock defeat. 'Didn't we agree to keep Hoffmann at arm's length until the maps are verified?'

'Hans wants to be involved at every stage,' said Inma. 'And this, as I'm sure you'd agree, is a fairly significant stage.'

Hunter shook his head. 'You're an idiot. We'll look like fools if these maps prove to be bogus. What if the equipment was playing up? Or the ink turns out to be modern? There are any number of reasons the results might be flawed.'

'The dates are sound,' said Inma. 'I just hope this expert you've lined up has the balls to back them publicly.'

'Cleary is the best in the field,' said Hunter. 'If she says the maps are real, they'll receive automatic credibility. Something you and I both lack at the moment.'

Inma scowled at him, flicking her shiny blonde fringe from her eyes. 'What is it with *you*? I know you are harbouring a grudge but I honestly don't know why. As I remember it, it was you who left me to rot in Brazil.'

'I left you? I left you? Is this your idea of a joke?' Hunter's cheeks reddened. 'We find a wreck, the like of which we've never seen before; the next day you disappear and I end up in prison. You sold me out and we both know it.'

'Prison, my arse. You didn't go near a prison. Is this the story you invented to cover the fact you ran away, leaving me at the mercy of those horrible men?'

The red mist descended. 'If by running away you mean, *rotted in a Rio jailhouse for two months*, then I'm sorry for not having had the wherewithal to send you a relocation card.'

'No you weren't, you can't have been. Were you?' said Inma, her venomous tone dissipating. 'They told me you escaped and fled the country.'

'And you trusted them? They tortured me for weeks. Imprisoned me in the mistaken belief I could give up a few classified secrets.' Hunter lifted his shirt to reveal several rows of pitted scar tissue, layered across his back. Inma's hard façade melted and she looked away. 'It got to the point I didn't know my name, let alone any official secrets.'

Inma took a sharp intake of breath and her eyes glistened. Was she holding back tears? Hunter examined her face. Her reaction at least looked genuine. She can't really have believed he'd escaped the country? And, worse still, that he'd left her imprisoned, never once trying to free her? He hung his head and his features softened. All this time he'd thought she'd double-crossed him merely to work with his captors. 'Eventually they realised I was a lost cause. One day they just removed my chains and literally threw me into the street.'

'But we were naval archaeologists, not agents,' Inma blurted. 'What were they after?'

'No idea,' said Hunter. 'Your spurious theory that we'd found Atlantean landing craft didn't help. They must have thought we were a right pair of idiots.'

'But we found convincing evidence they…'

Hunter held up a hand, stopping her in her tracks. 'Let's not go over old ground. Their interest in the boat was minimal. Their priority was the apparent agenda of the West to unearth proof of genetic superiority. Absolute rubbish of course.'

'It's not rubbish.' Inma broke eye contact. 'Actually it makes perfect sense. They tasked me with a huge research programme on that very theme. Warmongers have always thought themselves to be superior to their enemies: the Greeks, the Romans, the Mongols. Think about it, it's probably harder to name a successful civilisation that didn't view itself as a superior race.' She paused. 'Hitler infamously allocated huge sums of money in the pursuit of proving a link between Nazi Germany and an ancient race of superhumans.'

'A Nazi Atlantis, I know,' said Hunter.

Inma smiled. 'What would you say if I told you I've read documents signed by Hitler explicitly stating that uncovering the link between Atlantis and Aryan Germans was one of the Reich's top priorities? The discovery of the Master Race was to be a literal rubber stamp for legitimising the Holocaust.'

'But surely our government must have known of the plan? Weren't the allies carrying out counter research?'

'I doubt it. The defence of the realm was Churchill's chief priority, not some propaganda issue he probably deemed nonsense anyway.' She opened a bottle of water and took a swig. 'So what did you tell the Brazilians?'

'In between having my teeth knocked out, very little. They got my name, rank and a few details about the wreck. I didn't really have anything to tell,' said Hunter. 'Aside from your research project, what else did they get you to do?'

'Nothing sinister,' said Inma. 'They limited my freedom, but it was essentially business as usual. They let me continue with my Atlantis research and even let me supervise a few dives.'

'Alright for some. Did you find anything?'

'No, brick walls all the way. Eventually they gave up on me too; sent me back to Britain in return for the release of someone detained by MI6.'

'Then along came Hoffmann to sweep you off your feet.'

Inma snorted. 'Something like that. He offered me a job as in-house archaeologist on his team. It all happened so fast. I'm sure he'd deny it but I have a feeling Hans had more to do with my release than anything the British government ever did.'

Hunter stroked the stubble on his chin and mulled over her answers in his head. 'Maybe he did. Maybe he heard of your expertise in Atlantean research. He's a borderline fanatic; we spoke at length on the subject when we first met.'

'Really? He's never asked me to look into Atlantis.' Inma shrugged and sat at the library's boardroom-style table, spreading the maps out in front of her. 'You don't think Hans believes Lindow Man is somehow linked to Atlantis?'

'Yeah right,' Hunter snorted. 'Lindow Man was carrying ancient maps leading to a city lost to the sea ten thousand years before his birth.'

Inma stared at him in shock. 'Christ almighty, you could be bang on.'

Hunter's eyes narrowed. 'Bang on what? You can't be serious? Why would he leave us with the artefacts if he believed them to be that valuable?'

Hunter heard a slow clap and turned to see Hans Hoffmann materialise in the doorway. 'The answer, Dr Hunter, is he didn't know. But he knew if he left you alone for long enough you might confirm his suspicions.'

Hoffmann walked to the bar and poured himself a shot of a twenty-five-year-old Glenmorangie whisky from a skittle-shaped bottle.

'John, you are correct in thinking I have a healthy interest in finding Atlantis. One might even say it borders on the unhealthy.' He paused and downed his drink. 'You see, once I made my first billion my interest in the business world waned. My focus shifted, shifting as it has done for so many great men before me, to my legacy. How will I be remembered? What would I be remembered for? If I were a Roman it would be easy – just erect a statue or plough money into a public building with your name above the door and you were done.'

'Nothing's changed there then,' interrupted Inma. 'Although football teams and stadiums seem to be more the order of the day.'

Hoffmann poured himself a second shot and waggled a finger at Inma. 'You're right and it crossed my mind. However, I soon realised a physical legacy can only be as strong as one's descendants. A building or statue may last a generation or two but physical legacies will always fade into nothing. A fact I have no doubt has erased the names of thousands of powerful and influential men from the pages of history.'

'I suppose a statue can only stand for so long,' said Hunter. 'Saddam Hussein found that out during his lifetime.'

'A good example, Hunter,' said Hoffmann. 'As a result I focused my energies in a different direction and they landed on Howard Carter. This was a man of little wealth and low breeding, yet history will always remember him as the gallant archaeologist who discovered Tutankhamen. The same goes for Livingstone, Columbus, Armstrong and Marco Polo. Men who make great discoveries leave behind great legacies.' Hoffmann let the words hang in the air. 'So what is left for me?' he continued, slapping his hand against a wall for dramatic effect. 'What can I do to surpass the achievements of those great adventurers who have gone before me? The answer came when, by chance, I stumbled upon the work of a certain Charles Hapgood.'

Hunter nodded, familiar with Hapgood and his links with Atlantean lore. 'The geologist who developed the theory of Earth crust displacement.'

'The very same,' said Hoffmann. 'Although backed by Albert Einstein no less, his conclusions were widely discredited due to an inference that he'd discovered the resting place of Atlantis. This was my road-to-Damascus moment; something just clicked inside me. The fog lifted and for the first time I knew what I'd been put on this Earth to achieve. Dr Hunter, Dr Pérez, it is my destiny to unearth Atlantis.'

Hoffmann drained the remnants of his whisky and banged the empty glass on the bar's granite countertop. 'And you two are going to help me achieve it.'

Chapter Seven

Cambridge Police Station

Sergeant Paul McInerney was enjoying a strong cup of black coffee back at the station. Bored by the inaction of his nightshift, he'd constructed a crude target above a bin using a water bottle and a piece of card. He pulled the ball of wet paper from his mouth and placed it inside the empty shell of his biro. He lined it up and inhaled before blowing a burst of air from his lungs. The paper fizzed through the air, slapping against the centre of the target and dropping into the bin. Paul spun on his chair and pumped his fist in celebration. He was so bored.

He rubbed his eyes and glanced at the clock on his phone; still three more hours until he could knock off. He'd attended one call all night and then only to break up a low-level domestic incident. For the first time in months Paul was at a loss as to how to fill his time productively – even his paperwork was up to date, a first since his initial few months in post as an eager and diligent cadet. Five years policing the villages surrounding Cambridge had long since beaten any enthusiasm out of him. The experience had left him resigned to the drudgery of arresting low-value shoplifters and warning schoolchildren of the perils of drug taking.

A recorded England football match blared out of a small television behind him. Paul's partner, PC Jack Howse, screamed an obscenity at the screen and the team manager.

'What do you reckon, big man? This manager hasn't got a bloody clue has he? We need width on the left, and the two in the middle just can't play together. Where's the creativity? When are we going to unearth a Messi or a Maradona? I tell you what, that's why they've scored. We've got a team of idiots who can't keep the ball.'

'Jack, stop chatting rubbish and log the domestic.'

'I'll do it after this. There's only a few minutes left.'

Paul raised his eyes to the old, smoke-stained ceiling tiles and sighed. Three more hours – just three more hours and he could leave.

The ringing of a solitary phone in an adjacent office jolted him back to reality. He toyed with the idea of letting it ring out but the caller was relentless.

'Get the phone, chief? I'll get the next one,' said Jack.

Paul closed his eyes in defeat and swung his legs off the desk. He punched a pass code into his own phone and transferred the call. 'Cambridgeshire Police.' He grunted an acknowledgement and wrote an address down on his pad. 'Thank you, madam. We'll check it out.'

He put the phone down and balled up a piece of paper, throwing it at Jack. 'Time to suit up. We've got a suspected break-in. First-floor flat belonging to some academic.'

'Just five more minutes,' said Jack, dodging the projectile. 'Come on, sir, there's only five minutes left.'

'We lost 2–1, get over it.'

Jack slapped his desk and jumped to his feet. 'You bastard, you've been waiting to do that all night.'

Paul turned off the lights of the squad car a hundred or so metres before pulling up outside the flat. He double-checked the address and looked up at the first-floor window. This was the place, and the intruder was still inside, torchlight raking the walls just as the caller had described.

He turned to Jack and nudged his partner's arm. 'Stay sharp; looks like we've got a live one. Fancy assisting in an old-school takedown?'

Jack stared up at the house. 'I know this place. A friend of mine lives here.'

Paul nodded and opened the car door. 'Great, so play the hero for your mate and let's catch this guy in the act. I'll take point and you watch my back.'

Paul stepped onto the driveway fronting the flat and winced as wet gravel crunched under his boots. In the silence of the night, it sounded like fireworks. He froze and stared up at the window, expecting to see a face. None appeared. Satisfied the burglar hadn't been disturbed, he made a light-footed dash for the door and pushed. The slab of heavy oak swung open and thankfully without a creak. He glanced at Jack and jabbed a finger at the moonlit staircase dominating the entrance hall.

The pair entered with caution and Paul scanned the area for movement. They were still in the clear. He moved to the staircase and paused, his foot hovering above the first step. The wood was uncarpeted and appeared old. Would it take his weight without alerting their target? He eased his foot onto the step and applied a little pressure. It held firm. He shifted his full weight and froze as a horrifying creaking sound tore through the silence.

Cursing under his breath, Paul held up his hand and listened, trying to identify any signs of panic coming from the flat. But again there were none. Had they got away with it? He bit into his lower lip and signalled for Jack to press on. It was a slow and painful ascent, each footstep accompanied by the groan of protesting wood, long overdue repair.

Five steps from the summit, Paul stiffened and stopped Jack midstep in his wake. He pointed at the door to the flat. It stood ajar, its lock mechanism removed entirely. Something didn't feel right; every one of his instincts demanded he retreat. Something had changed, but what? Then it hit him: where was the torchlight? The flat was dark and the silence almost oppressive. His ears pricked, picking up a soft scrabbling sound. They'd been clocked. Spurred into action, Paul leapt the final few steps and grasped the door handle.

'Jack, get outside and cover the exits, he's making a break...'

The door flew open, striking Paul full in the chest. The force of the impact sent him staggering into the banister and he collapsed in a heap at the feet of a figure clad in black military fatigues. The figure paused in the doorway, glancing from side to side and presumably searching for Jack. Paul seized the opportunity and launched himself at the man's legs. His prey second-guessed the attack and stepped aside. The hallway flashed white and a clap of thunder roared through the house. A plume of smoke arced from the barrel of a recently discharged Beretta handgun.

Paul screamed as the bullet tore away the top few layers of skin on his left bicep. He dropped to the floor as the intruder emerged from the darkness, the Beretta's sights now centred on his forehead. Paul closed his eyes and waited for the second inevitable clap of thunder.

Instead he heard a heavy thud and a grunt of pain. He blinked, his eyes registering Jack's shoulder firmly planted in the gunman's midriff and driving him backwards. The intruder buckled and fell heavily against the banister. It gave way in a hail of splinters. A second gunshot illuminated the space and the two men tumbled over the edge, hitting the concrete floor below with a sickening crunch.

Paul dragged himself to the edge of the landing, squinting as his eyes picked out the two bodies through the gloom. 'Jack? Are you okay?'

Someone groaned and he saw a trace of movement. Paul closed his eyes, praying it wasn't the gunman. The groan gave way to a mumble and Jack's tobacco-roughened voice resonated about the space.

'I think so, Sarge. Although the same can't be said of my new best mate.'

'New best mate?' asked Paul.

'I think I owe him that much: his neck broke my fall.'

Chapter Eight
Cambridge

A swirling sickness rampaged in Hunter's stomach. Why would anyone break into his flat? He owned nothing of value. He didn't even
have a television for God's sake. There was his laptop, but luckily he'd
taken it with him to Manchester. He glanced at the message from Jack
Howse, an old school friend and now a member of Cambridgeshire
Constabulary. The police needed a statement; the burglar broke his
neck while escaping, an incident that elevated the case into something
warranting further investigation.

The executive jet touched down outside Cambridge on the freshly
mown grass of Coton village airstrip and taxied to a halt. The team
decided that Hunter should attend the police station after meeting
with Cleary. The dead burglar wasn't going anywhere and they
couldn't risk Cleary's wrath by asking to postpone at such short
notice. She would just tell Hunter to stick it. She'd done it before and
this time he couldn't afford to wait for one of her legendary moods to
dissipate. He was on thin ice as it was and it was safer to let the police
stomach the delay.

Hunter descended from the plane to find Darren pulling himself
free of the confines of yet another enormous Range Rover. He paused,
watching with amusement as the leather driver's seat squeaked and
groaned in a vain attempt to spit out the bodyguard's massive frame.

'Pleasant flight, sir?' asked Darren, addressing Hoffmann.

'Not bad,' said Hoffmann. 'Bit of turbulence over the Channel but
nothing too rough.'

'Glad to hear it. So where are we heading? Where does this professor live?'

'Over to you, John.'

Hunter opened the rear passenger door and stepped inside. 'Jesus

College. Her house isn't too far from here but it's rare she's home. She tends to live out of her collegiate rooms.'

'Really, why?' asked Darren, manoeuvring himself back into his seat.

'Most Cambridge academics do,' said Hunter. 'It means they're never too far from a library.'

Darren nodded and started the engine. Minutes later they were racing past the ugly modern colleges lining the city's periphery and on towards the famous Backs with their spectacular views of King's, St John's and Trinity College. Completed during the reign of Henry VIII, King's College Chapel dominated the vista. The chapel was the emblematic symbol of the university and the greatest example of Gothic design in the land, a building designed to inspire hearts and minds alike. Hunter sighed with contentment. Testing circumstances aside, it felt good to be home.

The car pulled up outside Jesus College with an hour to spare. Hunter suggested a quick coffee. After an early-morning start, his body was crying out for a shot of caffeine-induced stimulation. Hoffmann agreed and ordered Darren to drop them as close to the college buttery as possible. Hunter settled back into his chair, pleased with this unexpected chance to further quiz Hoffmann about his plans. There were still a few questions nagging at him; something just didn't feel right about the German's quest but he couldn't quite put his finger on exactly what.

Hunter threaded his way in and out of the rows of empty tables with a tray of coffee and pastries. He set them in front of Hoffmann to distribute and lowered himself into an uncomfortable armchair seemingly devoid of any functioning springs. He drained his espresso and slapped his cheeks as the strong Colombian blend reignited his senses.

'Are you coming in with us, Hans?' asked Inma.

'I'm not sure it would be a great idea,' said Hoffmann. 'Cleary is renowned as a woman with a long memory and a short temper. I doubt she'll have forgiven my conduct during our last encounter just yet.'

'True,' said Hunter. 'We're lucky she's agreed to see me; I wouldn't push her any further.'

Hoffmann nodded and his gaze flitted about the buttery. 'It sends shivers down my spine when I imagine the men who may have eaten in these halls: Newton, Wordsworth, Pepys, Cromwell.' He laughed. 'If all goes to plan, maybe future students will add my name to that illustrious list.'

'About that,' said Hunter, sensing an opportunity, 'Atlantis has remained hidden for thousands of years, its resting place eluding some of the finest minds the world has known. Many academics dismiss it as a mere literary invention.' Hoffmann nodded in acknowledgement. 'So what makes you think our quest will end differently? And while we're on the subject, how on earth did you link Lindow Man to this mystery?'

Hoffmann winked at Inma. 'Now would be a good time to fill Dr Hunter in on your research.'

She nodded and smiled. 'I suppose it isn't fair John is the only one in the dark. At the moment Darren's dog probably knows more than he does.'

Hunter raised an eyebrow. 'Thanks. Always nice to find out your security clearance is rated lower than that of a pet.'

'As I told you,' said Inma, lowering her voice as a student walked by their table, 'Hans hired me to focus on a specific research question.' She looked at Hoffmann. 'You didn't mention Atlantis, but I'm guessing there must be a link?'

'It was for your own good,' said Hoffmann. 'I didn't want to contaminate your research with any preconceptions or theories.'

'Makes sense,' said Hunter. 'What was the research question?'

'I drafted a paper on an obscure religious group known as the Order of Atum-Ra.'

She paused and let him mull over the name. It sounded familiar but he couldn't quite put his finger on why. He shrugged. 'And they are? They sound like an '80s electro-funk group.'

Inma rolled her eyes. 'As the focal point of our solar system, the veneration of the sun as a deity is nothing new and the practice can be traced throughout our planet's history. The most widely documented instance, however, occurred in ancient Egypt, or Khemet as the Nile region was originally known. The black land.'

'So we're talking about a sun-worshipping cult originating in Egypt or perhaps Ethiopia?'

'Yes and no,' said Inma. 'The origins of the Order are unclear but I have uncovered evidence of members going back as far as three thousand years. Although operating well under the radar of the man in the street, its members enjoyed a wide sphere of influence. I found references citing chapters in areas as far flung as India, South America and, of course, Africa.'

'Does it still exist?' asked Hunter.

Inma screwed up her nose and grimaced. 'The short answer is... maybe. The empirical trail disappears with the rise of Rome. Not a surprising coincidence. Certain emperors, and Claudius springs to mind, were keen to eradicate cults with the potential to unite indigenous peoples against Roman occupancy. The Order of Atum-Ra definitely came under this banner.'

Hunter nodded but raised an eyebrow. Although plausible, it all sounded a little like guesswork to him. 'Right, so assuming I take you at your word, can you tell me where Lindow Man and indeed where I fit into this little fairytale of yours?'

Inma's eyes narrowed but, to her credit, she didn't rise to his barbed comment. 'A few months ago Hans swung it for me to carry out work in the vaults of the British Library. A few days into the assignment, I stumbled upon a tome dating to the early fifteenth century. It belonged to a monastery located in the northwest of England.'

'Is the monastery still there?'

'It's under a housing estate,' said Hoffmann, waving a hand at Inma to continue. 'Not one of mine, I might add.'

'It took me some time,' said Inma, 'but as I deciphered more and more of the old English script, it became apparent the monks took an active interest in recording local history and, more importantly, folklore.'

'Stop building this up and just tell him what you found.'

Inma shot Hoffmann a venomous glance but relented. 'Most of the passages are tedious and mundane, but one caught the eye. It described a Roman ambush of a man the scribe described as a High Priest of the Sun. The Romans laid the trap with the aim of capturing and destroying an important symbol of the cult, an object they believed the High Priest carried. The plan failed and the priest evaded Roman capture, escaping inside a nearby bog. They pursued him but, although the Romans returned, neither the priest nor his package were ever seen again.'

'Although my team didn't recognise the importance of the legend at the time,' Hoffmann interrupted, 'Inma still recorded it as having possible links to the Order of Atum-Ra. A few months later a copy of your paper on Lindow Man hit my desk and your conclusions knocked me for six. They seemed to fit perfectly with the monastery's obscure legend.'

'So my paper prompted your excavation of the bog?' said Hunter.

Hoffmann nodded. 'I greased a few palms and it wasn't long before I was in a position to either prove or disprove your theory. I knew you were presenting a seminar on your paper at the end of last month and that became my deadline.'

Hunter frowned. 'Why did you need a deadline?'

'I couldn't be sure, but I knew if I'd put two and two together then so could our adversaries. I also wanted to use the platform of your seminar to lure them into the open and force their hand.' He winked at Hunter. 'And they certainly didn't disappoint. My intention was to capture one or two of their foot soldiers, but I guess you can't have everything.'

Hunter could not believe what he was hearing. 'What are you on about? Who are *they*? You aren't seriously trying to tell me an ancient sun-worshipping cult tried to rob my dig site?'

Hoffmann stood and placed his hands on Hunter's shoulders. 'John, look at me. And I mean really look at me. This is no joke. This is real. I believe... no scratch that... I *know* the Order of Atum-Ra still exists.'

Hunter shook his head. 'Come on, where's your evidence? You can't be basing all this on some obscure reference in a mediaeval story book?'

'Where's the evidence, Dr Hunter?' Laying down his metaphorical ace, Hoffmann nodded at the rucksack perched between Hunter's knees and tapped the outline of the cylinder. 'I think you'll find you're holding it.'

Chapter Nine

Hunter shifted in his chair and stretched his arms high above his head. Nerves were getting the better of him as he awaited the arrival of Professor Cleary. He felt like a pawn in some giant game of chess. Maybe Hoffmann and Inma were telling the truth and Atlantis and this Order were both real. It wouldn't be the first time the beliefs of the scientific community proved to be wrong. After all, before Galileo the world was flat and the sun orbited the Earth. Not that anyone believed him. In fact 'the father of modern physics' was tried by the Inquisition and forced to recant his theories by the Church. It wasn't until after his death that academia finally amended its stance.

Did Hunter really want to play the part of Galileo in uncovering the truth surrounding Atlantis? The proportion of risk seemed to be weighted very much in his corner at present. Hoffmann had little to lose besides money and Inma was an academic pariah already. If there was to be a fall guy, he was it.

He stared at the stone cylinder in his hands, its flawless golden-brown surface shimmering in the low light. On the other hand, if he could prove this find was of Atlantean origin, it would not only change the archaeological landscape but rewrite human history. Could he afford to pass up such a chance? His heart skipped at the thought and a long-repressed feeling stirred and bubbled in his psyche. It was the feeling that once underpinned his love for archaeology, a flaming desire to discover lost worlds, uncover forgotten history and tread the roads established academia dared not even recognise, let alone travel.

Inma coughed; the sharp sound pierced his daydream and brought him back to reality with a jolt. He looked around the office and wheezed as the damp, musty air wormed its way into his lungs. The professor's room was pretty much the literary stereotype of an archaeologist's office. Row upon row of dusty books lined bulging shelves, intermingled with yellowing scraps of paper and an indeterminate collection of objets d'art accumulated from a lifetime in the field.

As a student, Hunter had spent many long hours in this room

listening to and sometimes arguing with Cleary. In the early days, the professor played the part of sounding board and proved adept at pointing out the various flaws and pitfalls of Hunter's more outlandish theories. This was before he embarked on a career in the Navy. As one of the professor's most promising students, she still had not forgiven him for choosing to give up on academia to dive on wrecks. Although he had resumed an academic life after his Brazilian ordeal, if Cleary was pleased, she had yet to show it.

The door creaked open and Hunter rose to greet his old mentor. As was her way, she was formally dressed in a tweed trouser suit and tartan necktie, garb designed to emphasise her proud Scottish roots. She'd pulled her greying hair into a tight bun, emphasising her high forehead and wide, brown eyes.

'Dr Hunter,' she said, with a curt nod. 'And you must be Dr Pérez. Please sit down and make yourselves at home.' Inma's face reddened and she got to her feet. Professor Cleary strode past her, seeming to revel in the uncomfortable silence her comment induced. She sat and indicated Hunter and Inma should do the same. 'So what have I done to deserve the pleasure of entertaining two of the world's biggest proponents of historical bullcrap?'

Hunter looked at Inma, her face morphing from embarrassment into an angry shade of crimson. He cut in quick, hoping to diffuse the situation before she reacted. 'I am so sorry for what happened at my lecture, Professor, but I feel we both got caught up in the heat of the moment. From my point of view, I can assure you it was nothing personal.'

'You said you found maps at the dig site?' asked Cleary, glossing over the apology.

Hunter nodded and placed the cylinder on the desk. He shot Inma a severe look and hoped she would retain her cool. Surely she wouldn't dare rock the boat now, not when they were this close to possible answers? She knew what an important ally the professor could prove to be. At least for the moment, they needed her much more than she needed them.

Cleary lifted the cylinder and rotated it back and forth in her hands. 'What material is this?'

Inma jumped in before Hunter could respond. 'Possibly volcanic or extraterrestrial; remnants of a comet strike perhaps? We intend to clarify the rock type later today.'

Hunter winced and studied the professor's face, trying to gauge her thoughts. Did he imagine it or had her eyes flickered in recognition as they fixed on the inscribed symbol?

'Interesting,' she whispered.

Hunter held his breath. Was she going to elaborate? The professor placed the cylinder on the table and slid her chair backwards, stooping to scan one of the room's many bookcases. Her aggressive demeanour dissolved as a wide grin invaded her face.

'I know how you two must view me. Some conservative old fuddy-duddy with no sense of adventure, I expect.'

Hunter made what he thought to be a convincing stab at shaking his head in disagreement.

'Don't worry, I expect the twenty-five-year-old version of me would have reached the same conclusion.' She tapped the spines of a few books, grunting as she found what she was looking for and pulling a volume from the overfilled shelf. 'I too once dreamed of making world-changing discoveries. I wanted to shock my peers with irrefutable proof verifying outlandish claims and myths. And like you I became obsessed, perhaps even to the point of mania, with unearthing such evidence…'

Hunter furrowed his brow. 'So why have you always been so…'

'John, you were always a favourite of mine. You weren't like the endless dead-eyed clones I usually find staring back at me. You cared, showed a little passion; you reminded me of myself at your age. You followed your heart at the risk of your family disowning you.' She paused and flicked through the pages of the book in front of her. 'I may not have agreed with your choices since graduating but I'm pleased you're back on the right path. Although I'll deny it in public, this is the reason I'm helping you.'

She was right. Choosing archaeology had not proven an easy path to tread. His father wanted him to follow in his footsteps and attend Sandhurst at the earliest opportunity. He viewed Hunter's decision not to do so as selfish and misguided. The Army could offer so much more, make him a man instead of some sissy bookworm. They clashed regularly, sometimes with their fists, until the day Hunter left for university. Neither backed down from their respective stance and, much to the dismay of his mother, they had not spoken since. His stint with the Navy may have gone some way to appeasing his old man but he doubted anyone told him. Not that his father's opinion of naval personnel was much higher than that of academics anyway. His father fuelled the burning desire inside him to succeed, to prove him wrong on every level and then force him to admit it.

Hunter opened his mouth to thank Cleary for the compliment but she raised a hand to stop him.

'This is it.' She placed the book on the desk and turned it to face him. 'My memory is better than I gave it credit for.'

An artist's impression of a man in full druidic regalia stared back at him from the page. He looked at Cleary in confusion. The professor pointed at the Druid's hand. Hunter bent over the desk and looked closer. He caught a breath. It was the staff. The Druid's staff bore a familiar symbol carved into its apex: two circles, one carved within the other.

'The portrait depicts an English priest from a little-known group calling themselves the Order of Atum-Ra,' said Cleary. 'The drawing is credited to a Templar knight living during the twelfth century.'

Inma's jaw dropped. 'Where did you find this? I've been researching this cult for months and not come across anything like this.'

'You just weren't looking in the right places,' said Hunter.

'Don't beat yourself up. You need high-end connections to see works of this rarity. This tome is one of five copies and the others are all in private collections,' said Cleary, engaging with Inma for the first time since she'd sat down.

Inma crossed her arms and pretended to study the picture. 'At least this proves there was a link between the UK and the Order.'

Hunter smiled. In five minutes Cleary had found out more from her own bookshelves than Inma Pérez had managed in five months trawling through the catalogues of Europe's finest libraries.

'So you've been researching the Order?' asked the professor. 'Then I assume you discovered the cult's significance?'

'Well…' Inma flipped a pen lid between her fingers and broke eye contact. 'I cannot be sure. There's little written about them, merely the odd sentence here and there.' Cleary looked unimpressed. 'So little in fact, the cult's achievements can only have survived through an oral tradition. Senior members tutoring juniors…'

Cleary rapped her knuckles on her desk and stopped Inma in her tracks. 'Enough. Am I correct in assuming you know a little less than nothing?' Inma slumped into her seat and Hunter could see the resentment building inside her. He knew from experience Cleary's direct manner took some getting used to.

Cleary tutted and turned back to Hunter. 'Lucky for you I'm a more competent researcher and dug a little deeper than a Google search.'

Inma puffed out her chest and Hunter raised a hand to silence her. Any kind of outburst would do little to take the discussion forward and might end it altogether. He knew the professor needed handling with kid gloves. 'So who were these people, Professor? What did you find?'

Cleary stared at Inma, her dark, beady eyes daring her to react. Inma held her gaze for a second, but capitulated, breaking eye contact and buckling to Hunter's request. The professor snorted in triumph and jabbed a thin finger at the open book, tapping the circular image carved into the Druid's staff. 'This circle within a circle is a basic, yet ancient symbol,' she said. 'It has been used to represent the gods of heaven and earth, night and day, a god for the skies and another for the underworld. In this context the external disc represents the sun and the central disc is Sirius, the brightest star in the night sky. Although once common, this symbol has more or less disappeared from public consciousness. But if one were to look, you can still find it scattered throughout the world, omnipresent in our art and architecture, both ancient and modern.'

'Omnipresent?' asked Hunter.

'John Hunter,' said the professor, feigning surprise. 'How you ever got a first-class degree, I'll never know. Haven't you seen an aerial photograph of Stonehenge?' She plucked a selection of books from her shelves and dropped them one by one on the desk. 'Stonehenge;

Avebury; Thornborough. In fact Neolithic Europe as a whole is teeming with examples of this symbol. If you want modern examples, try looking at the dome of St Paul's Cathedral from the air; the Pantheon in Rome; St Peter's in Vatican City; the Dome of the Rock in Jerusalem; or indeed any domed building in the world. More often than not they are buildings with a religious connotation, either current or hidden in their past.'

Hunter nodded. 'So this Order was created to venerate the sun and the stars?'

'Well, yes and no. There is an alternative interpretation.' Hunter leant forward. 'During my research phase I discovered that, although the sun symbol remained, over time the inner circle came to represent something quite different. It symbolised a weapon of some sort, a weapon of such power it was said to displace the will of God into the hands of man.'

'What the hell does that mean?' Inma snorted. 'The will of God into the hands of man? Are you implying this group developed some kind of weapon of mass destruction?'

'I am not implying, Dr Pérez, I am telling you they achieved it. A weapon of such unparalleled power that, on the one occasion our ancestors activated it, it devastated and wiped out an entire civilisation.' She paused for effect. 'A civilisation now symbolised only by its capital.'

Inma rolled her eyes. 'Come on: a WMD sank Atlantis? No way. Do you not think that minor detail would have made it into Plato's account? You aren't buying this are you, John?'

Hunter ignored her and watched as the professor plucked a more familiar book from her shelves. Plato's dialogues of Timaeus and Critias, the starting block for any self-respecting Atlantis crank and conspiracy theorist. Cleary thumbed through its pages and found what she was looking for. Hunter knew the passage by heart.

"There occurred violent earthquakes and floods; and in a single day and night of misfortune all your warlike men in a body sank into the earth, and the island of Atlantis in like manner disappeared in the depths of the sea."

He wiped his brow. He expected this kind of talk from Inma but not from the professor. 'Are you telling me the Greeks destroyed Atlantis with this weapon during a phase of war?'

'Given Atlantis is a Greek word meaning daughter of Atlas, I doubt "Atlantis" was the name used to describe the land mass.'

'Agreed, but I must press you on this. Do you believe the Greeks destroyed it or not?'

'Inside this room I have certain theories, Dr Hunter.' Cleary cocked her head to one side. 'Outside this room this conversation never took place.'

'Assuming you are correct, where did you get this information?' asked Inma. 'It's certainly not clear from Plato.'

'From the horse's mouth, Dr Pérez,' whispered Cleary. 'From the horse's mouth…'

There was a brief silence as both Hunter and Inma processed the magnitude of this revelation. Hunter's jaw dropped. 'Shit, Professor, are you saying you have had contact with this Order of Atum-Ra?'

The professor nodded. 'They aggressively advised me to give up on my research and destroy my notes. In return they agreed to fund my first book and ensured the success of my application for professorship. These people are not amateurs, Hunter. Their ranks are brimming with power and influence, even now.'

'What would they have done if you'd refused?'

'For starters I doubt I'd be around to be talking to you.'

Hunter registered a little bile rising in his throat and coughed. He could hardly believe what he was hearing. If Cleary weren't the source and his yardstick for rational thought, he'd probably have walked out by now. 'So did these people know this cylinder could be found somewhere in the Lindow Bog? Is this the reason you tried to discredit my theory the other night?'

'I'm not proud of what I did and I apologise. The bog was an avenue the Order had not explored. They wanted the opportunity to search it themselves, but Mr Hans Hoffmann beat them to the punch.'

Hunter bit into his upper lip as he mulled over Cleary's words. 'What you've told me clears up a few issues.' He reached into his bag and pulled out a file. 'Before we leave can you give the three maps we found in the cylinder a once-over?'

Hunter pushed the papyrus documents in front of Cleary. She studied them for a few minutes in silence, placing each of them under a strong magnifying glass. She raised her gaze to meet Hunter's eyes and beamed. 'I believe the phase my students use is: OMG. If these maps are real, then you are sitting on the find of the century.'

'That's more like it,' said Inma.

'They look Egyptian,' said Cleary, sliding the maps back in front of Hunter. 'Could be some of the few examples to escape Caesar's fire in the Great Library.'

'So these maps are originals?' said Inma.

'I'd like to see your carbon date verified, but yes, my first impression is that they are genuine. If I'm wrong, they are exceptional forgeries.'

Hunter cleared his throat, delaying his response and plucking up the courage to ask what he knew Inma was thinking. 'Could these maps guide us to Atlantis? I mean, I know there aren't any land masses we can't account for, but...'

Cleary snorted, as if suppressing laughter. 'Are you kidding? In a word, no.' Hunter's heart sank. 'I doubt the maps are accurate enough to find anything.'

Inma smirked and rapped her fingers on the desk, eager to say her piece. 'Are you referring to the curvature of the Earth anomaly?'

Cleary nodded. 'Correct. The coastlines might be accurate but I expect little else will be.' She set each map down in front of her and scanned them one by one. 'Plus, you are right, John, there does not seem to be anything that could constitute the missing continent.'

'What about the Antarctica theory?' said Inma. 'Is there a chance the lost continent was forced underneath the ice cap by a comet strike?'

'It could have been, but you'd better pray it wasn't.' Cleary brushed her finger over the southern pole. 'There's the small matter of a few billion tonnes of ice covering the entire land mass. I doubt even Hoffmann has pockets deep enough to excavate that lot.'

She tapped the world map. 'Forget Atlantis; for me the more intriguing question is why the mapmaker has seen fit to scatter these circular symbols on each land mass. Give or take, they seem to correspond to several major religious sites around the world.' She paused and wrinkled her brow. 'Yes, I'm convinced of it. The symbols along the African and South American coastlines seem a little random but higher up…' She tapped the map. 'This one is printed above the Pyramids of Giza; the smaller one lower down the Nile must represent the Temple of Karnak.' She circled southern England. 'There's even one above Stonehenge. There is a correlation without question.'

Hunter dipped his head in agreement. 'What do you make of the hieroglyphs below each symbol? My first instinct screamed coordinates.'

Cleary frowned and perched a pair of wire-rimmed reading glasses on the end of her nose. 'My hieroglyphics are a little rusty but they do translate as sets of numbers. Then again, if they are coordinates, they don't relate to their modern counterparts. Take Stonehenge; they've labelled it 36-00-30. Now I know for a fact the actual coordinates are latitude 51° 10 0 N, longitude 1° 49 60 W.' She cocked her head to one side and pursed her lips, contemplating the problem. 'I guess they might make sense if one substituted the Greenwich Prime Meridian for another. We've only been using Greenwich since 1884 so I suppose it's no surprise they don't match up. The problem is the map's prime meridian could be anywhere in the world. Where do you start?'

Inma rose from her chair. 'Thank you, Professor,' she said. 'You have been most helpful, but I feel we have imposed upon you long enough.' Cleary nodded and watched her roll up the maps and slide them inside the cylinder.

'Yes, Professor,' said Hunter. 'Thank you so much for agreeing to see us at such short notice. Your insights have been most helpful. Can I assume you will not want your name to be linked with any of this?'

'You assume correct,' said Cleary. 'I tend to try and avoid professional suicide when I can.' She stood to see them out. 'If you truly want my advice I suggest you hand everything to the British Museum. Take the acclaim for the find and wash your hands of the matter. You are risking more than your careers by treading this dangerous path.'

Hunter shook the professor's hand and smiled, both of them aware the advice would fall on deaf ears. Inma waved a hand in thanks and left the room. He turned to follow.

'John?'

Hunter poked his head back through the door. 'Professor?'

'Should you choose to ignore my advice, and I am sure you will, I feel I should tell you the cylinder you're carrying is made from a material known as orichalcum. Look it up. Trust no one.'

Chapter Ten

Cambridge Police Station

Hunter stepped though the heavy fire door to a view of several offices, each labelled with the title of the occupant. He turned to look at his old friend, still finding it hard to take him seriously in his uniform. They'd attended the same schools throughout their formative years and shared an array of escapades in their journeys toward adulthood. 'Where now, Police Constable Howse?' Hunter smiled. 'Sorry, every time I look at you I still see my drunk eighteen-year-old mate trying to steal that Ferrari. By coincidence, the first and last time I visited this place.'

Jack stifled a laugh, and swept a lock of fiery red hair from his face. 'Can you not bring that story up in front of the Sarge, please?'

'I'm sure he already knows. What about the time we stole weed from your brother and then tried to hire a prostitute who turned out to be a friend of your mum?'

Jack mouthed an obscenity and steered him up the corridor. Hunter was powerless to resist. Jack always did have the upper hand physically and if anything the gulf in strength between the two of them as adults was even wider. 'Office on the left please, Dr Hunter.'

Hunter closed his eyes as he saw the nameplate, his stomach turning somersaults. His attempt to lighten the mood with jovial banter completely failed to ease the tension in his gut. Someone had died evading capture after breaking into his flat and he was struggling to get his head around why. The office belonged to a man named Sergeant Paul McInerney, presumably Jack's partner. He balled his fist to knock, but paused as an agitated voice carried through the door. To say its owner sounded upset was an understatement.

'What do you mean he's gone? How does a dead man walk out of a police morgue? Bloody amateurs, I'm surrounded by BLOODY

AMATEURS.' John jumped as something heavy crashed against the door.

'Okay, that didn't sound good; perhaps I better go in first. Give me a minute.' Jack eased Hunter aside and entered the office, closing the door behind him. The action did little to mute the voices. Hunter lowered himself into one of the plastic seats lining the corridor and tried to dissect the snippets of conversation.

'Can you believe the guard fell asleep on duty and the body of the burglar was lifted?' said the sergeant.

'You are kidding?' said Jack.

'Nope. They blacked out the CCTV; bypassed the swipe-card security system; entered the building and then just walked out with a thir-teen-stone body slung over their shoulders.'

'Shit,' said Jack. 'Sounds like an inside job. This has the whiff of pro-fessionals all over it. At least you're right about one thing. It confirms the dead man wasn't working alone. This break-in has to be part of something bigger. Also might explain why nothing was stolen. They were after something specific.'

'What were they after, Jack, what are we missing? The whole thing reeks of a cover-up. It doesn't help that the Super won't let up on receiving updates – something, I might add, he's never done before. It's all pretty unnerving. I'm actually surprised we haven't been shut down already.'

'Well until we are I suggest we run with it. I don't want to go back to petty criminals and domestic violence just yet, not while we still have a lead,' said Jack. 'Well, two if we count the weird tattoo on the intruder's neck and my mate sitting outside. We should show him the drawing. It might mean something to him.'

The door opened and Hunter stood, wiping his clammy hands against his trousers, his heart racing. Jack ushered him inside a sparsely decorated office and he smiled politely at the uniformed police officer sitting behind the room's only desk. 'Sarge, this is Dr John Hunter.'

'Good to finally meet you, Dr Hunter.' The man stood and Hunter shook his extended hand, struck by the aura of intelligence in the man's alert blue eyes. 'Paul McInerney, and of course you already know my partner, Jack Howse.' He smiled and indicated Hunter should sit. 'I've heard a few stories; all bad I'm afraid. You two must have been a right pair of pests in your youth.'

'I hope Jack managed to wedge a little good in there somewhere.' Hunter acknowledged the sergeant's heavily bandaged arm. 'Did that happen during the burglary?'

'Just a flesh wound. Unfortunate part of the job I'm afraid.' Paul flashed him a grin. 'But I guess that's why they pay us so well.'

Unsure of how to respond, Hunter dipped his head and smiled. He sat and placed his rucksack between his legs. 'So what can I do for you? Howse filled me in on the basics but I'm not sure if I can be much help in the circumstances.'

Paul plucked a pencil from his desktop and opened a notebook. 'I'm still hopeful you can shed a little light on a couple of issues.' Hunter nodded in anticipation. 'As far as you're aware nothing was removed from your apartment?' Hunter nodded again. 'We'll need your confirmation but the assailant didn't have anything on him.' Paul leant forward, his hands under his chin. 'But here's the rub, Dr Hunter. This guy was in your flat for at least the thirty minutes between the logging of the call and our arrival. In that time he pulled everything apart, and I mean everything. Floorboards, pillowcases, sofa cushions – hell, he even tore open the lining of your winter coat.' He tapped his pad with the pencil. 'There is no way this was a run-of-the-mill burglary and the evidence points to the perpetrator being hired or ordered to recover something very specific from you.' Paul stared into Hunter's eyes. 'What was this man searching for, Dr Hunter? What is it you're holding back?'

'He ripped my pillowcases apart?'

Jack nodded. 'And the hems of your curtains.'

Hunter ran a hand through his hair and closed his eyes. He was suddenly very aware of the orichalcum cylinder hidden inside the bag at his feet. Why hadn't he left it in the car? He'd just picked up his bag on instinct. The security blanket that rarely left his side. He shook his head in mock exasperation. 'Look, I'm sorry but I honestly don't have a clue.'

'Really?' Paul's eyes narrowed. 'No research or recent finds you've made that a collector might be interested in?'

Hunter bit into his lower lip and tried to fake he was thinking. This Paul fellow must have seen Hoffmann's article. If he hadn't, Jack definitely would have done. He decided to go with the truth. 'It's a possibility I guess. My name appeared in the press with links to a recent Iron Age excavation. Perhaps they thought I was storing finds at the flat.'

'And were you?' said Paul.

'Absolutely not.' He decided not to venture too far from the truth. 'The story in the press was only speculative anyway. My involvement in the excavation hadn't even begun when it was published.'

Paul nodded and pushed a piece of paper in front of him. 'These potential finds of yours, they wouldn't be linked to this symbol would they?'

The blood drained from Hunter's face. This must be the tattoo they'd been referring to earlier. 'Where did you find that?'

'It was tattooed on the neck of your intruder,' said Jack.

Paul circled the drawing. 'Can I assume by the expression on your face that you recognise it?'

Hunter tried to pull himself together. Maybe Jack could help. Hoffmann had instructed him to provide the police with as little information as possible, but surely this was just paranoia. There was no way Jack could be associated with this ancient Order; he'd never shown any interest in anything to do with archaeology and to think he was protecting some historical secret was laughable. The sergeant might be a member but then why would he be asking the question? Unless this was a test to see his reaction.

'Sorry, seeing it again so soon just came as a shock. I've just come from a meeting where this symbol was one of the talking points.' He cleared his throat and Jack passed him a glass of water. 'It was a symbol adopted by a religious cult operating in the Manchester area over two thousand years ago. They called themselves the Order of Atum-Ra. A bizarre coincidence but I doubt it is significant. Perhaps just a group of students getting too involved in their studies and playing dress-up.'

Paul shook his head. 'Do not underestimate these people, Dr Hunter. I cannot comment on your own experience, but in my day students didn't burn away the skin on their fingertips or carry semiautomatic handguns. Whatever your involvement is in this, I suggest you walk away now. I dread to think what I would have found had you been home the night of the burglary.'

Hunter gulped down the water and got to his feet. 'If there's nothing else?'

Paul waved his hand dismissively and passed him a card listing his contact details. 'Nothing for the moment, although I wouldn't mind a little more detail about the discoveries you were expecting to find at this site of yours. I'll be in touch if I have any further questions. In the meantime, please call me if you think of anything that might move the investigation forward.'

Hunter nodded and thanked Paul for his time.

Jack showed him to the door. 'Sorry about this, John. I'll ring you for a beer later in the week. Stay safe.'

Hunter managed to force a smile and backed out of the office, desperate to report this new turn of events to Hoffmann. It was clear the German was in the Order's sights, and their net was closing.

Chapter Eleven

Hunter paused for another cup of water in the reception of the police station. Still a little shaken at seeing the Atlantean symbol in a modern context, he needed a moment to compose himself. The implications were disturbing, and he was grateful circumstances had conspired to keep him away from his flat on the night in question. He shuddered and patted his rucksack, feeling the outline of the smooth cylindrical object inside. There was no question it was what the intruder had been after and by implication his burglar was therefore an operative acting on behalf of an ancient cult. It was shocking but the tattoo rubber stamped it as fact. Indeed, if Cleary was right and this Order did exist, then the robbery was a clear signal they meant business. Maybe he should take Paul's advice and just cut his losses. This surely wasn't worth risking his life for.

He drained his cup, gave the desk sergeant a cursory nod of thanks and pushed open the door to the street. He would hand Hoffmann the bag and tell him to stick it. He'd been in war zones safer than the situation the German had seen fit to involve him in. The entrance stood at the summit of a steep set of stairs leading to the roadside. Darren caught sight of him and waved a greeting.

Hunter raised a hand in response, his heart pumping hard as he contemplated the implications of leaving the team. He descended the first couple of steps and paused, staring down the street, bemused as the sharp sound of a car horn bounced off the buildings. The vehicle in question roared into view and Hunter watched in horror as a macabre scene unfurled. He stood rigid, unable to move as a military-style Hummer careered into a tiny Fiat, flipping it onto its roof. The world eased into slow motion as the huge vehicle showed no signs of slowing. If anything, it sped up. Darren screamed at Hunter to run for the car, but he knew he'd never make it.

With Darren's plea echoing in his ears, Hunter jumped the low railing bordering the stairs. He landed, twisting his head in time to see the Hummer slam into the rear of Hoffmann's Range Rover. He sprinted for cover, reaching an alleyway to the right of the police station and ducked behind a dustbin, recoiling as the chilling sound of crumpling metal and shattering glass filled the air.

Silence descended and Hunter risked a quick look. He surveyed the scene of devastation in stunned bewilderment. At first glance, the enemy Hummer seemed to have borne the brunt of the damage. If the Order was behind this attack, then its intelligence had miscalculated the resources of its intended victims. The bomb-proof Range Rover had taken the impact in its stride, the collision succeeding only in spinning the heavy vehicle into the centre of the road.

Hunter ducked back into cover as four men in black military fatigues jumped from the smoking Hummer. Unidentifiable due to their face helmets and body armour, each man cradled heavily modified SWAT-issue MP5 sub-machine guns. He stole another glance and watched in frustration as the soldiers surrounded the Range Rover, screaming at Hoffmann to surrender himself. What could he do? He didn't stand a chance against a group like that. The largest of them raised the stock of his MP5 and brought it down hard against one of the passenger windows.

Hunter closed his eyes and prayed the reinforced glass would prove too strong to crack. If the vehicle could only hold out until the mobilisation of an armed police unit, then the safety of the occupants would be assured. His only worry now was that the clips in their rifles might contain armour-piercing bullets. He covered his ears and watched as one of the men aimed point-blank at the rear window. Instead of the rattle of machine-gun fire, his eardrums channelled the sound of the Range Rover's huge engine firing up.

'At least Darren's okay,' he whispered.

The soldier opened fire but his weapon succeeded only in scratching the glass. The engine roared and found a gear, shunting the enormous car backwards. With no time to react, the soldier found himself pinned against the bumper by the Range Rover's momentum. He tried to wriggle free, but to no avail; his piercing scream snuffed out as the SUV's rear smashed into the bonnet of the Hummer, killing him instantly. The Range Rover snarled as it pulled itself free of the wreckage. Four giant tyres span as they fought for grip, encasing the

Hummer in a cloud of burnt rubber before biting and sending the SUV fishtailing down the street.

The three surviving soldiers opened fire, and it was with an eerie sense of peace that their silenced bullets ricocheted and sparked off the Range Rover's dark bodywork. Although making a mess of the paint-work, still nothing penetrated the car's well-armoured hide. The men realised the futility of their assault and returned to their vehicle, coax-ing it into life and driving over their fallen comrade to gain vital sec-onds on their prey.

Hunter emerged from his hiding place. He needed to act fast. The whole incident had lasted only sixty seconds and it wouldn't be long before the road was swarming with police officers. He sprinted to the fallen soldier and slid to the ground beside him. Although he hadn't been in active service for several years, his military training kicked in. He unsheathed the dead man's handgun, a Glock 9mm, checked the magazine and shoved it in his backpack. If nothing else the events of the last few minutes had emphasised the need to be armed. He'd not held a gun since his capture back in Brazil and the feeling of power and control was immediate, familiar and intoxicating.

On a whim he pulled back the thin layer of black material covering the dead mercenary's neck. He swallowed hard. The symbol stared up at him as clear as day. Two circles tattooed into the man's neck, one within the other. There could be no doubt now: the Order was real.

A crowd formed about him and he let the man's head fall back to the road. A siren whooped and signalled the time had come to disap-pear. He pushed his way to the rear of the throng, pulling up his collar and walking as casually as he dared towards the sanctuary of the city centre.

Chapter Twelve
Cambridge City Centre

Hunter made his way into the city centre without further incident, along the way purchasing a large hooded jumper with the logo of the Cambridge 'Light Blues' Rowing Club emblazoned across its front and back. He pulled it over his head and used it to blend in amongst the crowds of similarly attired American and Japanese tourists patrolling the streets.

With his heartbeat returning to normal and confident he'd escaped detection, Hunter ducked inside a nearby coffee shop. It was a non-chain establishment and empty as a consequence, giving up most of its custom to the tax-dodging conglomerate opposite. He needed a few moments of calm to clear his head and mull over his rather limited options. He was alone without a passport or a phone and God only knew how many armed men were looking for him. He swung the rucksack from his shoulder and unzipped the main compartment. The flat top of the undamaged cylinder glinted in the light. He shook his head, frustrated at seeing the source of his current predicament, the artefact for which a not-so-mythical brotherhood was willing to die and kill to retrieve. The shoot-first policy he'd just witnessed wasn't particularly conducive to allowing him to simply walk away; so until he could figure out an exit plan, he was stuck, his only option being to plod on with his unwanted quest. Ever the optimist, it was possible that unearthing a few answers might make him useful enough to keep alive if caught.

Hunter ordered a black coffee and settled down at a small table towards the rear of the shop. He closed his eyes and took a deep breath, taking a moment to let the hustle and bustle of Cambridge on a Saturday morning wash over him. He needed a dose of normality after his latest ordeal. Five minutes passed before Hunter allowed his guard to lower. No one knew of his whereabouts and it was reassuring to know he was safe, at least for the moment.

Aside from the barista whose head was buried in a book, Hunter was alone. It was time to get to work. He retrieved the cylinder from his bag, tipping it on its side and watching as the three maps slid onto the table. The maps must hold the key to unravelling this mess. If only he could figure out their secret, perhaps he would have a much better handle on what was at stake. He thought back to the meeting with Cleary. She'd told him the Order had been formed to prevent the use of an ancient weapon and then dismissed the notion the maps might lead to Atlantis itself. If this were true then what were they signposting? If not a lost city, then the weapon itself must be the most obvious candidate. He touched a few of the curious circular symbols and their hieroglyphic numbers. He needed to decipher their meaning.

Hunter pulled out his laptop and flipped it open. Although dismissing Atlantis, Professor Cleary did give a little life to the theory the symbols shared a link with sites of religious importance. For the want of a better idea, he opened up Google.

Thirty minutes later and with a little help from the coffee shop's free Wi-Fi, he'd identified just over half the locations. Given the age of the maps, the cartographer's grasp of world geography was leaps and bounds beyond any of his contemporaries'. Not only were Stonehenge and the Great Pyramid accounted for but, based on his rough calculations, there were links with Gozo in Malta; Xi'an in China; Susa in Iran; Göbekli Tepe; Machu Picchu, the holiest city of the Incans; Easter Island; Jerusalem; Carthage; Luxor; Rhodes; Babylon; Avebury; Canterbury; and Pyongyang, the capital of North Korea. The list stretched on.

Hunter paused and linked his hands behind his head, stretching his spine. He was hitting brick walls and try as he might several labelled sites were eluding him. A site deep in the Brazilian rainforest was returning no hits at all, a result all the more annoying given it was labelled with the second largest of the circular symbols after Giza. The associated hieroglyphs were also leaving him confused. He'd translated them but, if coordinates, the sets of numbers didn't relate to their modern counterparts in the slightest.

On the plus side, his workings at least proved the symbols did correlate with various sites of religious or ritualistic significance. There were surprises – Canterbury for one. He knew the Saxons erected the first cathedral atop an old Roman church in 597 CE but wasn't aware of any prior religious connotations. That said, the Romans often erected temples on land considered holy to conquered peoples, a tactic used to symbolise the submission of a people to their new rulers. Given this policy, Canterbury's religious significance might stretch much further back in time than current thinking gave it credit for.

Hunter tapped his pen against the table and sucked a breath in through his clenched teeth. He downed the remains of his coffee and shut his eyes, hoping the strong beans might somehow awaken a dormant part of his brain and spark some much-needed inspiration. The maps must mean something to someone; it was just unfortunate he wasn't that someone.

He grimaced and, for what seemed the thousandth time, reviewed the list of translated numbers scrawled in his notepad. It was still possible they could be coordinates. He needed a different perspective, someone trustworthy with a keen and analytical mind.

'George,' he whispered. 'This is George's area.'

George Goodheart was a geologist working out of the nearby Fitzwilliam Museum. A world-leading researcher in the field of paleoclimatology, George's faculty had recently granted him a six-month secondment to the museum for the purpose of creating a global-warming exhibit. Whether or not George could help might be a long shot, but it was a calculated one. Given his lack of options, Hunter was willing to let him try.

He closed the laptop and leant to his right, slipping the computer inside his rucksack. He jumped as something fizzed over his shoulder and thudded into the soft wood of his chair back. Hunter rolled to the floor on instinct, turning his head as the rear of the chair exploded into a cloud of razor-sharp splinters, the cheap furniture putting up little resistance as it was peppered by automatic gunfire. Before the gunmen could adjust their aim, Hunter grabbed the maps and shoved the table on its side. He knew it wouldn't last much longer than the chair but it was cover, if only temporary. He needed a plan and fast.

With no visible target, the gunfire ceased. Hunter peered out from behind the table. Two men were homing in on his position, the soldiers shoving aside swathes of oblivious tourists with the barrels of their assault rifles. Could no one see the danger? For Christ's sake, surely it was obvious these were not rag-week students playing dress-up? Hunter looked for the barista but he'd disappeared. With luck he'd recognised the threat and wouldn't reappear. Hunter ducked behind his table and cursed. How had they found him?

A camera-phone bulb flashed, a brave, or more likely stupid, tourist interrupting the unerring progress of the soldiers with a picture. Hunter watched as the smaller of the men wrenched the phone from the tourist's hand and, much to the dismay of its protesting owner, smashed it against the pavement. This was Hunter's window of opportunity. He gritted his teeth and bolted, scrambling on all fours towards the café's toilets. He lunged for the door, crashing through it as a second volley of bullets ripped through the space he'd vacated.

Hunter kicked the door shut and threw the lock. He patted his body, checking for blood, and sighed in relief. There were a few splinters to remove but otherwise he was still in one piece. His gaze flitted about the room and landed upon the three-by-three-foot window centred on the rear wall. Although nailed shut he knew it overlooked an alleyway and at least offered a glimmer of hope. He crawled towards it and peered through the dirty glass.

He pulled away and bit his lip, slumping alongside a ripe-smelling urinal. There was a third gunman covering the alley and the café's rear door.

Hunter hit his head with the palm of his hand. 'Stupid, stupid, stupid. Come on man, think.' The crash of tables overturning served to heighten the need for action. He pulled the stolen handgun from his rucksack and scrambled to the far end of the toilet. He released the trigger safety on the Glock and sprinted for the window, instinct and adrenaline diluting any fear. He raised his gun and fired four shots at the soldier outside. The glass shattered and he leapt into the air, following the bullets through the obliterated window.

Rounds one and two slammed harmlessly into the Kevlar armour protecting his target's shoulders. The man glanced skyward, a look of surprise on his face as he registered Hunter's airborne assault. He swung his rifle to meet the threat, but too late as the next two bullets found their mark. The first severed his windpipe and the second ripped through his jugular, a fountain of blood erupting from his throat. The soldier wobbled and collapsed to his knees, clutching at his neck with the desperation of a man knowing death was close.

Hunter crashed into the man's chest and knocked him to the ground. In one smooth action, he kicked the rifle out of reach and pulled his enemy's handgun from its holster, extinguishing the chance of retaliation. The toilet door crashed open behind him, its ageing lock and hinges unable to keep his assailants at bay for long.

'My cue to leave,' whispered Hunter, turning and emptying the remainder of his clip through the broken window. He heard someone swear and retreat. Hunter twisted his body in the direction of the road and pushed forward. He stumbled and yelped in pain as something gripped his right ankle. He turned to see a commando knife arcing towards his calf.

Hunter dropped to his knee; the movement was enough for the knife to miss its target and slice through his jeans. He could see blood but no pain followed, certainly none the adrenaline coursing through him couldn't handle. Hunter flipped the Glock and lashed out with the butt of the gun, landing a blow on the man's wrist. The soldier lost his grip and Hunter jerked forward like a sprinter from the blocks. If he could only make it as far as the museum...

Chapter Thirteen

Hoffmann swore under his breath and thumped the seat next to him, his blood boiling. How could he have been so stupid? How had he overlooked Hunter taking the bloody cylinder with him into the police station? Had he just been played? Surely the archaeologist couldn't be working both sides – he seemed too honest.

'What did you do that for?' said Inma, shying away from his fist.

He glanced at her and looked away. 'Sorry, just worried Hunter has screwed us.'

'Not a chance. Anyone else but not John. I may not be his greatest fan, but it's something that just isn't in his make-up.' The car jerked to the left and Inma winced as her shoulder collided with her door. 'Forget him and do something about the bastards trying to kill us.'

Hoffmann pulled open a hatch hidden under the driver's seat and his hand emerged with a bottle of Scotch. He showed the label to Inma, but she shook her head. He reached for a glass but thought better of it as a pothole jolted him. He put the bottle to his lips, took a deep swig and wiped his lips dry. 'Now, Dr Pérez, now I'm ready to wage war.'

Hoffmann leapt into the front passenger seat and his eyes widened, panic dissolving his bravado in an instant. The huge Range Rover veered from the path of an oncoming bus and clipped the wing mirror of a parked Fiat 500, snapping it and sending it spinning into the road. He turned, wincing as the chasing Hummer lurched around a corner and finished the job, smashing into the Fiat's rear and knocking it through the window of a nearby souvenir shop. The massive machine barely slowed, its driver ruthless in his pursuit and unfazed by the trail of destruction left in his wake.

Hoffmann pushed away from the door, clicked his seatbelt into place and rubbed a bump on his head. 'Calm it down, Darren. Any chance you can avoid hitting anything too solid?'

'Doing my best, Mr Hoffmann,' said Darren, mashing the horn and swerving again to avoid a luckless pedestrian.

Hoffmann gritted his teeth and turned to look at the battered outline of the pursuing Hummer and its three occupants. If this was to be the end of the road, at least they'd killed one of the bastards. Not that he believed this was to be the end – far from it. Hoffmann smiled and licked the top row of his teeth as his car broke free of the restrictive, congested city streets. Both drivers opened their throttles in unison. The noise was intoxicating, a tsunami of sound reverberating through the open countryside as the two drivers pushed the massive engines to their limits.

Hoffmann nodded as he saw Darren glancing at him through the rear-view mirror. 'How do you feel about ridding ourselves of the chasing wolf pack? It won't be long before we're joined by a police helicopter and being detained isn't high on my wish list.'

Inma ducked as a hail of machine-gun fire struck the rear window.

Hoffmann grinned. 'They may as well be firing spitballs. No bullet will penetrate the hide of this gorgeous lady.' Inma nodded and rubbed her neck. She looked shaken. He knew she'd experienced hostile exchanges before, but he'd lay good odds this was the first time she'd been shot at. The front line was far from a field archaeologist's natural habitat.

Darren flicked a switch on the satnav console and replaced the route planner with a high definition image of the road behind. 'Whereas we have something a little more potent than a spit ball.' The system beeped and a variety of white squares flooded the screen, each one tracking the movements of the enemy vehicle.

Hoffmann gripped his seat as Darren accelerated into a tight bend. The Land Rover's tyres screeched and squealed as they hung onto the ageing tarmac. He looked ahead and allowed himself a fleeting smile. In front of them lay the arrow-straight Roman road he knew Darren had been targeting. It was time for the endgame to begin.

He turned in time to see the Hummer round the corner in a haze of burning rubber. Losing grip, the back end kicked out and ploughed into the hedgerow, flattening the fence beyond. The giant machine fishtailed and lurched back onto the road, undeterred by its brief misadventure. With no more bends to hide behind, Hoffmann clenched his teeth as it became clear their pursuers had also decided it was time to put an end to the chase. He pointed at the close-up of the Hummer on the dashboard. 'It's now or never, Darren.'

'Shit, they're preparing an RPG.'

'A little crude.' Hoffmann tutted. 'I would have expected a little more finesse from such an esteemed and ancient Order. I guess it's time to find out if my "optional extras" were worth installing.'

Darren grimaced. 'I suggest you hold onto something, Miss Pérez. This weapon is still in the development phase. There is a recoil issue.'

'Just keep her steady and we'll be fine,' said Hoffmann.

Darren flicked a second switch on the console and mopped his brow. In response, and oblivious to the tension in the cabin, an androgynous voice boomed through the speakers.

'Acquiring targets.'

Hoffmann held his breath as the voice gave way to the faint, whirring sound of a computer hard at work. One by one the white squares turned red.

'Six targets acquired. Please select a target.'

A twinge of anticipation churned in Hoffmann's stomach and he swept away a bead of perspiration as it slid down his cheek. Time was not on their side. The soldier with the RPG was clambering through the sunroof and it wouldn't be long before he was in position. Darren prodded the touch screen display and selected two targets: the face of the driver and the Hummer's engine.

'Brace yourself, Dr Pérez,' said Hoffmann. 'We're about to hit a little turbulence.'

'Invalid target, please try again.'

'Darren, what's happening? The bad men are about to open fire,' hissed Hoffmann.

Darren wiped his fingers against his shirt and tapped another option.

'Invalid target, please try again.'

Darren slapped the screen in frustration. 'Bloody computer. WORK GODDAMN YOU, WORK.'

'Target valid.'

There was a trio of sharp cracks as three high-velocity armour-piercing bullets flew from the rear of the Range Rover. Hoffmann held on for dear life as the recoil from the Vulcan 20mm cannon snapped the big car forward, propelling it from eighty to 140 miles per hour in less than a second. The car wobbled and he could see Darren tugging the wheel hard to the left and then to the right, struggling to keep control. Inma screamed as the car tipped onto two wheels.

'Weight to the left, weight to the left,' screamed Darren. Hoffmann launched himself against his door, yelping in pain as the Range Rover dropped back onto all fours, whipping his skull hard against the bulletproof window. The car span to a stop, tyres smoking and bumper to bumper with the smouldering remains of its victim.

'Target destroyed,' announced the computer. A little dazed, Hoffmann glanced at the monitor and allowed himself a brief smile as he watched it replay the action. Each shell found its target with deadly efficiency and the results were as immediate as they were devastating. After decapitating the driver, the rounds had exited his corpse at over two thousand miles per hour and entered the right leg of the soldier clambering through the sunroof, ripping it clean from his hip. The RPG launched its round, point-blank into the vehicle's cabin. The Hummer exploded in a mushroom of fire, reinforced glass and molten metal, the concoction coating the surface of the road like confetti at a wedding of the damned.

'Fuck me… Well, I think we got them,' said Darren.

Inma pulled herself upright. 'That's an understatement and a half. The only thing you didn't do was drown them!'

Hoffmann grinned and patted her leg. 'I'll mention it to the engineers.' He turned back to Darren. 'If this thing still works, I suggest you get us out of here and fast. It won't be long before this road is crawling with blue lights.' He ran his hands through his hair, grimacing as his fingers disturbed a variety of bumps and bruises. 'Have you got any painkillers in here? They might help me figure out how the hell we're going to find Hunter and his damned rucksack.'

Darren threw a pack of paracetamol into his lap. 'As for Hunter…' He flipped a switch on the dashboard and map of Cambridge appeared on the screen, a red dot flashing at its centre. 'I took the liberty of tagging both him and his bag. A lucky precaution in hindsight.'

Chapter Fourteen

Fitzwilliam Museum, Cambridge

Hunter flung open the door to the Fitzwilliam Museum and headed for the basement, pausing only to acknowledge the security guard and flash his university identification. He smiled in anticipation. Hunter and Dr George Goodheart went back years. They'd first met as undergraduates at Jesus College in a boat on the banks of the River Cam and bonded during the subsequent club dinner over a shared passion for all things Atlantis. The subject matter generated enough heated debates to ensure a lifelong, banter-fuelled friendship.

Panting, Hunter skidded to a stop outside the door to his friend's dingy office. He leant against one of the ageing, black-oak pillars holding up the ceiling and caught his breath. He plucked a Bronze Age arrowhead from a nearby table and flipped it through his fingers. The sheer quantity of priceless artefacts just lying about unguarded and awaiting categorisation never failed to amaze him. He replaced the arrowhead and coughed. Since opening in 1848, the lower levels of the museum had undergone limited modernisation and each year the damp was becoming more and more noticeable.

Suitably rested, Hunter pushed open George's door and stepped inside without knocking. He scanned the room, his eyes taking a few seconds to acclimatise to the gloom. He spotted George, crouched over a microscope and immersed in whatever he was doing. The door closed with a bang and the diminutive geologist jumped and turned to face him. He looked angry. Hunter gave him a sheepish grin and waved. George's hostile demeanour vanished in an instant.

'Hunter, old boy, good to see you. I've not seen you for days, where have you been hiding, old bean?'

Hunter shrugged. 'I've been about, ducking and diving, you know the drill.'

'I thought you were the cleaner. Old bag has been nagging at me to clear up for weeks now. Claims she can't do her job as she doesn't know where the floor is. The cheek of the woman...'

Hunter looked at the rock samples and archaeological artefacts mingling with the rivers of paper flowing across the floors and tables of the office. He winked at his friend. 'Up to your usual standards I'd say. I assume you told her the liberal use of fire is the only way to clean a Goodheart office?'

George laughed and got to his feet. 'Don't give her any ideas.'

George had the makings of a handsome man but he'd never shown much appetite for fulfilling his physical potential. His long, dark, matted hair straddled his shoulders and framed his bearded face. The look was in keeping with the dirty black jeans and ageing Metallica *Master of Puppets* T-shirt Hunter's friend never seemed to remove.

'So what brings a "famous" archaeologist like you to my humble lair?' he asked.

Hunter's face reddened. 'I take it you saw the article?'

'Saw it, read it, laughed at it and then used it for my chips. Quite an evening by all accounts. Almost wish I'd turned up. Almost...'

'Cheers mate. If you enjoy an uncomfortable silence, it was the place to be.'

'So did you find the elusive treasure of your troubled bog man?'

Hunter removed his rucksack and, without saying a word, emptied the bag's contents onto George's desk. The cylinder rolled to the table edge.

George stopped it from falling with the tip of a finger and raised an eyebrow. 'What the hell is this?'

'The treasure of my troubled bog man.' George's eyes widened. 'As for what it is... As the number one geologist in my life, I was sort of hoping you would tell me. I've shown it to Cleary and she reckons its orichalcum.'

George gawped at him, staring into his eyes and searching for evidence of an elaborate joke. 'As in Atlantean orichalcum? You're kidding, right?'

'Not this time.'

George grabbed a nearby magnifying glass and bent over the cylinder. 'Can I take a sample?'

'Be my guest.'

He rummaged about in a nearby drawer and pulled out a small razor blade. He pinned the cylinder into a padded vice and, with a degree of precision a surgeon would be proud of, cut a tiny sliver from its edge. He transferred the shard onto a glass slide and slipped it under the lens of an impressive-looking digital microscope. A blurred image appeared on an adjacent monitor. George fiddled with the focus for a few seconds until a clear image of the metal appeared. He grinned.

'So? What's the verdict?'

'John, can you remember any of the mythical properties of orichalcum?'

Hunter scratched his head. 'Plato described it in *Critias* as a golden-coloured bronze alloy. If I remember correctly it was a widely mined metal second only in value to gold.'

'Yes, but that's not what I'm getting at. What about the alloy's potential as a source of fuel and power for our lost continent? The American psychic Edgar Cayce alleged this stuff could generate four times the power of uranium. Plus he went further and claimed it could do it without the waste problems associated with nuclear. Might be a load of balls but…'

Hunter looked at the shard in front of him. 'I'm not so sure we should take his word as gospel. Cayce also claimed the ancients powered Atlantis using a massive crystal ball and its people carried death-ray guns.' He placed a hand on George's shoulder. 'If this is a power source, how might we go about testing it?'

'Let's go with… unscientifically.' Before Hunter could protest, George slipped the slide from under the microscope and launched it into the nearby fireplace. 'We may want to stand back,' said George, pulling Hunter behind a large workbench.

The dying embers sparked at the impact but, after several diligent hours spent warming the room, the charred wood did little more than glow a little brighter. Sixty seconds ticked by and nothing more happened.

'Hmmm.' George frowned. 'I was convinced it would react with heat. I guess the whole fuel thing really is just a myth. On the other hand, I guess the cylinder may not even be orichalcum.'

'You did use a really small piece.'

'Yes, but I'd still have expected some reaction.'

George stood and walked towards the fireplace, dusting himself down. As he got closer, the fire hissed and spat out an ember. Hunter recognised the danger and grabbed George by the collar of his shirt, pulling him backwards. The fire's dull orange embers continued to rage and hiss, spitting red-hot splinters into the room. Hunter pushed George aside for a better view and regretted it as the movement coincided with an explosion of bright white light from the hearth. He clamped his hands to his eye sockets, rubbing them hard until the pain subsided and his vision returned.

He joined George, watching open mouthed as the fire whipped itself into a frenzied climax. The purity of the white flames was almost supernatural. They didn't look real, instead resembling a Disney animation spluttering into life before them. If it were not for the blistering heat kicking out into the room, Hunter wouldn't have believed it. The legends were true. The energy produced by such an insignificant shard was incredible. If somehow harnessed and channelled, he didn't doubt the whole cylinder could heat the entire building, perhaps even the whole block.

George wiped his forehead free of perspiration. He turned to face Hunter and the orichalcum cylinder in his hands.

'You know I don't swear much,' said George, 'but this is truly a "fuck me" moment. If a flake can do this, your cylinder could probably heat Cambridge for the next twenty years. Have you seriously just been carrying it around in your backpack?'

Hunter blew the air from his lungs and shuddered involuntarily. 'That might be a bit of a leap but even so, just imagine what would happen if this stuff ever made it onto the open market.'

'The coal, oil and nuclear energy industries would literally collapse overnight.' George massaged his temples. 'Christ, this would render the Middle East nigh-on redundant and shift the world's power bases in God-only-knows what direction.'

'At least now I know why people are willing to kill for it.'

George's face morphed in slow motion as Hunter's throwaway

comment hung in the air. 'Say what? Back up. People are killing for this? Who? Am I in danger?'

Hunter smiled and spent the next ten minutes filling George in on the events of the past week. He started with Hans Hoffmann's offer and ended with the moment he'd pushed open George's door. George sat in silence, making notes and analysing each shred of evidence passed down to him. As the tale concluded he sucked in a deep breath and bit on the end of his pen.

'So, as you embarked on your trip down a certain creek and without a certain paddle, you thought of me. A wise choice.' He glanced at his notes and tapped a word he'd ringed. 'You mentioned the maps were created using differing north points. Show me how you came to this conclusion? Use my computer. I'm just going to grab one or two things from another lab. Can you manage on your own?'

Hunter nodded and slid in front of George's keyboard. His decision to involve the geologist was proving inspired, and to be honest it was just nice to be with someone he could trust. His relationship with Hoffmann was a very different beast and, although he was seemingly singing from the same hymn sheet, something still didn't sit right about the German. The man was holding something back and Hunter was certain Mr Hans Hoffmann knew a lot more than he let on.

George re-entered the room just as Hunter hit the final couple of keys to complete his on-screen map. There was an air of triumph about him, pricking Hunter's curiosity as he placed three large, carved squares of rock onto the nearest workbench.

'Ok, so we're talking the Yukon and the Hudson Bay,' said George, peering at the results on Hunter's screen.

He looked up at him in surprise. 'Bit of a snap conclusion.'

'You may have to work with me here, John. I know this might be hard for you to accept but geology may hold the key to solving your little mystery and not your new-age, tinpot subject.' He nodded at the three rocks. 'Those samples form part of a display I created two years back. The museum's suits rejected it, but for our purposes it's perfect.' He arranged the samples into a neat row. 'Before we start, note I've aligned each rock exactly as they were found.' Hunter nodded and ran his fingers over the smooth surfaces of each of the dark rocks. 'Do me a favour and tell me what you see.'

Hunter rubbed the stubble on his cheek and watched in confusion as George placed a metal arrow atop each rock. The three arrows each pointed in different directions.

George turned to face him. 'Any ideas?'

'None...'

'What if I tell you they are all volcanic?' Hunter took a little time to think, but still didn't have a clue. He shrugged his shoulders. 'And you call yourself an academic.' George grinned. 'Shall I go back to Geology 101? Molten rock is thrown up during a volcanic eruption...'

'Thanks mate, I'm not that stupid.'

'I disagree. If you aren't "that" stupid, should I assume you're aware the temperature of molten rock is above the Curie temperature of any ferrous oxide it may contain?' Hunter looked blank and the reaction prompted an arrogant snigger from George. 'In ignorant man's terms, the rock gets so hot any magnetism present resets itself. As the rock cools the ferrous oxides regain their magnetic properties and, unless melted again, they hold onto these properties until the end of time.'

'And now in English?'

'Volcanic rocks can give you a very accurate reading of the whereabouts of magnetic north at the time of their respective eruptions.' He paused and picked up the first rock, polishing it on his shirt. 'Now to blow your mind. This first rock represents magnetic north as we know it now. The second represents magnetic north when it lay somewhere in the Hudson Bay. That was 12,500 years ago. And last but not least, this third rock represents a magnetic north somewhere in the Yukon valley.' He paused for effect. 'The last time it was in the Yukon was 80,000 years ago.'

Hunter frowned and tried to digest what George was telling him. Then the answer hit him, his gaze flitting back and forth between his map and the rocks. 'You're surely not implying someone mapped the Earth over 80,000 years ago?'

'Not at all, Dr Hunter, this is what your maps are telling you.' He shuffled through the three documents. 'These must be copies of a much older set. Given the discrepancies, I'd guess an amalgamation of a few.'

Hunter giggled as a surge of nervous energy bubbled up inside him. 'I cannot believe you're the one telling me this. You used to be my greatest critic and now... Now, not only are you presenting me with watertight proof of an Atlantean civilisation, but you're advocating a people advanced enough to traverse and map their planet 70,000 years before modern man even learnt to write.'

'It's your evidence, not mine.' George grinned. 'Their cartographers must have used a kind of grid system, hence all these duplicated numbers,' he continued, tapping Hunter's figures. 'I'd be willing to bet good money they placed markers at each site.'

Hunter nodded. 'Markers that over time became significant to the locals in a religious context once the original meaning disappeared.'

'Bingo,' said George. 'It would explain why so many religious sites exist at these longitudes and latitudes today.'

'George,' said Hunter, getting to his feet. 'I need to get hold of Hans Hoffmann. Any chance I can borrow your phone?'

George opened his mouth, but before he could reply they both looked to the door as something crashed to the floor in the corridor outside. 'Bloody kids,' George hissed, moving towards the source of the noise.

Hunter grabbed his arm and pulled him to the floor. He cupped a hand across George's mouth and raised a finger to his lips. 'Give me your mobile,' he whispered. George passed it over and Hunter dialled Hoffmann. An answerphone kicked in after three rings. The German's cheery voice informed him he was far too important to answer his phone and to leave a name and number after the tone.

'Hans, it's John, I'm in the Fitzwilliam. I have company, repeat I...'

'Room 4 clear.'

Hunter froze as the unmistakable sound of a man in radio contact with another interrupted his message.

'Jesus, the bang must have been a door being kicked in,' said George, pulling Hunter's hand from his mouth. 'Whoever is out there, they are only two rooms away.'

Hunter mouthed an apology and motioned for George to slide

under the workbench and hide. Once satisfied George was safe, he transferred his attention to the room's lighting. He noticed the soldiers from the café carried night vision. Given the gloom prevalent in the basement, he was gambling on this new group carrying it. He scanned the walls and noticed a bank of switches by the door. He pushed himself upright and, trying not to make any noise, crept towards them.

Hunter stumbled as his phone beeped, yelping as he caught his hip against the corner of a desk. He froze but heard nothing. It was a message from Jack Howse.

'Mate, I'm in pursuit of our superintendent. They know your position. I have your back. Jack.'

Hunter locked his jaw, channelling his emotions and using every ounce of his willpower to stay put and not burst into the corridor, confronting his enemy with all guns blazing. He took a deep breath and drew his handgun, deftly replacing the empty clip with a full one. He cocked the deadly weapon.

Chapter Fifteen

The door creaked open and Hunter welcomed the cool breeze wafting in from the corridor. The heat was intense in the office. If he'd not witnessed it first hand, Hunter would never have believed such a small flake of metal could generate heat of this magnitude – and for so long. The flames were burning white and showing no signs of abating. If anything, the temperature was still rising.

The dark shape of an armed soldier paused in the doorway. Hunter held his breath and flattened himself against the wall.

'Bloody hell,' hissed a male voice. Somewhere about the soldier's person, a radio crackled into life.

'Delta two, confirm your status. Over.'

'Room five unlocked. Lights out but lit by a fire. Proceeding with caution. Christ, it's hot in here. Over.'

'Check it out. Over.'

'Roger that. Over.'

The soldier entered the room and inched his way towards the fire, his index finger hovering above the trigger on his rifle. Hunter glanced at George and signalled for him to keep still. This man wasn't playing at soldiers and Hunter doubted his orders included taking prisoners. The footsteps of their enemy closed in on George's makeshift hiding place. Hunter's muscles tensed in anticipation.

The footsteps stopped. Hunter closed his eyes and prayed the geologist hadn't been spotted.

'If you know what's good for you, you'll get out from under there now.'

Hunter glanced around the door and bit into his lip. He could see the barrel of a rifle trained on George's hiding place. Worse still, the soldier had removed his night-vision goggles.

The man tapped something on his chest. 'Delta one, suspected primary in seven. Over.'

'Confirm target. Over.'

Hunter held his breath as George rolled from under the workbench and stood.

'Negative. It's not him. Primary target still at large. Over,' said the soldier. He pushed George against the bench and pressed the business end of his rifle deep into his neck. 'Where is John Hunter?'

'Who? And who are you? What gives you the right to come into my place of work and point a gun at me? I want to see your supervisor.'

The intruder grinned and rammed the butt of the rifle into George's midriff. 'Supervise that you cheeky prick.'

George collapsed to the floor and held his stomach, struggling for breath. The soldier grabbed the geologist's long hair and pulled him to his knees. It was the distraction Hunter had been hoping for.

The soldier must have sensed movement in his peripheral vision but reacted too late. Hunter grabbed a rock sample and launched it at the man's face. His aim was true and with a sickening crunch the soldier's nose exploded amidst a spray of blood. Using the momentum of his attack, Hunter drove his shoulder into the man's chest. His target stumbled backwards and tripped, crashing headfirst into the roaring fire. He screamed. Hunter recoiled and covered his nose, expecting the foul stench of burning hair and flesh to follow.

Instead the soldier rolled clear and looked down in confusion at his unburnt hands. The man was unharmed. He smiled at Hunter and made a grab for his rifle, still engulfed in the flames. He let out a guttural scream that sent a shiver down Hunter's spine. He averted his eyes as the molten metal remains of the weapon seared through the soldier's flesh. Unable to bear witness to such pain, Hunter smashed the butt of his handgun against the soldier's temple.

'Bloody hell, John. Is he dead?' said George.

Hunter shrugged and pulled his friend to his feet. 'I did him a favour. I'd expect the same myself.'

'What the hell just happened? He should've been ash. His head was in the middle of the flames.'

Hunter walked to the fire's edge and held a hand to his face, shielding himself from the heat. The flake of orichalcum was still glowing bright at its epicentre. With a degree of trepidation, he reached into the flames and pulled back, scouring his fingers for marks. He frowned. There was no evidence of a burn or in fact any trauma at all; certainly no pain. He reinserted his hand and raised an eyebrow as the white flames lapped at his fingers, cocooning them in coronas of supernatural light. He glanced at George and smiled at the sight of his friend's shocked face, the geologist's jaw opening and closing like a goldfish starved of oxygen.

Hunter looked around the room. 'I need something metallic. Can you pass me that fire axe?' George obliged and handed it over without question. Hunter adopted a strong grip and, little by little, lowered the steel head into the flames. It bubbled on contact, the metal dripping into the hearth as it melted to nothing. Within seconds the fire stripped the axe of its steel, but inconceivably the wooden handle showed no signs of the fire's wrath.

· 'How on earth?' said George. 'It attacks metal but not wood?'

'It would appear so.' Hunter stood to face the geologist. 'Have you ever come across anything like this before? To your knowledge has anyone in your field even written an article suggesting such a material might exist?'

George shook his head. 'It would be ridiculed without proof.' George grimaced, held his ribs and reached into the fire, pulling the flake of metal free of the flames. 'This can't have been mined here on Earth. Perhaps it was part of an asteroid...' He threw it to Hunter. 'It's still cool to the touch. Feels the same as when I threw it in.' George rubbed his face free of perspiration and watched as the fire returned to its natural golden colour, dying almost to the point of going out.

The unconscious soldier's radio crackled into life and transmitted the sound of someone stifling a cough. Hunter's heart sank. The bloody thing was still switched on. Whoever and wherever he was, Delta One had heard everything. Hunter grabbed his backpack from the floor and scooped up the artefacts.

'George, I'll make a run for it and draw this second guy away from you. You go and hide. It's me they're after.'

'Get stuffed, John. I'm not about to let you take all the glory for this...' George paused. 'And what makes you think hiding under my desk will be any safer? I might be wrong, but I don't think this second gun-toting psychopath is here to share a cup of tea with me.'

Hunter shrugged and pushed the rucksack into George's arms. He ejected the magazine from his gun and checked the number of bullets. He chambered a round and knelt beside the unconscious soldier, relieving him of his Colt handgun. The safety was on. He offered it to George. 'If you're coming, you'll need this.'

'Wow. Does this mean I can officially justify all the hours I spend playing *Call of Duty*?' He reached for the gun.

Hunter pulled away, arcing the weapon and slamming its butt hard into George's temple. He crumpled to the floor. *Sorry, mate,* Hunter thought, *but this is for your own good. You won't be out for long but I'm afraid coming with me isn't an option. I can't risk the cylinder falling into enemy hands if I'm caught.* He smeared blood over George's face and pulled him across the floor, shoving him inside the cleaner's cupboard with the rucksack still on his back.

He returned to the radio and raised his gun. 'What are you doing? Don't you dare try and interfere with my plans. Keep away from those rocks. Stand down, Goodheart. Stand down or I swear I'll shoot. Don't test me.' He pulled the trigger, the gunshot thunderous in the silent basement. 'I said don't test me.' He crushed the radio under his boot and smiled to himself. *Hopefully that will put the cat amongst the pigeons and buy George a little time.* He kicked the debris under a workbench and returned to the corridor, peering out into the dark void beyond. Someone had cut the lights…

'Shit.' Hunter pulled back in the nick of time, turning his head as a high-velocity bullet whistled past his ear and ploughed into the door frame. Whoever Delta One was, he'd covered their only exit and had it in his crosshairs. A red dot danced on the door frame above Hunter's head. The soldier was on the move.

He crouched down in the doorway. He needed a plan and needed it quick. He couldn't make a run for it: he'd be mown down on sight, quicker still if the sniper was equipped with a night-vision scope. 'Just stick with the original plan, John. Trust your plan.' It was still his best chance of survival; perhaps his only chance. He killed the lights.

Hunter gripped his gun and closed his eyes, focusing on the regularisation of his heartbeat. The fear threatening to overwhelm him was palpable and he couldn't give into it. He needed to stay strong. This was his only chance of escape and he didn't intend to waste it.

The door crashed open, concealing him behind it. He couldn't see Delta One but heard his rubber-soled boots squeaking as he entered the room. He steadied his breathing and tensed as the soldier's laser sight scythed the room. A spot of blood dripped to the floor as his grip tightened about the rock. It was now or never. He shifted onto his haunches and tossed the rock into the dying fire. The effect was instantaneous. Automatic fire peppered the area, cutting through the ageing bricks, and spraying debris and dust about the room.

Hunter flicked on the lights. Exaggerated by the night-vision goggles, it was akin to detonating a flash grenade in the soldier's face. He heard a guttural scream as the blinding artificial light pierced the man's retinas without mercy. Hunter dipped his shoulder and charged, catching his prey square in the chest. The force of the impact sent both men crashing into a workbench. Hunter reversed his momentum and, using a throw from an aikido textbook, sent the soldier careening back through the battered door and into the corridor beyond. Hunter ducked as bullets from the soldier's rifle continued to slam indiscriminately into walls and priceless artefacts alike. He grasped the soldier's arm, kicking his rifle aside and pinning him to the floor with a knee. He pushed the barrel of his handgun into the man's throat and pulled the helmet and balaclava free of his face.

'Speak you bastard. Who the hell are you, and why are you trying to kill me?' He pressed the gun deeper into the man's throat, making him choke.

'O-O-Orders. I'm only following orders,' he rasped.

Hunter grabbed a handful of dyed, blond hair and raised the soldier's head, tapping his gun against the tattooed neck. 'What the hell does this mean? Who are you working for?'

The soldier coughed and shook his head. 'Who are you? You were meant to be a green target.'

Hunter got to his feet and righted an upturned chair, pushing it in his prisoner's direction. 'Sit.' The man complied and let Hunter bind his hands and feet.

'If you want to live, you better start singing.' The soldier stared straight ahead and hummed an Elvis song. Hunter threw his elbow hard into the mouth of his captive. 'Still feeling clever?'

The man's lip split on impact and he spat blood. 'You are the idiot, Hunter. You should question the people you're working with. My conscience is clear.' Hunter's left eye twitched as the soldier landed upon his biggest insecurity, and the man clearly knew it. A contemptuous leer spread over his prisoner's bloodied lips, wrinkling an elongated scar running the length of his left cheek. Did he know this man? There was something familiar but he couldn't place him. 'Just how much do you know about your glorious leader, Hans Hoffmann?'

Hunter grasped his collar and placed his gun against the man's temple. 'Explain yourself,' he hissed, 'before I give that scar of yours a companion.'

'I bet he's fed you some bull about legacy or something. This is about money and power, Dr Hunter, nothing else. You cannot let him find the weapon. Now look down at your chest and drop your gun. You're coming with us. '

Hunter glanced down and closed his eyes. The red dot of a laser sight trembled above his unprotected heart. Somewhere down the corridor lay Delta Three.

His prisoner grinned up at him. 'Now you know why I didn't struggle. Now tell me where your mate is and we can get out of this dump.'

Hunter hung his head in mock defeat. 'He tried to steal the three rock artefacts from me. I shot him. I locked him in the cleaner's cupboard.'

Hunter winced as something popped and fizzed through the darkness, thumping into his body at high velocity. He fell to his knees, his gun clattering as it dropped to the tiled floor. His gaze flitted in disbelief between the tranquilliser dart protruding from his chest and his prisoner.

Chapter Sixteen

Hunter regained consciousness, his head throbbing. He tried moving but found his wrists bound behind his back. He could hear the throaty drone of an engine; it must belong to the Order soldiers from the museum. Hunter raised his head to look through a window. It was pitch black outside. How long had he been out? His vision was blurred but he could still make out the outline of his two kidnappers. They appeared unaware of his recovery and continued a conversation in hushed tones. Hunter strained to hear what they were saying, cursing the volume of the vehicle's engine as he tried to make sense of the snippets loud enough for him to process.

They appeared agitated about something. The driver kept chastising the scarred man in the passenger seat, accusing him of losing men and reinforcing the importance of finding 'the full package'. Could this mean George was still alive?

'I cannot believe Cleary just let them leave her office. If she'd just signalled for us we'd be walking away from this with a full team,' said the driver.

The hairs on the back of Hunter's neck stood on end. At least this corroborated Cleary's story, and apparently she was still on the payroll, albeit with confused principles.

'I can't believe you thought that guy in the cupboard was dead.'

'What was I supposed to think? He was covered in blood and that idiot in the back did say he shot him. We didn't exactly have much time to check.'

'True, we were lucky to get out of there before the German's team arrived. Thank Christ for our eye in the sky.'

'It's not a problem, the satellite will find him again,' said the scarred man. 'Hoffmann's money can only hide someone away for so long.'

The driver nodded at Hunter. 'Especially since we've got a juicy bit of bait to flush the bastard out.'

The car slowed and took a sharp left, the purring sound of tarmac giving way to the crunch of gravel beneath its tyres. It continued for a further five minutes before coming to a stop. Hunter held his breath, fearful of what might happen next.

Someone yanked the passenger door open and Hunter shivered as a waft of freezing cold air replaced the warmth of the previously soporific cabin. He winced as someone grabbed his wrists and dragged him from his seat, pulling a sack over his head before he could take in his new surroundings. It stank of stale soil and rotting vegetables. He gagged and fell forwards. A strong arm wrenched him upright, pulling him mercilessly along a gravel pathway. His legs flailed as he struggled to keep pace with his captors. The ordeal ended with a sharp shove in the small of his back. Hunter lost his balance and collapsed to his knees, the gravel biting into his kneecaps through his jeans.

Hunter made out the shape of his captors through the distressed weave of the sack. The smaller man stared into a camera to the side of an ornate set of double doors, his hand hovering over their handle. A locking mechanism clicked and the doors swung open at his touch. Hunter grunted in pain as the second man pulled his collar taut against his throat, using the handhold to launch him through the entrance and into a well-lit foyer. He stumbled and collided with a stocky bull-dog of a man dressed in the black robes of a Catholic priest. The man buckled but somehow retained his balance while also managing to prevent Hunter from face-planting the polished marble floor.

'Rutter, you bloody idiot, what are you trying to do, kill me?' The priest held Hunter at arm's length and pulled the sack from his head. 'I presume you must be Dr John Hunter?'

Hunter glanced at the man referred to as Rutter. He was a clean-shaven, heavyset man in his late forties. His dark, receding hairline released a bead of sweat as he lowered his gaze to the floor. This priest must be a man of some importance. It was clear his captors hadn't expected him.

'This is Hunter, sir,' said Rutter, looking at his feet. 'Sorry, sir, I'm a little thrown. We were told you'd be arriving tomorrow.'

The priest threw the empty sack at Rutter and cut Hunter's bonds. 'And that gives you the excuse to treat my guest like this?'

'No, sir. I apologise, but I assumed you wouldn't want him knowing our location.'

'You assumed wrong.' He paused. 'Did you at least take care of your two police officers? Are they off the case?'

'Sorted,' said Rutter. 'They won't cause us any more problems.'

'Good, at least you've done something right. And the other academic from the museum?' he asked, this time addressing the scarred man. 'Mr Anderson, am I right to assume your men dealt with him? Do we have control of the legacy package?'

Anderson cracked his knuckles and made a fist. 'Not quite. Intelligence advised us Hoffmann's men were closing in on the museum. I removed a computer and some rocks Hunter indicated are relevant. Hunter claimed to have shot the other man. He looked dead.'

The priest exhaled, showing his frustration. 'Looked dead? What do you mean, he looked dead?'

Anderson bit his lip. 'Unfortunately, we later received CCTV images of him walking away with Hoffmann's rottweiler of a bodyguard. The rottweiler carried a rucksack he didn't enter with.'

Hunter grinned. George was still alive and, even better, had managed to escape with the artefacts. His head twisted as a stinging slap connected with his cheek.

'What are you smiling at? You murdered some of my best operatives.' The priest raised his hand to strike him again.

This time Hunter was ready and caught hold of the man's wrist, blocking the blow. 'If they were your best, perhaps you need to revisit your recruitment criteria. While you're at it, you might want to check how your intelligence goons didn't pick up that I'm an SBS-trained operative.'

It was a borderline lie: he'd trained with the Royal Navy's Special Boat Service for only a week or so, but it had the desired effect. Using the priest's momentary shock to his advantage, Hunter twisted his wrist into a lock and swung it behind his back. He may not have been an active member of the SBS but the course focused on mastering the basics of hand-to-hand combat. He positioned his free arm around the priest's neck, and simultaneously pulled his forearm hard against the man's Adam's apple whilst spinning him about to face Rutter and Anderson.

'I want answers and I want them now. Who are you and what do you want with me?'

Rutter unholstered his gun and trained it on Hunter. Anderson did the same and paced in an arc to his left.

'I'm not kidding around here. Drop your guns or I swear I'll break his neck.' Rutter responded by mirroring Anderson's movement and arcing right. Hunter registered the tactic and shuffled into a corner, effectively closing the door on their flanking manoeuvre. 'Don't take me for a fool. Now stand down.' He twisted his prisoner's wrist, making him yelp in pain.

'Drop your guns, you idiots,' he screeched. 'Dr Hunter, I give you my word I will tell you everything you wish to know. I have nothing to hide. Just release my damn arm.'

Hunter scanned the huge hallway. There was a chance he could make it to the door using the priest as a shield but where would he go? They were in the middle of nowhere. He was also unarmed and really didn't fancy his chances against the two gunmen if forced to engage them. He wiped sweat from his forehead as the reality of his futile situation hit home. There was no course of action other than trusting the odd little man in his arms. He loosened his grip and pushed his captive into Rutter, not daring to speak for fear his voice would reveal the extent of the panic in his gut. Anderson leapt forward, shoving Hunter against the wall, and pressing a gun to his head.

'You shouldn't be so trusting, Dr Hunter,' said the priest, flexing his wrist. 'But in this case your instincts are correct.' He waved a dismissive hand at Anderson. 'Please escort our guest somewhere a little more… comfortable. We have much to discuss.'

'Is the gun necessary?' Hunter stuttered. 'Where am I going to go?'

'You must excuse Mr Anderson for keeping his weapon raised. If you are indeed ex-Special Forces, you'll understand why.'

Anderson grabbed Hunter's wrist and strong-armed him in the direction of a nondescript metal door set into the side of the main staircase. Rutter opened it and urged him to enter. He resisted, pushing against the gun in his back. What fresh hell was this? The dark hole in front of him looked to all extent and purposes like a prison cell. His defiance proved futile as Anderson's hand replaced the gun and shunted him through the door. Hunter lost his balance and fell. He tensed, bracing himself for the pain of skidding across an unforgiving concrete floor. On the contrary, his shoulder met something soft.

A light illuminated the space and, to his astonishment, Hunter found himself wrist deep in a thick pile rug. Anderson gave him a vindictive glare and passed George's museum laptop to the priest as he entered.

'You are aware that laptop belongs to someone else,' said Hunter.

The priest ignored his protestations and turned it on. 'I suggest you take a seat, Dr Hunter.' The computer cycled through its usual routine of beeps and whirrs as it booted up. 'How rude of me. In all the excitement I don't think I gave you the courtesy of a proper introduction.' He offered his hand. 'I should begin by apologising for the slap. I do not take the loss of my men well.'

Hunter shook the hand and nodded at Anderson. 'I'll accept when your monkey lowers his gun.'

'Do as he says and take the laptop to the table in the corner. See if you can find anything useful.' Anderson glared at Hunter and took back the computer. 'My name is Jacob Knight,' said the priest. 'My friends and I are members of an organisation founded many generations ago. You are standing in our Bath headquarters.'

'You're part of the Order of Atum-Ra. I already know.' Hunter studied him properly for the first time. Knight looked Italian but spoke English with an Etonian plum. The grey flecks in his dark, curly hair and the expanding crow's feet framing his eyes betrayed a man in his forties. He was evidently comfortable in his own skin and his flushed, round face and rotund stomach implied a penchant for good food and expensive wine.

Knight snorted. 'The Order of Atum-Ra; it's been a while since I've heard that variation. There have been plenty of others: Templars, Druids, Freemasons, Rosicrucians… Would you believe we can even be credited with the origins of the Klu Klux Klan?' He placed his hands behind his neck and stretched. 'Don't get me wrong, we don't share all the beliefs fostered and practised by these societies. Far from it – we are more overseers than active participants.'

'I'm not sure I follow,' said Hunter.

Knight winked at him. 'A group can only be manipulated for so long before the puppets become aware of the puppeteer.' He grinned. 'And to be honest, my brothers and I aren't bothered about maintaining control. The primary function of infiltration is recruitment.'

'Recruitment?'

'Yes, recruitment to our… Order, as you term it.'

'And once recruited, what happens then? Aside from attempting to murder innocent academics, what do they do?' Hunter jumped as a blood-curdling scream penetrated the room. 'What the hell was that?'

Knight's dark eyes flashed with spite. 'Something else my people do. You see, John, Rutter failed me. The police officers he spoke of did not stand down. Indeed, they are currently wandering through the grounds of my estate. Rutter is now paying the price for leading them here.' A second agonised scream echoed about the space.

'Are you playing it through a speaker?'

'It serves to warn my men of the price of failure. Now shall we continue? I believe you were in the process of chastising me over an attempt on your life.'

'Why keep me alive? The trio in the Cambridge café weren't there to take prisoners.'

'They received fresh orders. The more I learnt of you, the more hopeful I became we might work together to achieve a common aim.' He sighed and tapped his chin with a pen. 'We shall see. So back to what happens once they're recruited,' he mused, pausing as another scream interrupted his sentence. 'Tough question. You see our society is not a society in the truest sense of the word. It might be easier if you looked upon us as a kind of unseen global police force.' He leant forward and stared into Hunter's eyes. 'We were founded over eight thousand years ago, with the raison d'être of protecting humanity.'

'Protecting humanity? Sounds a little self-absorbed don't you think? Protect it from what?'

'Why, John, from itself, of course.'

'Given what you're doing to Rutter, humanity needs protection *from* your organisation, not to be protected *by* it.'

Knight exhaled and got to his feet. He strolled over to a mahogany drinks cabinet and poured two glasses of 77 Croft vintage port. Hunter did his best not to show it but, as a connoisseur, he could not help but be impressed. The organisation must be wealthy to afford bottles of such acclaim. He used the break to take in his opulent surroundings. The mahogany walls supported a number of acclaimed paintings. He paused as his mini tour of the room reached the fireplace. He cocked his head to one side. 'Is that a print? Surely it can't be real.'

Knight looked up and chuckled. 'Van Gogh's sunflowers? Yes, it is real. A loan from a collector for a job well done.'

Hunter shook his head. 'Who are you people?'

Knight returned to his seat and passed him a glass of the port. 'I can see I must start from the beginning. Can I assume, Dr Hunter, you are not a creationist?'

Hunter shook his head. 'Rejecting the principles of evolution would prove quite a limiting exercise in my field, don't you think?'

'True. Then we are agreed the Earth has existed for four-and-a-half billion years?' Hunter nodded. 'And during said time frame, our animalistic *Homo sapiens* ancestors can only claim to have experienced life for the last two to three hundred thousand. The mere batting of an eyelid in time.' He paused. 'Don't get me wrong, granted we are advanced animals, but nonetheless we humans are still animals at heart.'

'Your point being?'

'No matter how advanced we profess to be, the base mentality of humankind is as it is for the rest of the animal kingdom: firstly to survive and secondly to propagate.'

Hunter nodded. 'Simplistic, but I'll go along with that.'

'Humanity has spent the last four million years evolving from a bipedal ape into the Earth's ultimate predator. Would you concur that our species has achieved this goal over the course of the last three to four thousand years?'

'I guess that's true,' said Hunter, raising his eyes as a sizzling sound could be heard.

'He's being branded,' interrupted Anderson. 'Screaming has stopped. Must have passed out.'

Knight ignored the torturous sound and pressed on. 'Well then, and here's the crux of the matter, in achieving what we both agree are our innate animalistic goals, we have created a paradox. What does one do with oneself when there are no predators to fear, no threats to one's young and, crucially, no masters to serve?'

Hunter didn't know how to react. A man was being tortured and these two weren't batting an eyelid. How often did this happen? 'I don't know... Sit back and enjoy life?'

'War, Dr Hunter, war. In the absence of a worthy adversary and motivated by an innate lust for power, man has turned on himself. History is littered with everything from localised conflict amongst neighbouring tribes all the way up to massive modern conflicts in Europe.' Knight leant forward and whispered conspiratorially. 'Now what do you think might happen if you introduced starvation into this already warmongering mindset of ours?'

Hunter shrugged. Where was this strange priest going with this?

Knight grinned. 'World war, Dr Hunter, and a world war in the truest sense of the term – every man, woman and child forced to bear arms.

'Okay,' said Hunter. 'So what are you getting at? You think we are on the brink of war because of a shortage of food? I've not even heard a whisper of this amongst the conspiracy fanatics on the web.'

Knight snorted, almost falling from the edge of his seat. 'God no. This is historic. In fact, given your background, you probably know as much as I do. Plato documented sketchy details of the first global war in his books *Timaeus* and *Critias*.' Knight moistened his mouth with another drop of port. 'Twelve-and-a-half thousand years ago a comet smashed into Earth, punching a hole in the crust near Canada's Yukon Bay. The event was cataclysmic and of the same intensity that wiped out the dinosaurs sixty-five million years ago. The world's volcanoes erupted in unison, jettisoning an ash cloud so vast it blocked the sun for a year. Earthquakes ripped apart the land and tsunamis rolled around the globe, devastating landscapes long after the original impact.'

'I know the theory,' said Hunter, trying to retain his calm.

'This is no theory, Dr Hunter. It decimated the human population. Pockets of survivors fled into the mountains, seeking refuge from the floods and noxious volcanic fumes polluting the atmosphere. Months went by before the waters subsided and the sun reappeared in the skies. Forced from the caves by starvation, a planet-wide food shortage sparked a war of survival. It escalated into a campaign of such intensity that, in a matter of years, the human race faced extinction.'

Hunter raised his eyebrows, distracted by Knight's bold disclosure. 'So the war Plato speaks of actually occurred? But the Greeks were not a military force until around four thousand years ago.'

Knight shook his head. 'Do not confuse the classical Greeks you know of in books with the exploits of their prehistoric ancestors.' Hunter frowned but yielded and let him continue. 'The war Plato mentions between Greece and Atlantis was not the start by any means. It was the culmination of hundreds of tribal battles fought all around the world. Thousands died and many more surrendered to the armies of Atlantis. Their military superiority resulted in the creation of a unique piece of military technology. Order legends speak of a super weapon. A weapon of such power it could lay waste to entire armies without loss.'

'And you believe this?'

Knight smiled and refilled Hunter's empty glass. 'In an audacious attempt to protect his people, Captain Zeus of the Greek army led a small team disguised as Atlanteans deep behind enemy lines. They located the weapon and killed the guards ordered to protect it. His group barricaded themselves from the enemy long enough to activate the weapon and turn it against the city of its creation. Atlantis sank without a trace.'

'So you are saying the comet strike didn't flood and sink the island? Instead it was some kind of super weapon?'

Knight nodded. 'The Atlantean army executed the Greeks or whatever label their predecessors gave themselves, but their memory lived on. As a tribute for saving their homeland, their names passed into legend and then myth, eventually becoming synonymous with the gods.'

'If true, why didn't Plato report it?'

'The knowledge was suppressed.' Knight shifted in his seat. 'But even if Plato did know the truth, you must understand he wasn't writing a history. The concept of Atlantis was a mechanism to illustrate certain philosophical points. In this context, I'd be more surprised if his account didn't exhibit a little artistic licence.'

'Is this how you explain away the possibility the Atlantis myth stemmed from the destruction of Minoan Thera? His facts were a little muddied.'

Knight grinned. 'Ah, the Santorini quandary. Nothing more than a coincidence, Dr Hunter. A lucky coincidence for my organisation, which continues to both confuse and appease academics and conspiracy theorists the world over.'

'But there are so many matches: excavations have even verified the multicoloured bricks Plato described. Given half the island disappeared underwater in the wake of a massive volcanic eruption, it is easy to see why people have made the link.'

Knight nodded. 'In reality we believe Plato must have known of both stories: the fall of Atlantis and the fall of Thera. As I've told you, Plato's objectives did not lie in writing history. He appears to have combined the two events to fit his rhetoric. You should revisit his work. Read it objectively and you'll find that, when gaps arise in his knowledge of Atlantis, Plato inserts descriptions of the Minoan city of Akrotiri.'

Hunter shook his head, although he could see merit in this explanation. 'So why suppress the truth? What possible benefit could there be?'

Knight leant forward conspiratorially, his eyes twinkling with excitement. 'Ah, now we come to the crux of the matter.'

'Sir, is it wise to divulge so much of our past? This person is not one of us,' Anderson interrupted.

'What does it matter?' snapped Knight. 'Who will he tell? And to be frank, who the hell would believe him?' Anderson shrugged and continued tapping away on George's computer. 'Apologies, Dr Hunter. Where was I?'

'Suppressing the truth?'

'Ah yes. After the destruction of the Atlantean citadel, the majority of survivors took to the sea as refugees, integrating themselves into any community which would accept them. One group decided to take a different path. They were led by a certain General Ra, the soldier responsible for killing Zeus and recapturing the weapon. Realising he was too late to save his people, Ra made a vow to protect humankind from itself and ensure the weapon would never be used again.'

'Did he destroy it, or hide it?'

'He took the weapon to what is now Brazil, founding a city deep within the rainforest, its sole purpose being to protect the weapon and make certain humanity never came so close to annihilation again.'

'So he set himself up as an ancient United Nations or NATO?'

Knight cocked his head to one side and nodded. 'There are similarities I guess. Unfortunately, the city's location has been lost to time. We believe the occupation phase only lasted two or three generations before its people abandoned it. The elders decided there was a more effective way of ensuring peace and it was not to act as a recognisable controlling force. Instead they followed the lead of their ancestors and attempted to integrate themselves into societies around the world, exerting their influence from within.'

'And your Order resulted from this integration?' Knight nodded. Hunter frowned. 'So if this weapon is lost, why are you worried?'

'A month ago my reply would have been different.' He gripped the arms of his chair and pulled himself forward. 'Now my answer rather depends on you.' He smiled. 'Generations ago the whereabouts of both the city and the weapon were known only to the highest-ranking member of my Order. This knowledge was accompanied by the means of activating the weapon should it ever be needed.' Hunter nodded. 'It was a secret passed from generation to generation until the custom abruptly stopped sometime around the birth of Christ. We believe the Romans killed the keyholder and stole what he was carrying. Although accepted as fact amongst my people, there has never been proof... That is, until now.'

'You believe Hoffmann stumbled upon this key?'

'From what I know of the find, the activation device has yet to be unearthed. However, if the maps you pulled from the cylinder hold the key to finding our lost city...' Knight slumped back in his seat and sighed. 'Put it this way: I am anxious they may also pinpoint the whereabouts of the associated weapon.'

'Does Hoffmann know about this?'

'We are not sure what he knows. We can prove he has killed for information, but I still harbour hopes he is a mere fanatical follower of the Atlantis myth who got lucky. My men are delving into his past as we speak. I shall have more of an insight soon enough. Given he still possesses the maps, all I can do at present is pray his motives are nothing more sinister.'

Hunter looked into Knight's eyes and wondered if the priest knew the extent of Hans Hoffmann's resources. He must know Hoffmann was an adversary not to be taken lightly. He mulled over Knight's words and examined his face for any telltale signs of lying: a lack of eye contact; sweaty palms; fiddling with his clothes or hands. He found nothing. Could the Order actually be the good guys here? Surely not, given what he'd witnessed both in Cambridge and here in this house. He closed his eyes and exhaled, the weight of the world on his shoulders. 'Why are you telling me all this? What do you want from me, Mr Knight?'

Knight rose from his chair and paced the room. He stopped and looked him in the eyes. 'To be honest I'm not sure. I'd hoped the artefacts would be in your possession. But given they aren't, I guess you could say we're back to square one.' He gave Anderson a menacing stare. 'Especially since my incompetent men appear to have lost Hoffmann and his team yet again.' He turned to face him. There was a certain vulnerability in his eyes. 'Given what you've heard here today, would you be prepared to help us acquire the artefacts?'

Hunter let the question hang in the air and screwed up his face, breaking eye contact. He stared at the priest's black leather loafers and contemplated his response. The silence verged on the uncomfortable and he was pleased when Anderson broke the deadlock with a triumphant yelp.

'Sir, I've had a result with the laptop. He's saved the three maps on the hard drive. We can't verify the rest of the package but I'd say this is a damn good start.'

Hunter winced, shielding his eyes as a blinding light filled the room.

He heard Knight sigh and rise from his seat. 'Looks like Rutter's men have triggered a tripwire, and right on cue. Come on, Anderson, and you Hunter. I understand you count one of these men as a friend.' Hunter remained stony faced. 'I didn't think you'd give anything away. Even so, you may want to intercede should our trigger-happy guards start getting too... happy.'

Chapter Seventeen

Order Headquarters, Bath

Hunter arrived at the outsized, first-floor window just as one of the police officers slid over the bonnet of a car, narrowly avoiding a blast of buckshot from a pursuing guard. Several of the security spotlights turned, their operator training each beam on the treeline and focusing on the fleeing man. There was nowhere to hide. Hunter looked at the second of the police officers and clawed at his face in horror. Jack Howse lay prostrate on the manicured lawn, a gun at his back and his right leg snared in some kind of wire trap. Hunter felt detached from the scene, as if it were happening in slow motion to someone else. He needed to do something, but what? The Order held all the cards.

A second gunshot roared, the shot obliterating the driver's window and showering the area in a hail of cubed safety glass. Two of Anderson's men freed Jack from the snare and hauled him to his feet, a shotgun levelled between his shoulder blades.

Hunter felt something jab him in the side and turned to find Jacob Knight grinning beside him. 'I suggest you make up your mind, Hunter.' He opened the window. 'Only fair you can hear what's going on. Be advised my men are operating on a shoot-to-kill order. You're lucky your friend on the lawn hasn't already been taken out.'

'Order them to stop. I'll do whatever you want.' He was operating on autopilot and capitulation seemed the only option. He couldn't watch Jack die, not for this.

Hunter raised his eyes to the heavens as the situation worsened and Paul McInerney shuffled into the open, his ID held high above his head. 'Stand down. Police officers. I repeat, we are both police officers. Please lower your weapons and stand down. We are on a call to investigate a suspected burglary. I repeat, please lower your weapons, we are both police officers. Do not shoot.'

Anderson activated a radio transmitter in his ear. 'Mr Knight, the boys are awaiting your orders.'

'So, Dr Hunter, you say you'll do whatever I want?' The priest tutted. 'The question now is whether I believe you... Perhaps I should show you how serious I am and maybe execute one and hold the other in reserve. What do you think?'

Hunter's gaze flitted between Jack and Paul, panic rising in his gut. He needed to buy some time and there was only one way he could do it. 'I said I'm in and I'm a man of my word. Killing these men won't change my mind. They mean nothing to me. Just cut them loose.'

Knight smiled and patted Anderson on the back. 'Then you won't mind if I use them as target practice. Mr Anderson, give the word.'

Hunter screamed a warning and beat his fists against the window, his senses deserting him. He heard Anderson give the kill command and felt his body go numb. This couldn't be happening. He turned, fists raised and ready to avenge his friend. What he saw stopped him in his tracks. They all ignored him, each of them gazing skyward, their jaws dropping in almost comedic unison. Hunter turned in confusion and then he heard it: the unmistakable sound of whipping helicopter blades.

He saw one of Jack's guards raise his weapon to meet the threat. Hunter tensed, expecting gunfire, but nothing happened. The guard dropped to his knees, his body shuddering as a volley of apparently silenced, high-calibre sniper rounds pummelled into his chest.

Hunter's gaze flitted between his captors and the window in front of him. Before they could react, he shoved Knight into Anderson and leapt from the window. He landed in the thick shrubbery, yelping in agony as his left shoulder took the brunt of the impact. There was no time to take stock. He scrambled to his feet, fighting to bury the overwhelming pain shooting through him with each step. He ran without knowing why or even where he was going, only aware he needed to escape. The remainder of the guards fled for the safety of the house amongst a hail of bullets. It wouldn't be long before reinforcements arrived.

An arm snaked about his waist and he struck out, trying to beat it away. The grip tightened. 'John, it's me, Jack, stop hitting me. The chopper has lowered a rope ladder. Are you okay to climb? Looked like a thumping fall you took there.'

Hunter blinked back tears and shook his head, his left arm hanging limp at his side.

'Okay,' said Jack. 'We're beneath the ladder. Can you hold on? They'll have to winch us in.'

Hunter grabbed for the ladder, looping as best he could through the rungs. He felt Jack's legs wrap around his torso, forcibly pinning him to the ladder as the thrust generated by the rotors buffeted them back and forth. He could see Paul's outline above him, his limbs similarly clamped inside the thick, rope rungs. He looked back to the house. They were sitting ducks. Why had the Order refrained from returning fire? Did the priest still believe he'd switched allegiance? I suppose he had given the man his word.

He heard Hoffmann shouting directions to Darren as the helicopter's winch hauled him inside the cabin. Someone banged the cockpit door and the sleek helicopter banked right and gained altitude. Hunter winced, closing his eyes as Jack limped towards him. The breath was forced from his lungs as the burly man straddled his chest, and he felt something being pushed between his teeth. He screamed, snapping whatever it was in two as the police officer wrenched his dislocated shoulder back into its socket.

Chapter Eighteen

Hunter's stomach lurched as the helicopter veered to the left. The 200mph Eurocopter was no slouch when it came to speed.

Hoffmann appeared from the cockpit and collapsed into the seat opposite Hunter and the police officers. 'Late night, boys?'

Hunter nodded. 'You could say that, and thank you. How on earth did you find me?'

Hoffmann bent forward and fished something from Hunter's jacket pocket. He held up the GPS bug and dropped it on the table. 'Darren's idea, but I'm bloody glad he ran with it. He put one on your rucksack, which is how we managed to pick up your mate George.' He grinned. 'Nice fellow by the way, if a little greasy. He's actually been a busy bee while you've been playing hide and seek.'

A hand clamped on Hunter's left shoulder and he batted it away, wincing in pain. He didn't have to look to know who it was.

'Shit, sorry, John, I forgot.'

'Just sit down, George, you dozy clown.'

'A dozy clown with information,' said George.

'Before you dive in,' interrupted Hoffmann, 'I need to know what the Order wanted. Last I heard they were shooting at you in Cambridge. Jumping from a first-floor window tells me they probably didn't get what they wanted.'

'They wanted the cylinder.' Hunter decided the truth wouldn't do any harm. 'They also tried to persuade me to double-cross you. Fed me some baloney about the fall of Atlantis and that you plan to destroy the world.'

Hoffmann snorted back a laugh. 'I'm glad you didn't take them seriously.'

'I'm just happy you turned up when you did. Their leader was on the verge of executing my friends.'

Hoffmann frowned. 'Friends? So you know these two?'

'I've known Jack since birth and this is his partner, Paul McInerney. They are the police officers assigned to investigate the burglary of my flat.'

'I see,' said Hoffmann. 'Good job, guys. Well... ish. Did you follow John from the museum?'

'Yes, sir,' said Paul. 'Our superintendent warned us off the case but my gut just wouldn't let it lie. We decided to tail Hunter and... well I guess you saw how it panned out.'

'We're headed for Gibraltar,' Darren interjected. 'You two can make your own way back to England from there.'

'No, no, no. That won't do at all; we can use the skills these men possess,' said Hoffmann. 'We can't just abandon them. We'd be throwing them to the dogs. They're screwed until they have proper evidence to expose their superintendent. I'm sorry chaps, but until then you can no longer consider yourselves police officers.' The two men exchanged confused looks. 'Come on guys,' Hoffmann continued. 'If your boss is any kind of bad guy, he'll have the deaths of those two guards pinned on you already. You'll be fugitives by morning.'

'He has a point,' said Paul. 'We have little choice. Although I'm not sure what kind of work we could do for you, Mr Hoffmann. There is little we can share about the case. What did you have in mind?'

Hoffmann grinned. 'Oh, I'm sure I can find you a role.' He turned to George. 'Now I suggest we all turn our attention back to Dr Goodheart here. Particularly you, John; he's been champing at the bit to tell you something.'

George beamed at his audience and pushed a slip of paper into Hunter's hand. Hunter flipped it and raised an eyebrow. George had drawn a fish and scrawled the name 'Percy' through its centre. He glanced at his friend and back at the fish. 'Percy?' George nodded. 'You've drawn a picture of Percy, my goldfish.'

George nodded again. 'Come on, John, I thought you'd be quicker than this. Who did you name him after?'

'Fawcett, Colonel Percy Fawcett.'

'Who was?'

'A British explorer from the 1920s, famous for a number of expeditions into the Brazilian rainforest.'

George grinned. 'Surely you can do better than that? I remember the stories you used to tell us of this ill-equipped, Indiana Jones-style character, stumbling about the rainforest and happening by chance upon the ruins of an ancient city, a city he believed to be founded by refugees from Atlantis. If memory serves, he returned to Brazil in 1925, determined to bring evidence of the discovery back to London, but he never reappeared and is presumed dead.'

Hunter nodded. 'The lost city of Z. So you did learn something useful as an undergrad.' He slapped the table in triumph. *The lost city of Z. Colonel Fawcett: of course. It was so obvious in hindsight. Why hadn't he made the connection? It was years since he'd read Fawcett's journals but, from memory, the theory certainly fitted their scenario.* He frowned. 'Do the locations match? I have a vague recollection Fawcett's location for Z is nowhere near the mystery site on the Lindow map.'

George leafed through his notes and pointed to a set of ringed numbers. 'These are Fawcett's coordinates.'

Hunter stood and peered over the geologist's shoulder. His eyes widened and a triumphant smile spread across his face. 'Christ, George, they match. Twenty degrees north and twenty degrees west.'

George laid out a photocopy of the relevant Lindow map. 'The same numbers are repeated here; a fact that can only mean…'

'Fawcett didn't randomly chance upon Z, did he? He found it with a copy of our map,' said Hunter, his hands trembling.

George raised a finger and tapped the map of Brazil. 'Yes, but as you have pointed out, Fawcett's location is way down here somewhere.'

Hunter nodded. 'And all later expeditions searching those coordinates drew a blank.'

George peeled the next paper from his pile, his smile evolving into a full-blown grin as he slid it under Hunter's nose. Hunter bit his lip. This was big. 'They didn't find anything because the silly buggers were all using the wrong meridian.'

Hunter's stomach lurched in unison with a patch of turbulence as his friend's words found their mark. He could feel the excitement building. Could the answer really be as simple as the mathematics being wrong? He laid the copy of the ancient South American map beside George's calculations.

'Look at the Giza Pyramid complex in Egypt,' said George, tapping the map. 'And the glyph underneath it. It translates as the number zero?' Hunter nodded. 'There's a modern atlas on the seat beside you. Can you open it to show London, please?' He obliged and spread it over the table. 'Now find me the longitude of Greenwich.'

Hunter found the London borough and, more for the benefit of the watching onlookers around the table, traced his finger to the map's edge. 'Zero. So you believe all later explorers calculated their destination using modern longitudes?'

'Don't forget about the latitude.' John looked at George quizzically. 'The equator was in a very different position when these maps were compiled.' He drummed his fingers on the table top. 'Do you remember the paper I wrote a few years back? The one hypothesising the Earth is hit by a sizeable meteor every hundred thousand years or so.'

'Vaguely, why?' said Hunter.

'Hmm, how can I put this?' George pursed his lips. 'Imagine the Earth as a tennis ball with a golf ball knocking about inside to represent its core.' Hunter nodded. 'Now imagine the vacant area between the two balls is filled with a gel.' Jack nodded again. 'If I flicked the tennis ball hard with my finger, the impact would be absorbed by both the crust and the gel. Depending on the angle of the strike, the tennis ball may shift before stabilising again. Conversely, the golf ball at the core would remain unaffected and stay in the same position.'

Hunter rubbed the stubble covering his chin. 'I remember now. So you're saying if a comet crashed into the Earth, depending on the angle, the crust might be shoved around the planet?'

'Correct. An amazing quirk of nature which has enabled the Earth to enjoy, more or less, the same orbit since the big bang. Without this safety mechanism, it is arguable life on this planet would have ceased long before it evolved past single-cell organisms.' George pointed at Egypt and tapped it with his finger. 'Twelve-and-a-half thousand years ago, the estimated time frame for the last great impact, Giza must have lain directly on the equator. For whatever reason, be it religious, the Nile matching the Milky Way or whatever theory you choose to believe, our ancestors decided this point should be the site of the Earth's first prime meridian.'

Hunter nodded, his voice cracking as the final pieces of the puzzle fell into place. 'And it was with this starting point that this ancient race mapped our world.'

George winked at him and scribbled another set of numbers on his pad. 'All of which means… If I use a prime meridian focused on the Giza complex… Fawcett's city is…' His pencil hovered above the modern map of South America and plunged, making a hole in the paper deep within the Brazilian rainforest. 'Here.'

Hunter stared at the hole in the map, not knowing how to react. His heart certainly didn't seem to be beating. He raised his head and stared at George in disbelief. Could this really be the missing link he'd spent his life trying to discover? Something vibrated against his leg. It felt like a phone, but it couldn't be his as Hoffmann had yet to return it. He reached into his pocket and withdrew the latest iteration of the iPhone. The screen lit and a simple seven-word message filled the screen. His heart stopped for the second time in as many minutes. 'I hope I can count on you.'

Part Two

The Lost City of Z, Mato Grosso

Chapter Nineteen

Monaco

Hunter grinned as Inma clapped in excitement, her face a picture of undiluted astonishment. George concluded his ad-hoc presentation with a flourish of his pen in the Aurelian's on-board library. 'I knew there was something wrong with the Brazilian theories,' she said. 'Six years wasted because no one picked up on the fact we were using the wrong bloody prime meridian.'

'Why hasn't this city been found before now?' asked Paul. 'Surely it should have been picked up by a satellite or a drone or something?'

'The forest is too dense,' said Hoffmann. 'You'd be surprised how little is known about the Amazon rainforest. It is vast. The basin alone stretches over five and a half million square kilometres. Without co-ordinates, you'd have more luck finding a defined particle of dust on the carpet.'

'Sounds like you've got experience,' said Jack.

Hoffmann puffed out his cheeks. 'I've wasted millions on this folly. I've even paid for a military-grade satellite to search hundreds of square miles of this forest and found nothing. Well nothing bar a tribe of cannibals and a few species of rare bird.'

'Cannibals?' asked Jack.

'You've searched for Fawcett's city?' said George, brushing Jack's comment to one side.

'You sound surprised. Of course I have; I own the man's original notebooks. Plato aside, he's the starting point for Atlantis fanatics the world over.'

A flare of anger blossomed in Hunter's stomach. 'Why is this the first time I'm hearing this?'

Hoffmann shrugged. 'I'd discounted Fawcett as a dead end until now. I can count myself amongst the goons using the wrong prime meridian.'

'I'm sorry but I still don't understand; satellites do more than take photos. What about thermal imaging or radar? I've watched *Time Team*. There must be some way of locating something the size of a city,' said Paul.

Hoffmann shook his head. 'You need to see it to believe it. In most areas, the canopy is not only dense enough to block out light, but it also negates the possibility of obtaining clear images of the forest floor below. Sonar and thermal are pretty much useless.'

'What about at ground level? It must be easier once you're on the ground?' said Jack.

'Then you're in for a shock. Even in the midday sun, it's difficult to see your own feet, let alone anything else. The rainforest is an eerie, disorientating place, full of chattering birds, biting insects and a fierce array of deadly reptiles. Not that you'll see any... well not until they attack.' He smiled at George and slapped the geologist's knee. 'But what am I saying? My days of blind exploration are behind me. Isn't that right, George?'

George cleared his throat and nodded.

'So even though it's dangerous and you hate the place,' said Paul, 'you still want to go back?'

'With the chance of eternal and worldwide celebrity on offer...' Hoffmann snorted. 'Yes, PC Paul, in this instance I am more than willing to overlook my misgivings and get back on the metaphorical horse.'

'So this job you're offering, does it have a dental plan?' asked Jack.

Hoffmann grinned. 'And all the mosquito repellent you can drench yourself in.' He turned to Hunter. 'John, do we have a drop zone?'

Hunter nodded. 'We've been back and forth but yes, I think we're ready.' He turned the map of Mato Grosso to face his benefactor and ignored George's irreverent mumbling. Hoffmann examined the area ringed red by Inma.

'Is this it?' Hoffmann sounded surprised.

'Why? What's wrong?' asked Hunter.

'That's cannibal country.'

'Cannibal country?' interrupted George. He glared at Hunter. 'I told you my suggestion made more sense. But no, you have to pander to the lady.' Inma raised two fingers in George's direction. 'Whatever, princess. Look, there is no way I'm signing up for cannibals. This was not in the guidebook. I want to be toasted in Cambridge, not roasted in Brazil.'

Inma rolled her eyes. 'You are such a try-hard.'

'Enough, the pair of you,' said Hunter. 'We've been through this and, George, your suggestion was a non-starter then and still is. There isn't enough room for error. Half of us would end up hanging from the canopy with a hundred-foot drop to the ground.'

George shook his head but didn't counter the argument.

Hoffmann glanced at Darren. 'I assume you can arrange for suitable arms to be provided to minimise the risk?'

'We're covered, sir.'

'Minimise the risk?' said George. 'Is there a good chance we'll run into these people?'

'You'll be fine,' snapped Hoffmann. 'Cannibals go for leaner specimens as a rule. A better quality of meat I guess.'

George's face reddened as the connotation struck home. 'What are you implying? My body is a temple.'

'A temple to what, the McChicken Sandwich?' snorted Darren. George glared at him. 'What you gonna do, chubby?' Darren grinned and flexed his pectoral muscles, making them dance in time to the classical music playing quietly through the room's speakers.

There was only one winner in this fight and it didn't surprise Hunter when George backed down. The geologist's face reddened and he turned to address Hoffmann. 'On the off chance you have a point about my physique, what might a cannibal do with a "less than lean" gentleman? Would they just let him go?'

Hoffmann smiled. 'Not quite. The fattier meat usually winds up with the dogs or sometimes on the plates of the elderly.'

George took a deep breath. 'Well that's fine then, my mind is at ease. When do we leave? I'm really starting to strain at the leash now.'

'Come on, George, he's only pulling your leg,' said Hunter. 'No one is getting eaten.'

The ensuing uncomfortable silence spoke volumes. A rapping on the door broke the tension. Hoffmann sprang to his feet. 'Ah, that'll be the pilot. So, to answer your question, George: our kit is packed and we're leaving now.'

Chapter Twenty

Hunter held the door to the helipad open and waited for Inma to pass through. This was it, leg one of the adventure of a lifetime. He stared up at the helicopter's mesmeric rotors whipping round and round above his head. They would soon be in Gibraltar and boarding a plane bound for Rio. He looked at the straits beyond the bow of the yacht and smiled. Plato described Atlantis as lying 'beyond the Straits of Gibraltar' so this was a fitting location for their quest to begin.

He let the door slam and walked towards the huge machine. It was a Boeing Sea Knight, the transport helicopter favoured by the US Marine Corps. Capable of carrying twenty-five, there was more than enough room for the team and all their equipment.

He paused to take a final gulp of fresh sea air and clambered aboard, heading for the vacant seat next to George. He belted up, surprised to find his friend engaged in a discussion bordering on amicable with Inma Pérez. No doubt Inma's enthusiasm and feminine charms were working overtime in persuading George of the merits of one of her far-fetched theories. He nodded a greeting and winked at Inma. 'Morning, guys. You two look cosy. I hope she's not filling your head with any unsubstantiated twaddle, Georgie?'

George tutted. 'Not at all. Dr Pérez was just giving me the low-down on some research she's completed on early man. It's fascinating stuff.'

Hunter groaned; he'd been here before. 'Not Bigfoot again?'

Inma scowled. 'There was a time when you would at least have looked at the evidence. It's still at the theoretical stage but I'm convinced there must be a link between the Asian genus of giant men and the legends in America.'

Hunter rolled his eyes. 'I wanted to sleep with you then. That time has long passed.'

'Come on,' Inma continued. 'You can't be so blinkered you cannot even entertain the idea of interspecies breeding. Interbreeding could easily have resulted in the manifestation of a rare genetic anomaly harking back to early man.'

Hunter sighed and looked away from her. He was not in the mood to debate the pros and cons of gigantism. 'Okay, if I agree it's possible, can we wrap up this conversation? If you hadn't noticed, we're already neck deep in a more pressing, fantastical theory. Can we leave Bigfoot to someone else for the moment?' Inma folded her arms and pouted, looking out to sea. 'Oh come on. Are you serious? What are you, ten?'

The arrival of Hoffmann and his entourage of hired guns and ex-police officers saved Hunter from further argument. The men scrambled aboard, joking with one another as they secured an array of deadly weaponry to the shell of the helicopter. Hunter raised an eyebrow and exchanged a glance with George.

'Handguns, machine guns and RPGs?' hissed George. 'I thought we were searching for a lost city, not staging a coup.'

Hunter grinned and gave Hoffmann a wave as he entered, a little shocked by the German's choice of attire. He looked like a throwback to the days of Dr Livingstone. He was dressed from head to toe in khaki; a matching explorer's helmet adorned his head and brown leather boots, cut just below the knee, covered his legs.

'Someone woke up in the wrong century this morning.'

'I know, what a hero,' said George.

Hunter winced as something buzzed in his pocket. He knew exactly what it was and who it would be. The Order's smartphone was a lead weight around his neck. He still hadn't decided what to do about Jacob Knight and his convincing assertion he was working for the wrong side.

'Time to belt up, people,' Hoffmann yelled. 'Our ride is waiting for us in the shadow of the great rock. It's time for the talking to stop and the action to begin.'

Chapter Twenty-One
Order Headquarters, Bath

Jacob Knight slumped into his chair and awaited the return of his companion. He pursed his lips and stared into the dying embers, smouldering red hot in the hearth of the room's oversized, gothic fireplace. He took an unconscious bite of his fingernails and swilled the contents of his glass. The situation was spiralling out of control and he knew his next move would be critical. If what he'd just discovered were true, then the threat posed by the German was off the chart. He needed to tread carefully or this could spell the end for the brotherhood.

He lifted his phone and smiled at the text message on its screen. At least something was going to plan. His impassioned speech to Dr Hunter must have resonated and found its mark.

En route to Brazil.

Dr Hunter had nailed his colours to the mast. There was still scope for a double cross, but given his trusted status with the Order's current enemy, the risk was worth taking.

The door creaked open and a short, plump woman in a woollen trouser suit strode inside. She exuded a confidence rarely seen in Knight's presence. He rose to his feet and glowered down at her. Knight enjoyed cultivating feelings of fear amongst his colleagues and it galled him that this woman dared show him so little respect.

Professor Cleary returned to her chair and plucked a glass of red wine from the side table to her right. She wafted it under her nose and took a swig. Knight retook his seat and followed her example, letting the unmistakable perfume of minerals, cedar, graphite and red fruits envelop his senses. He took a sip, sucking the liquid through his teeth to amplify the tannins and momentarily holding it in his mouth before allowing it to slide down his throat. It was a heavenly, well-textured blend from one of the world's finest vineyards. Designed to intimidate his visitors, at £1000 a bottle the 1990 Lafite Rothschild was a clear statement of his organisation's power and wealth. Although he doubted the underlying implication would go unnoticed, it was a statement the professor was happily ignoring.

Knight tapped the sketch laid out on the table. 'You're sure this tube isn't a fake?'

'I'm certain,' said Cleary. 'I admit I've never seen it in this quantity, but I know orichalcum when I see it.'

Knight nodded. 'It's a nice find. It'll make an excellent addition to our collection.'

Cleary rolled her eyes. 'Are you purposely choosing to ignore the significance of this tube? Or has your IQ taken a dip since we last met?'

'Enlighten me,' said Knight, finding it hard to keep his cool with this obnoxious woman.

'A month before your group... how should I put this... dissuaded me from continuing with my research back in the '80s, I made a significant breakthrough. A black-market contact of mine in Paris forwarded a request to help sell a set of hieroglyphic inscriptions. They alleged they'd been removed from the base of the Giza Sphinx by Napoleon's soldiers during the French occupation. My man claimed he'd never seen glyphs of such quality and thought I might be interested in seeing them. I agreed and, posing as a buyer, certainly didn't regret the trip.'

'Where are they now?'

'The glyphs? I understand they ended up in Germany but, as I said, my interest ended soon afterwards and I lost any incentive to monitor them.'

'Germany? Might the buyer have been Hoffmann?'

'His father perhaps. It would explain a few of our blanks.' Cleary frowned. 'But we're veering off track. The identity of the owner is not the issue.'

'Okay, what did the glyphs tell you?'

'It wasn't just what they said, it was everything about them. Although dated to a period five or six thousand years before the Egyptians perfected their own style, these glyphs were already perfect. Each symbol had been carved and styled by what could only have been a master artisan. To put it in context, they were created at a time when cuneiform was undergoing its first stage of development in Mesopotamia. Here in England, we were still thousands of years from expressing ourselves using the written word. It didn't seem possible but there I was, standing in a Parisian cellar and gazing at a fully formed expression of written language at the peak of development.'

'What did the glyphs say?' Knight asked again, irritated by the professor's continued insistence on sidestepping the question.

'Mr Knight, my understanding of Egyptian hieroglyphics is second to none.' Professor Cleary leant back in her chair and took a deep breath. 'But these glyphs were something very different to the norm. Imagine trying to translate Old English into its modern form and you'll begin to understand the problem. Although the Egyptians based their later form of hieroglyphics on this original one, over time they'd adapted and developed it in a different direction. I could make out a few words and a few phrases, but much of it was still unintelligible.'

'Enough of the disclaimers. Just tell me what the damned thing said.'

Professor Cleary reached into the recesses of her jacket and pulled out a small piece of folded paper. She shook it open and handed it to Knight.

*"********* the ***** might of *********** the great warrior ***** in memory of our **** city. ********* inactive *** reminder ****** the perils of war. The key ********* held ****** descendants of ******* the ******** ***** people of Mu."*

Knight bit into his top lip and turned the words over in his head. 'I see what you mean about the blanks. So what's your assessment? Alongside the war references, the wording "in memory of our city" suggests the Sphinx to be some kind of memorial does it not?'

'I'm inclined to agree,' said Cleary. 'Given we erect memorials for every conflict we engage in, it's not a huge leap to assume past civilisations may have engaged in a similar practice.' The professor extended a finger and jabbed at the text. 'I believe this "key" is a reference to the key your Order was created to protect.'

'It's possible,' said Knight. He cocked his head to one side and fixed his gaze on the paper in his hand. 'Is the word "Mu" significant?'

Cleary smiled. 'It's the name of an ancient city said to be lost amongst the trees in the Amazon rainforest. There is a wide acceptance by many a crackpot that the city's origins lie in Atlantis.'

'So this might be our lost city? Surely the weapon can't still be housed there?'

'Why not? Your mate, Hans Hoffmann, seems to think so.'

'Don't worry about Hoffmann. We have that base covered. The German may have found maps and a little orichalcum, but he can do little without the key.'

Cleary pulled a second piece of paper from her pocket, changing the subject. 'The symbol of the Order, have you ever given it much thought?'

Knight shrugged his shoulders. 'I believe the explanation put forward by our academics. They tell me it's a representation of man surrounded by the divine. I have no reason to question the interpretation.'

Cleary nodded and slid the piece of paper over the table. 'This is a copy of a rubbing I took in Paris. I translated the glyph as representing the word… key.'

Knight unfurled the paper and stared at it in disbelief. Two sets of the Order's symbol were merged as one. They formed a set of intertwining circles. The edges of the central circles touched to form a horizontal figure of eight, the mathematical symbol for infinity.

'So, Mr Knight, if you happened upon an Atlantean artefact stamped with one half of this symbol…' Cleary grinned. 'An artefact carved from a material with the power to light up Europe. What, pray tell, do you suppose said artefact might be?'

As the significance of Cleary's words sank in, a chill rushed about Knight's person and he shivered. 'Hoffmann has the key…'

Chapter Twenty-Two
Mato Grosso, Brazil

The familiar mechanical clunk and whirr of gears echoed about the cargo hold as the rear door of the Hercules slid open. Hunter winced, the roar of an angry wind engulfing his senses as it battered the aircraft's fuselage. The leader of Hoffmann's mercenary team, Tyler Dent, motioned for him to approach the exit ramp.

Hunter rose to his feet and glanced with unease at the altimeter above his head. It was flickering at the three-thousand-feet mark. Hunter knew the jump altitude should pose him few problems, yet he still couldn't help but worry. It wasn't the jump itself – he'd clocked up over a hundred at this height with the Navy – it was a fear of the unknown. The landing zone was a complete mystery and for all the aerial reconnaissance completed by Hoffmann's team, they might still land on a rocky outcrop or something worse. The less experienced of their number could so easily snag their chutes on high branches or even miss the landing zone altogether; ending their journey at the bottom of some uncharted ravine. Certain risks were inevitable, but these were incalculable.

Hunter shivered and slapped his cheeks. 'Focus man, just keep calm and concentrate on hitting your mark.'

Dent grabbed Hunter's arm and yelled into his ear. 'We're above the LZ. This is go time, mister. You need a shove?'

Hunter looked back inside the cavernous aircraft. George and Inma were readying themselves, both fiddling with their equipment to ease their nerves. He winked at them, hoping his apparent indifference would mask the knot of dread in his stomach and reassure them all was well. He turned and shook his head at Dent, pulling a pair of goggles over his eyes.

Dent grinned and clamped an enormous hand in the small of

Hunter's back. He yelled something over the sound of the screaming wind. 'Hop and pop.'

Hunter signalled he was ready by raising his right thumb and stared at the ramp in front of him. He took a breath, held it and rocked back and forth on his heels, building his confidence. Unable to delay the inevitable any longer, he sprinted towards the blue sky and launched his body into the void. The instant rush of adrenaline was intoxicating and he drank it in, enjoying the hushed silence of his new world.

He spread his arms and legs, stabilising his body as it broke free from the forward throw of the plane. He looked at his altimeter. The dial read two thousand feet, decreasing by the second as his body accelerated towards terminal velocity. He tapped his chest, searching for the ripcord. His gloved fingers closed about the familiar toggle and he held his breath as he tugged it. Any malfunction could spell death. The pilot chute shot out above him, dragging the bridle line behind it. The mechanism pulled the pin from the closing loop on the deployment bag and, on cue, the parachute's large silk canopy punched free of its nylon prison. His body jerked and, with painful efficiency, his descent slowed from 120 to a mere twelve miles per hour. Hunter allowed his body to relax into the straps, confident of his survival for at least another few minutes.

He groped at his waist and freed a set of binoculars from their case, determined to enjoy the sublime beauty of the landscape into which he was drifting. As far as the eye could see, a carpet of rich greenery, teeming with wildlife, stretched towards every horizon, a vista only disturbed by the imposing quartzite-sandstone mountain range to the north. He smiled. If George's calculations proved correct, their journey's end lay somewhere out there, buried beneath the canopy and in the vast shadow of the mountains.

Hunter trained his binoculars on the treeline below and watched as a colourful collection of birds shrieked and fluttered through the high treetops. His heart skipped a beat, and he zoomed in for a close-up. A blue speck came into focus. His instincts were on the money. A bright blue hyacinth macaw flapped its wings and pecked at its torso. It was a good spot. Due to its beauty and resultant popularity as a black-market pet, Hunter knew it was high on the endangered species list. He raised an eyebrow and couldn't help but smirk. His father was a fanat-ical twitcher and Hunter knew his old man would've given up a kid-ney to have a wild blue macaw on his list.

A nearby tree branch shook and startled the macaw into flight. Hunter adjusted his lens, hoping to see another bird or perhaps a play-ful monkey emerge from the leaves. Without warning a flash of white light seared his retinas, blinding him. He shook his head and dropped the binoculars, the strap biting into his neck. He rubbed his eyes, blinking until the red and black dots dancing across them subsided.

He looked to the ground, surprised to see the same intermittent fleck of light. It was as if the sun was glinting off some kind of mirror stuck in the treetops... or a rifle scope. Hunter's blood ran cold. Were their movements being monitored? He gulped, suddenly very aware of what an easy target he presented. The erratic flashing ceased. Hunter grabbed at his binoculars and fiddled with the zoom, hoping to grab a fleeting glimpse of its source.

He jumped as a sharp crack and a puff of smoke answered his ques-tion.

He fumbled for his radio in panic and screamed into the receiver. 'Sniper! Tyler, come in. There's a bloody sniper in the trees. Can any-one hear me? I repeat, we have a sniper in the canopy. We're sit-ting ducks up here. Abort, abort.' He heard nothing but the sound of crackling interference. 'Tyler, come in. Do you read me?'

'Hunter? I read you. Over.'

Hunter gulped, trying to generate saliva to moisten his dry throat. 'Thank god, I thought we'd lost comms. There is a sniper in the trees. Repeat, there's a sniper in the trees, over.'

'Calm yourself, man,' Dent hissed. 'It's being dealt with, over.'

Another crack from the trees echoed up and into the air. The sniper's aim was improving and this time Hunter heard the round whistle past his shoulder, missing him by a matter of centimetres. 'Whatever you're doing, can you do it quicker?'

'Got him,' said Dent.

Hunter craned his neck skyward, curious as to the lithe mercenary's plan. Something fizzed and exploded just above him. It sounded like an RPG. He was right; the rocket raced by and, knocking Hunter's chute in its wake, bashed him sideways. His limbs flailed, and it took all his strength to retain a measure of control over his descent. He steadied and stared at the forest, following the rocket's progress. The shell found its mark with unerring accuracy and the sniper's position exploded in a ball of orange flame.

Hunter looked up, intending to signal his thanks to Dent. In an instant his mood switched from gratitude to one of horror. He gulped back the bile rising in his throat. Flames licked his parachute's canopy. He'd be free-falling in seconds. He closed his eyes and attempted rational thought. Although square inside the 'less than ideal' category, Hunter knew the situation was not yet critical. He checked his altimeter. A thousand feet. More than enough time to jettison the flaming chute and activate the reserve. He needed to remain calm and let his training kick in.

He reached for the cutaway handle to the right of his chest and let out a sign of relief as his fingers closed around the small metal hoop. He wrenched it hard, plummeting as the flaming canopy detached and his body returned to terminal velocity. Free of the main chute, Hunter reached for the second handle on the front left of his harness. He found it and pulled... Nothing happened. Through his goggles, he looked at the pull cord clamped tight inside his clenched fist and his heart stopped. It was severed in two. The sniper had found his mark after all.

'Tyler, come in. I need help,' Hunter yelped. 'Main canopy jettisoned and reserve chute damaged beyond repair. Repeat, I need help.'

High above him, he saw Dent jettison his chute and arrow towards his position.

'John,' Dent yelled. 'Spread your legs and arms as wide as you can. You need to slow your descent. We only have a window of a few seconds.'

Hunter bit into his lip and followed his orders. Dent was closing fast but, unfortunately, so was the ground. On the verge of giving into despair, he jumped as a strong hand grabbed his ankle. He looked to the sky and found his would-be rescuer within spitting distance. A rogue gust of wind caught them both off guard and Dent lost his grip, losing him for a couple more metres. With one last-ditch effort, the mercenary freed his rifle and, using it to extend the length of his arm, beckoned for Hunter to grasp hold.

Hunter swiped his hand at the gun, but missed. He gritted his teeth and lunged again, forcing his body to defy the constraints of gravity. The relief as his gloved hand grasped hold of the hard metal was palpable and he choked back the tears as it overwhelmed him. Dent hauled him in and curled a thick arm about his chest. Hunter gripped hold of the arm and closed his eyes as the ground came roaring up at him. Dent's spring-loaded pilot chute ejected and the reserve parachute billowed into the sky. He dared a brief look downward and instantly wished he hadn't. They'd fallen below the hard-deck decision altitude.

'Brace yourself,' Dent yelled.

They hit the ground at three times the recommended landing speed. Dent took the brunt of the impact, and the big mercenary screamed in pain as his knees buckled under him. His grip on Hunter loosened and the archaeologist hit the ground hard, landing on his back and careering head over heels across the hard, sun-baked mud. It was a few seconds before the contorted bodies of the two men came rolling and twisting to a painful halt.

Hunter was the first to stir. 'Tyler? Are you dead?'

With a pained groan, Dent croaked a response. 'This'll chafe in the morning. But I don't think anything's broken. You?'

Hunter pushed himself onto his forearms. His muscles felt as though they were on fire but he could wiggle his fingers and toes. It could have been so much worse. He forced a grin and gave his rescuer a thumbs up.

Dent beamed back. The moment was short-lived. Hunter's grin turned to one of shock as a gust of wind caught the mercenary's open canopy, yanking him into the air and dumping him back down hard on the forest floor.

Stunned, Hunter summoned every last ounce of energy and, fighting to block the pain in his legs, scrambled to Dent's stricken body. Something was wrong. He was motionless, his body hanging limp from the straps of his parachute as the relentless Brazilian wind dragged him further away with each gust. Within touching distance, he recoiled as another blast twisted Dent's flaccid torso onto its back. Hunter's legs collapsed under him. He bent forward and vomited, continuing to retch until his brain gave up the fight and he slipped into unconsciousness.

Dent's body came to a rest a few metres ahead, the canopy of his parachute halting as it tangled with the high branches of a nearby tree. His head lolled to one side, exposing an open wound and a cobweb of bloody trails. To his right, an innocent rock protruded from the ground, its tip a mass of coagulating blood and flecks of bone.

Chapter Twenty-Three

'John? John, are you okay? George, he's coming round. Call Inma. John, what the hell happened out there?'

Hunter opened his eyes, punch drunk and groggy. Someone mopped his brow, and he turned to acknowledge the gesture. 'Hans, is that you? Where the hell am I? Is this a hospital?'

'Good boy. So you haven't lost your mind then,' said George.

'You're in a tent,' Hoffmann continued. 'We're still in the clearing you landed in. You're a very lucky boy. Only a few scratches and little bruising. We've sewn up a deepish cut in your back but that aside you've no permanent damage.' He punched Hunter's shoulder. 'Just a decent scar and a damn good story you can impress the ladies with.'

'What about Tyler – where is he?'

Hoffmann screwed up his nose and shuffled his feet. 'I'm sorry to say he didn't make it. He took a nasty blow to the head.'

'Where is he?'

'I've alerted our pilot and requested a pick-up. It'll be twenty-four hours before they arrive though.' Hunter frowned. 'Don't worry, I've made sure he's in a spot where the birds can't get to him.'

'Are you serious? Why aren't we flying back with him? You aren't intending to carry on with the expedition? That man died saving my life.'

George placed a hand on Hunter's shoulder. 'I'm glad you're feeling better, mate, but rather than stew in your own juices, don't you think it would be better to carry on?' He paused. 'Tyler sacrificed himself so you could carry on. It would be wrong to turn back now. It's only right we all press on, if only to honour his memory.'

'Is this a sick joke?' said Hunter, his senses returning.

'George is right,' said Hoffmann. 'The best way you can honour Tyler is to find this city. We're on the verge of creating history, John. Success would virtually deify the name of Tyler Dent and the whole world would know of the extraordinary bravery he showed whilst saving your life.'

Hunter looked away and shook his head. They had a point. 'Screw you both.'

George smiled at Hoffmann. 'That means he'll do it.'

Hunter started as Inma bundled her way through the tent flap and shoved George to one side. She'd been running and was short of breath. 'Is – is he alright?' Hunter scowled at her. 'Back to normal I see.'

'A few hours' rest and he'll be fine,' said George.

Inma grimaced. 'That may not be possible. We've encountered an incy-wincy problem.' Hunter jumped, almost falling from his bed as the crackle of automatic gunfire echoed about the clearing.

Inma stood aside and lifted the tent flap to reveal a scene of chaos. Hoffmann's miniature army was racing around the makeshift camp, constructing a barricade around thirty metres from the edge of the rainforest. They were shoving crates of food alongside ammunition; fallen branches alongside uprooted foliage; in fact anything to give them cover. But cover from what?

Hoffmann's jaw dropped. 'What the hell is this? Who authorised…'

Before he could finish, one of Hoffmann's troops glanced in their direction, distracted from his task by the anger of his employer. Something fizzed and whistled through the humid air and thumped hard into the soldier's neck, knifing through the soft tissue under his ear. Hunter retraced its flight path and lost it somewhere amongst the shadows on the edge of the rainforest.

The soldier dropped the crate he was carrying and grabbed at his neck. He pulled a small dart free of his skin and raised it aloft, grinning. 'No harm done. Lucky this one wasn't using a gun.'

Hoffmann stroked his cheek and glanced at Inma. 'What do you think? Sixty seconds?'

'Maybe two minutes; he was quick on the draw to pull it out.'

'Sixty seconds? What are you talking about?' Hunter shook his head, trying to clear the fog from his brain. Whatever was going on, he needed to be alert. The question hung in the air as the soldier's eyes rolled back into his head and he collapsed to his knees, mouth foaming and a trickle of blood dribbling from his left nostril. He pitched forward and lay motionless in the dry mud.

Inma ignored him, her eyes wide in shock. 'Bloody hell, that was quick. What do you think it was, dendrobatids?'

'Dendro what?' said George. 'Isn't that something to do with tree rings?'

'They're talking about poisonous frogs, you idiot,' said Hunter. He rubbed his temples in a futile attempt to rid himself of the claustrophobic feeling of being trapped rising in his gut. If surrounded, there was no means of escape. 'This tribe must coat their darts with venom.'

'And damned potent venom at that,' Inma added. 'I've never seen frog juice take down a man of that size so fast. They must have found a way to refine it.'

Hunter shifted as George slumped beside him on the makeshift bed. 'What the hell is going on? Aren't the baddies meant to get us as we're about to solve a riddle or find some treasure? We've not even left base camp.'

Hunter pushed himself upright, wincing as he did his best to ignore the painful bruising on his back. He slid to the floor and unsteadily shifted round to confront Hoffmann. 'It's time to earn your stripes, Hoffmann. What's the plan? How many more of us do you intend to sacrifice on behalf of your ego?'

Hoffmann snorted in defiance, his eyes flashing in anger. Hunter braced himself for a barrage of abuse and took an aggressive stance, but it failed to materialise. Instead the German's face lost all colour and he broke eye contact, seemingly staring straight through him. Hunter clicked his fingers, trying to break the trance. Hoffmann didn't react and instead continued to stare at something beyond his right shoulder. Then, little by little, he raised both hands above his head.

Hunter felt his body go numb and he shivered. What, or rather who, was behind him? He turned, following Hoffmann's gaze. Hunter's jaw fell slack, his heart skipping a beat as his brain processed the danger presented by the colossal shape blocking the tent's only exit. A hefty hand shot from its centre, the open palm catching him square in the chest and shoving him over the bed and onto the floor beyond. The haloed figure flung the tent flaps aside and in strode a gigantic, red-skinned native adorned with fur and a plethora of colourful parrot feathers.

'He looks friendly,' whispered George, pulling Hunter to his feet.

'For our sake, I hope he's a vegetarian,' said Hunter, trying to rub away the fresh pain in his ribs.

The man licked his lips, his scarred features contorting into a wide grin as he scanned the fear-soaked faces of the four intruders lined up in front of him. He seemed to bask in the panic his presence was generating – that is, until his gaze locked on Hoffmann. Hunter noticed the native's face twitch and his previous self-assurance fade into a confused frown. Hoffmann walked around Hunter and beckoned the native forward. He stepped further inside the tent, his eyes narrowing as he studied Hoffmann's face. Without warning, he grabbed the German by his cheeks, pinching them in a father-like manner, albeit a potentially abusive one.

Hoffmann pulled free of the strange embrace and bent forward, whispering something inaudible into the Brazilian's ear. The native's face erupted into another beaming smile. This time however, the eyes were definitely friendly. He pulled Hoffmann into a full-on clutch and, in an inhuman display of strength, tossed him into the air like a rag doll before catching him again.

Hunter looked at George and raised an eyebrow. 'What on earth?'

'Just roll with it my mate, roll with it. If this keeps us off his dinner plate, I'm all for it.'

'You don't really think he's a cannibal do you?' Inma asked.

'Given where we are, I'd say there's a bloody good chance, wouldn't you?' said George.

Hunter tapped Hoffmann on the shoulder. 'Are you okay in there, mate?'

A muffled groan came from the suffocating depths of the warrior's armpit. The Brazilian laughed, releasing Hoffmann with a hearty slap in the small of his back. Leaving him gasping for breath and off balance, the blow was strong enough to knock the German clean through the tent flap and into the clearing beyond. Their new friend smiled and gestured for everyone to follow, marshalling them into the bright sunshine.

Hunter shielded his eyes and blinked, blinded for a moment as his retinas adjusted to the afternoon sun. He heard Inma retch to his right and felt her grab his arm, steadying herself. As the world came into focus he realised why, his own legs threatening to give way as he drank in the horror of the terrifying scene unfolding before him.

Hoffmann's remaining men stumbled about the camp in defeat, dropping to the ground as they were rounded up by groups of men dressed in a similar fashion to their new ally. As far as the eye could see, the scantily clad warriors appeared to be at an advanced stage of cleansing the battlefield and claiming their spoils. Hunter squinted, surprised to see several of them carrying German-made firearms from the Second World War era. Although the how and why were still a mystery, at least this explained the presence of the sniper rifle. The Nazis must have embarked on a similar expedition and stumbled upon the same tribe sometime during the war.

Aside from the occasional lustful glance at Inma, the group were largely ignored. The clearing was a hive of activity, the warriors more focused on dragging the dead and wounded into different areas. They were binding the arms and legs of their victims using twine. Hunter frowned. Alive he could understand, but this seemed a rather unnecessary precaution to bestow on a dead man.

A crackling sound to his right answered his question. Hunter turned to find another group of the warriors clustered around a roaring fire. They were cooking up a feast on a makeshift spit, two of them turning a large animal above the red-hot flames. He looked closer as a limb of the unfortunate animal slipped from its tether and dropped toward the fire. His blood froze. The limb lolled back and forth, unidentifiable if it weren't for the standard-issue military boot, stubborn in its refusal to part company with its owner.

Hunter rubbed his eyes, his vision impaired by the trails of fear-induced sweat snaking into his eyes. He glanced at Hoffmann. The German's face was devoid of emotion, barely registering the inhumanity of the situation unfolding about him. Hoffmann beckoned for their captor to join him. He wasn't close enough to hear Hoffmann's command, but whatever it was, it did the trick. The Brazilian took two steps forward and boomed out a command in the local dialect. The effect was immediate and, as if under a spell, everyone stopped what they were doing and congregated around their spokesman.

'Do you think this chap could be their leader?' said George, nudging Hunter in his aching ribs.

He shrugged, irritated by his friend's seeming lack of empathy, and nodded at the growing crowd. They were chanting the same words over and over. 'Him-A-Lar, Him-A-Lar, Him-A-Lar.'

The volume increased in line with the intensity, rising until, at the point of frenzied crescendo, a wave of calm fanned about the clearing. The crowd fell silent as one. Stunned, Hunter racked his brain for a clue. What the hell was going on? The words sounded familiar but his grasp of the dialect was non-existent and the meaning evaded him. He looked at his companions for inspiration, but their vacant expressions gave nothing away.

Hoffmann stepped forward. What was he doing? He surely couldn't be contemplating addressing the crowd. Hunter made a grab for the German's arm. 'Don't do anything stupid. You'll get us killed.' Hoffmann's eyes seemed to sparkle as he pulled his arm free. He grinned at Hunter and pushed past the tribe's spokesperson, taking centre stage.

He held his arms in front of him and spoke. 'Thank you for your kind welcome.'

Hunter rubbed his hands as nerves got the better of him. Whatever the plan, it'd better work. It was no exaggeration that their lives depended on it. Hoffmann's voice at least sounded authoritative, even if 'kind welcome' was stretching the truth a little far.

Hoffmann waited for his words to be translated before continuing. 'It is clear you all know of my eminent grandfather. I am glad his memory is still as strong in your culture as it is in mine.' He smiled, amused by the comment. Hunter frowned at Inma and she shrugged, similarly confused by this development.

'He made you all a promise. The day will come when his descendant would arrive in your village, a saviour dressed in white and ready to complete the work he started. Well, my friends, that day has arrived and I am that descendant.' He paused as the crowd roared its approval. 'I will take up my grandfather's fight and restore your tribe to its rightful position at the summit of a new world order.' He lowered his head in apparent regret. 'I must apologise for the delay in my arrival.

It is unfortunate but, in his haste to conceal the find, my grandfather's clues were a little too ambiguous. Even for his rightful descendant to follow.' An amused titter rippled through the crowd as Hoffmann's translated words found their mark.

Hunter was dumbstruck. What was Hoffmann talking about? Who was this 'eminent grandfather' of his? It couldn't have been Percy Fawcett, could it? He looked at George, who was mouthing something at him.

'Not, Him-A-Lar – it's Himm-ler.'

Hunter stopped breathing as the enormity of the truth struck him like a dagger to the heart. He bent forward, this time unable to stop vomit gushing from his mouth. It wasn't a local chant at all. And it wasn't three words, it was one... Himmler. Hoffmann's grandfather was Heinrich bloody Himmler.

Chapter Twenty-Four

Mato Grosso, Brazil, 1939

Heinrich Himmler lay in the sun-kissed clearing, a pair of screeching monkeys mocking him from a perch high in the trees. He'd informed Hitler and the rest of the Party that he was travelling to North Africa in search of a solution to the Jewish problem. Not for the first time he wished the lie were true. He was certain he wouldn't have been fighting for his life in Tunis. The skirmish was not turning out as planned. He lifted his head and scanned the battlefield. Only two of his men and the translator remained.

He wiped away the sweat accumulating in his hairline and checked his Luger. A wisp of smoke lingered at the tip of its barrel. The forest air, thick with humidity, was silent. Himmler squirmed further under the dead man he was using for cover. This new, eerie silence was almost as deafening as the screaming chatter of machine-gun fire it had replaced. He grimaced and ejected the weapon's magazine. He cursed and smashed it back inside the gun. Only two rounds; what the hell could he do with only two rounds?

If Himmler was to survive, he needed to act fast. He made a decision and shoved aside the dead German shielding him. He scrambled to his feet and raised both hands high above his head. Hitler would not be pleased when he learnt of his surrender to these savages, but what choice did he have? He shook his head, disappointed in himself. How had he, the great Heinrich Himmler, allowed himself to be captured by men no better than the Untermensch scum sitting in his extermination camp at Dachau? Noticing movement to his right, he heaved the cowering translator onto his feet and beckoned his two remaining soldiers to join him in surrender.

'Translate me,' he snarled, kicking out at the orange-skinned man quivering at his side. Even in defeat, Himmler cut an imposing figure. A meticulous man in every sense of the word, every aspect of his persona and dress had been carefully selected to promote fear and panic amongst those unlucky enough to encounter him. Back in the Fatherland, he was widely acknowledged as the second most powerful man in Nazi Germany. Hitler was quick to recognise Himmler's value to the Party, and it wasn't long before the Führer promoted him to Chief of the German Police and the Minister of the Interior. In addition, the role gave him control over the German security forces, including the infamous SS and the Gestapo.

Himmler straightened the circular, wire-framed glasses adorning his pointed nose and brushed down his short dark hair. Appointed to head up the Lebensborn programme back in Germany, it was ironic he was the antithesis of the blond-haired, blue-eyed children he'd been commissioned to promote.

'I have food and weapons. Grant me a safe passage through the trees and they are yours.' He paused, waiting for the translator to relay the message to the dark trees. 'This is all a misunderstanding; I mean you no harm. I am a mere explorer, a German politician searching for his ancestors and their lost city.' He pursed his thin lips, mulling over a variety of strategies and scenarios in his mind. 'If any of you know of this city and can take me to it, I will reward you beyond your wildest dreams. Kill me and my people will obliterate you from the skies.'

The translator finished speaking and Himmler relaxed his grip on the man's hair. He collapsed to his knees and sobbed into his hands. The undergrowth rustled to Himmler's right, and he turned to meet the threat, standing tall as three, half-naked savages emerged in front of him. He must show these creatures no fear.

The largest of them reached out and touched the SS lightning bolt insignia attached to his lapels. The hot breath of the savage prickled the hairs on his neck and he recoiled as the smell of rancid, rotting meat overwhelmed his senses. He turned his head and retched, unable to stomach the intoxicating stench. His tormentor grinned, grasped Himmler by his chin and spat in his face.

Overcome by revulsion and inflamed by the audacity of this vile specimen of subhumanity, Himmler reacted on instinct and smashed his forehead against the bridge of the man's nose. The native's knees buckled and he hit the ground, screaming in agony and holding his nose as blood oozed between his fingers. Himmler licked his lips, a cruel smile spreading across his mouth as he enjoyed the man's anguished cries.

He lowered his gun and placed the barrel against the native's forehead. If today was to be the day he met his maker, then this scum would join him. He sneered at the other two savages, daring them to attack and give him an excuse to pull the trigger. Behind him, he could hear his remaining soldiers diving for cover. They would pay for that later.

A loud bellow echoed through the trees and a monster of a man burst into the clearing. His skin glistened under stripes of green and yellow warpaint, exaggerating a set of bulging biceps and a huge barrel-like chest. Caught unawares, Himmler grimaced as the sharp edge of an obsidian knife pressed against his throat. The man continued to yell, frantic in his gestures between Himmler and his captive.

Himmler kicked out at his whimpering translator. 'Do your job.'

'Man under gun is son of chief.' The fear in the translator's voice was palpable. 'This man, Chief Tibiriçá.'

'Is he?' Himmler's eyes narrowed. 'Then I suggest you tell this Tibiriçá to let me go. In return I won't decorate the forest with his son's brain.'

The translator looked at his feet. 'Not so easy. You draw blood. Chief already want revenge.'

Tibiriçá yelled something at the translator and pointed at Himmler.

'He demands blood offering. What I say?'

Himmler smiled and drew the translator close to him. 'Is that all? Well in that case tell the nice man the two cowards behind me are my sons. Do you understand?'

'What? Please no, Mr Himmler, sir. They your men. They loyal. Follow you anywhere.'

Shoving the knife to one side, Himmler grabbed a handful of the old man's lank, dirty hair and forced his head back, raking the barrel of his gun across the exposed throat. 'It's them or you. Now make your choice.'

The translator didn't need to be asked twice and, with a glance at the cowering soldiers, he gabbled out the message. Tibiriçá nodded.

Himmler returned the nod and shoved the translator back to the ground, turning his attention to the two soldiers. They scrambled to their feet. The fools must think he'd negotiated their freedom. They stood to attention, their right arms at a forty-five-degree angle.

'Heil Hitler.'

Himmler raised his Luger and fired his remaining bullets in rapid succession, shooting both men at point-blank range in the head. They crumpled to the ground, a look of fear and shock emblazoned across their bloodied faces.

Himmler reached down and retrieved a standard-issue cap, placing it firmly on his head. He noticed the previous owner had embroidered his SS membership number on the side. Although an impressive 616, Himmler was glad his own number, 168, was lower. It still grated it wasn't lower. He didn't begrudge Hitler's number one spot, but why he wasn't number two was beyond him. After all, he effectively ran both the SS and the Gestapo single-handed.

He ran his thumb and forefinger along the rim of the cap and straightened his black tie, locking his eyes on the chief. 'Can I assume we are now even?' said Himmler.

The crowd of onlookers was growing. There were at least two dozen of them now, each armed to the teeth with a variety of decorated spears, knives and thin, two-foot tubes. They no longer looked aggressive, more inquisitive. They must be intrigued by the tiny weapon in his hand and how it could have caused the excessive gore dribbling from the heads of the dead soldiers.

Himmler shuddered as he assessed his present vulnerability, which was compounded by the empty clip in his handgun. With no other options, he threw the Luger at Tibiriçá's feet and placed his hands on his head.

The chief growled and, gripping his knife with ominous intent, motioned for his men to advance. Himmler didn't fancy his chances in a fist fight, but given the choice of surrendering to these savages or dying with dignity on the battlefield, death was the only option. He balled his fists.

Instead of striking him, Tibiriçá frowned and lowered his spear, stooping to stroke the number on his cap. Himmler stared in defiance, meeting the chief's angry gaze head on. The chief's meaty hands shot around his waist, enveloping him in a vice-like grip and forcing the air from his lungs. Himmler coughed, his feet jerking about in thin air as Tibiriçá hoisted him astride his broad shoulders. He sucked in deep breaths of the humid air, and stared at the group of painted warriors surrounding him, wary of the razor-sharp spears pointed at his torso.

Tibiriçá strode to the centre of the crowd and halted. Himmler jerked forward, clinging on for dear life as the giant man arched his back and roared out a single phrase. It resonated through the trees, silencing the wildlife and natives alike.

'É ele, É ele, É ele.'

Whatever the meaning, the response it drew was overwhelming and instantaneous. Himmler watched on as the savages collapsed to the ground in unison, flinging their arms forward in a deep bow. The whole display was baffling. He clicked his fingers, and caught the attention of the translator, pointing to the baying chief beneath him.

The small man wiped the tears from his face and cleared his throat. 'They ch-chanting,' he stammered. 'É ele, É ele. It is him, it is him.'

Chapter Twenty-Five
Mato Grosso, Brazil

Hunter stared at the back of Hoffmann's head. He didn't know what else to do. It was shocking, but Hoffmann appeared proud to have Himmler as his grandfather. The disclosure explained the origin of his family fortune. History recorded Heinrich Himmler as having amassed a huge fortune in stolen paintings and gold bullion during the Nazi occupation, a fortune only partially recovered after the war. Hunter bit into his lip. As unpalatable as the foundations of Hoffmann's empire were, they didn't concern him. The immediate issue was more what impact the revelation might have on the safety of his team.

Hunter knew Himmler as having been one of the crazier members of Hitler's Third Reich, an achievement given the competition. Known for fronting the infamous SS, Himmler presided over the Holocaust and is believed to have been responsible for coordinating the deaths of over ten million 'enemies' of Germany. As one of the most dangerous and influential men in the Third Reich, it was a shame his cowardly suicide robbed the West of its chance to put him on trial in Nuremberg.

Hunter shuffled his feet. He also knew there was more to Heinrich Himmler than the cold and calculating war criminal history painted him as. As an undergraduate, Hunter's passion for all things Atlantis had led him to a copy of Himmler's war diaries. Its contents were both appalling and exciting. The entries confirmed Himmler as the absolute definition of a racist and his hatred of foreigners and, in particular Jews, was overwhelming in its ferocity.

The Reichsführer was never shy in voicing his views and thrived on his fearsome reputation. Backed by Hitler and the Party, Himmler chose archaeology and anthropology as his weapons to justify his racist stance. This led to the creation of the Ahnenerbe, the ancestral heritage branch of the SS. Under Himmler's direct command, the unit undertook numerous projects with the goal of evidencing a link between the Germanic-based Aryan race and the survivors of the Atlantean apocalypse. He believed that, as rightful descendants of this 'super race', it was their divine right to conquer and rule the world taken from their ancestors by the Untermensch or subhumans.

In 1938 the search for physical evidence took the Ahnenerbe to Tibet and allegedly struck gold. Their discovery was never publicised but many sources confirm the expedition leader, Ernst Schäfer, presented Himmler with a document pertaining to the origins of the Aryan race. Unfortunately for Atlantophiles, this supposed evidence was lost at the end of the war when the Ahnenerbe's work came to a grinding halt. Himmler's subsequent suicide proved to be the final nail in the coffin of Aryan research and the trail went cold.

With no leads, Hunter chose not to pursue the legend during his own hunt for the lost city, dismissing it as mere Nazi propaganda. He wished he'd given it more credence now. If Himmler had led an expedition to Brazil himself, there was no doubting Schäfer's document must have been real.

Hoffmann continued his speech, his foot slipping a little on the rock he'd used to elevate his position. The crowd of natives barely noticed, all of them hanging on his every word. Hunter zoned out as the German persisted in grinding out a few minutes of overprepared prose about family ties and the importance of his grandfather's work. Given the extent of Himmler's crimes this love-in was making him cringe. He only hoped Hoffmann was referring to the archaeological aspects of Himmler's career, as opposed to the genocidal.

Hunter's heart sank as Hoffmann answered this question by pulling an old, polished Luger from a chest holster under his shirt. He held it aloft, letting it glint in the sunlight. The natives apparently recognised the handgun and gasped in unison. Hunter shifted his feet as George leant to whisper into his ear. 'What do you think this bit is about? I'm assuming the gun must have belonged to grandpappy Himmlie?'

Hunter shrugged. 'Just be ready to make a break if we get the chance. Himmler wasn't adverse to the odd killing spree, and it seems his grandson has inherited a similar passion. This Luger is being brandished for a reason.'

'Darren? Darren? Where are you?' said Hoffmann. Darren stepped into view. 'Ah, there you are. Do me a favour and fetch my sons please.'

Hunter frowned. Sons? What was this crazy man talking about now? He watched Darren turn and enter a nearby patch of dense foliage. He appeared to be pulling at something heavy. Even with the inhuman well of strength Darren could call upon, he was struggling. Hunter squinted and his heart skipped a beat as he suddenly realised why. The bodyguard's massive hands were clamped around the ankles of two writhing bodies. Hunter swallowed hard, recognising the bandaged arm jutting from the smaller man's torso. It was Jack and Paul. He turned away and closed his eyes, a feeling of utter helplessness threatening to overwhelm him.

He heard Darren kick out at his captives. Hunter flinched as the steel toecap in Darren's boot connected with Paul's thigh. He opened his eyes and saw Darren ditch Paul, focusing instead on clamping both his hands around Jack's ankles. He must have decided dragging both men was a little ambitious, even for him. With a firm tug, he pulled Jack clear of the treeline and into full view of the baying crowd.

Hoffmann clicked his fingers and pointed at the bare ground in front of him. Darren nodded and shoved the police officer into position. In a deliberate and exuberant manner, Himmler's grandson gripped Jack's jaw and yanked the terrified man onto his knees. 'How's it going, Constable?' said Hoffmann. 'I trust you're looking forward to playing your part in history? You should treat this as an honour. You'll be remembered for something. Most of your kind will not be so lucky.'

'Your kind? W-w-what's going on, Hans?' said Inma, finding her voice. 'What are you doing? Why have you tied up Jack?'

'Quiet,' he snapped. 'And that goes for the rest of you. Any nonsense and I swear none of you will live to see out the day.' George sniffed as fear-fuelled tears ran down his cheeks. 'Shut him up, Hunter. If you don't my Luger will do it for you.'

Inma grabbed George's head and pulled his cheek to her chest, stroking his head to calm him. Hunter scanned the clearing. He needed a gun. If any of them were to survive, he definitely needed a gun. Disarming Hoffmann was a possibility but the distance between them was a little wide. The German would have time to get off at least one shot and maybe two. Even if his bullets missed, he was certain Darren's wouldn't, and he was carrying an AK-47. Responsible for thousands of deaths in the hands of terrorists and militants worldwide, it wasn't a weapon to be taken lightly. Hunter steadied his breathing and tried to relax. He needed to bide his time and wait for his moment. Given time, Hoffmann would make a mistake. The bad guys always made a mistake.

Darren hauled Paul over the final few metres of the stony ground and dropped him at Hoffmann's feet. Paul flopped forwards, knocking into Hoffmann's legs and causing him to stumble backwards. Hoffmann cursed and lashed out, catching Paul flush in the ribs. Hunter flinched as he heard the sound of a bone cracking. Darren reached forward and grabbed a handful of Paul's hair, pulling him upright and forcing him to face Hoffmann. The German turned to the expectant crowd and aimed his gun at the bruised and battered police officers.

'Ladies and gentlemen, boys and girls, let me introduce… my sons.' The corners of his mouth rose into a tight smile and a hush descended. He pulled the trigger.

Hunter looked in disbelief as a splash of warm blood hit Jack in the face. This couldn't be happening. He felt like a voyeur in a cheap horror movie. And yet it was happening; Paul was dead. Hans Hoffmann had murdered Paul, a police officer. A shrill and unbearable tinnitus rang in his ears as he watched Paul's body slide in slow motion from Jack's shoulder and crumple to the forest floor. A tear trickled down Hunter's cheek and he raised his head to the heavens, praying for a miracle from a god he'd long stopped believing in.

He watched Hoffmann cock his head to one side, pausing both to heighten the tension and apparently revel in Jack's supplicatory reaction to the death of his partner. Hunter wondered if he'd pulled the trigger on anyone before. The bloodlust in the man's eyes suggested he probably had. Hoffmann eased the sight of his gun to the right, stopping only when centred in the middle of Jack's sweat-laden forehead. His index finger caressed the trigger of Himmler's gun. What was he waiting for?

It was disgusting. Hoffmann was actually savouring the moment. His eyes narrowed and a thin, sadistic smile spread over his lips. He traced the Luger's barrel around Jack's face, circling his chin, lips and nose. Then, as the cold steel returned to the police officer's clammy forehead, Hunter closed his eyes, averting his gaze as the German squeezed the trigger.

Chapter Twenty-Six

Mato Grosso, Brazil, 1939

Himmler's head was spinning. In the hours following his decision to execute his men, the Brazilians had embarked on a swift and all-encompassing campaign of unabated hero worship. They hoisted him into the air, carrying him with reverence back to their village. On their arrival, Chief Tibiriçá himself offered up his own residence for Himmler and his translator to use as their own. He gave them food, a choice of women to lie with and a beverage which, based on his pounding headache, must have been near pure alcohol.

Himmler swept aside the animal hide concealing the hut's entrance and took a deep breath, sucking the fresh morning air into his lungs. It was a far cry from the polluted offering he inhaled in Berlin. Even the pain from his habitual stomach cramps seemed to have eased. As a long-time sufferer, it was good to know there were alternatives to the healing hands of Dr Kersten, his masseur.

Himmler shielded his eyes as they became accustomed to the bright sunlight and scanned his surroundings. He raised an eyebrow, struck by the order shown by this savage community. His preconceptions of jungle society dictated he should find an assortment of badly built mud huts, their number correlating with the size of the population. Growth through necessity, one might say. The reality was a different beast entirely. It was clear the village had been built according to an overarching architectural master plan, a plan its people were advanced enough to execute. Two concentric rings of huts surrounded a large central fire, each hut spaced at regular intervals and built to the same specification, size and shape. Only Chief Tibiriçá's differed, and then only in its size.

Himmler took a step backwards as two groups of naked children sprinted past, the second pursuing the first with murderous intent. Himmler frowned and stared with morbid fascination as the back marker from the front group tripped and crashed to the ground. The chasing pack pounced and, with an unrelenting efficiency, took turns kicking and punching the torso of the fallen boy. They left his head untouched, an oddity given the ferocity of the attack. Himmler looked back into the hut and picked out his translator slouched against a wall in the gloom. He gave him an inquisitive nod and pointed at the fight.

The translator grimaced at the pain of getting up and joined Himmler in the doorway. 'Ah, it how you say – rite passage? Only way they learn. If boy survive, he become man. This warrior tribe. Ritual make sure weak not survive to breed.'

'Why are they avoiding the head?'

The translator smiled. 'Boy must be given chance to survive. Kicks to head fatal.'

'And what of those fast enough to escape a beating?'

'If boy avoid capture ten time, they also become man.' Himmler nodded, impressed by the philosophy. Maybe these savages were not so different. If the German people underwent similar rituals, perhaps his soldiers would have fared better in the earlier battle.

Lost in thought, Himmler started as a slender pair of arms grasped and eased their way around his waist. He turned, angry at the intrusion into his personal space. It was the woman he'd known carnally the previous night. With no further need of her services, he grabbed her wrists and threw her aside. The woman careered into the wall of the hut, knocking free a section of the dried-mud coating. She picked herself up, her pretty face contorted in a mix of fear and confusion. On the verge of tears, she scurried off into the depths of Tibiriçá's residence. A sadistic leer spread across Himmler's face as he watched her go. The terror in the woman's eyes both thrilled and aroused him in equal measure. He glanced at the bare section of wall the girl damaged during her fall and his eyes narrowed in curiosity. He bent to examine it and brushed away the remaining mud. It was concealing bricks: modern-looking, greyish bricks. How could a society such as this have developed the means of building with bricks?

A roar of laughter echoed through the clearing. Himmler spun on his heels, tensing his muscles and clenching his fists, ready for a confrontation. It was Tibiriçá. The gargantuan figure leant towards him and clamped a huge hand on Himmler's shoulder, forcing him against the wall of the hut. The giant man said something incomprehensible in his native tongue. Himmler shrugged, pleased the native was prattling on with a smile on his face.

There were few men the Reichsführer feared but this man would be counted amongst them. He could see Tibiriçá's coward of a son skulking in his father's shadow, the boy's nose still bloodied and bent out of shape from their earlier encounter. Himmler clicked his fingers and beckoned for his translator to do his job.

'He pleased to see you discipline woman,' said the translator. 'Respect you more. He want to know where you from and why you have fire rods… I think he mean your guns.'

Himmler frowned, unsure how to play this. He stroked his chin and, unable to see a downside, opted for the truth. 'Tell him I'm from the Fatherland, a land thousands of miles northeast of where we stand. I am here to discover the origins of my people. We are the descendants of the race who once populated these lands. Tell him the fire rods are our weapons, just as spears are theirs.' He paused, only continuing once satisfied the chief had understood. 'If he can provide evidence of my ancestors, tell him I will share the secrets of our fire rods.'

This final sentence provoked Tibiriçá into babbling at a heightened decibel level. He grabbed Himmler under his armpits and lifted him off his feet, swinging him in a circle. Himmler gritted his teeth and tried to force a smile, glad none of his men were alive to witness his embarrassment. After what seemed an eternity, the chief dropped him and continued spouting a stream of nonsensical chatter at his translator.

The translator shrugged. 'He speak too quick.' Tibiriçá grasped Himmler's arm and pointed at the tall trees surrounding the village. He yanked at his arm and pulled him forward. 'I got it. He want to take you into the rainforest.'

Chapter Twenty-Seven

Mato Grosso, Brazil

Knight shoved the note aside. Its contents were concerning. 'Para-troopers delayed due to enemy activity at the LZ.' He gazed up at the huge blanket of webbing rustling above his head and pondered what 'enemy activity' might mean. A battle perhaps. He shrugged, gripping his armrest as the Lockheed Martin C-130 Hercules transport plane banked right, the eight-blade NP2000 propellers cutting through the night sky as they found the new heading. He'd been in the air for hours and at last the plane was descending towards the agreed jump zone, deep inside the boundaries of the Brazilian state of Mato Grosso. He peered through the tiny window to his left and saw nothing but absolute darkness, not even the merest pinprick of light to indicate life. The rainforest really was one of the few remaining frontiers man had yet to dominate.

Knight settled back into his seat and contemplated his options. Having his men land at the secondary landing zone was frustrating but in the grand scheme of things he supposed it didn't matter – an insignificant delay to the mission's inevitable success. The detour at least meant Hoffmann must still believe his party was alone in the rainforest. Given the recent change in circumstances back in Bath, the delay had also given him the opportunity to order his men to bed down and await his arrival.

A few hours earlier the brotherhood had decided Knight himself should take the lead in the operation against Hoffmann. Although the Order's special-ops team could be trusted, Professor Cleary's revelations certainly raised the stakes. The mission was now far too important to leave in the hands of mere subordinates. If her analysis was right, everything the Order stood for was under attack and, to all intents and purposes, they were at war. Knight shuddered. He was in a position his predecessors hadn't faced since the Crusades.

He thought back to the Templars' accidental discovery deep inside the Temple Mount in Jerusalem. Facing exposure and extermination, the Order had bought the Templars' silence and, united as one, they thrived, albeit not for long. The Templars underestimated their new bedfellow and, two hundred years later, the Order exacted its revenge.

On Friday 13 October 1307, in its most open display of power, the Order, through King Philip IV of France, commanded the French Army to arrest and slaughter every Templar Knight it could find. It was a black day in history; even today, Friday the 13th is still treated with mistrust all around the world. He shook his head. If only he could dispose of his own adversaries with such clinical ease.

Knight squirmed in his seat and cursed his wardrobe. The military fatigues and body armour were a necessity, but the fact didn't make them any more comfortable for a man of his build. A loud klaxon sounded, making him jump. The rear doors of the Hercules jerked, crunching and grinding on their hinges as they opened to reveal the eerie, moonlit vista below. The scene fuelled his imagination and he could only wonder what secrets lay undiscovered, hidden for generations in amongst the blanket of trees and chattering wildlife. With a renewed sense of determination, Knight punched open his safety belt and sprang to his feet. The time to face his nemesis was nigh, and he was ready for the fight.

Chapter Twenty-Eight

Hunter bowed his head and closed his eyes. He couldn't bear witnessing a second execution, but what other choice did he have? The presence of Darren's AK-47 alone extinguished the possibility of anything other than a kamikaze attack. If alone, he might have chanced it, but there were the lives of his companions to consider. Paralysed by circumstance, there was nothing for it but to bide his time and stay alert for any opportunities to escape. His heart, however, refused to comply, stirring his senses by replaying childhood memories of his time with Jack over and over in his brain. This was his oldest friend. He couldn't stand by and let this happen. He tensed his muscles. If these were to be Jack's final moments, Hunter was newly determined they would also be Hoffmann's.

The piercing crack of a single gunshot echoed about the clearing. Inma gripped Hunter's arm as a cry of anguish followed the bullet's thunderclap. Puzzled, he raised his head and opened his eyes. A cry of anguish? Surely Hoffmann couldn't have missed?

A wave of nausea and relief hit Hunter like a train, his brain questioning the reality of the panicked scene unfolding in front of him. As unbelievable as it seemed, Jack was still alive, the police officer's eyes stretched wide in terror as he teetered back and forth on his knees. Instead it was Hoffmann screaming blue murder, clutching his right hand as blood oozed between his fingers, hitting the ground and staining the parched earth about him. Hunter scanned the treeline. Was this the work of a sniper?

Hunter hit the dirt, spinning in the air as Darren knocked him aside, tackling his boss and dragging him to cover. The bodyguard ripped a sleeve from his shirt and tied it around the wound, stemming the bleeding. It was the first time Hunter had seen Darren's feathers ruffled. Clearly the events of the past few seconds were not in the script. Darren grabbed Hoffmann under his arm and waved his machine gun at the trees, unloading a full clip in the vague direction of the sniper to cover his retreat.

Hunter couldn't believe his luck and pulled a Stanley knife from his belt. He crawled alongside Jack and sawed at the bonds holding the petrified man captive. 'Jack, can you walk? We need to move.'

Jack rolled onto his front and attempted to push himself upright. He pointed at the fleeing German, his eyes red and raw with emotion. He attempted to shout something but his voice box refused to cooperate and instead only a rasping, guttural noise escaped his mouth.

Inma grabbed him around the waist, righting him before his arms buckled beneath him. 'Don't try to speak. Your vocal cords must be damaged.'

Jack pulled away from her and lurched in Hoffmann's direction, tears running down his face. He balled a fist and stumbled, adrenaline alone not enough to support his weight. Hunter caught hold of him, ducking under his friend's arm before he hit the floor.

'Jack, we need to leave. You can fight this fight another day. Do you understand me?' said Hunter. 'I've no idea what's going on but if we stay we die. What good will that do Paul?' Hunter's gaze raked their surroundings. The natives were following Hoffmann's example and ducking for cover. This was their chance. A window to slip away, unnoticed in the chaos.

Hunter spotted movement in the trees and beckoned for everyone to follow, gambling on the loyalty of the sniper. He kept the group low, trying to stay inconspicuous as he plotted a course between bushes and rocky outcrops. He adjusted his grip on Jack's sweat-drenched torso and urged him forward. They were close.

'Wait, what about the maps and the canister?' rasped Jack, spitting each word out in obvious pain.

Hunter's stomach took a dive and he looked at Inma in despair. 'Tell me you've still got the artefacts?'

Her lips tightened. 'No.'

'Jesus, Inma, where are they, then? I left them with you.'

'I know,' she snapped. 'They're in my rucksack.'

Hunter bit his lip. 'This isn't a game. Where's your bloody rucksack?'

She looked to the ground. 'Darren asked if I needed help. I was struggling with the weight so I let him take it.'

George rolled his eyes. 'Okay, so who's going to ask the heavily armed psychopath if we can have our ball back?'

'Shut up, George,' said Hunter. 'Let's just focus on getting out of here before we're missed. We can worry about the cylinder later.'

The colour drained from George's face. 'Oh shite.'

'What?' Hunter twisted and collided with a wall of solid, orange-brown skin. He screamed in pain as five meaty fingers bit into his shoulder and shoved him to the ground. Jack followed suit, knocking himself unconscious as the side of his head smacked against the baked earth. Hunter winced as the dead weight of Jack's muscular frame landed across his legs, pinning him to the ground. He tried to lever the policeman aside, but the effort was futile; he was trapped. The colossal figure of the once-friendly tribesman stepped forward, his welcoming grin replaced by a menacing look of contempt. He levelled an antique machine gun at Hunter.

Hunter bent forward, redoubling his efforts to heave Jack's torso from his legs. The Brazilian smiled, satisfied Hunter posed no immediate threat. He swung the gun in Inma's direction and waved it at her chest.

'Remover, remover,' he growled.

Inma touched her shirt. 'You must be kidding. Piss…' The native's hand caught her cheek, his thick fingers leaving an angry red mark.

'Remover, remover.'

'Just do as he says,' George urged. 'At least it'll buy us a little time.'

Hunter watched Inma turn her head and gaze into the eyes of her attacker. 'Don't break eye contact, don't break eye contact,' he whispered under his breath. He was pleased her naval training had kicked in. It was imperative she show no sign of fear or weakness. He watched Inma dab the cut on her lower lip and defiantly grasp the top button of her shirt, flicking it undone. The man grinned, waving his gun at her again, trying to hurry the process.

Hunter kicked out again, desperate to free himself. If rape was the intention of the Brazilian, then he would die trying to prevent it. The crack of a rifle stalled his progress, and he screamed as Jack's full weight rolled back onto his ankle. He glanced at the native, surprised to find the man's leer replaced by a look of shock. The dark eyes rolled in his head and he collapsed face first into the long grass, a trail of dark blood trickling from a small hole in the side of his skull.

'Our sniper's back,' said Hunter. 'George, Inma, find cover.' Jack stirred, giving Hunter the chance to wriggle free. He hobbled to the dead tribesman and grabbed the machine gun, hurling himself behind the stump of a fallen tree. He examined his prize and raised an eyebrow. A German Mauser with half a clip of ammunition. No doubt a relic dating from Himmler's expedition. A bullet hammered into the trunk of his tree. Surely this sniper must be on their side? Why were they being shot at? He slumped to the ground. They were pinned in no-man's-land, enemies to their front and rear, and with no means of escape.

Countless bullets whistled through the air above him, cutting down all in their path with indiscriminate ease and unerring accuracy. Whoever was shooting, it was clear they were professionals.

Hunter tensed as a bullet fizzed above his head and another native hit the dust. Whoever this new group were, taking prisoners didn't appear high on their agenda. The chattering gunfire dissipated as the surviving members of the tribe abandoned their positions and fled into the sanctuary of their rainforest.

'John Hunter?' boomed a deep baritone voice. 'If you are alive please show yourself.'

A wave of relief swept over Hunter like a tsunami. He made a move to get to his feet. George lunged for his leg, pulling him beside him. 'What are you doing?' he hissed. 'Are you crazy?'

'Get off me, you idiot.' He shook his leg free of George's hand. 'These are the good guys.' He grinned and waved his hands above his head. 'At least I hope they are,' he whispered. 'Cease fire, cease fire. Jacob Knight, is that really you? Your timing is impeccable.'

Hunter poked his head above cover and squinted in the bright light. His heart skipped a beat, as he made out the familiar figure of a rotund man in black military fatigues striding toward him. As the distance reduced he saw the unmistakable shape of an SAS-endorsed L96A1 sniper rifle slung around his shoulders. A group of twenty or so soldiers followed in his wake, each of them breaking cover with a little more caution than their leader; trigger fingers alert to the potential dangers hidden within the wispy grasses of the clearing.

'Where are the artefacts?' shouted Knight.

Hunter pointed to the trees behind him. 'Hoffmann has them.' Knight rolled his eyes and motioned for his men to follow.

'Why didn't you kill the bastard when you had the chance?' shouted George.

Knight glanced at George, his left eye twitching in irritation. 'He is still of use. Is the same true of you, Dr Goodheart?'

Chapter Twenty-Nine
Mato Grosso, Brazil, 1939

Himmler paused, bending to examine a black, broken piece of rock discarded on the forest floor. He turned it in his hand, frowning as he swept a finger over its impeccable, marble-like finish. It must have been chipped from a statue or pillar. It was impressive workmanship and Himmler doubted even the largest construction companies in Germany would have done any better, even with their modern machinery and tooling techniques. He slipped the fragment into his pocket, a tingle of childlike excitement building in his stomach.

After years of ploughing Nazi resources into the Ahnenerbe, he was at last on the verge of completing his quest. If the papers found in Tibet by the short-sighted idiot, Ernst Schäfer, were to be believed, then it wouldn't be long before he possessed the evidence he craved: solid, indisputable proof linking Aryan Germany to prehistory's greatest lost empire, the kingdom of Atlantis. Armed with this knowledge, Himmler was convinced the Aryans of Europe would rally under the Nazi banner, joining forces with the Führer to form an unstoppable alliance tasked with reclaiming the lands and legendary technologies of their ancestors.

Tibiriçá barked a command in Himmler's direction, snapping him out of the daydream. There were still several steps he needed to tread along this path and he needed to focus on the present. Proving his doubters wrong would have to wait. A month earlier, Hitler himself had dismissed the Ahnenerbe as mere folly and the criticism still smarted his ego. Luckily for him, his reputation ensured the majority of Party members were still happy to indulge the quest. Himmler wasn't a man anyone wanted as an enemy, and the Party viewed their support as an easy way to appease his infamous temper.

Up ahead, Tibiriçá swept aside a dense section of foliage and signalled for Himmler to follow. He disappeared through the gap with his son and the vines dropped back in place. Himmler looked down at the diminutive translator. His hate for the man welled inside his gut. He despised the reliance his current predicament demanded he place on such an insignificant being. Back in occupied Europe he would have ordered the creature's execution without even batting an eyelid. But out here... He shook his head. Out here this dirt-encrusted man was irreplaceable.

'You go first and tell me if it's safe,' said Himmler.

'W-w-what if it t-t-trap?' stuttered the petrified translator.

'That is why you are going first.' Himmler shoved him in the small of his back and propelled him through the foliage, sending him crashing into whatever lay beyond. With a bone-crunching thud the translator hit something solid and yelped in pain. He staggered backwards and lost his footing, returning through the greenery and landing at the feet of his employer. He whimpered and pulled a mucky rag from his pocket, pressing it against his broken and bloodied nose.

'Well?' asked Himmler, suppressing laughter. 'How did you get on?'

'Wall... Wall on other side.'

Himmler frowned and slipped a hand through the thick, leafy foliage. His hand barely cleared the flora when it met something solid, something sharing the same smooth surface as the strange flake of rock in his pocket. Himmler's eyes widened in anticipation. Could he really be touching the walls of the lost city? It was an incredible feat of engineering. He couldn't have been closer, and yet, if it weren't for Tibiriçá, he and his men would have walked on by, never knowing how close he'd come to his goal. Not for the first time, he offered up a quick word of thanks to Lady Luck. This information alone more than made up for the loss of life inflicted on his Gruppe.

Himmler forced the rest of his body through the tight opening. The greenery dropped in place behind him and his world plunged into darkness. Surprised and a little disorientated, he stumbled forwards, both hands slapping hard against the rock wall. An eerie echo bounced back and forth through the oppressive, airless atmosphere. Torrents of perspiration snaked his body, drenching his already moist uniform. He battled to keep it from his eyes and cursed his decision to wear the black SS uniform. One of his men had advised otherwise but Himmler had refused to heed the advice, stubborn in his belief the officer concerned was testing his authority.

Himmler took a moment and regained his composure. He groped for the torch strapped to his belt and flicked it on. The thin beam penetrated the gloom, casting ghostly shadows and exaggerating the size of the obstacles littering the overgrown path ahead. With a sense of foreboding and familiar feelings of claustrophobia creeping up on him, Himmler waved the torch to his left, illuminating the black wall of rock holding his weight. It seemed to stretch on forever. He stroked its surface and moved forward a few steps. There weren't any breaks or cracks anywhere, the wall's surface seamless in its construction. No joins, no cement holding it together, in fact no discernible clues as to its construction at all. He smiled, marvelling at the thought of his ancestors possessing such advanced skills in engineering. The Reich had so much to learn from this ancient people.

Himmler froze as the torch registered movement up ahead, the beam picking out the shadow of something hidden in the under-growth. He cocked his handgun and held his breath, poised and ready to react to the merest hint of hostility. A male voice split the tension. Tibiriçá's son called out to his father. The two tribesmen must have realised he was no longer following and retraced their steps. Himmler lowered his gun and reached for his translator, grabbing his hair and forcing him to take point. He wanted to trust Tibiriçá but his instincts advised him otherwise. Trust was a luxury a man in his position could little often afford to give freely. He prodded the translator in the back with his gun and shoved him towards the two tribesmen.

'Tell them to stay where they are,' he said. 'If they disappear again, we'll never find them.' The translator repeated the order, his speech muffled by the cloth still pressed to his nose. A minute later, after slip-ping and sliding their way down the rocky passage, Himmler arrived alongside his two guides. They flanked him and prodded the torch, both fascinated by the magical shaft of light it emitted. Himmler kept them at arm's length, making a mental note of the greed in the younger man's eyes.

'Ask them where we are headed,' he ordered, trying to distract them.

The translator obliged, and Tibiriçá's response sounded curt.

'Well?' said Himmler.

The translator frowned. 'He say we walk through wall. I ask where door. He only repeat same words and point at wall.'

'I don't pay you to question what he says, just do your job and translate.' Himmler shoved him aside and raked the torch beam across the wall, searching for evidence of an entrance.

The proximity of the magical light source suddenly became too much for Tibiriçá's son. In a mix of lust, greed and perhaps revenge for his broken nose, he lunged at Himmler. Catching him unawares, he shoved Himmler's gun arm behind his back and punched him in the kidneys. Himmler tensed his muscles and flung the elbow of his free arm into the Brazilian's gut. The blow connected, but found little purchase on the boy's greasy stomach. A thick forearm snuck around his neck, while the other made a grab for the torch. The attempt failed but the force of the attack was enough to knock it from his grasp and send it crashing to the ground. Himmler grimaced, grinding his teeth as the bulb shattered on impact, engulfing the passage in darkness.

The sudden disappearance of the light took the young warrior by surprise and his grip slackened. Himmler whirled on the ball of his foot, simultaneously smashing the palm of his hand into his attacker's already broken nose. The Brazilian didn't even have time to scream, dying where he stood as numerous splinters of bone penetrated his brain. Himmler shoved the corpse aside and smoothed the creases from his uniform.

'Translator, please inform Chief Tibiriçá to proceed. His son has met with a little "accident" and I wouldn't want a similar one to befall him.' The translator didn't respond. Himmler clenched his fist. The little bastard must have made a bolt for it. He stared into the darkness, his index finger hovering above the Luger's trigger as he searched for a target. The silence was deafening – even the birds appeared to have abandoned this long-forgotten piece of forest. The Nazi shuddered, straining his ears for the merest hint of sound. His life was in danger, and he knew it. A faint clicking sound, two or three metres to his left, disturbed the silence. He turned to greet it, gun levelled and ready to open fire.

'Translator? Is that you?' Himmler whispered. 'Answer me or I'll shoot.' A bead of blue light flickered in response, illuminating a small clearing up ahead. Himmler tensed as a large shape loomed into view. It was Tibiriçá. He stepped forward, only to see Tibiriçá raise an arm and halt his progress. The chief extended a long finger and pointed at Himmler's feet.

Himmler crouched and scanned the ground ahead. There was something blocking the path. His arm snaked towards it, tentative but determined to confirm his suspicions. He scowled as his fingers met the soft, warm flesh of his stricken translator. How would he understand the bloody chief now? He pulled the old man onto his back and recoiled at the brutal efficiency of the kill; the head ripped clear of the neck. It was a sight that left Himmler in no doubt of the suppressed rage Tibiriçá must be harbouring. To break a man's neck was easy, but to rip it clean from the spine took a strength and skill rare in a world where the gun ruled the battlefield. He looked up at the chief. Did this mean they were even again? An eye for an eye and all that?

The stoical Brazilian nodded and jabbed a finger at the glowing light in the wall. The result was as immediate as it was spectacular. A semi-circular shaft of light shot from the rock and illuminated the clearing brighter than the midday sun. Himmler raised an arm to shield his eyes and staggered backwards. What black magic was this?

Tibiriçá sniffed and wiped a smattering of blood from his face. He turned away from Himmler and ducked his head, sliding his ample frame through the newly formed gap in the wall. Himmler scrambled up the slope to join him and darted through before the thing closed. He didn't have a choice; his life was now in the hands of the chief and he knew it. He stepped from the makeshift doorway, buoyed to find natural light on the other side. His elation was tempered as Tibiriçá's massive hand clamped around his shoulder, hauling him through the gap as it closed behind him. He yelped in pain, feeling a rib crack as he landed on something solid. He pressed his chest. No harm done, just another bruise to add to his ever-growing collection. He pushed himself upright. Where was he? It almost looked like a gutter of a paved road. The corners of his mouth twisted upward into a tight smile and he glanced at Tibiriçá.

'If this place is what I think it is, Untermensch scum,' he whispered, 'then you have assured my place in history.'

If Tibiriçá understood the German language, he'd have killed Himmler then and there. Instead he managed only a look of puzzlement. For the sake of his son, the chief could do little more than pray Himmler was the messiah his tribe were expecting. Himmler's smile widened. Luck was indeed on his side.

Chapter Thirty
Mato Grosso, Brazil

'What the hell just happened?' Hoffmann hissed. 'I pulled the trigger and my whole frigging hand exploded. Some bloody bodyguard you are.'

'Sniper in the trees. You're lucky the bullet only nicked you,' said Darren. 'It's my fault. We should have done a sweep of the area. We were sitting ducks out there.'

'Too bloody right it's your fault.' Hoffmann flexed his fingers. Darren was right, though. He had been lucky, the bullet missing anything vital and punching through the meaty part of his hand to the left of his thumb. It was painful, but he still seemed to have a full range of movement.

'Does this change the plan?' said Darren.

Hoffmann rounded a bend in the trail and stopped in his tracks, eyes wide and full of wonder.

'Sir?' asked Darren. Hoffmann pointed over his bodyguard's shoulder, the enormity of the scene opening up before him hitting home. They'd arrived. A circle of huts surrounded communal fire, just as Himmler's letters described. He grinned, relief as palpable as triumph. At last, after millions of pounds and euros wasted on so many dead ends, the Hoffmann, or rather, Himmler legacy was within his grasp.

'This is the village. After all these years searching, I can't believe I'm really here.' He clutched at his breast pocket, blinking back tears as he retrieved an old, tattered piece of paper. For the thousandth time he unfolded it and pored over his grandfather's faded prose:

Invisible from the air, the layout was the first thing I noticed upon being accepted into the community. It became clear the colourful huts were not random constructs, but rather they'd been built and organised in a very deliberate manner. They surround a central fire in a series of concentric rings, each identical bar one. Chief Tibiriçá's hut is markedly larger and the only residence to be stained bright blue.

Hoffmann raised his head and stumbled into a run, scanning the circular buildings and yelping as his eyes fixed upon the largest. The blue-stained exterior was a little washed out, but now there was no doubting this was the self-same village his grandfather had arrived in over seventy years earlier. A huge, barrel-chested figure emerged from the doorway of the chief's hut. Long, lank, grey hair straddled broad, caramel shoulders. Although bare of clothing, tattoos dominated the man's torso, a multitude of designs emphasising the toned musculature of his upper body. He cut an imposing and fearsome figure. If it weren't for the elasticity of his facial skin, Hoffmann would have guessed his age at around fifty rather than the hundred plus years he must be.

'That can't be Tibiriçá. He shouldn't be alive, let alone mobile,' Hoffmann whispered. With the pain in his hand forgotten, Hoffmann bounded toward the old man. His lips curled into a self-satisfied grin as an iconic image came in to focus. He bore the mark of a swastika. Hoffmann pulled his sleeve to his shoulder and showed Tibiriçá an identical image.

The chief stared at Hoffmann and, without uttering a word, turned and strode off through the village.

'I'm not certain, but I get the impression he likes us,' said Hoffmann. 'So what do you think? Should we follow?'

Darren frowned and gripped the handle of his machete. 'What other choice do we have?'

Darren motioned for the remainder of his crew to fall in. 'Silenced weapons lads. We don't want to attract attention. Treat any movement as hostile. Shoot first, questions later.' He pointed at the disappearing chief. 'Keep tight and don't lose him. I'm on point. Let's roll out. Lock and load.'

Foliage whipped against Hoffmann's chest, knocking the breath from his lungs. He stumbled, his knee hitting the forest floor. Something scurried up his thigh and he batted it away, shuddering. This place was relentless. Darren pulled him upright and pointed at their guide. Tibiriçá raised an arm and brought the team to an abrupt halt.

Hoffmann raised his gun, sweeping the sight around the shadowy clearing and still pool of water on their right. There didn't appear to be any obvious danger unless the chattering monkeys swinging through the branches above them posed a threat. Why did the old man keep stopping? If anything, they needed to pick up the pace to stand any chance of reaching the city before their pursuers.

'Encantdos,' Tibiriçá hissed.

'Encant a what?' asked Hoffmann, a little too loudly.

Tibiriçá silenced him with a look and unsheathed a hefty knife from his belt. He eased onto his haunches and faced the stagnant pool. His every muscle looked taut and primed for action. Darren waved the mercenaries to follow the Brazilian's lead and in seconds they were mimicking his stance. Hoffmann ducked behind the line of men, his heart rate quickening.

'What is going on?' whispered a wiry mercenary. 'Why is he afraid of the water? What's he seen? Do they get gators around here?' The mercenary shuffled forward, rifle raised, and peered into the dark, dank water.

Unbeknown to the seasoned veteran, a quicker and much more experienced hunter was going through a similar routine. The surface of the pool detonated in an explosion of water and mud, saturating the stunned group. The mercenary toppled backwards and squeezed off a single round as sharp fangs penetrated the soft skin of his exposed neck, severing his jugular and killing him instantly. The enormous snake floundered on the ground, straining as it fought to pull the dead soldier towards a watery grave.

'Don't shoot,' shouted Darren, physically lowering the rifles of the men lined up beside him. To their credit, both men held their ground.

'What the shitting hell is that?' hissed Hoffmann, scrambling behind Tibiriçá.

Tibiriçá returned to his feet and pointed at the snake, unfazed by the brutal death he'd just witnessed. 'Encantdos.'

'I'm guessing Encantdos is their word for anaconda,' said Darren. 'Mr Hoffmann, I'd like to introduce the world-famous green, or as it's better known, *giant* anaconda.' For the moment the huge reptile appeared relaxed, its muscles hypnotic as they pulsed back and forth across its enormous, two-hundred-pound body, easing its kill, inch by inch, back into its watery habitat.

Hoffmann shuddered. This being one of the few remaining predators of man left on the planet, it was no wonder the locals both revered and feared this creature. 'I don't think "giant" quite does it justice. Bloody thing must be five or six metres long. Why can't we shoot it? What's stopping it from attacking us again?'

'As long as its mouth is wrapped around our mate, we're safe,' said Darren. He pointed at the remaining mercenaries. 'It's lucky these two can follow orders. If we'd injured it, the chances are it would have dropped him and gone for someone else. Just stay calm and keep quiet. As long as we don't interfere with dinnertime, we should be fine.'

Hoffmann took a deep breath, his heart rate normalising. 'What a way to go. Let's hope he's ready for another meal when our friends walk past.' He watched, fascinated as the anaconda pulled the dead mercenary under the murky water, all evidence of the attack disappearing into nothing more than a series of fading ripples.

Chapter Thirty-One

Mato Grosso, Brazil, 1939

Himmler assessed his new environment, searching for threats but struck by the sense of desolation permeating through the long-abandoned streets. He hurried to catch Tibiriçá, a little surprised by the Brazilian's lack of emotion following the death of his son. He strode ahead, focused on his mission and negotiating the maze of derelict roadways with the assured gait of a man who'd travelled this path many times before.

Himmler's mind was in overdrive, taking in as much of the urban jungle surrounding him as his brain would allow. In fairness there was not much to write home about; row upon row of shabby grey stone buildings littered the streets in varying states of decay. It must have been a depressing place to live. The scene was devoid of colour. It was as if the city itself was in mourning over some long-forgotten event. He shuddered. He couldn't put his finger on why he found the setting disturbing, but he did. There was no sense of the population dwindling over time and dying out through the passage of time. In a few of the dwellings there were plates still set for a dinnertime that never came. He'd once holidayed near the Roman town of Pompeii, and the similarities were palpable. The destruction of this city must have been quick and violent.

Stone pots, broken clay plates and even children's toys lay discarded, scattered about the chipped, scarred floors and lying where they'd been dropped perhaps thousands of years before. It was clear the inhabitants were removed by force. The parallels with the campaign his party was waging against the Jews weren't lost on him. He shook his head and tried to clear his mind, but the images of SS officers breaking down doors and throwing screaming residents into the streets were hard to ignore.

Himmler bent to examine an inscription carved into a nearby wall, using the distraction to rid his mind of any empathy for the Jews. He'd noticed the strange pictorial scrawl on buildings throughout the city, but the one in front of him was in an excellent state of repair. Himmler registered the image of a bright ball of light surrounded by dying men. He frowned. Tibiriçá saw him stop and retraced his steps, pulling him from the wall and shoving him into the road. He pointed at something ahead.

Himmler grinned and dismissed the strange artwork as a sideshow. Chief Tibiriçá had come through for him. It was a ruin but this must be it, Schäfer's Atlantis Pyramid. Yes, just as described in the letter, he could see the outline of a central casket, the fabled Casket of Kings. Himmler yelped in joy. He was staring at the end of the war and certain victory for Germany.

As he closed in, Himmler made out more and more of the stone casket, decorated in a plain fashion and sunk into a shallow recess at the pyramid's centre.

'This building must mark the centre of the city,' mumbled Himmler. 'I wonder why they destroyed it?' He kicked aside a lump of rubble and sprinted the final few yards, kneeling beside the casket. It bore similarities to the stone sarcophagi of the Egyptian pharaohs. His hands shook as his fingers caressed and snaked their way over the container's smooth contours. Dare he believe this artefact might represent his journey's end? If it contained the remains of the Atlantean ruler alluded to in Schäfer's report, the link between Germany and the Aryan race would soon be irrefutable.

He needed time to think. He rose and paced the footprint of the building. Although mostly destroyed, jagged sections of wall protruded from the rubble still in situ. They were a rich black colour, matching the floor and constructed from the same material. It was clear from their angle they formed part of the fabled pyramid, each side sloping towards a long-lost point high above the forest canopy. In its pomp it must have been an impressive building, a symbol of tribal power which would have dominated the landscape for miles in every direction.

Tibiriçá remained seated beside the casket. Himmler watched him reach into his clothing and pull out what looked to be a small bead.

The huge man bent over the casket and slid the bead into the centre of a circular symbol carved into the lid. Is this how he'd opened the city gates? Did the beads double as some kind of key?

Tibiriçá pulled his hand away, revealing lines of the same blue light Himmler had seen enveloping the city's entrance. It appeared to pulsate inside the stone, leisurely tracing its way around some kind of symbol. Himmler stepped closer and received final confirmation that this was indeed the Casket of Kings. A circle within a circle – the royal seal of Atlantis.

The Brazilian signalled for Himmler to approach and tapped the casket as the strange light completed its circuit of the symbol. The lines of light throbbed, maintaining a steady beat. It was almost hypnotic. Himmler frowned and cocked his head. Could it be mimicking the heartbeat of its long-entombed resident?

Himmler started as the ground shuddered. 'What the hell?'

He heard a loud crack and a puff of dust blew into his face as the casket's seal broke. He stepped back as the lid of the casket moved, sliding on an unseen pivot and shifting sideways.

Himmler leant forward with caution, half expecting a ghostly apparition to drift from the floor. Tibiriçá clapped a hand on his back and stabbed a finger deep into the recesses of the dark box. It was a captivating object. He watched as the interior illuminated in a similar fashion to its lid, the same inexplicable light source tracing its way around a series of fascinating, yet meaningless carvings. They bore a resemblance to the pictographic writing used by the ancient Egyptians, but not being an expert, Himmler couldn't be sure how far the similarity went. He cursed the death of his archaeologist at the hands of Tibiriçá's tribe. Without him there was nothing he could do but stare in ignorance at the symbols, able only to admire the technical brilliance and artistry of their creators.

Himmler retracted his arm from the empty casket and slapped the ground in defeat. He pushed himself upright, anger swelling in his belly as the implications slapped him about the face. The casket: the bloody thing was empty. He couldn't fail now. Not being so close. The evidence must be inside somewhere. He ducked his head inside and swept a hand over each of the casket's smooth surfaces. Illuminated inscriptions were still appearing, their lines as crisp and clean as the day of their creation. He shook his head. Whatever their original purpose, they now highlighted an inescapable truth: the bones of the King were no more.

An eerie echo reverberated around the ruined buildings as the devastated Nazi leader drummed his fingers on the casket's lid. He felt like crying, something he hadn't done since learning to absorb the blows from his father's belt so many years before.

'Where is he?' he said. 'This is the tomb of the founding father. All the evidence points to him being here, so where the hell is he?' Fuelled by frustration he turned on Tibiriçá, his fear of the man evaporating under a cloud of anger. 'Where's the body? The man they buried here: where have you put him?' He paused. 'Christ, this is ridiculous. You will never understand me.'

Himmler took a deep breath and closed his eyes, rubbing his face in his hands. 'Calm down Heinrich, just take a moment and think.'

He slipped his hand into his breast pocket and pulled out the folded report given to him by Ernst Schäfer. Himmler wasn't ready to give up on the Casket of Kings just yet; he'd invested too much time and Party funds to fail now. He opened it, his eyes skipping over the crude map and scanning the familiar words scrawled underneath.

'*Beneath the Pyramid in the second city rests our reason for being. It is order we seek and in order we trust and only with order can the keys to the kingdom of heaven lie.*'

It still meant nothing to him. He'd always been confident of finding the city and assumed the paragraph's meaning would somehow present itself on arrival. There must have been a body in the casket; there was no other explanation. He ran through his options and realised all remaining hope rested squarely on the shoulders of his Brazilian guide.

Himmler made his decision and strode with purpose to the brightly lit casket, sliding his legs inside. He maintained eye contact with the chief and jabbed a finger at the bare interior. Tibiriçá stared back in apparent bemusement.

'Where are bones? Where are the bones of the man buried here?' He continued with his impromptu game of charades by lying inside the box and feigning death. 'Come on, you brainless bastard, look what I'm doing. Where's the corpse?'

The moment Himmler's sweat-drenched head touched the cool base of the casket, he yelped in pain. A surge of electrifying energy rushed through him, contracting every muscle in unison and engulfing him in a state of paralysis. His eyes widened in fear as the gut-wrenching sound of whirring gears assaulted his senses. The casket lid jerked and slid shut.

Petrified by the prospect of suffocation, Himmler screamed and fought to release himself from the unyielding force pinning him inside. The effort was futile. The heavy stone locked in place above him, snuffing his cries and bathing the city in a sea of deathly silence.

Unmoved by the stranger's protestations, Tibiriçá knelt beside the casket and planted a huge hand inside the circular symbol. The carvings were messages from his god, messages passed down from generation to generation, father to son, chief to chief.

He bowed his head, closed his eyes and recited the chant. 'Resting beneath the eastern waves, Ñanderú will rise when her children fall. She will blacken skies and unleash the fires of hell. The earth will tremble in the wake of her fury and her tears will cleanse all. As above as below, the seven numbered beasts of revelation will ascend to bring order to those with none. Only in order will light return and the number of beast shall guide your key.'

The stranger possessed the sacred number and sacrificed his children to prove his worth. Whether Ñanderú herself or her emissary, the apocalypse was close. Soon the cleansing would begin, the Motherland rising to baptise humanity in the fires of her underbelly and give rise, as prophesied, to the golden age of humankind.

Himmler closed his eyes and took a deep breath. 'Calm yourself, Heinrich,' he muttered. 'Panicking will just waste precious oxygen.' The energy surge yielded as the lid clicked into place. He blinked as his eyes adjusted, his body feeling strangely reinvigorated. The light from the strange carvings continued to illuminate every corner of the tight space but, rather than offering hope, the glow only exaggerated the futility of his position.

An outpouring of panic erupted inside him. This time he couldn't control it as a familiar foe reared its head. The claustrophobia attacked his consciousness with an inexplicable ferocity. His heart rate sped up and his limbs convulsed. It wouldn't be long before the nausea and hyperventilation kicked in. Himmler was rocketing towards the point of no return, a tortuous descent into madness and eventual death.

He smashed and clawed his hands against the lid of his prison, hoping upon hope it might give way under his manic onslaught. Blood dripped from his red-raw knuckles, yet still he continued. In a final act of desperation, Himmler kicked out at the casket's base, shoving his body towards it to maximise the blow.

His feet met thin air. Himmler yelped and dug his nails into the casket's walls, trying to slow himself as his body shot into darkness. He only fell about a metre but the drop felt much further in the pitch black. Himmler landed on his feet, but unable to prepare himself for the impact, he turned an ankle and tumbled forward. He cursed as his body crashed into something solid. A little dazed, Himmler rubbed his head and gasped for breath as his claustrophobia faded.

'What fresh hell is this?' he asked, wiping spittle and blood from his hands and mouth.

The light from the casket illuminated the chamber enough for Himmler to observe its pyramidal shape. The floor space was approximately twelve by twelve feet and devoid of decoration. He rose and ran a hand over the surface of a wall, smooth like marble and cool to the touch. It was incredible to think of the man hours required to hue such a room from solid rock and to such a high standard.

Himmler stepped back to get a better view and lost his footing, his heel striking something solid. Knocked off balance, he twisted and landed on all fours. He froze, his heart stopping as he found himself face to face with a small hunched creature staring at him through a pair of unblinking, brilliant blue eyes.

'Jesus?' he said. The creature remained motionless. 'Calm yourself, Heinrich, it's a statue… it's just a statue.' He took two deep breaths to normalise his heart rate and shuffled forwards, reaching out to touch one of the figure's outstretched limbs. Whatever it represented, it wasn't human. The creature's arms were not arms at all, they were paws. And the head... with a huge pair of horns and a snub nose, it was a bull.

He moved closer and noticed something flicker between the creature's paws. Himmler's eyes narrowed and he bent for a closer look. The light wasn't strong enough to pick out the anomaly, and he swept his hand blindly over the area. His fingers found and traced around a small, notched, circular indentation in the chamber floor.

'And what might you be hiding?' he muttered. 'What's meant to go in here?' He lowered his head in defeat. 'A key?'

Himmler bit his lip and slapped the ground in frustration. The notch was too big for one of the chief's beads and, with no other artefacts, this marked the end of the road. The Ahnenerbe had failed him. No, that sceptical bastard Schäfer had failed him. Vowing to have the ornithologist shot upon his return to Germany, Himmler grasped the face of the bull and stared into its motionless eyes.

'My descendants will return, bull. I swear a Himmler will one day set your secrets free.'

Chapter Thirty-Two
The Lost City of Z

Hunter batted away yet another wave of bloodthirsty insects and glanced back at George and Inma, both of them engaged in similar battles. He smiled as the geologist slapped his cheek and looked up at him in disgust, raising a hand to display the squashed mess on his palm.

They'd been travelling in the midst of the Order soldiers for the best part of an hour now, trailing in the wake of a guide Knight had captured on the battleground. Hunter strained his eyes, staring at the improvised trail ahead of them. The geography felt somewhat familiar, sparking a distant memory he couldn't quite access. He yelped in excitement. George appeared at his side.

'What? What have you seen?'

'It's the city, George,' said Hunter. 'We've arrived. Look around you; it all fits with Fawcett's description. We're descending into a valley around ten miles wide. A valley surmounted by mountains.' He dropped to the ground. 'Now we've just got to hope Hoffmann is still in there somewhere with the artefacts.'

'Bit of a vague leap but I guess it sort of fits,' said George, knocking away another insect. 'I just hope you're right. I've had more than enough of this journey.'

At the head of the group, their guide suddenly darted left into a section of thick foliage. Knight swept the greenery to one side and indicated that his men should follow.

'This is it, George. This has to be the entrance.' He shook George by the arm in excitement. 'We are about to enter an Atlantean outpost.'

Hunter pushed his way into the concealed passageway and stumbled through the undergrowth in near darkness, trepidation mounting with every footfall. His excitement waned, overtaken by an overriding sense of foreboding and impending danger. Something just didn't feel right. He felt his way around a thick tree trunk and stopped in his tracks, the scene before him almost stopping him from breathing. A thin blue line highlighted an arch-like shape cut into what looked like a pitch-black wall. Someone behind Hunter cursed as they knocked into his back but he barely noticed. He felt a hand grasp his arm, hauling him through the gap and into the light beyond.

Hunter picked himself up and dusted himself down, scanning the ruined street in trepidation. Where was the resistance? Where was Hoffmann? The Order had located and entered the ruined city far too easily. What was Hoffmann waiting for? They'd passed through numerous pinch points perfect for an ambush, but so far encountered nothing more than a screeching monkey. He'd initially put it down to Hoffmann's arrogance rather than an inability to cover his tracks, but the deeper the team advanced inside the ancient city, the more a nagging sense of unease and dread took hold of him. He glanced at his two companions. If they were in danger, both Inma and George seemed oblivious to it. He wished he could turn off the paranoia in his brain and enjoy this experience. He was living one of his childhood dreams and the pessimistic dread in his heart was killing it for him.

Inma, on the other hand, may as well have been in Disneyland. She'd morphed into an excitable teenager the moment the team stepped through the walls. He watched as she darted back and forth, skipping in and out of buildings and chattering nineteen to the dozen, giving a running commentary of find after find to anyone who would listen. She'd even swept George along on her wave of enthusiasm. He'd put aside his fears and trailed her like an excitable puppy, savouring the astonishing archaeology.

Hunter could barely believe what he was seeing either and forced himself to stop seeing shadows and shapes where none existed. For god's sake, in the last five minutes alone they'd discovered evidence of a foundry, a kiln and a working millstone, each of them within a hundred yards of each other. The finds were extraordinary in their own right but together, and given the suspected date of occupation, they would change the face of archaeology forever.

Inma sprinted from a small hut and turned a corner. She stopped in her tracks and dropped what she was holding.

'Inma? Inma, what's the matter?' said Hunter, hurrying to her side and hoping it wasn't Hoffmann. He followed her line of sight and his jaw dropped.

'Is that what I think it is?' asked George. Unable to speak, Hunter just nodded. Knight's men dominated the road ahead, busy securing the perimeter around the remains of a huge, jet-black pyramid. A weird glow emanated from its centre. 'What's the deal with the light?'

'I've no idea,' said Hunter. 'But this confirms beyond doubt this is Colonel Percy Fawcett's lost city.' He wiped his brow, his gaze flitting between the derelict buildings and the ruins of the grandiose pyramid. 'Are either of you finding this a little too easy?' he asked. 'I'm not saying I was expecting Herculean trials and booby traps, but I'd have thought Hoffmann might have tried something to stop the Order. He must be around here somewhere. There is no way he'd have missed something the size of this pyramid, especially if he has a guide.'

Inma shrugged. 'Maybe they didn't make it. There's enough venomous wildlife to kill an army in the rainforest.'

'We're not that lucky. That bastard is out there somewhere,' said George. 'I expect he has eyes on us right now.'

'I'm inclined to side with George on this one,' said Hunter. 'This feels like a set-up.' He scanned the dreary, apocalyptic landscape and bit into his lower lip. If this was a trap, what was Hoffmann waiting for? Reinforcements? Possibly... Then it hit him. Hoffmann was waiting for him. With no experts left in his team, Hoffmann didn't have anyone left to decipher the pyramid's secrets. He must be waiting for Hunter or Inma to do it for him.

'John, get over here,' boomed Knight, his voice carrying across the pyramid. Hunter shook off the daydream and focused on the stocky priest. 'There's something glowing in the middle of this monument and I need you to give me an appraisal. I assume this must be the reason that bloody German dragged you out here.'

Hunter's legs trembled. He could empathise with those approaching their deaths at Tyburn. Somewhere in the gloom, he knew the crosshairs of a rifle must be following his every move and he could do nothing but continue to offer the shooter a target. He jogged to Knight's side and fended off the sickening feeling in his stomach by focusing on the glowing rock at the pyramid's centre. 'It looks like a sunken sarcophagus,' said Hunter. 'Those lines criss-crossing the surface are similar to the ones you activated at the city entrance.'

Knight nodded. 'Maybe. Now, get yourself over there and confirm it. You're meant to be the expert here.'

Hunter's gaze flitted about the derelict ruins. 'Are you sure Hoffmann isn't around? There's no cover; I may as well paint a target on my forehead and be done with it.'

'Recon is under way. If he's out there we'll find him. You'll be fine; the German needed you for something and I assume still does…' Knight punched his shoulder playfully. 'And if I'm wrong, I promise to shoot back.'

'That's comforting.' Hunter pulled out his handgun and checked its magazine. 'Just stay alert to any movement. If Hoffmann does get what he wants, we'll all be in danger.' Hunter scrambled up and over the shallow wall, pausing as a slender arm snaked about his waist. It was Inma.

'John, you don't have to go through with this. This isn't worth risking your life for,' she said, her voice tight with emotion.

Knight scowled and grabbed Inma's arm, pulling her aside. His earlier amiability vanished, replaced by soulless eyes flickering with resentment. 'Dr Pérez is right, John, you do have a choice. Either help me, risk a German bullet and claim your place in history. Or stand against me and my men will happily shoot you all where you stand.'

Anderson stepped forward, licked his lower lip and cocked his gun. 'Make my day, Hunter.'

'Do it,' said Hunter, defiantly staring into the man's eyes. 'Shoot me and there will be no one to translate the casket.'

Knight unsheathed his Glock and placed it against George's forehead. 'Good point. So get out there and do your job.'

'Let him go,' hissed Inma. 'What the hell do you think you're doing?'

Knight met her gaze and pushed her backwards. 'Whatever it takes, Dr Pérez. Now make your mind up.' He shot a bullet into the ground at Inma's feet. She hopped backwards and fell to the floor. 'Believe me, I'm not an enemy you want to make.'

Hunter moved to help her, but Anderson blocked his path. He glared at the priest and balled his knuckles in frustration. There was no alternative but to press on. 'Inma, are you alright?'

She nodded. 'Fine. Just get this over with and do as he says.'

'Yes, do as he says,' Knight repeated. 'I'll look after your friends.'

Hunter turned and inched forward, wishing he were entering in better circumstances. Even so, he could not help but marvel at the metre-thick walls and the complexity of the building he was entering. In its pomp it must have rivalled the Great Pyramid in Egypt, albeit on a smaller scale. The hypnotic halo of blue light continued to pulsate from the buried sarcophagus, drawing him ever closer. He surveyed the shadowy landscape and wondered which of the toppled walls or derelict buildings masked his covert potential killers.

Hunter's brow creased as he glimpsed the mountain range through gaps in the oppressive foliage high above his head. It struck him how odd a location this was for the Atlantean refugees to choose as their home. Dominated by the same black stone as the city walls, it must have been a depressing place to live. Why hide in the shadows and cut themselves off from the rest of humanity? There must have been a reason, but what? What were they hiding from – or perhaps the question should be, what were they hiding?

He stooped to pick up the torso of a damaged statuette and admired the intricate muscular detailing on its chest. Even with its head and legs missing, it was clear the Atlantean refugees were so much more than the warmongering race painted by Plato's dialogues. Carved in jade, the scale and toning captured to perfection, it was reminiscent of the best of the marbles carved during the Greek Hellenistic period; but this was so much older, perhaps fashioned thousands of years before the Greeks even picked up tools. If he ever made it home, there would be several hundred archaeologists revisiting their theories.

'Get on with it,' said Knight, his voice startling Hunter as it resonated through his earpiece. 'Or are you simply waiting for me to kill your friends?' Catching his anger before it manifested into speech,

Hunter clenched his fists and knelt beside the open casket. 'Well, what can you see?'

'Give me a chance,' Hunter hissed. 'The sides are covered in symbols. They look Egyptian. If these are the precursor to hieroglyphics, then we're in luck.' He frowned and brushed his trembling fingers over the smooth black surface. He could hardly believe where he was. Science fiction morphing into science fact before his eyes. 'God only knows how this light is being generated. There must be a chemical reaction going on. Perhaps an early form of electroluminescence?'

'This is all very interesting but can you get on with translating the script,' said Knight. 'There'll be plenty of time for analysis later. For now, can you deal with Pandora's box so we can all get the hell out of this hole?'

'Fine by me,' said Hunter. He opened a notebook and jotted down the symbols one by one. 'This is crazy but the script bears an extraordinary similarity to an early form of Old Kingdom hieroglyphics.'

'Is that good?' asked Knight.

'It means I can at least have a stab at a translation,' said Hunter. He paused, scribbling his thoughts on his pad. 'I think it's a statement. Something about Nan... Nan... Damn, I can't make it out.'

'Ñanderú perhaps?' said Inma, her voice crackling in his ear.

'Ñanderú – of course,' said Hunter. 'The pre-Christian god of Brazil. The great creator of all nature, the sea and the moon. But why would the reference appear here? Maybe the Amazonians adopted Ñanderú from a culture whose origins lay much further back in time. An Atlantean god perhaps or maybe even one of their kings.' He snorted. There was so much to uncover and he was barely scratching the surface. 'If the rest of this text is anything to go by, this Ñanderú was not a nice chap. He is pencilled in to rise from the sea and cleanse humanity of its sins. Nice story to tell the kiddies.' He shuffled closer to the inscriptions. 'I'm not convinced I understand the meaning of this second section though. It sounds almost Masonic: *As above as below, the seven numbered beasts of revelation will ascend to bring order to those with none. Only in order will light return and the number of the beast shall guide your key.*'

'The beast's number? The number of the beast... might be a reference to six, six, six,' said George. 'It sounds like the biblical apocalypse.'

A flash of lightning lit the pyramid and a spot of rain landed on the back of Hunter's neck. 'Did we just anger Ñanderú?' He glanced upward as the droplets increased in their ferocity. 'Anyone have a brolly?'

'Just get on with it,' said Knight. 'It's only water.'

Hunter pulled his shirt up around his ears as the rain lashed down around him, the drops landing so hard they stung on impact. The rainforest was living up to its name, the only positive being the temporary disappearance of the oppressive humidity. He tried to concentrate his mind. The quicker he finished, the quicker he could seek shelter.

He reread the inscription. There was no doubting the reference to the number of the beast. George's guess of three sixes was in fact now a historical inaccuracy. A recent cache of several third-century manuscripts flagged a mistranslation and proved beyond doubt the Antichrist would rise bearing the number six, one, six.

'Jesus,' whispered Hunter, to himself more than the others. 'I was right; the rebirth of Atlantis is documented in the Bible.' A paper written whilst a young postgraduate flooded into his consciousness. 'It's all there in Revelation 13:1: and I stood upon the sand of the sea,' he recited. 'And saw a beast rise up out of the sea, having seven heads and ten horns, and upon his horns ten crowns, and upon his heads the name of blasphemy. Starter for ten. How many kingdoms is Atlantis alleged to have had?'

He heard a clapping sound through the earpiece. 'Bloody hell, John, brilliant,' said Inma.

'What's brilliant? What the hell are you talking about?' said Knight.

'Come on,' said George. 'There's no way the Atlantis myth is in the Bible.'

'Not on its own,' said Hunter, sweeping away the water obscuring the inscription. 'Plato talks of Atlantis having ten kingdoms ruled by ten kings, right?' George grunted in affirmation. 'Ten horns and ten crowns ring any bells?'

'What about the seven heads?' said Knight.

'They probably relate to the seven circular bands of the Acropolis,' whispered George, conceding defeat. 'Or more likely it's a reference to the seven islands Atlantis allegedly occupied.'

'Bingo,' said Hunter. 'I have another convert.'

'Okay, I admit the evidence is promising...'

Hunter cleared his throat. 'I'm impressed, although you missed the third possibility. The number seven may be a veiled reference to a civil war Plato mentions. It resulted in the ten kings being whittled down to seven, one ruler for each of the seven islands.' He paused, shielding his eyes from the rain. 'Not the easiest translation I've worked on but the final sentence is a little cryptic. *Only in death can the journey to enlightenment begin.*'

'What does that mean? Does someone need to die? Because that can be arranged,' said Knight. 'Is there anything inside the casket itself? I'm assuming not given the bloody thing is already open.'

'Nothing but water. It's sunk about half a metre into the floor,' said Hunter. He rapped his knuckles against each of its surfaces. 'It's a solid build, but a dead end by the look of things.'

'Fine,' said Knight. 'Take some photographs and we'll get the hell out of here. We'll return in a few weeks with a bigger team and some proper equipment. We won't have the threat of a German lunatic shooting at us then either.'

Hunter complied as best he could and slipped the thankfully waterproof camera into his rucksack. He turned to leave, eager to return to the safety of the collapsed pyramid walls. He took a step and jerked to a halt, paralysed as a series of ear-splitting cracks echoed about the city. The smooth floor of the ancient temple disintegrated at his feet, showering him in pieces of chipped basalt. He stumbled backwards as a second hail of bullets ripped into the temple floor, finding their mark centimetres from his toes. With nowhere to run and no other cover within fifty feet, Hunter slung his rucksack into the casket and followed it into the rising water.

He heard Knight barking orders to his soldiers and at last they returned fire. A wave of relief rolled over him as the enemy bullets shifted from his position to target the Order. The reprieve was short lived. Hunter's eyes widened, his body seized by a wave of electrical energy, stripping him of his motor skills and pinning him to the base of the sarcophagus. He stared up in terror as an ancient mechanism clicked into gear and, accompanied by a low hum, the heavy lid slid shut.

Chapter Thirty-Three

Hunter coughed, spitting water and straining to keep his nose above the waterline. This couldn't be how it ended. The rain continued its relentless assault, water pouring in on all sides as the casket's lid eased shut. He screamed for help, but the continuing echo of gunfire meant no one would dare answer his call. At least the lid would block the rain, but there really wasn't much to choose between drowning and suffocation. He closed his eyes as the lid closed with a thud. Water seeped into his mouth. This was it. He held a breath, desperate not to inhale and flood his lungs. There had to be a way out. The casket must be more than an instrument of torture. Panic tore through him and, unable to bare the pain, he succumbed and took a breath. He gurgled and spluttered, his body fighting to process the non-existent oxygen.

Without warning, his limbs freed and the water rushed away. He coughed, water pouring from his nose and mouth, his head knocking against the basalt rock wall as his muscles convulsed erratically. He collapsed in a heap and touched the rising lump on the rear of his skull. Could he really be alive? He kicked his legs in the direction of the remains of the dripping water, his feet meeting nothing but thin air. The closing lid must have opened a passageway.

"Only in death can the journey to enlightenment begin."

Of course, it seemed so obvious now; to gain access one simply had to lie in the sarcophagus and play dead. Although he doubted the builders had ever envisaged the lucky participant would be joined by a few litres of rainwater. His feet found the tunnel's end and Hunter thrust himself forward, eager to wriggle free of what could so easily have become his tomb. The drop was further than he'd anticipated and he hit the ground hard, tumbling over as his legs collapsed under him. He came to a halt in the midst of a cloud of dust and coughed, blinking hard as his eyes adjusted to the lack of light. He lifted his head and drew a quick breath, scurrying backwards on all fours. A pair of steely blue eyes was staring at him through the gloom. He was not alone.

'Who's there? Show yourself,' said Hunter, fumbling for his torch.

A sharp crackle of radio static made him jump. 'John, come in. Are you okay? Were you hit? Where are you?' He relaxed as the familiarity of Inma's voice dissolved the fear in his stomach. The dust settled.

He snorted and shook his head as the face behind the mysterious blue eyes showed itself in the torchlight. He tapped his earpiece. 'This thing is still working?'

'We're in a rainforest,' interrupted Knight. 'Surprise surprise, we anticipated rain.'

'I'm a little bruised but all good otherwise. I'm inside a chamber under the sarcophagus,' said Hunter. 'I almost punched a statue but nothing else to report. What's happening up top?'

'We're alive,' said Inma. 'Jacob's men seem to have scared Hans off for the moment. Two or three of them took hits but it could have been worse.'

'John, what's your status?' said Knight. 'Do you need us to hold our position?'

'Yes please. Can you buy me a few minutes to look around?'

'No problem, you've got ten.'

He shone the torch around the chamber, illuminating the surfaces. 'Inma, can you record what I'm saying?'

'Way ahead of you, John. Say your piece.'

'I should start by saying the architect wouldn't win many interior design awards. Minimalist springs to mind. The room is empty bar the statue.' He ran his hand over the walls. 'The craftsmanship is amazing, though. So smooth… and the room is a perfect geometric pyramid, I'm guessing a mirror of the building above.' He shook his head in disbelief. 'So we can add advanced mathematics and engineering to the Atlantean CV.'

'There's nothing inside? Nothing at all?' asked Knight. 'Describe the statue? Is it relevant?'

'I expect so,' said Hunter, stooping to examine it. 'It's a horned bull head perched on the body of a lion.'

'A sphinx,' said Inma.

'Yes, or rather a couchant or reclining sphinx to be exact,' said Hunter. 'It's not such a surprising find. The veneration of bulls is quite common through history, usually celebrated as symbols of strength and virility.' Hunter smiled. 'Years ago I theorised a bull's head once sat atop the Egyptian Sphinx.'

'Really? Not the Pharaoh?' said Knight.

'Long before Khafra. If you study the proportions of the body against the head, Khafra's face is much smaller than it should be, the only explanation being that Khafra must have ordered his image replace the larger original. Proportion was important to the Egyptians. Had they carved the head and body during the same build phase, the sculptors would never have made such an obvious error. It's perhaps the most famous and yet overlooked example of defacing the gods of an earlier generation in the world.'

'So the ancient Egyptians adopted the Sphinx?' said Knight. 'And its origins are in fact tied to a much older civilisation?'

'Something like that...' said Hunter, leaving the unsaid link to Atlantis hanging in the air. The beam of his torch caught a depression on the floor. He knelt to examine it. 'Guys, I was wrong. There is something else in the room.' His fingertip found the shallow hole. 'Strange. There's a small circular imprint depressed into the floor.' He traced his hand around the area. 'Approximately five millimetres deep and five centimetres across. I can see a pair of straight lines extending from its centre and ending at the sphinx's paws.' He shifted position. 'There are more lines fanning away from the statue.' He illuminated the floor. 'They run from the depressed circle all the way to the chamber walls.' He paused and pursed his lips. 'So, anyone got any ideas?'

'What about the Lindow cylinder?' asked Inma. 'Would it fit?'

'Good idea, but the hole is much too small.'

Hunter reached forward and slipped his hand under the mythical creature's chest, looking for clues or maybe a concealed switch. It was cool to the touch and smooth as the chamber walls, almost like polished steel. He pulled away and knocked his head against the bull's nose. He cursed and bent forward, holding his head to ease the pain. The Atlantis medallion he'd stolen from the orichalcum canister fell from his shirt. It knocked against the right paw of the sphinx.

Hunter stared down at it, his eyes widening as he drank in its familiar shape and the centred linear markings adorning its face. His gaze flitted between the medallion and the hole in the floor. A broad smile spread across his dust-covered face as two and two suddenly made four.

'Mr Knight, I think this thing on the floor is some kind of switch. How much more time can you give me?'

A crackle of static followed before the priest's voice resonated in his ear. 'Good work, Hunter. Still quiet up here. Happy for you to proceed. Over.'

Hunter removed the medallion from its leather necklace. He held his breath and lined up the edges with the indent... They matched.

It was all he could do to stop his hands from trembling as he pressed down and eased the disc into position. An audible click confirmed success, cueing his muscles to tense in anticipation. A minute passed... and then another. He must have missed something, but what? Surely something should have happened by now. Hunter stood and paced the chamber, running through each piece of evidence in his head.

'This must be the trigger; it has to be,' he thought. He paused, decluttering his mind with a series of deep breaths. 'There must be a clue in the text,' he muttered. 'Think, John, think.' *Only in order will light return and the number of the beast shall guide your key.* 'Six, one, six, shall guide your key. Six, one, six...' he repeated. Could the answer be so simple?

Hunter crouched between the paws of the sphinx and wiped his brow. He placed his palm on the medallion and held his breath, exerting a little pressure. It moved. The mechanism was stiff, but with a low clicking sound, it nudged one notch to the right. This was it, his Tutankhamen moment. Could this really be happening?

Hunter counted out the clicks under his breath, twisting the medallion further and further until the second, third, fourth, fifth and sixth vibrated through his fingertips. He paused and tried to control his breathing. His heart rate was up in the high hundreds and he needed to calm himself. He wiped his clammy fingers against his trousers and positioned them back on the medallion. He moved it left and then a further five clicks to the right before pausing again. The disc was one twist away from linking the horizontal lines on the floor and connecting the paws of the sphinx. Hunter took a final, nervy breath and tapped the bull's forehead, staring into its unblinking eyes as he shifted the medallion to the right.

'Time you gave up your secrets, my friend,' he whispered.

Somewhere beneath his feet, he heard the sound of whirring machinery, hushed but still audible in the silence of the chamber. The lines linking the paws of the sphinx lit, miniature lava flows of blue light arrowing towards the medallion's centre. Hunter winced as the lines met, but the collision just spawned a series of secondary lines rather than any fireworks. There were seven in total. He watched them fan beyond the medallion, heading for the chamber walls.

'Seven lines,' he whispered. 'Seven lines for the seven islands of Atlantis.'

With a wall at his back, Hunter let his knees buckle. He dropped to the floor in a trance, his mind spinning. He, Dr John Hunter, was sitting in the legendary city of the survivors. It was almost too much to take in; it didn't feel real. There were still so many questions, the biggest of them being 'why?'. Why would a small band of ancient mariners travel thousands of gruelling miles only to stop and build a city in such an inhospitable location? Hunter had struggled for years with the question. It was part of the reason he believed Fawcett may have been a fraud.

Hunter frowned. The room was getting lighter. He shook himself free of his trance and looked about the chamber. The line of light reached the wall and split. 'Oh my god,' he whispered. The bland and featureless walls exploded in a sea of blue light, the smooth basalt awash with the linear artwork of Atlantis.

In a mild state of shock, Hunter touched his earpiece. 'Guys, if you're listening, I believe the appropriate phrase I'm looking for rhymes with clucking bell.'

'John, what's happening? Are you okay?' said George. 'The casket has gone mental up here. It looks more like a Vegas searchlight than a tomb.'

'I'm not surprised,' said Hunter. 'Do any of you recall the time when The Beatles claimed they were bigger than Jesus?'

'Yes.'

'Well this is bigger than The Beatles,' said Hunter. 'I wish you were down here to see this, it is breathtaking. The chamber literally awoke when I flipped the switch.'

'What are you seeing?' said Inma. 'Text? Pictures? Describe it.'

'It'll take hours to translate everything, but there is a map – a detailed and, from the look of it, accurate world map. Your analysis in Cambridge was spot on.'

'Tell me there's a grid system,' said George.

'There is a grid system. They mapped it using ten-degree intervals.' Hunter smiled. 'And you'll love this bit: where the latitudes and longitudes coincide on land, more often than not the locations correspond to modern religious sites.'

'Good god,' said George.

'John, Jacob here again, is there any mention of a weapon?'

'Hang on, I'm not finished. Another two maps are appearing either side...'

'You're kidding me,' said George. 'Come on Johnny boy; tell Papa what he already knows.'

Hunter laughed. 'Take a bow, Papa Goodheart, each map is aligned to a different pole. The first we know about; the second is somewhere in the Hudson Bay and the third...'

'Is in the Yukon Valley?' screamed George.

'Bingo. You were right: Atlantis, or whatever they called their city, has existed for at least one hundred thousand years.' Hunter paused, letting the bombshell filter through to his captivated audience. 'And in case any of you were wondering, the older maps show an island, a large island of seven parts lying beyond the straits of Gibraltar. At a guess I'd say its land mass is about that of Libya and Asia combined.'

'Just as Plato described,' said George.

Hunter rubbed his face, giddy with excitement. 'It looks like we've found Atlantis. Or at least where it once was twelve thousand years ago.'

'Excellent work, Hunter. Is your camera still operational? Can you get a record of the text?' asked Knight.

'Yes, but it will take me a while. This place is dripping with information.'

Hunter raised the viewfinder of his SLR to his eye and heard a soft buzzing sound high above his head. He frowned and stared into the dark apex of the underground pyramid. What could have made a noise like that? It sounded out of place and almost modern in the otherwise silent chamber. He lifted his torch and his heart fluttered. Caught in the powerful beam, the lens of a tiny surveillance camera glinted in the darkness. Hunter tensed as its significance struck him a devastating blow.

He fiddled with his earpiece and whispered, 'Jacob, we have a problem. A big problem.'

Chapter Thirty-Four

Hunter grabbed George's hand and let his friend pull him free of the casket. 'Thank God, I was thinking I'd be trapped down there forever.'

'I saw the lid slide open and...'

'Grew a pair,' said Hunter.

George tapped Hunter's cheek. 'Couldn't have you taking all the glory.'

'You have all the glory you want. I'm just glad the rain's stopped.' A loud fizz pierced the silence. Hunter followed the sound skyward and heard something explode above the forest canopy. A bright flare drifted through the treetops, sparking as it stabilised and bathing the ancient city in an eerie purple haze. Hoffmann's decision to expose his location could only mean one thing: the German was executing an escape plan.

'Out of the frying pan,' he whispered. The crackle of machine-gun fire filled the air, bullets pinging off rocks and embedding in walls as the Order's soldiers advanced on the flare's launch site.

'George, we need to move. This is going to get messy,' said Hunter. 'Keep your head low and aim for the doorway to our left, beyond the pyramid.' George hesitated, his head twisting left and right, his eyes manic. Hunter grabbed his friend's arm and pulled him from danger, skidding to a halt behind a sturdy wall as a series of dull thuds pounded into the space they'd just vacated. 'Don't move,' he shouted. He waited for a lull in fire and risked a look at Inma's position, Hunter gritting his teeth as two of the Order's team crumpled in her vicinity.

'They're using silenced rifles,' hissed Hunter, ducking beside George. 'Watch for the muzzle flash next time they fire, they can't be far from us.'

Enraged and galvanised by their losses, Knight's men returned fire to Hoffmann's position with a reckless abandon, bullets ripping into and sparking off the scarred basalt walls that must be concealing the German. Hunter's eyes narrowed. A new noise had entered the fray, a repetitive thumping sound building to a crescendo and replacing the crackle of rifle fire. It was coming from somewhere above the trees. He clapped his hands to his ears and stared at the gap in the forest canopy, snorting as he recognised the distinctive sound of whipping rotary blades.

As the sound bordered on unbearable, a dark shape replaced the bright hole in the treetops. Knight screamed for his men to fall back but the order fell on deaf ears. Hunter ducked and wiped a torrent of panic-induced sweat from his face. This was bad. He'd been expecting an armoured transport but the descending beast was a different proposition altogether. A Mil Mi-24 Gunship, or as it was more commonly known, 'the Hind'.

Although it was predominantly associated with Russia, Hunter knew the Brazilian Army numbered amongst the Hind's fans. Someone high up must owe Hans Hoffmann a huge favour. Hunter had experienced the machine during a training mission in Afghanistan and the encounter left him in no doubt why the Soviets nicknamed the machine 'the flying tank'. Knight was wise to sound the retreat. Besides having space for eight passengers, the Hind packed one hell of a punch.

Hunter shuddered. Even at this distance the flexible 12.7mm Gatling gun was visible, perched in its usual position under the bulbous fuselage. The huge barrels twitched, jerking left and right as they searched for a viable mark. With it capable of unloading 1500 rounds of armour-piercing ammo into a target in under twenty seconds, no one in Order colours was safe.

The helicopter continued its descent, the dual-bubble cockpit giving it the look of a cautious, oversized dragonfly surveying its surroundings. It slowed as it neared the ground, the colossal machine hovering ten metres above Hoffmann's location. Hunter saw the side door slide open and a heavy rope ladder drop inside a near-decimated residential building.

Hunter slapped the wall, frustration boiling over as Hoffmann and the remainder of his crew ascended the ladder. Hoffmann still possessed the cylinder and he knew they were now in a race against time. If the German translated the chamber text and unearthed the weapon, there was no telling what he'd use it for. The events of the previous twenty-four hours made it clear Hoffmann hadn't embarked on this quest for the good of humanity or science. Whatever power the weapon possessed, Hunter was confident Heinrich Himmler's grandson intended to abuse it.

In his periphery, Hunter noticed an Order soldier lift his gun. 'No,' he hissed, as loud as he dared. 'Don't...' The warning came too late as a flurry of 7.62 rounds hammered against the helicopter's armoured underbelly. Knight screamed for a ceasefire but it was too late: the Hind had a target.

Hunter's stomach lurched as the barrels of the helicopter's massive guns started their ominous revolutions. He grabbed George about the neck and scrambled as far from the area as he dared. George tripped and they both hit the ground, rolling into the gutter of a stone-paved roadway. He clamped his hands to his ears as the deafening roar of the Hind avenging its scratched paintwork cracked and thundered in the air. They needed to keep moving. Hunter forced himself onto his elbows and crept forward, sneaking a peak at Knight's position as they passed an obliterated section of wall. His stomach convulsed and a jet of bile hit the road. He fought on, not daring to look back for fear of seeing the Hind's mini-gun vaporising yet more of Knight's men.

The armour-piercing rounds showed no mercy, ripping through bone and stone alike in their unwavering quest for retribution. It was the longest twenty seconds of Hunter's life and he swept away real tears, thanking God as the smoking gun slowed and span to a stop. The Hind ascended, no doubt with Hoffmann and his team safely ensconced inside, its murderous rage placated. A door gunner continued to pepper the city with automatic fire, minimising any retaliation. This time the Order's remaining soldiers kept well hidden.

Hunter stumbled into the open as the noise of the machine's huge rotors faded. He fell to his knees and dried his eyes. The pyramid floor and the casket lay in pieces, ripped apart and exposing the hidden chamber. He could see its walls, alive with light minutes earlier but now pitted and scarred, destroyed beyond repair by a hail of unrelenting bullets. Clearly the Order's soldiers were not the Hind's only target.

He heard someone shout his name and turned to see Inma stumbling over the debris, Knight hobbling in her wake. She threw her arms around him and kissed his cheek and neck. 'Tell me you aren't hurt.' She rubbed her tear-stained eyes. 'I thought you were still inside.'

'I've had better days,' said Hunter, cracking a few vertebrae as he straightened his spine. 'I'm glad I wasn't inside.' He looked into the pit of mangled and cracked basalt and shook his head. 'I feel like crying again. The evidence is gone. Who's going to believe us now?'

'I hope you managed to save the pictures,' said Knight.

Hunter opened his fist and held up his camera's memory card. 'You try anything and I'll snap it in two. My friends and I are out. You understand. Take us home and you'll have your photographs.'

Knight stopped in his tracks and held his arms in mock supplication. 'Let's not be hasty, Dr Hunter. I know you're angry and I apologise for my previous actions. I know my good intentions can sometimes be misconstrued.'

'Misconstrued? Are you kidding?' said George, joining Hunter. 'You put a gun to my head. You're a bloody psychopath.'

'I prefer to think of it as evidence of my dedication,' said Knight. 'You'll soon understand why I did what I did. Our very existence hangs in the balance. We must put aside our petty differences and work as a cohesive unit. The clock is ticking and we have a common enemy who must be stopped at all costs.'

Part Three

The Giza Plateau, Cairo

Chapter Thirty-Five
Somewhere above the Atlantic

Hunter clasped his hands behind his head and reclined in his first-class British Airways seat. He thought about Jack. The police officer had struggled with his wounds during the flight to Rio, his body not reacting well to the vibrations of air travel. Rather than continue to London and risk worsening his condition, Knight reasoned Jack be left to recuperate in a local hospital. Albeit with reluctance, he agreed to stay, swayed by Knight's request for a little time to clear his name with the constabulary back home. Hunter smiled; Jack might even receive a promotion once the dust settled. An unthinkable prospect a week ago.

He returned to work, tapping the map of the Giza plateau laid out in front of him. The flight to London was a long one and Hunter was determined to make good use of his time. Photographs from the chamber lay scattered atop the map, developed and blown up as A3 prints during their stopover in Rio. He'd spent the majority of the flight exchanging ideas and translations with Inma and they'd already made several astonishing discoveries. He sucked on the end of his pen and looked across the aisle. George, on the other hand, was also doing what he did best: sleeping.

Hunter returned to his notebook and the intriguing text stared back at him – text discovered at the apex of the underground pyramid and which he hoped might prove to be the key to finding this so-called weapon of Atlantis. Unfortunately it was a damn riddle. *For those who follow we hath returned whence we came. It is in the heavens with our god that our might doth lie where the sky and earth embrace.*

'Where the sky and earth embrace,' he whispered. This must be a reference to the Giza plateau. The theory that the Great Pyramid and its two lesser siblings matched up with the belt of Orion was not new to archaeology. Many did not accept the assertion but in

Hunter's mind the similarities could not be ignored. Could this mean the weapon might still be hidden somewhere within the Giza complex? Surely, given the number of ongoing excavations, it would have turned up by now. He shook his head, and ran a finger around the outline of the Sphinx on his map. The pyramid texts referred to it as a monument to their past, a monument celebrating humanity's first encounter with a vengeful God. Could it be so simple as the weapon being buried beneath the paws of the Sphinx?

'Are you still at it?' said George, stretching his arms. 'Come on, get some sleep and turn your bloody light off.'

'I'm so close, George,' said Hunter. 'Can you just cast your eye over this for a second?'

George sighed. 'Come on then. If it's the only way I'm going to get some shut-eye, I guess I have to.'

'This weapon or whatever it is must be located somewhere on the Giza plateau. It's the only place that makes any sense.'

'If it is, it's going to be somewhere with meaning to these people. We just need to work out what's important to them and go from there.'

'True. Everything on the plateau is planned to the nth degree, all monuments built or sited for a specific purpose or reason. It is clear Atlantis was home to a measured and precise race of people. If they hid something in the desert, you're right, they would have buried it somewhere meaningful.'

George struggled to spread out a larger map of the pyramid complex on the table in front of them. 'I was going to share this once we landed, but since we're up... The Giza Pyramids are renowned for their extraordinary geometry.' He smiled. 'In fact I remember you bludgeoning me with facts and figures about the Great Pyramid as a student.'

'You dismissed them as hokum or mere coincidences.'

'Yes, but now... well, now I'm a believer.'

Hunter leant forward to examine George's notes. '36,524 divided by 11,625.96 equals 3.14159.' He grinned at his friend. 'The final figure is pi. Ah, so you've been looking into Taylor's pyramid inch.'

Hunter had himself spent many hours building upon the work of the English publisher, John Taylor. In his 1859 opus, *The Great Pyramid*, Taylor developed the theory of the pyramid inch, a measurement equal to 1.00106 British inches. He mooted this measurement as having been used by the Egyptians to build the Great Pyramid. This first of George's figures, 36,524, was the sum total of the four sides of the pyramid in pyramid inches. Placing a decimal point between the five and the two gave the figure 365.24, the exact length of the solar year. The second figure in George's notebook, 11,625.96, was twice the height of the Great Pyramid. Hunter reflected on how these so-called 'coincidences' exist throughout the construction, from the alignment of the narrow entrance passage pointing at the North Star, to the physical positioning of the three pyramids on the desert floor, mirroring Orion's belt in the heavens.

'With such precision evident in the build, if a hidden chamber exists, my money is on a site of astronomical significance,' said George.

'But didn't you once tell me the pyramid inch isn't an accepted scientific unit of measurement?'

George huffed. 'Given our recent experiences, I've been forced to re-evaluate rather a lot, haven't I?'

'Fine, but aside from giving me a reason to gloat, I still fail to see how it brings us any closer to establishing a dig site.'

'There is one site that leaps to mind.' George paused. 'I've looked into it and the theory fits the reality of what's on the ground.'

'Go on,' said Hunter, his interest piqued. The aircraft shuddered, and George stumbled and fell across the sleeping Inma. She awoke with a cry of pain.

'Idiot. What are you doing, pervert?'

'Sorry, Inma, turbulence.'

'Inma, leave him alone, we're in the middle of something,' said Hunter. 'George thinks he may have found us a dig site.'

Inma slipped out of her belt and joined George at the table. He stared at her a little too long. 'Well go on then, or are you intending to touch my chest again?'

George fumbled with his map, flustered by Inma's aggression. 'You're aware I've been studying the Giza plateau from the air.'

Hunter nodded, waving a hand to hurry him. 'Given the relationship of the site to the stars above, I superimposed the night sky of twelve thousand years ago onto a plan to see if anything matched up.'

Inma nodded. 'And obtained a correlation. We know this. If this is all you've got, I'm going back to my seat.'

'With respect, this is a little more advanced.' George winked at Inma, and she reacted with a dismissive flick of the wrist. 'Rather than proving the Orion theory, I've been concentrating on implementing it in the hope of discovering a possible dig site. There are a few possibilities.' He tapped the plan in front of him, and circled a small area to the southeast of the Menkaure Pyramid, the smallest of the three Giza pyramids. 'But this is the cheeky chappy I'm most excited by. This area mirrors the location of Nebula Messier 78.'

'Messier 78,' said Hunter. 'Why does that ring a bell?'

'Unless you are an avid comic book reader or up on your astronomy, I'm not sure. M78 is where one might find the Land of Light, the home planet of Ultraman.'

Inma snorted in derision. 'Are you telling me you want to dig at this spot on the basis of a comic book hero I've never heard of?'

George cocked his head to one side and smiled. 'Not enough for you? Okay, from an academic point of view, Nebula M78 is accepted as a point in the universe where many young stars have been born. At present, scientists have documented sixty-two and counting.'

'Okay, now impress me. I'm still not sold on why I should care,' said Inma.

'Did you know the ancient Egyptians believed their pharaohs are reborn after their mortal death, reborn as stars in the Sahu?'

Hunter pursed his lips. 'The Sahu? Of course, the Egyptian name for Orion.'

'Makes sense,' said Inma. 'And it fits with the inscription in the chamber about the sky and earth embracing.'

Hunter nodded. 'If the Egyptians believed Orion held the key to the rebirth of their pharaohs, a class they deemed gods, it's plausible they celebrated the fact with a secret chamber. Do you have an idea where?'

George laid a second map over the first. 'If I draw a straight line connecting each of the south-east corners of the three pyramids and then draw a second perpendicular line originating at the right paw of the Sphinx...' He sketched the lines onto the map. 'Then, if I extend a line south along the eastern edge of the Khafre Pyramid...' He completed the drawing. 'Like so. And finally I add a diagonal line which runs through the northwest and southeast corners of the Menkaure Pyramid.' George flicked back and forth between the two maps, amused at the blank looks from his audience. 'Come on guys, you must be able to see the correlation now.'

Inma clapped. 'They intersect at the same point.'

George gave her an enthusiastic nod, as if explaining a difficult concept to a group of undergrads slow on the uptake. 'Yes, but remember what we've been discussing. What do you suppose this point might correspond to?'

Hunter let out a long exhalation. 'Jesus... are you saying they intersect at the centre of M78's mirror?'

Chapter Thirty-Six

Order Headquarters, Bath

Forty-eight hours later and Hunter was ready to present his findings. He flicked the microphone on the lectern and blew into it. A high-pitched squeal of static echoed through the purpose-built lecture room. George and Inma winced in unison, covering their ears. He raised a hand in apology and twiddled with the volume. 'Sorry guys.'

Built deep inside the bowels of the seventeenth-century estate doubling as the Order's headquarters, the oak-panelled room was equipped with the latest in audiovisual technology. In addition to the huge touch-screen display framing his head, each seat had its own built-in private television and translation device. Given the cultural diversity of the delegates present, these added extras were crucial.

Beyond the back row, a heavy wooden door swung back and forth as the various attendees filed back inside after their meal. Knight's Order was certainly well connected. The majority were politicians, but there were representatives from the military, several recognisable religious figures and a smattering of high-profile industrialists. A pang of anxiety gnawed at Hunter's gut. Why would such a high-profile collective want to hear him speak? And even if they did, why would they act on his conclusions?

He turned to his companions. George squirmed under his gaze, confirming he was well outside his comfort zone. The geologist had delivered a briefing before the break on the events leading up to their Brazilian expedition, and it hadn't gone well. To say the room had received George's material with a lack of interest was an understatement, and the stoical look on his friend's face made it clear he'd taken the snub to heart. Hunter couldn't be certain, but put the apathy down to the possibility George's material was old news rather than a reflection on his lecturing style.

Inma broke the tension and nudged George playfully. 'How long does it take to grab something to eat? You don't think you bored a few of them into needing forty winks do you?'

'These guys are weird,' George snapped. 'I can't think of anyone who wouldn't have been blown away by my presentation. Or at the very least reacted. Even a few angry questions would have been nice. I show them evidence of an orichalcum cylinder and genuine Atlantean maps and what do they do? Nothing. They just sit there in muted silence. I'm telling you, these guys are a bunch of emotional retards.'

The door creaked open and Knight stuck his head round the door. 'I assume you're ready to start, Dr Hunter? The emotional retards are eager to hear part two.'

George went white. 'Sorry, what? Oh God. I didn't mean...'

'No worries, Goodheart.' Knight winked. 'To be honest, I'm inclined to agree.' He tapped his earpiece. 'Next time just remember to turn your microphone off before bad-mouthing your audience.'

Turning from white to a deep shade of crimson, George flicked off his microphone and slumped into his seat.

'What's it like to insult people in a hundred different languages?' Inma asked.

'Don't worry about it,' said Hunter. 'I'm sure most of them have been called worse. Not sure about the cardinal though.'

George ignored him, raising a file in front of his face and pretending to read. Hunter ruffled the geologist's hair, grinning as George batted his hand away.

The heavy auditorium door swung open again and the last of the delegates retook their seats. Hunter returned to the lectern and caught Knight's eye as he opened the door for an elderly woman to enter. Caught off guard, Hunter dug his nails into the soft wood of the podium, struggling to maintain his composure.

Dressed in her trademark tweed, the woman took her seat in the front row and nodded with nonchalance in his direction. 'Dr Hunter.'

Hunter took a breath and nodded back. 'Professor Cleary.'

A hundred miles east, Hans Hoffmann gritted his teeth as a wave of pain coursed through him, his knuckles whitening against the arms of his chair. He fought to retain consciousness, thanking whatever god was responsible, when the clank of metal on metal at last signalled the end to his ordeal. He let out a long breath and released his grip on the chair, cursing his decision against having a general anaesthetic.

'All done, Mr Hoffmann, you can open your eyes now. You'll be limping for several days, but all in all you've been lucky, there's no lasting damage.'

Hoffmann opened his eyes as instructed, blinking as they adjusted to the fluorescent lighting in the Harley Street office. He looked down and forced a smile at the pretty nurse bandaging his bloodied thigh. Darren stood at the door, looking relieved. As well he should. A ricocheting bullet had found Hoffmann's leg during their escape from the lost city, and he hadn't let his bodyguard forget it.

Hoffmann glanced at the big man, tearing his gaze from the voluptuous cleavage of the nurse. 'Any luck finding someone to translate the chamber images?'

'We're still trying, sir,' said Darren. 'We tried Hunter's Cambridge colleague, Professor Cleary.' Darren paused.

'Let me guess: no luck?' Hoffmann snapped.

'She's in the field working on a book. I was told she doesn't like to be disturbed and never leaves any means of contacting her.'

Hoffmann shook his head. 'Bloody academics, why can't they live in the real world with the rest of us? Is there no way we can trace her whereabouts?'

'We can, but it will take time.'

'And what of our original trio? Any word on where they've taken Hunter?'

'There's better news on that front,' said Darren. 'They flew them to the Order estate in the Bath hills. Our intelligence hasn't picked up any movement from them since.'

Hoffmann nodded. 'Excellent. Have you assessed the building? Any chance of mounting a successful retrieval? Keep in mind this would be my preference.'

Darren sucked in a breath through clenched teeth. 'Slim. Security is tighter than a duck's arse. I fired off a few rounds at the windows last time we were there...'

'Bulletproof?' interrupted Hoffmann.

'More like blastproof. And given we know they've got a small army kitted out with the latest in military tech, it might be easier for us to break into Fort Knox.'

Hoffmann rubbed his temples, wincing as the nurse tightened the bandage. 'Still, I suggest you start the planning process. For the moment it's our only lead. If we don't translate the text in the next twenty-four hours, we can kiss goodbye to my grandfather's legacy. The Order already have a head start they don't deserve. If the Cleary woman can't be located, we need Hunter back in the fold. We're losing ground with every passing minute and need him to get back in the game.'

Chapter Thirty-Seven

Professor Esmeralda Cleary – what the hell was she doing here? Hunter pursed his lips, recalling Cleary's admission that the Order had funded and fast-tracked her application for professorship. In hindsight, there must have been more to the deal than burying her Atlantis quest. It was obvious they recruited her, but why, if she was one of them, had she encouraged him to continue with his own quest? Hunter shook his head, hoping it was a case of academic curiosity rather than anything more sinister.

With everyone seated and the expectant murmuring dying, Hunter straightened his papers and moistened his mouth with a swig from his water bottle.

'Good evening, gentlemen… and ladies.' He nodded a silent greeting at Professor Cleary. 'I trust you are all suitably refreshed.' He waved an arm in George's direction. 'Before dinner, my colleague ended his presentation with a bang. The revelation that Plato's Atlantean civilisation mapped the world they inhabited with an unimaginable degree of accuracy. A feat confirming they were a race of both accomplished sailors and skilled cartographers.'

Hunter tapped the computer and waited for his first slide to appear. 'I took this photo inside the pyramid chamber in Brazil. These are the chamber walls found close to the pyramid's tip. Note the series of random, perhaps decorative, dots of light.' He circled the dots with a laser pointer. 'However, I've learnt this is a civilisation which didn't do random.' He glanced at Inma. 'Now as much as I would love to take the credit, the plaudits must go to Dr Pérez. Inma, would you do the honours?'

Inma nodded and took her place at the lectern. 'Thank you, Dr Hunter.' She took the laser pen and highlighted part of the picture. 'What you are looking at is a prehistoric map of the night sky. In a similar fashion to the mariners of recent history, I believe this was how the Atlantean sailors navigated the oceans of our planet.'

'But that looks nothing like our night sky,' asked a well-known

American politician in the second row. 'Which constellations are they meant to be?'

'A good question,' said Inma. 'And one that can be explained by the precession of the equinoxes.' The politician looked blank. 'The positions of the stars have altered significantly throughout Earth's history. They do move themselves, but the radical change is more the fault of the Earth. We don't feel it, but even now our planet is twisting back and forth on its axis, something akin to a spinning top before it topples. As a result the constellations can be seen to move up and down over the sky, travelling through cycles of about 26,000 years.'

The politician nodded as Inma moved to her next slide. 'What you are seeing on this slide,' she said, 'is a modern star map sat alongside its Atlantean counterpart.' She fiddled with the keyboard. 'Now if I can just switch on my program.' Hunter smiled and leant forward, tapping a button and activating an animated short.

'Thanks, John.' Hunter nodded and looked up at the screen, watching as the familiar constellations shifted and morphed into those depicted on the chamber walls. A number flashed up on the screen. Inma highlighted it in triumph. '12,530 BP.' She paused for effect. 'This, my esteemed colleagues, is the last time the stars occupied the positions recorded in the chamber.' She circled a constellation. 'I'd like us to focus upon one constellation in particular. This is Orion.'

On cue a magnified image of Orion appeared on the screen. 'Now compare it to this.' An aerial photograph of the pyramid complex at Giza slid beneath the constellation. 'Note Orion's belt and the position of the pyramids. They are an exact match. Now look at the Nile and the Milky Way.'

Inma gazed out at her audience, her face flushed with excitement. 'The Giza complex is a mirror of Earth's skies as they were twelve-and-a-half thousand years ago. When they were built is irrelevant. This proves the site must have been planned by a group predating Egyptian civilisation. Perhaps to commemorate an important event in their history.' She cocked her head to one side. 'The destruction of their homeland perhaps?' Inma paused, holding her breath and waiting for feedback. But, like George before her, nothing but stony silence greeted her words.

'Thank you,' said Hunter, replacing Inma at the podium. 'In my mind Dr Pérez has shown the link between Egypt and Atlantis to be irrefutable. But to cement the deal, I have a little extra to add.' Behind his head a familiar photograph of the Egyptian Sphinx filled the screen. 'It has long been theorised by individuals my profession deem as credulous...' Hunter glanced at Professor Cleary, 'that the Sphinx is not of Egyptian origin but instead harks back to a long-forgotten era of prehistory. The largely ignored, but conclusive proof has come not from archaeology, but instead from its sister subject, geology.' Hunter turned to acknowledge George. 'As my colleague Dr Goodheart will attest, the weathering patterns covering the body of the Sphinx were created not by sand as is the accepted view, but by water.'

George stood, joining Hunter as a close-up of the famous monument appeared on the screen. He pointed at a series of vertical lines dissecting it. 'These lines are a clear sign of weathering caused by water. If caused by wind-blown sand, we would see harder layers of rock jutting out beyond the soft, the reason being the softer material would be eroded at a faster rate. In my professional opinion, there is no question that anything other than water caused the weathering on the Sphinx.' He threw Hunter a sly look, aware he was on the verge of another revelation. 'And this gives us a build date of at least nine thousand years ago, the last time frame the weather systems in Egypt could have supported such weathering.' George grinned, this time unfazed by the vacant faces lined up in front of him. 'The floor is yours, Dr Hunter.'

'Thanks George,' said Hunter, easing him away from the podium. He shuffled his feet. The final part of the lecture was a tough sell, and he was doubtful as to how it would be received. He tapped the keyboard, and an image of a text-covered wall appeared behind him. 'Although groundbreaking evidence, I am aware this is not the reason the majority of you have turned up to hear us speak.' He tapped the screen with his laser pen. 'This is another photo taken inside the Brazilian chamber. Dr Pérez and I have spent the last two days piecing together a rough translation of this text. In doing so we uncovered the true legacy of Atlantis.'

A murmur rippled around the room. Inma stepped from the podium and distributed a series of A4 sheets amongst the re-energised attendees.

'Although more advanced in its construction, the text bears an extraordinary resemblance to early Egyptian hieroglyphics. There were a few anomalies, but once Dr Pérez and I realised what we were dealing with, it proved an easy language to crack. As a disclaimer, I should say the translation isn't perfect. We've filled gaps with best guesses and reordered the words to ensure the passages can be understood.'

Hunter paused, allowing the room time to digest the material. 'The earliest inscriptions, those inscribed towards the pyramid's tip, suggest the chamber existed as a memorial. A memorial to the citizens of Atlantis who lost their lives in the great flood.' He held a hard copy of the translation aloft. 'I'd like to draw your attention to paragraph two. Lines of text that blow current archaeological thinking out the water.'

'With our armies engaged in conflict with the god-fearing Greeks, the Atun and Sopdet rose and sent a raging bull with the tail of a lion to their aid. Day by day, the bull grew until on the fifth day it filled the skies, spraying our lands with fire and burning our crops and cities. Forced to the seas, the people sailed forth from Atuntis and sought sanctuary amongst our armies. On the ninth day, we found dry land in the country of the black-skinned. It was here that the great Bull did deem it time to strike. The earth screamed under our feet and the sky did darken above our heads. Waters rose and mountains fell before silence reigned supreme. It was many cycles before we felt warmth from the Atun once more. Our godless punishment was complete.'

Hunter clapped his hands against the lectern. 'We can finally put paid to the question as to how Atlantis, or Atuntis, was lost. The passage also explains why the North Pole moved so dramatically twelve thousand years ago from the Hudson Bay to its current position. A comet strike of a sufficient size, punching into the Earth at an angle, would have had more than enough power to shove the crust hundreds of miles over the plastic flowing rock of the mantle below. Such dramatic and geologically instantaneous changes in the Earth's crustal positioning would account for many of the anomalies in our planet's history – anomalies modern academics tend to gloss over. The plight of the Siberian mammoth, for example.'

Hunter looked at Professor Cleary, a little perturbed as to why she hadn't tried to interrupt. If anything she almost looked impressed. 'Over the last few decades, we've uncovered thousands of mammoths frozen deep within the Siberian ice sheets. In some cases the beasts were frozen in mid-step, their meat in a state fresh enough to eat. I believe one was even found with half-digested buttercups still in its mouth.'

Hunter cycled through various slides depicting the destructive power of nature. 'I'd like you to imagine the consequences of a crust displacement episode. Hundreds of Krakataus erupting in unison. Tidal waves and tsunamis a mile high striking every coastline. Earthquakes, avalanches, hurricanes… the list goes on. The chances of survival would have been minimal. Food sources bordering non-existent. Volcanic ash would have blocked the sun for months and life on Earth would have ground to a halt.' He took a sip of water. 'It should come as no surprise that these people believed this circumstance to be a punishment. They adopted the bull-headed sphinx as their god, and it was through prayer and sacrifice that this ancient civilisation found the strength to survive. If you remember your Plato, he described Atlantis as a complacent race and one that wholeheartedly rejected the gods.'

Hunter tapped the screen in front of him. 'This passage suggests he was right, and further than that, the Atlanteans appear to have blamed their atheism for the disaster. As a consequence they evolved their thinking and embraced the notion of living in the shadow of a vengeful God.' He skirted over the next few lines and continued. 'There follows a potted history and evolution of what they saw as God and how, upon their return to the motherland, it was their intention to build a temple to commemorate and give thanks to the God that had spared them.'

Hunter stopped, his eyes flitting between Inma and the words scrolling down the screen. How had he been so stupid? That was it. How could he have overlooked something so obvious?

Inma rose from her seat, thinking he might be struggling, and grabbed his arm. 'John, are you okay? You look like you're about to pass out.'

'You're not far off,' said Hunter, thankful for her steadying arm. He covered his microphone and leant into her ear. 'Any chance you can wrap this up without me? I need to check something.'

Chapter Thirty-Eight
Hoffmann Headquarters Building, London

Hoffmann stared at the image on his tablet. It showed Darren, hunched down in the driver's seat of a modified, bulletproof Range Rover Sport. His bodyguard raised a pair of binoculars, presumably trained on the grand entrance of the Order's country house headquarters. Darren was going above and beyond on this mission; he'd certainly earned the long stretch of R&R Hoffmann had promised him when all this was over.

Hoffmann shifted the dashboard camera to show the rear seats, comforted by the sight of the two blacked-up ex-members of the British Special Forces. With these boys in tow, the extraction should be a breeze. He moved the camera back and saw Darren check his watch. 21:32. Hoffmann winced, aware his London team was well behind schedule.

Hoffmann rose from his seat and gazed around the sea of faces, all tapping away and engrossed in their respective screens. He shook his head; the job was way beyond the capabilities of his staff. But he'd expected that. What he'd not catered for was the distinct lack of anyone in England with the capability, or even the willingness to at least attempt, the hack he required.

Three hours had passed since he'd been passed the dossier: details of a viable spy satellite with thermal capabilities scheduled to pass over England. The target was an American, military-grade surveillance satellite due to orbit over England in the next three hours or, rather, right about now. The stats were impressive. Launched in 2000, the MTI, or Multispectral Thermal Imager satellite, could provide up to five-metre resolution, which made it more than capable of achieving Hoffmann's objectives. Operatives controlled the machine from their base inside the ultra-secure Los Alamos National Laboratory, a secret government building hidden in the New Mexico desert landscape. All they needed to do was alter this minor inconvenience and shift the base of operations a little. How hard could it be?

'So, you must be the Hoff. I'm told you require my genius to hack Los Alamos?'

Hoffmann spun on his heels, surprised to find himself face to face with a short, skinny boy of apparent Asian descent. Hoffmann looked him up and down. He was a cliché of working-class London. From the obligatory beanie hat, black hoodie and baggy jeans, down to the oversized tan Caterpillar boots on his feet. A series of lank stands of dark, unwashed hair poked out from under his hat and framed his acne-scarred face. In an attempt to age himself, the boy sported a fine covering of dark hair on his upper lip.

'Who the hell are you?' asked Hoffmann. 'And how the hell did you get past security?'

'I, Mr Hoff, am your saviour. I'm a board jockey, a sick board jockey,' the boy replied, his thick East End accent giving away his roots.

Hoffmann frowned and shook his head. 'You're sick? Is this a joke? I'll ask again, how did you get past security?' Hoffmann started as the door to the stairwell crashed open and James, a member of his IT team, bundled through it.

The man stopped in the doorway, doubling over and fighting for breath. 'So sorry, Mr Hoffmann, he ran on ahead. Little bastard blocked the lifts and forced me to take the stairs.' He stood upright and placed a hand on the boy's shoulder, his breathing regularising. 'I've come up trumps for you, sir. This is Ninja Star. He'll be your hacker for the evening.'

'Ninja Star? Are you pulling my leg? An acne-riddled teenage oik is the best we can do?'

'He's the best anyone can do, sir. This kid is only seventeen and already on the FBI's most-wanted list.'

The boy snapped his right hand at Hoffmann. 'Eighteenth if you're counting, but today's update hasn't been published yet.'

Hoffmann rolled his eyes, but James continued unperturbed. 'His CV is impressive; includes the FBI, the CIA, the Home Office and MI6. Boy claims to be looking for evidence of aliens.'

The boy nodded. 'The truth is out there.'

Hoffmann stroked his unshaven chin and contemplated his some-what limited options. 'The real truth is that nothing is out there, but I can overlook the crazy if your CV is as impressive as my colleague is making out.' He offered his hand. 'What do I call you? Mr Star? Ninja?' Hoffmann pulled his hand away, cutting the boy off before he could answer. 'Not that I care; all I need to know is your capability of hacking Los Alamos for... shall we call it a round twenty grand?'

'The MTI is protected by five firewalls, each more complicated than the last. The systems in this facility are better protected than God. I'm thinking ten per wall. Minimum. And another ten if you want me to assume control of the satellite. You want me, those are the terms.' He handed Hoffmann a card. 'Wire the dough to this account. When it hits, I start work.'

'Sixty thousand?' said Hoffmann, amused by the front of the teenager. 'You better be good for that kind of money. How long will it take?'

'I'll need state-of-the-art juice. And I'm talking some proper sick equipment. Round here, Grace is the only accessible badass super-computer able to crack Los Alamos open. Three hundred and forty-one teraflops and eleven thousand processor cores. An hour with that kind of lady and I can guarantee results.'

Hoffmann gave his IT manager a blank look. 'Grace is a Lenovo-made supercomputer owned by University College London. I may need to grease a palm or two, but at this time of night I'm confident we can get him a couple of hours, no questions asked.'

Hoffmann nodded. 'Excellent, wire the money and take him to UCL.' He scribbled the address of the Order's headquarters on the back of a business card and handed it to the young hacker. 'I need you to provide a thermal-image feed of this building.' He tapped the card. 'It needs to be transmitted to these three devices. Don't be fooled by the look of the building. We are dealing with a top-end, high-tech construct. The walls are a metre thick and lead-lined. They can block out any kind of ground-operated imagery.' He tapped the picture of the MTI in front of him. 'I'm gambling this satellite will pack more of a punch.'

The hacker nodded and turned to leave.

'One more thing,' said Hoffmann. The boy turned and eyeballed him. 'Screw me over and I'll boil you alive inside that stupid hat of yours.'

Chapter Thirty-Nine
Order Headquarters, Bath

Knight was bordering on the apoplectic as he stormed through the oak-panelled corridors and opulent gothic-style rooms of his so-called impregnable fortress. Hoffman's foot soldiers had executed a smash and grab with a meticulous and almost enviable level of planning. He didn't care they'd taken Hunter. The Order had his notes and that made the academic expendable. No, what galled him was the incompetence and general complacency his men had demonstrated in their defence of the building.

He kicked aside one of the many dead bodies littering Hoffmann's escape route, cursing himself for once again underestimating his foe. Knight banged his fist against a wall. The whole thing stank of Special Forces. Only men trained in the art of war could have overridden and evaded his million-pound security system with such ease.

Knight arrived at the building's control room and hesitated before entering. The unlocked door stood ajar. He nudged it open and rolled his eyes in disgust. The two guards lay dead, stripped of their uniforms and slumped against their desks, bullet wounds still oozing blood from the back of their skulls. At least the uniforms explained how the intruders had navigated the house without arousing suspicion.

Knight gnashed his teeth as his gaze landed upon the bank of screens in front of him. He reached for the nearest screen and ripped it from the wall, hurling it to the ground. The small LCD shattered on impact, erasing the image burnt into its screen forever. He sank to his knees, grimacing as shards of broken glass and plastic sliced through his clothing. Every one of the thirty-nine remaining screens displayed the same provocative image: the auditorium. How much had Hoffmann seen? At a loss as to his next move, Knight squinted as the image faded and a line of text scrolled across the screen.

"You lose!!! Now get off the floor, you're embarrassing yourself."

The words swirled about the screens in a dazzling array of colour and deformed images. Knight gasped as the visuals settled down. It was a live feed with his upper torso at its centre, a goatee and horns drawn onto his face. Overwhelmed by rage, he grabbed a vacant chair and hurled it into the screens.

Knight turned and strode from the room, leaving the satisfying sounds of cracking glass and exploding monitors in his wake. Anderson fell in step beside him. 'What do you want?' The burly man mumbled something incoherent. 'Are you trying to antagonise me? Speak up man.'

'We've lost contact,' Anderson stammered. 'We've lost contact, sir.'

Knight stopped in his tracks and slowly closed his eyes. 'What do you mean we've lost contact?' He slowly spat out each word with venom. 'What kind of imbecile do you have to be to lose an entire bloody satellite?'

'I was stood behind the satellite technician when it happened.' Knight narrowed his eyes, enjoying the sole positive from the situation and making this usually arrogant man squirm. Anderson gulped down a breath and continued. 'It was tracking the path of the car and the screen just froze. I made him reboot, but the access programme has gone. We've lost everything.'

Knight strode the few extra metres to the satellite technician's office and shoved open the door. 'For Christ's sake, what is that?' he hissed, stabbing a finger at the technician's computer screen. The man it belonged to turned a shade of scarlet and cowered down in his chair.

Anderson stared at the screen in disbelief, unaware of what Knight already knew. 'The bastards have hacked us.'

Knight slapped the desk and felt the red mist descend. A fist unfurled a middle finger on an animated loop in the centre of the monitor. He studied the image. 'Does the star-shaped ring on the finger mean anything to you?'

The technician shrugged, unable to speak.

'Find out. Hunt this hacker down. Then I want that finger removed and shoved down his throat.' He paused and glared at his employees. 'Either that or hire him. Heaven knows we could do with some real talent in this place.'

'I'll find him, sir,' said Anderson.

Knight rolled his eyes and stiffly left the room. He returned to the auditorium, not entirely sure how to deliver such bad news. The excited babble of chattering voices subsided as he entered, everyone focusing on him as he took to the podium. He saw George comforting Inma as they bemoaned the loss of their colleague. Knight waved the snivelling pair aside and tapped the microphone, making sure it was still functional.

'Fellow members, I am sad to report we have been the victim of a new kind of warfare. Our enemies have breached the walls of our organisation not by traditional means, but via the electronic superhighway. Cyber warriors are bombarding us from afar, hidden behind their keyboards and well beyond the range of our conventional weapons. We are at war, ladies and gentlemen, and this war has already escalated to an unimaginable level. Our security systems are down. We've lost our satellite and, with it, the ability to track those seeking to destroy us.' He shuffled his feet, his mind searching for a few positives. Something the members could rally around. He settled on revenge. 'Be assured we will not take this lying down. We know where this godless German heathen is headed and I suggest we organise a welcome party for the wily little bastard.'

Chapter Forty
Cairo

A bucket of freezing water jolted Hunter back into consciousness. He raised his head and shook the drips from his unwashed, greasy blond hair. He flexed his fingers, but found them bound to the rear of a hardwood chair. Hans Hoffmann leant into his eyeline, grinning as he intruded on Hunter's personal space, inches from his face. Hunter refused to react, staring at his kidnapper as a cocktail of hate and anger welled up inside him. The memories flooded back. The blow to the back of the head and the tortuous car journey, compressed in the boot of a car.

'Wakey wakey, Dr Hunter. Welcome back.'

Hunter jerked his chair, forcing Hoffmann to retreat. 'Fuck you, Nazi. Yeah, you better stay out of range.'

'Tut tut, John, not the language I'd expect of a Jesus alumnus.' He ruffled Hunter's hair and gave him a condescending smile.

'You're a genetic freak,' hissed Hunter. 'Grandson of Heinrich Himmler. You should be ashamed of your past, not basking in it. Your life is built on the spoils of the most detestable and indefensible event in history. How do you sleep at night?'

Hoffmann leant in again, nose to nose with Hunter. 'Whatever my grandfather did, Dr John Hunter, it was for the good of humanity. I can't say I agree with his execution of the plan, but the theory was sound. The Untermensch or subhuman scum were and still are a plague ravaging our planet of its resources. If you could see beyond the spineless programme of media-driven propaganda and spin, you'd know I speak the truth.' He wiped spittle from his mouth. 'Heinrich was doing his duty as a good German and as a better Aryan.'

'His duty as a better Aryan? Are you for real? He's the antithesis of the Aryan ideal, not that such a race ever even existed. It's a nineteenth-century literary myth, a misinterpreted racial category found in the works of Arthur de Gobineau.'

'You know your stuff, Dr Hunter, but how can you dispute the existence of a master race after what you've seen, Aryan or otherwise?'

'You're mad. What do you hope to achieve from expounding this claptrap? Who is it you expect to support a campaign of selective genocide? No one will care if your master race is real or not. It doesn't matter how you spin it.'

'Selective genocide?' Hoffmann laughed. 'That was my grandfather's plan, not mine. He lived in a different era and didn't know better.'

'I guess that's something,' said Hunter.

Hoffmann gripped the arms of Hunter's chair and crouched in front of him. 'I'm hoping once you learn of my objectives, your adopted stance will change.'

'Don't bank on it,' Hunter snorted. 'Kidnap and forced imprisonment is not really route one to getting me onside.'

'The talk of this ancient weapon is what interests me. It's so much more exciting than simply proving a politically motivated link between my people and a long-forgotten society. As you pointed out, apart from the extreme right, who would really care?'

Hoffmann retrieved an envelope from his blazer pocket. 'A week before he died, my father gave me a key to a safe-deposit box.' He let Hunter scan the first paragraph. 'Expecting gold or cash, I opened it on my eighteenth birthday. You can imagine my disappointment when all I found was an old gun and a letter, addressed not to me, but to my father. In hindsight a rather short-sighted reaction, wouldn't you say, John?'

Hunter shrugged. 'You're an idiot now, you were an idiot then.'

Hoffmann smiled and rose to his feet. 'You're a brave man, John, braver than I gave you credit for.' He tapped Hunter's head with the letter. 'This letter detailed my origins alongside Heinrich Himmler's quest to link Germany with Atlantis. It includes a log of all his evidence, evidence including our lost Brazilian city and a description of the underground chamber.'

'Your origins?'

'My father was created as part of my grandfather's involvement with the Lebensborn programme.'

'Created?' said Hunter, immediately wishing he'd shown greater lack of interest.

Hoffmann knocked the top of his head with condescension. 'I'm so glad you care and, yes, created, my dear John. Heinrich arrested a number of blue-eyed, blonde-haired beauties and, to put it bluntly, inseminated them with his seed. Helga Hoffmann, my grandmother, was the lucky winner.'

Hunter pulled against his bonds, overwhelmed with disgust. How could anyone treat something as precious as life with such disdain? 'What about...'

Hoffmann cut him off. 'The rest found their way to Dachau.'

'You're an animal. Instead of righting this horrific wrong you squander Nazi gold on a folly like Atlantis.'

'What can I say? The implications of the city's existence intrigued me more than paying off the families of a few long-forgotten women.' Hunter spat at Hoffmann, but he neatly sidestepped the projectile and grinned. 'It wasn't actually Atlantis that sold me on the quest,' he continued, ignoring Hunter's attempted assault. 'Grandfather also uncovered evidence of an ancient order, formed to protect humanity from a weapon capable of destroying...' He rubbed his hands conspiratorially. '...or creating civilisation. Now that, Dr Hunter, piqued my interest.'

Hunter's eyes narrowed. 'Creating civilisation?'

Hoffmann shrugged. 'I was sceptical myself, but a chance encounter with an Order member looking to induct me changed my perspective. I persuaded him to take a look at the letter, and he verified the accuracy of its contents. Not only that, but he confirmed the failure of the Order in its ancient mission. They lost their key around the time of Christ and my contact described the group as being in turmoil ever since, paranoid the weapon might resurface, its power harnessed and used against them.' Hoffmann smiled. 'The conversation sealed my destiny. What could an organisation as powerful as this Order possibly be afraid of? Whatever it was, I vowed it would be mine.'

'You are such a cliché. Who do you think you are, a Bond villain? Sorry to burst your bubble, Hoffmann, but Blofeld's plans for world domination didn't amount to much and neither will yours.'

Hoffmann's mouth tightened. 'Given the weakness of your present position, you would do well to retain a modicum of respect.'

Hunter shook his head and exhaled through his nose. 'What do you want, Hans? You must need me for something. If you wanted me dead, I'm sure you'd have done it by now.'

Hoffmann shrugged and ignored the comment. 'It's not world domination I desire.' A smile flickered about his lips. 'Well, not yet. For now I'm looking at this Atlantis weapon more as a foundation, a foundation stone for a new Europe. Although Adolf Hitler's methods were a little questionable, I'm convinced he was on the right lines in his ham-fisted attempt to create a United States of Europe.'

Hunter closed his eyes. 'A little questionable? Christ, you really are casting yourself as a Bond villain.'

'Times are changing, Dr Hunter, and we're the group being left behind. Europe is a dying force in world politics. We're nothing more than a fragmented group of bitter governments living off past glories.

'I take it you aren't a believer in the European Union then?'

'A bunch of useless, self-serving, pen-pushing bureaucrats. They've presided over an era in which Europe is weaker than it's ever been in recorded history. And these are the same bureaucrats you expect to lead us into a brighter future?'

'So with you at the helm, you believe the good ship Europe would thrive?'

'The political climate is ripe for a dictatorship. People are running scared, John. The Euro is weak, inflation is high; unemployment and export figures are heading in the wrong direction. Europe is crying out for a leader to implement the drastic measures required for change.'

Hunter raised his eyebrows at the ferocity of Hoffmann's delivery, surprised the German hadn't gone the whole hog and ended his speech with a Nazi salute. 'You're crazy. No one in their right mind will support the rise of a fourth Reich. Or do you need reminding how that particular story panned out last time?'

Hoffmann grinned. 'It's true the logo may have to change.'

'Do you think this is a joke? Have you no concept of what you're proposing? These are the foundations for another world war.'

'If the world requires a stick, I will use one,' Hoffmann replied, all traces of warmth in his demeanour vanishing. 'Can war be any worse than living in a world controlled by Jacob Knight and his Order?'

'You are mad. And you believe this weapon, a weapon that's over twelve thousand years old, will be your stick.' Hunter shook his head. 'We don't even know if it still exists, let alone if it's operational.'

Hoffmann slapped his hands down on the arms of Hunter's chair. 'Himmler uncovered evidence suggesting the Atlanteans developed a technology allowing them to boil water in a matter of seconds.'

'What?' Hunter snorted. 'This is what we're fighting over, a prehistoric kettle? What are you planning, a tea party? I'll invite my niece, but only if she can bring her teddy bear.'

'The human body is sixty percent water,' said Hoffmann, his eyes narrowing as he strove to control his temper. 'Imagine having the tech to boil it away in seconds. It is little wonder many battles fought by Atlantis ended before they started.'

Hunter bit his lip and mulled over this new information. If true and Hoffmann actually managed to find and activate such a weapon, the armies of the world wouldn't stand a chance. Depending on its range, the effect of such a weapon on the modern battlefield would be seismic, potentially greater than the atomic bomb and machine gun combined. They were talking of an invisible weapon of mass destruction, able to strike without warning and devastate targets without any environmental repercussion. The hair on Hunter's arms rose and he shivered at the thought. 'So now you've revealed your evil plan, what now? You can't believe I'm going to help you find this thing?'

'I take it by your use of the word "evil" as oppose to "noble" that I have not quite convinced you?'

'Just kill me or let me walk. I'll never join forces with a psychopath like you.'

'So you think siding with the Order is the better option? Search your soul, Dr Hunter. Once you'd served your period of use, what do you think they intended to do with you? Pat you on the back, present you with a fat cheque and show you the door?' He clipped Hunter around the head. 'Get real, John, you're a dead man walking and you know it. As are your friends, George and Inma.' He bent to his haunches and gazed into Hunter's eyes. 'If you want to save them, you must surely see you have no choice but to help me. You translated the pyramid text; all you need to do is tell me where this weapon is located and you'll walk free.'

'Why don't you find someone else? I'm not the only specialist in this area.'

'True, but you've already translated it. Unfortunately I appear to have found myself in a race with that podgy priest heading up the Order and he has your notes. So, as you can imagine, time is rather of the essence.'

Hunter pulled at his bonds and spat at the German. Hoffmann turned his cheek as the globule of phlegm hit his right ear. He wiped the spittle away with his sleeve, a mixture of disgust and hatred in his eyes.

'Your final mistake,' he hissed. 'Darren tells me you SBS boys go through an intensive programme of interrogation training.' He rose and patted Hunter's defiant face. 'As much as I would like to discover your breaking point, time is against us. Darren has suggested a far simpler method of breaking you.'

The door behind Hoffmann opened. The unexpected injection of bright light forced Hunter to avert his eyes from the stout figure entering the room. It was Darren. He squinted as his eyes acclimatised and noticed the bodyguard struggling to drag something through the doorway. It was another prisoner. In one fluid motion, Darren kicked a chair in front of Hunter and forced his captive to sit. The man was naked bar a pair of handcuffs and a black sack encasing his head. Hunter noted the various cuts and bruises covering the man's broad shoulders and naked torso, evidence of recent torture.

Unconcerned by the condition of his second prisoner, Hoffmann met Hunter's repulsed look head on. 'Any change of heart, Hunter?'

'Why should I care what you do with some near-dead idiot?' said Hunter, trying to feign indifference.

'The label could also apply to you,' Hoffmann snorted.

'You're a quick one; no wonder you were accepted at Cambridge.'

Hoffmann lost his cool and thumped his fist hard into Hunter's stomach. Hunter tensed and absorbed the blow. He winked at the German. 'If you want a bit of slap and tickle, at least be a gentleman and buy me dinner first.'

Hoffmann scowled and ripped the hood from his prisoner. 'Perhaps this will curb your penchant for insolence.'

Hunter sucked the cell's stale air into his lungs and coughed. Although there was little reaction from the man opposite, their eyes met and Hunter could have sworn he saw the faint sparkle of hope.

'Jack? Jesus Christ, Hans, what the hell have you done to him?'

'What do you mean, what did I do? You must have known there was no way I could let him live, not after what he'd witnessed.'

'You snatched him from the hospital?'

'I did. The trail your entourage left wasn't hard to follow. I couldn't believe my luck when you left him in Rio. It made our day, didn't it Darren?'

'It did, sir,' said Darren.

'I guess you had better things to do than protect a friend,' Hoffmann hissed.

'Jack, that's not true,' said Hunter. 'You have to believe me. The doctor told us you might not survive the flight home. You agreed, remember. I swear to you, I'll get us out of this. Hoffmann will pay for what he's done to you, and to Paul.'

'Oh no Hoffmann won't, Dr Hunter. Our disgraced police officer is here to die.' The German tapped Jack's head. 'Unfortunately you weren't a very helpful bean-spilling monkey, were you?' Hoffmann turned Jack's head to face Hunter. 'Luckily for us, this particular monkey can still be used to extract the beans from the organ grinder.' He bent forward and gripped Hunter's chin in his hand. 'The question for you, John, is how much more pain you want dearest Jack to endure before giving up your aforementioned beans.'

'You are one sick bastard,' whispered Hunter. Once again the situation was hopeless. He'd not recovered from the emotional turmoil experienced in Brazil. Days later and Hoffmann was squeezing him once again. Jack was his oldest friend and, although work and general adulthood had diluted their time spent together, the man was the closest thing to a brother he'd ever know. He would fight to the bitter end to save him.

'Darren, I feel Dr Hunter needs a brief introduction to the techniques of torture used by my grandfather's SS. Would you be so good as to indulge him in a history lesson?'

The bodyguard stepped into Hunter's eyeline, his immense frame blocking the light from the open door. 'It would be my pleasure.'

It was clear this was not the first time Hoffmann had requested Darren execute such a brutal order. The bodyguard disappeared into the corridor, returning with a hacksaw and a large hammer. A jet of bile raced into Hunter's throat, and he fought the urge to vomit.

'You have twenty minutes to get a result. Failure is not an option.' Hoffmann turned and vacated the room, apparently unwilling to bear witness to his employee's upcoming bloodlust.

Darren nodded and crouched in front of Hunter. 'I like you, Doc, but a job is a job.' He ran the cold steel tip of a screwdriver across Hunter's cheek. 'Now do me a favour and tell Mr Hoffmann what he needs to know. Dignify your friend with a swift death and tell us where to find the weapon.'

Hunter sensed his opportunity and launched his head forward. The blow connected and caught Darren off guard, striking him clean on the bridge of his nose. He scrambled backwards and lost his balance, falling to the floor with a thump.

Hunter winced and grinned at Jack. 'Not the most sensible thing I've ever done, but when in Rome.'

Jack forced a weak smile and raised his hands. Hunter frowned; what was he doing? The policeman's face contorted into a grimace and, using all his remaining energy reserves, he jangled the bracelets of his handcuffs. Hunter did a double take. Jack's right hand was free of the cuff. Of course, how could he forget Jack's Houdini pick-up trick? He smiled, remembering his friend's efforts to impress the local girls, his thick right wrist allowing him to escape a pair of handcuffs only to cuff himself to his target. A crunching blow came out of nowhere, striking him in the stomach and driving the air from his lungs. Hunter gasped for breath, closing his eyes as one of Darren's huge hands grasped him about the throat.

'I swear you'll pay for that.' The bodyguard steadied himself and drew back his fist. Hunter turned his cheek. If this punch connected, he knew it could kill him. He braced himself for impact. But it never came. Instead, a hoarse, scratchy voice cut through the tension.

'Hey idiot, kill him and your boss won't get his information.'

Darren wavered and opened his fist, slapping Hunter hard about the face. 'You're a lucky man, Hunter, which is more than can be said for your friend.'

Hunter opened his eyes, watching in horror as Darren plucked his hammer from the floor and slid a nearby table in front of Jack. Both Jack's hands were back in the cuffs and Darren grabbed them, forcing his friend's fingers flat on the polished metal surface.

'So are you going to squeal for me, Hunter?'

Devoid of ideas, Hunter lowered his head and prayed Jack would forgive him. If he was to die anyway, he couldn't risk caving in to Hoffmann's demands just to facilitate a painless death. But what of the Houdini trick? If he could just engineer some time alone with Jack.

Darren smiled. 'Is it wrong I'm genuinely pleased you're refusing to speak? Now comes the fun bit.' He raised the hammer and glanced at Hunter, giving him a final chance to save his friend.

'Wait.' The hammer quivered in mid-air, still ready to strike. 'Stop this nonsense. Leave him be and I'll tell you what you want to know. You hurt him and you'll get nothing.'

Darren tapped something in his ear and huffed. 'Boss is giving you one chance. Shame. Although I don't suppose one little tap would hurt anyone. Well, apart from this poor bastard.'

'No,' screamed Hunter, straining at his bonds. Darren licked a droplet of blood from his bleeding nose and, with a blood-curdling roar, smashed his hammer into the table. Hunter held his breath, his body numb with shock. He could see the hammer lodged in the table and, behind it, Jack's chair had toppled on its side, the police officer prostrate on the dusty floor. He wasn't moving.

'Better not be playing me, John.' Darren kicked Jack in the ribs. 'Or next time that's his head.'

Jack groaned and raised a pair of uninjured hands in the air, rattling his cuffs. He was alive, thank God. Hunter let out the breath he'd been holding and coughed up phlegm. They were safe, at least for now.

Chapter Forty-One
The Giza Plateau, Cairo

George strolled through the lobby with Inma and entered the spectacular gardens of the Le Meridien Pyramids Hotel. They spent the first few minutes in silence, gazing in awe at the ancient landscape sprawled out before them. With an unrivalled panorama dominated by the Great Pyramid of Khufu and the equally imposing Sphinx, Jacob Knight's choice of hotel was inspired. The daily sound and light show started and George jumped as the first few bars of eerie Egyptian music drifted across the dusk-drenched desert. He glanced at Inma as a series of spotlights sparked into life, giving him goosebumps as they added to the extraordinary sense of mysticism the ancient structures evoked.

He nodded at the Sphinx. 'Do you really believe this beautiful creature might be of Atlantean origin?'

'Who knows?' said Inma. 'I just wish John was here. We've had our differences but, as stupid as it sounds, there's a part of me still in love with the damn fool. I can't bear the thought he's in danger.'

'If it helps, he didn't get over you either.'

Inma blushed. 'Why does he insist on keeping me at arm's length then?'

'Why do you think? You sold him out in Brazil. You betrayed his trust to save yourself.'

'But that isn't true; they threatened to kill him if I didn't give in to their demands. They promised to release him if I collaborated.'

George lowered his head and kicked a loose stone into a nearby bush. 'Surely you aren't that naive. Why didn't you try to escape?'

'Put yourself in my shoes. This group possessed solid evidence of Atlantis. Why would I try and escape a situation I would have given my right arm to be a part of? I couldn't just walk away.'

'I suppose. So what did they ask of you? Did you find anything?'

'Same thing I did for the Navy; I dived on wrecks. As for finding anything, I actually don't know. Everyone contributed to the overall research question in parts. They didn't allow any of the various research teams to interact. Served to lessen the impact of a confidentiality breach, I guess.'

'Did your team unearth anything?' asked George.

'When John and I were captured, we were diving on a group of rocks about twenty miles north of Rio. The Navy tasked us with finding a British frigate sunk during the '40s. It was just the two of us as the dive was categorised low risk and of no interest to the locals.' Inma sighed. 'Two hours into a series of scoping dives we were pulled from the sea and thrown into cells.'

George frowned. 'I wonder what they wanted with an old frigate?'

'Nothing. I discovered later the site was an alleged port used by Atlantean refugees landing in Brazil. In hindsight I don't really blame them for picking us up. Bit of a red flag to find two archaeologists diving on the site, particularly when said archaeologists are prominent figures in Atlantean research.'

George yawned. 'Sorry, long day. I take it you found nothing?'

'There were plenty of wrecks, but so little remained we dismissed them as fishing boats. Perhaps we were a little hasty with that conclusion.'

George frowned. 'Why hasty? Nothing we've found pinpoints a port.'

'During my final dive I found a tiny broken box buried deep in the silt. It contained nothing but tiny beads. I logged them as either luxury items or jewellery, imported goods on their way to a local market. I said nothing at the time, and I probably should have done sooner once I knew the material the Lindow cylinder was made from but...' Inma reached into her blouse and pulled out a plain, black-cord necklace. She held it up to one of the poolside lights. 'I had a hole drilled through one of them.'

'Holy...' George let the bead lie in his hand. 'That's orichalcum.'

'So this is where you two have been hiding,' boomed a familiar voice from across the garden.

George turned, shielding Inma as she stuffed the bead back inside her blouse. Professor Cleary and Jacob Knight strode towards him.

'Breathtaking isn't it?' said the professor. 'I always insist on staying here when I'm in Cairo. It doesn't matter what I'm working on, this view never fails to inspire.'

Knight gave George an affable slap on the back and shook his head in mock defeat. 'All the time and money we've wasted chasing this artefact and the bloody thing was sitting under our noses at the first site we ever investigated.'

Cleary's mouth tightened. 'We'd have made the breakthrough sooner if you'd indulged my academic curiosity instead of stifling it all those years ago.'

'Get off your high horse, woman. You've worked on this project for years since then. None of your excavations have turned up so much as an Atlantean pisspot.'

'Perhaps, but if I'd concentrated on the weapon rather than the key, I might have had more luck. No one could have found that bloody cylinder except by chance.'

'It's a shame that lucky soul turned out to be a lunatic, Nazi wannabe,' George interjected.

Knight scowled. 'Slippery bastard. I half expected to find him sitting in the hotel reception when we arrived.'

'I doubt we've seen the last of him,' said Inma.

George turned to Cleary. 'Professor, it's obvious you know more of the Atlantis story than you've let on. Is there anything we're overlooking? Perhaps a discovery you've made that may help us?'

Cleary gave Knight a furtive glance. He responded with a dismissive wave of his hand. 'We're beyond the bounds of confidentiality, wouldn't you say? Answer him.'

The professor pointed to a nearby table and took a seat. She drained the drink in her hand and presented the empty glass to a passing waiter for a refill. 'Where do I start?'

'From the beginning would help,' said George.

'As good a place as any.' She wiped a sheen of perspiration from her hairline. 'Let me take you back to the early '70s, a time when making a name for myself on the academic circuit consumed me. I chose the

Giza Sphinx as my mechanism and went for it, all guns blazing. By chance, or as a result of incessant pestering, my proposal landed in the lap of a group willing and connected enough to fund my research.'

'What did you propose?' asked Inma.

'A full excavation of the site to ascertain the true age of the Sphinx and confirm my suspicions the sculpture is much older than the accepted estimate.' She cocked her head to one side.

'How did you get on? I don't believe I've ever come across your findings.'

'No, you wouldn't have done. The Egyptian authorities intervened three days into the excavation and, although I possessed all the correct consents and permits, they shut me down.'

'They didn't give you a reason?' asked George.

Cleary shook her head. 'They claimed I wasn't using enough Egyptian labourers. Later I found out Jacob here paid them to kick me off the site.'

Knight chuckled and slapped his thigh. 'And she's still bitter. You wouldn't have found anything anyway. There have been hundreds of excavations on the Giza plateau and nothing out of the ordinary has ever turned up.' The professor glared at the priest but refused to rise to the bait.

'Why do you believe the accepted date is wrong? Did you analyse the patterns of erosion?' asked George.

'No, the hypothesis came about as a result of fortuitous circumstance. Early in my career I completed a little work for the British Museum, logging forgotten Egyptian artefacts in their vault. The work was tedious, so when I chanced upon a sandstone slab taken from the base of the Sphinx, I pushed my brain into overdrive. Although damaged, my effort paid off and I uncovered an early form of hieroglyphics inscribed into the stone. My time with the epigraph was restricted, but my rushed translation was enough to convince me the origins of the Giza Sphinx do not lie in Egypt.'

George felt his eyes widen. 'What did it say?'

Cleary cleared her throat. 'It stated the Sphinx was to be a memorial to the destruction of the Motherland. Hunter was right, Dr Goodheart. Think of it along the lines of the Cenotaph in London: the

Sphinx is a reminder to the survivors of an unknown cataclysmic event to remember their fallen brethren.'

'And you suspect this to be the fall of Atlantis?' said George.

'I didn't voice the possibility, but it crossed my mind,' said Cleary.

'Did it say anything more?' asked Inma.

'A little. The hieroglyphs referenced a key, the key to unlocking the "might" of their civilisation.'

Inma mulled over the words. 'Okay, so there is a definite correlation between your find and the transcriptions taken from Mato Grosso.' Cleary nodded. 'Did you glean anything more?'

Cleary frowned. 'What more do you want?'

Inma massaged her temples. 'Confirmation of George's Sahu theory would be nice. Are we digging in the right place, Professor?' The professor shifted in her seat and looked at the ground.

'Why did you concentrate your efforts on finding the key rather than the weapon?' asked George, changing the subject and addressing Knight.

'Watch your tone, Goodheart,' Knight snapped. 'Why would I fund the search for a weapon I can't activate?'

George rolled his eyes. 'Why would you fund the search for a key with nothing to activate?'

'I assume to keep it out of the hands of potential German psychopaths who might want to activate it?' said Inma. 'Oh dear.'

Chapter Forty-Two

Cairo

Hunter heaved at his bonds and attempted to straighten his aching back on the thin, well-worn mattress. He sniffed the air. It smelt like central Cairo, a heady mix of spice and sweat hanging in the humid air like a suffocating blanket. The airless hotel room wasn't helping. Hunter elbowed Jack in the ribs, making him yelp in protest. He could almost feel the neurons sparking in his brain, overriding any discomfort experienced during the journey. They had a plan and it needed implementing.

'Sorry, mate,' he whispered. 'How are you doing?'

Jack forced a smile. 'I'm getting there. Although I'll be writing to that airline – the level of service was abysmal.' A little colour had returned to his friend's gaunt face, and it pleased Hunter that their current predicament hadn't dampened his sense of humour.

Hunter rattled his cuffs against the steel tube doubling as the bed's headboard and surveyed the sparse room. It was an excellent example of the soulless two-star hotels proliferating in Cairo. The patterned orange walls were peeling and in need of urgent repair. Dark layers of dust and dirt coated the room's surfaces and blocked the light from the only window. The furniture was basic yet functional, comprising two bedside tables, one chair and a small desk in the corner. His notebooks littered the desk's surface, no doubt removed by Hoffmann's stooges during his kidnap. Underneath it, and infinitely more important, stood the rucksack containing the orichalcum tube. Hunter shuddered as a cockroach scurried the length of the wall. It paused before disappearing through the open window. Evidently the room didn't meet its standards either.

'Both of you, shut it and stop moving,' growled a stooge from the foot of the bed.

Hunter raised his head, pulling his chin into his chest and straining to get a decent view of their guard. The man returned his gaze with callous lack of interest. His guard's name escaped him, but Hunter recognised the man as one of Hoffmann's hired guns from Brazil. The man turned the chair to face his prisoners and slumped into its comfortless, plastic recess. He was awaiting the return of Hoffmann and, even after ten minutes, looked thoroughly bored.

Hunter let his head drop back into the pillow. With only one apathetic guard to overcome, this might be their best opportunity to escape; perhaps their only opportunity. He'd overheard Darren saying a few members of the Order, plus Inma and George, were already in Cairo. They'd checked into a hotel somewhere near the Sphinx. Hoffmann and his bodyguard had decided to engage in some long-distance reconnaissance, probably in the hope of confirming the rumour and gauging the capabilities of their enemy.

Frustrated by his lot, the guard knocked the barrel of his Uzi submachine gun against his forehead. 'I so can't be arsed with this shit. I should just shoot the pair of you and be done with it. Bloody Hoffmann. Where the fuck is he? He said he'd be back by now.' He tugged at the bed sheet and wiped his forehead. 'I'm boiling up in here.'

Hunter nudged Jack in the side. 'Disgusting oaf. Do you seriously expect us to give a crap about you?' As they'd agreed on the plane, Jack rolled onto his side and slid his cuffed wrists under a pillow.

The soldier lifted his gun and pointed it at Hunter. 'Don't test me, Doc.'

Hunter lifted his head again. 'You're a joke mate, complaining about the heat. What kind of soldier are you? Is your gun a little too heavy for you as well? Poor princess, do you need help finding your balls?'

The guard took the bait, launching himself at Hunter and striking him hard in the midriff with the butt of his gun. The acne-scarred man swung a leg over the winded academic and sat on his chest. He flipped the gun around and jabbed its barrel against Hunter's temple. 'How brave are you feeling now, funny man?'

Hunter grinned and pushed against the cold steel of the Uzi. 'Fairly brave as it goes.'

Hunter's gaze flicked to his left. Confused, the soldier turned his head. Jack's fist connected with a sickening crunch, breaking the bridge of the guard's nose and knocking him off balance. Blinded by pain, he dropped the Uzi and rolled to the floor, clutching his bleeding face. Hunter seized upon his momentary vulnerability, wrapping his legs around the guard's neck and ensnaring him within his thighs.

'He's pulling a knife,' Jack shouted.

Hunter arched his back and, using every last sinew of muscle in his exhausted body, jerked his waist hard left. A sharp crack of snapping bone punctuated the air and a knife tumbled across the tiled floor.

'Nice work, Jack,' said Hunter. 'But we aren't out of the woods just yet.' He released the dead guard and shoved him onto his back. 'The keys to our cuffs are in his right trouser pocket. Get me out of these things and make it quick, we have no time to lose.'

Jack gave Hunter a blank look and didn't move, apparently struggling to process the brutality of the execution he'd just witnessed. 'Christ, John,' he stammered. 'You killed him.'

'You need to pull yourself together, Jack. It was him or us.' Hunter winced and rubbed his bruised ribs. 'I know which of those outcomes I prefer.'

Jack bit his lip and to Hunter's relief accepted the urgency of their situation. He vaulted the bed and knelt beside the dead guard, frisking the man's body for a set of keys.

Hoffmann raised his silenced Beretta handgun and emptied five 9mm rounds into the body of the dead guard.

'Shit, Darren, shit… I knew I should have left you here. Stupid bloody idiot. How did he let some half-starved moron and a witless lecturer get the better of him?'

Darren shrugged. 'What do you want me to do? Shoot him again?'

Theo, the last of Hoffmann's original group of mercenaries, appeared in the bathroom door. 'They escaped through the window in here. There's a fire escape below.'

Hoffmann kicked the body and scowled as the dead man's blood stained his suede shoe. 'Well, thanks to this useless sack of shit, we're back to square one. Hunter has his notes and the damned cylinder to boot.' He looked at his remaining men, his plans unravelling by the second. 'Have either of you anything worthwhile to contribute?'

Darren moved to the window and pushed it open. They peered out and gazed upon a busy market in full swing. His bodyguard raised an eyebrow. 'We could chase them.'

Hoffmann's breathing quickened, a combination of exasperation and panic welling inside his gut. 'I beg your pardon?'

'The bastards are still here.'

Hoffmann shielded his eyes and again scanned the hustle and bustle of Egyptian life. His heart skipped a beat. Seven storeys below, Hunter and Jack stood out like clownfish in a tank, their white faces bobbing up and down like beacons amongst the darker-skinned marketgoers. He looked at Darren. 'We need those notes.'

Darren pulled a pistol from his jacket, and fired.

Hunter heard a dull thud as Darren's bullet penetrated the loose clothing of the unfortunate Egyptian buying rice to the left of him. A dark, maroon shape expanded under the man's cream, cotton robe and he fell to his knees, screaming in pain and fear. Hunter lunged at Jack and pulled him to the ground, shielding his friend from harm. He twisted his head and stared at Hoffmann's hotel room, his heart rate quickening as he saw Darren leap onto the fire escape. He unsheathed his weapon and, oblivious to the surrounding panic, returned fire at the bodyguard. The move might only buy them a few seconds, but they were seconds crucial to their survival.

Hunter rolled onto his haunches and assessed his options. The area was awash with screaming women and crying children, all of them pushing and shoving as they tried to flee the crime scene. The mêlée moved out into the adjacent road, blocking traffic and giving Hunter the spark of an idea. He grabbed Jack's arm and, dispensing with any social niceties, shoved his gun in the face of the first moped owner he came across. He shoved the man to the ground and jumped astride the small machine. He revved the engine hard and fired a volley of shots into the air to part the crowd. The rear tyre screeched as he engaged first gear, sliding to the left and right as it strained to bite into the baked mud and gravel road surface. The bike finally lurched forward, arrowing through the newly formed gap and onto the tarmac beyond.

Hunter smiled, satisfied with the chaos in their wake. 'That should hold them up for a while.' Jack didn't respond, his vice-like grip tightening as they weaved dangerously in and out of the battered cars and horse-drawn carriages littering Cairo's streets.

An engine roared to their left. Hunter glanced in his mirrors, grimacing as a black Audi S6 careened around the corner and slotted into the traffic behind them. He veered hard right and cycled through the gears, heading away from the Nile and eking as much power as he dared from the moped's tiny whistling engine. The tyres groaned, squealing as they struggled to grip the corroding tarmac and hold each corner Hunter threw at them.

A smattering of gunfire confirmed they were not yet in the clear, the bullets ricocheting off the boot of a nearby hatchback and shattering its rear window. The driver lost control and veered sideways, smashing into the passenger door of a Fiat Panda. Unable to compete with the power of the larger car, the Fiat's driver found himself squeezed against a row of parked cars. The small car clipped the rear of a heavy, series seven BMW and all hell broke loose. With nowhere to go the collision catapulted the Panda into the air and flipped it onto its roof. Unable to react, the next three cars ploughed into the immobile vehicle one after another. Windows shattered and airbags deployed, the situation swiftly escalating out of control. Cars swerved to avoid the incident but crashed into others, and in seconds the pile-up blocked the road. The hustle and bustle of Egyptian life was quickly replaced by a gruesome, apocalyptic scene of torn metal, blood and broken glass.

Hoffmann stepped from the stationary Audi and slammed the car door in frustration, shaking his head as Hunter disappeared into the distance. 'You are one lucky son of a bitch, Hunter. Your guardian angel is doing you proud.' He keyed a number into his phone, whispering to himself as he pushed the green phone icon. 'And that being the case, I feel the need to shift the odds back in my favour.'

The call connected. 'Yes, this is Hans Hoffmann. Can one of you please get hold of that Ninja Star fellow? I've got a little task for our recently acquired eye in the sky.'

Chapter Forty-Three

The wheels of the rusty moped cut into the soft sand, the rear one spinning. Hunter and Jack slid from the saddle and dumped the machine, scrambling up the nearest sandbank.

Jack reached the top first. 'Wow…'

Hunter joined him, hands on his knees as he tried to regulate his breathing. When this was all over, a little time in the gym would not go amiss. He stood, taking a moment to drink in the spectacular vista laid out before him. Goosebumps prickled his skin. He watched as the hot Egyptian sun dipped below the horizon of the West Bank, its fading rays sparkling on each of the lazy ripples littering the Nile's surface. In this context it was easy to see why the early settlers associated it with the Milky Way. The hazy coronas, radiating behind each pyramid, only succeeding in adding to the mysticism the site engendered. Hunter shivered, wishing for a jumper as a cool breeze replaced the warmth of the day. He plucked the binoculars from Jack's neck. They'd been on the brink of paying for them when Darren's bullet found its mark. Hunter vowed to repay the debt and held them to his eyes, scanning the plateau for unusual activity.

'Why have we stopped here?' asked Jack. 'We're about a mile from the Pyramids and the Order hotel. Surely the quicker we get there, the safer we'll be.'

Hunter glanced at Jack and nibbled his lower lip. 'Something doesn't feel right. As nutty as Hoffmann is, he still might prove to be the lesser of our two evils.'

'Why? He killed Paul and hardly treated me any better.'

'Call it a hunch.' Hunter brushed a hand through his hair. 'This "Order" has kept itself hidden from the world for perhaps as long as ten thousand years, correct?' Jack nodded. 'Now, given their propensity for violence, and the fact they've attempted to kill me on more than one occasion, you'll have to pardon my cynical outlook as regards their actual agenda. Hoffmann might be right. What's stopping them silencing the four of us once we've outlived our usefulness?'

'But they let me live. Back in Rio, remember?'

'They did, but how do we know they'd have let you survive the night?' Hunter smiled. 'It's ironic, but Hoffmann might have saved your life when he busted you out.'

Jack rubbed his eyes and sat down in the sand. 'Come to think of it, I was due to receive a pain-killing injection that evening. The medics insisted I wouldn't sleep without it.'

'I'm not saying the Order are nailed-on bad guys,' said Hunter, clambering to the highest point of the bank. 'I'd just prefer to err on the side of caution until I know for sure.' He raised the binoculars and swore, jumping as a booming voice blasted through the silence. 'The sound and light show. I should've expected that.' He smiled, watching numerous flashlights slice through the night air in time to music. 'I haven't seen this in years. I bet it hasn't changed – the narrator certainly sounds the same.' He pursed his lips and let the binoculars fall to his chest. 'Damn it. The fact it's going ahead suggests the Order haven't worked out where to dig. George obviously hasn't managed to convince them of his theory.'

'So what's the plan?' asked Jack.

A little deflated, Hunter turned to look at their prostrate moped. 'I suppose we'll have to find ourselves anoth…' He stopped mid-sentence. The narrator's voice cut out, replaced by the intrusive sound of a wailing alarm. Hunter darted back to the bank's summit and raised his binoculars. 'Or maybe he has.'

'Why? What's happening? What can you see?'

'That, dear Jack, is the fire alarm. I'd put my house on the fact the Order are using it as cover to clear the area of tourists.'

Jack pointed to the left of the Pyramids. 'Look. Over there. Two JCBs.'

'And they're making their way to an area southeast of the Menkaure Pyramid.' Hunter grinned and pumped his fist. 'Get in. Good old George, I knew I could count on him.'

'What's George done?'

Hunter raised an eyebrow. 'Everything. I won't bore you with detail; those diggers are heading for an area George highlighted as the resting place of the weapon.'

Jack wrinkled his brow. 'And you're happy about that, why?'

'Because he is wrong.' Hunter cracked his knuckles. 'You're aware the Giza plateau is a mirror of the sky as it was twelve thousand years ago?'

Jack shook his head. 'No… but okay.'

'On the plane we both fell into a stupid trap.' Jack looked confused. 'George used a modern star map to prove the dig site mirrored a neb-ula important to the ancient Egyptians. Minutes before Hoffmann captured me, I realised the nebula correlated with the Great Sphinx and not my intended dig site at all. I expect it's a reason why the Sphinx is sited where it is, but that's a journal submission for another time.'

'So George is directing the Order to the wrong site and you're say-ing we should head for the Sphinx?'

Hunter gave him a smug grin. 'Not quite.'

'But you just said…' Jack shook his head. 'Okay, why not?'

'Because it's not there either.' Hunter fished around inside his jacket and pulled out the notes retrieved from Hoffmann's hotel room. He sifted through the pages and, finding what he was looking for, shoved a sheet of paper into Jack's hand.

Jack looked at it in confusion. 'It's a number.'

'Not just a number, Jack, those are coordinates.'

'The coordinates of our hidden chamber? Are you serious? How did you get them?'

'The answer slapped me about the face during my presentation to the Order. It was in front of me all the time.'

Jack nodded, urging Hunter to continue. 'Where did they come from? More importantly, where do they take us?'

'I found them hidden in the bigger picture.'

'Are you about to blind me with science? Because I'm not sure my brain can cope,' said Jack, massaging his forehead.

Hunter smiled. 'I'll be gentle.' He jabbed a finger at the Pyramids. 'Those majestic creatures mirror Orion's belt. Agreed?'

Jack nodded. 'If you say so.'

'Given the extent of Atlantean cartographic and astronomical awareness and the clear importance of Orion to them, do you not find it strange they only planned a mirror of the belt?'

'I suppose.'

'Planned is the key word here. You see, what was built and what was planned are two very different beasts. As important as Giza evidently was, standing at the lectern in Bath I realised I should have been casting my celestial net a little wider.'

Jack grinned. 'I'm guessing you discovered sites mirroring the other stars of Orion.'

'Unfortunately not. That line of thinking proved a dead end. If a wider plan ever existed, none of the other stars ever made it into the construction phase.'

Jack looked disappointed. 'So what's the plan? Are we going to search the sites where monuments should have been? Or are we back to square one?'

'Well, yes and no. My research into the positions of other key Egyptian sites threw up an interesting anomaly.' Hunter bent and traced a line in the sand. 'If this line represents the Nile with the Giza plateau here, there are two other important, but much less impressive, pyramid complexes here and here.' He stabbed his finger into the sand. 'At Saqqara and at Abusir. Saqqara was the precursor to Giza, and dates back as far as the First Dynasty. The Abusir Pyramids followed Giza, and they date to the Fifth Dynasty.'

Jack nodded cautiously. 'Okay, I'm following, but why is it a surprise burial sites existed before and after the Giza Pyramids? Why do we care?'

'In each of the complexes there are three or, in the case of Saqqara, four pyramids with corners aligned in a straight line.'

'Aligned? What do you mean aligned?' asked Jack. 'The Giza Pyramids are all different sizes for a start.'

'I didn't say all the corners, just one,' snapped Hunter. He rummaged through his papers again and pulled out an archaeological plan of the Giza complex along with a pen. He laid it flat and traced a straight line through each of the south-eastern corners of the monuments.

'Point taken,' said Jack. 'And this exists at the other two sites?'

CHAPTER FORTY-THREE

'It does.'

'Okay,' said Jack. 'I don't get it. Why are parallel lines important?'

'I don't think I ever said they were parallel.' Hunter returned to his diagram in the sand. 'Behold my epiphany. If I extended the lines from Giza, then Saqqara and lastly from Abusir, what happens?'

Jack looked between Hunter and the diagram in shock. 'Holy sh… is that right? They intersect at the same point?' The policeman shook his head and looked at the numbers on the paper in front of him. 'And these are the coordinates.' He cocked his head to one side. 'Hold on, why is this any different to your Sphinx theory? Why should the weapon's location be there and not here?'

Hunter grinned and tapped the paper. 'These coordinates aren't random, Jack. They lie over one of the oldest cities in Egypt, Heliopolis.'

'Heliopolis?'

'I know, shocking I didn't put two and two together earlier. Translated as "Sun City" or "Eye of the Sun" from its Arabic name, at the height of its power the city was the capital of the Lower Egyptian *nome*. There is even evidence suggesting occupation as far back as the pre-dynastic period.'

Jack pursed his lips, looking impressed. 'How old are we talking?'

'At least six thousand years.'

'So this could be our puppy, so to speak?'

'I think so. The link to the sun intrigues me, and it fits with the evidence we uncovered in Brazil. *It is in the heavens with our god that our might doth lie where the sky and earth embrace.*'

'Now you've lost me.'

'In ancient Egypt, although the people worshipped many gods, two were more prominent than others, the sun god Ra and his Old Kingdom son, Anubis, Anubis being the original god of the dead before Osiris replaced him during the Middle Kingdom.' Hunter tapped the dissecting lines in the sand. 'The link to Ra is obvious, but what of Anubis? Could Heliopolis be the point where the heavens meet the underworld? Where the sky and earth embrace?'

Jack answered the questions with a blank stare.

'What if I were to refer you back to our celestial map?' Hunter looked up into the night sky. 'It's not up there now but what's the brightest star in the sky?'

Jack squinted and pointed to a bright spot.

Hunter smiled. 'No, that's Venus, you plum. I said it wasn't out at the moment.'

'Sorry, I didn't prepare for a test.'

'Sirius,' said Hunter. 'Sirius is our brightest star, and a star often associated with Anubis. Now, given what we've been discussing…' He paused. 'Where do you think we might find the mirror of Sirius if we use Giza as our scale and starting point?'

Jack raised his eyebrows, his speech slow and measured. 'Not Heliopolis?'

Hunter wiped the sand from his hands and rose to his feet. 'Got it in one, hombre. There are signposts everywhere once you know where to look. There's even a link with Fawcett's Brazilian city. Do you remember the region we were in?'

Jack pleaded ignorance and shook his head.

'Mato Grosso, a region which by coincidence is represented on the Brazilian flag by the star…'

'Sirius?' said Jack, clapping his hands together.

Hunter nodded, looking away as the sound of a revving diesel engine distracted him. He looked through his binoculars and fiddled with the zoom. 'Excellent, they've made a start on their excavation. I suggest now might be a good time to collect Inma and George. With any luck this diversionary dig will occupy our bloodthirsty benefactors long enough for us to make it to the real site without being noticed.'

Jack grinned. 'I may need to grab a Big Mac before I pass out but, that aside, I'm good to go.'

Chapter Forty-Four

Hoffmann tapped his phone against his cheek before returning it to his ear. 'Ninja Star, can you hear me? For Christ's sake where is he? The reception is so crap in this place.' The atmosphere was electric, everyone in the room aware the success of their mission hinged on the call connecting.

Finally, the phone's speaker crackled into life, the tinny echo of the hacker's voice serving only to exaggerate the tension. 'Loud and clear, Mr Hoff. What service do you require now?'

Hoffmann pulled a face at Darren and made a rude hand gesture. Darren nodded and mouthed a descriptive obscenity in agreement.

'Mr Star, Hans Hoffmann here. Any chance you can get our borrowed satellite back online?'

'I'm using it to look right at you, right now, sir. And if those gesticulations were aimed in my direction, I can assure you the price for my services has just incurred an inflationary rise. If I fancy a little abuse, I'll phone my mother. Are we clear?'

Thrown by the hacker's reply, Hoffmann scanned the room, uncomfortable at the thought the boy was watching him. 'You're good; I'm impressed. I apologise if I offended; it's a condition. Do this and I promise to seek therapy. Given time I'll blend back into society a changed man.'

Hoffmann grimaced as his attempt to lighten the mood was met by a telling silence.

'Okay, bad joke. Look I'm sorry, Ninja, it won't happen again. As I think you young guys say, my bad? Incidentally, whilst we're having this heart to heart, can you tell me your real name? Calling you Ninja just feels so wrong.'

'Apology accepted. My fee is twenty grand and, no, you can't have my real name.'

'Fine, I'll just call you Colin from now on.' Hoffmann chuckled. 'A good solid name for someone working in IT.'

'Come on, you agreed not to abuse me.'

'Fine, I'll wire the money to your account as before. While we wait, can you do me a small favour and point our eye in the sky at the Egyptian Pyramids. I'd like to know if there's anything out of the ordinary going on. An excavation perhaps?'

'No problem. Just got to type in the coordinates and… bingo von dingo.'

'Colin, you are certainly a unique individual. Can you see anything unusual?'

'No. Not many people kicking about. Just the odd worker dotted about here and there.'

'There's no one around? Strange. It's only half-past seven; the area should be teeming with tourists watching the sound and light show. Colin, please zoom in on one of the workmen. What is he doing? Is he stationary or moving about?'

'Affirmative. One moment.' Ninja Star sucked on his teeth. 'Woooh, now that shit is cool.'

'What? What shit is cool?'

'This guy is packing some serious hardware.'

'They're not workmen, they're guards,' interrupted Darren. 'The Order must have found somewhere to dig. They've somehow evacuated the pyramid complex. These chaps are in place to ensure the perimeter remains secure. Nothing like an armed guard to deter prying eyes.'

'Colin, there must be a dig site somewhere. It could be anywhere in the vicinity – can you zoom out far enough to take in the entire area?' asked Hoffmann. At last they were making progress, however limited.

'Already on it and… Got it. There's a lot of activity going on around the small pyramid. Looks to be around twenty men clustered around a pair of diggers.'

Hoffmann looked at Darren. 'Twenty? We may need a few more bodies. As good as the two of you are, even I can recognise a suicide mission when I see one.'

'I'll see what I can do, Mr Hoffmann. Throw a few dollars in the air, and there'll always be someone willing to catch them.'

'NICE,' Ninja Star screamed.

Hoffmann jumped. 'Jesus, what now, you bloody idiot? Don't shout out like that, I damn well almost shot a hole in my foot.'

'Sorry, but you will love this. It appears the secure perimeter...' he said, mimicking's Darren's cold Midlands English accent, '...has already been breached. There are two guys behind enemy lines. They are running and ducking behind any cover they find. I'm guessing they are not meant to be there.'

'Good spot, Colin.' Hoffmann addressed Darren. 'It appears we've found our resident Indiana Jones and his policeman sidekick.'

'Are they heading for the dig site?' asked Darren.

'No,' said Colin. 'They appear to be aiming for a hotel.'

Hoffmann screwed up his face, perplexed by this latest turn of events. 'The Le Meridien Pyramids I expect; but why go there first and why go undercover? Hunter must know the dig is going on. I wouldn't be surprised if the Order are digging at that site on his advice.' He stroked his chin. 'So why, Dr Hunter, wouldn't you want to be part of the find? Why aren't you playing the hero and accepting the inevitable pat on the back for executing a daring escape from the clutches of the evil German?'

'Unless...' Darren mused.

'What?'

'Unless Hunter knows the Order are digging in the wrong place and your speech gave him food for thought as to whom he can trust. If I'm right, and he knows the real location of the weapon, maybe what we're seeing is an attempt to make a grab for his friends and take them to the real site.'

Hoffmann clapped his hands together. 'You may be onto something there, Darren.' He paused. 'You know what, let's take a punt on Hunter and forget the Order. If he's trying to free his mates, I want you and Theo to do everything you can to make sure he succeeds.'

Darren frowned. 'You want me to help Hunter?'

'Trust me. Now grab what you need and move. I'll ask Colin the Ninja to stream live images of the hotel and Hunter's position to your devices. Just make sure he gets in and out unnoticed. If they encounter resistance, I suggest you neutralise it with extreme prejudice.'

Darren turned to Theo and threw him an American M21 sniper rifle. Although out of general service since the late '80s, the rifle was all Hoffmann's money could get on such short notice. Theo caught it and stood to attention. 'You heard the man, soldier. It's time to make shit happen.'

Hoffmann watched the two ex-soldiers pull balaclavas over their heads and descend into the hustle and bustle of the Cairo night. They jumped astride a pair of waiting motocross bikes and took pleasure in over-revving their engines to part the crowds. With a burst of acceleration they were gone, their helmets intermittently bobbing in and out of the rush-hour traffic.

Hoffmann glanced at his phone and smiled. Whatever his misgivings over Colin's character, he could not deny the talent of the boy. Five minutes had not yet ticked by and he already had live infrared and thermal feeds of the hotel up and running.

'Mr Hoffmann,' said the hacker. 'I've hacked the hotel database. Pérez and Goodheart are both staying in the Royal suite. The heat sigs suggest they are home but have company. Two guards packing heat are sitting outside their door. They look chilled; I don't suppose they're expecting any action.'

Hoffmann squinted at the yellow and orange images of the Order soldiers and tapped the screen. 'The idiot on the right may even be asleep.'

Ninja Star laughed. 'Could be a long sleep.'

Chapter Forty-Five

The rear door to the Le Meridien Pyramids Hotel kitchen creaked open and Hunter peered inside, pleased to find the hustle and bustle of after-dinner service well under way. Dressed in the borrowed uniform of a kitchen porter, no one gave him a second glance as he entered. He beckoned Jack to follow and grinned. His friend hadn't fared quite so well with the limited clothing available in the laundry room and his uniform was a little tight. Hunter froze as someone barked a command in his direction. He turned to face the chef in question.

'يا لك. اتخاذ هذا الترولى إلى الغرفة,' the dumpy man repeated.

'God, John, he's talking to us,' whispered Jack. 'What do we do?'

'Keep your cool. He's asking us to take a trolley to one of the rooms. Just smile and nod.'

Jack did as he was told and grimaced as the chef shoved a trolley into his midriff. He looked angry. 'وقم بتغيير سراويل نظرتم غبية.'

Jack retained the fake smile and pushed the food towards a row of lifts. The chef continued to scream at his back. 'What the hell is that lunatic squawking about?'

'He's telling you to smarten yourself up. Says you're dressed like a clown and an embarrassment to the hotel,' said Hunter. He pulled the other end of the trolley. 'Make a beeline for the service lift and select the top floor. Whatever you do, don't look back.'

The lift mechanism hummed as they rose through the floors, slowing to a stop as a ping announced their arrival. The doors slid open. 'What can you see?' whispered Jack.

'Four doors and a pair of guards. They look Egyptian; probably local militia.' Hunter grinned. 'One of them is snoring, which makes life easier.' He eased the trolley from the service lift. 'Get behind the trolley and use the tablecloth to hide those bloody half-mast trousers.'

The silver, domed plate covers jangled and rattled against the tray, announcing their arrival to the dozing guards. They jerked awake in unison and stared with suspicion at the approaching trolley. 'Room service,' mumbled Hunter in English, mimicking an Egyptian accent.

The nearest guard rose from his seat. Without breaking eye contact, he moved a hand to his holstered handgun and banged on the door. 'Did either of you order room service?'

Hunter took a punt and raised his voice, banking on George being the one to answer. 'It's the Jesus College special, as requested.' He paused and heard a pair of muffled voices debating something behind the closed door.

After a moment's delay, George's distinctive monotone voice penetrated the corridor. 'The JC special? Yup, let them in, we're bloody starving in here.'

Jack held the door open and the guards parted, scowling as Hunter wheeled the food inside the room. Jack released the door and the return mechanism dragged it shut behind them. Hunter raised his head and winked. 'So when were you two going to get round to saving me?'

Inma yelped and took a running jump into his arms. He took her weight and accepted the embrace, swinging her in an arc before letting her drop to the floor. 'I can't believe it's you. Are you hurt?' she asked, wiping tears of elation from her eyes. 'I thought I'd lost you for good this time.'

'No, I'm fine,' said Hunter. 'A little worse for wear but nothing I couldn't handle. I'm just pleased you're both awake.'

'Five in the morning isn't early when awaiting news of this magnitude. They've promised to credit us with the find,' said George. He leant forward, squinting as he examined Jack, clearly struggling to recognise the policeman's emaciated face. 'Do I know... Jack? Is that you?' he asked. 'It is you. You look bloody awful. What the hell are you doing here? I thought you'd still be sunning it up on a Rio beach.'

Jack coughed and lifted a plate cover, his eyes widening as a selection of cold meats and cheese revealed itself. 'Long story. Bit unfortunate, but my holiday was cut short by our old friend Mr Hoffmann. Poor guy was operating under the mistaken belief I possessed information worth trying to kick out of me.' Jack reached for a bread roll but George intercepted his hand, pulling up his sleeve to examine the various sores littering his skin.

'Jesus, what did the bastard do to you?'

Jack glared up at the geologist. 'Withholding food was part of it.'

'Sorry, go ahead,' said George, releasing his hand. 'We can talk later.' George turned to Hunter. 'So what's going on? Why the cloak-and-dagger entrance? Jacob will be ecstatic when he hears of your escape.'

'You need to trust me and listen,' said Hunter. 'We aren't safe here.'

'But the dig is going on as we speak. You won't know this yet, but I got Jacob to dig at our location. Leave now, and we'll be leaving behind our chance to make our mark on history. This is our Howard Carter moment, remember?'

'Grow up, George. If true, why has he locked you in a hotel room? Jacob and his group have kept this secret safe for thousands of years. It's all sweetness and light for the moment but, given what we witnessed in Brazil, what makes you think he won't dispose of us once he finds what he's after? Don't be so naive.'

'So you think we're only here until he finds this weapon? Then what, you think he'll shoot us?' said George.

'You think he won't?' Hunter walked to the window, admiring the uninterrupted view it offered of the last of the Seven Wonders. 'I wouldn't worry for the moment, though. They won't find it anytime soon.'

'What do you mean by that?' said Inma. 'The site they're excavating is based on your research.'

Hunter shrugged. 'I made a mistake. Happens sometimes.'

'Or you led George down the garden path to claim all the credit for yourself?'

'Come on, Pérez, these are bad men we are dealing with,' interrupted Jack. 'The only reason you're still alive is because they still think you might be of use.'

'Mere conjecture. You don't know that,' said Inma. 'Even if you are right, you can't honestly believe Jacob will let you set up your own dig and then just leave you alone?'

'She's got a point, mate,' said George.

'Will you guys give the poor man a break,' said Jack, mumbling through a mouthful of food. 'The weapon isn't at Giza.'

The academics exchanged confused glances. 'If it isn't out there,' said Inma, thumbing the Giza complex behind her, 'then where is it?'

Hunter clapped his hands together. 'Tell you what, why don't I just take you? Come on, chop chop, we haven't much time. It won't be long before the Order realise their current dig site is a red herring. When they do, this room will be their first port...'

The door to the suite swung open, banging against the wall and cutting his sentence in two. Hunter hurled himself to the floor, scrambling behind a sofa as a familiar silhouette stepped into the doorway. 'I'm afraid your sands of time are already spent, Dr Hunter,' said Jacob Knight.

Chapter Forty-Six

'How are our boys getting on, Colin?' asked Hoffmann. 'My screen is a little too small to make much out.'

'I can confirm they are in position with a view of the suite on the eastern roof,' replied the hacker, his voice a little squeaky over the phone's loudspeaker. 'Two shots fired. No dead bodies so at a guess they've taken out the CCTV cameras.'

Hoffmann nibbled his lower lip. 'Nice work. They definitely have a clear view of the suite?'

'Affirmative.'

Hoffmann grinned. 'Affirmative? You're certainly embracing your new role. You'll have me calling you Q next.'

Hoffmann jumped, wincing as the phone transmitted a loud bang. The sound of breaking glass followed and his blood ran cold. 'Colin, what the hell is going on? Are you okay?'

'Move away from the keyboard, Ninja Star,' barked a gruff, male voice. Hoffmann's muscles tensed and he gripped the desk in front of him, his knuckles whitening as his fingernails dug into the soft pine. 'Do it now.' A volley of ear-splitting automatic fire ensued. Hoffmann flinched, fearing the gunfire might blow the little speaker. 'I said move,' yelled the gunman.

'Mr Hoffmann, we have a breach, attempt to cover tracks failed,' garbled the hacker.

Hoffmann shook his head in disbelief. 'Why on earth would you use my name, you bloody idiot?'

'Hoffmann, eh?' the gunman acknowledged. 'Is he listening right now?' There was a pause during which Hoffmann guessed Colin must have nodded. 'Hey, Hoffmann. A little message from our chairman: you fuck with us and we'll fuck with you harder.' A second volley of machine-gun fire boomed through the handset and the line went dead.

'Bastards.' He kicked over his chair and hurled a mug of tea at the wall. It shattered in a satisfying explosion. 'Utter bastards.'

'I suggest you show yourself, Hunter. You too, Dr Pérez. Or would you prefer I put a bullet in one of your associates?' Hunter could see Knight's reflection in the window. He looked Jack up and down, his eyes narrowing in recognition. 'Aren't you the policeman we left in Brazil?'

Jack nodded, unable to speak through a mouthful of food, his jaw locked in shock at the unexpected intrusion.

'You're more resilient than I gave you credit for. How did you survive the hospital?' Knight clipped the nearest guard on the back of the head and snarled. 'Why wasn't I informed of this man's escape? What is it you people don't understand about security risks?'

Hunter pursed his lips and searched for the hilt of the gun shoved into the back of his trousers. As long as he remained armed, there was still the chance of getting through this alive, however one sided the odds. He knelt and raised his hands, hanging his head in mock defeat. Inma followed suit and emerged from underneath a desk.

'Oh, Dr Hunter.' Knight tutted. 'And I thought we were friends.'

Hunter furrowed his brow, feigning confusion. 'What's going on, Jacob? Why are you pointing guns at us? We're on your side.'

'I fear returning to academia has softened you, Dr Hunter.' The corners of Knight's mouth curled into a leer. 'How else can you explain how someone with Special Forces training didn't do a quick bug sweep?' Hunter's heart sank as the priest reached into a lampshade and plucked a black dot from inside its rim. 'A wise precaution in hindsight, wouldn't you say?' He lifted his arm and showed Hunter the small MP3 player clasped between his fingers.

Hunter bit into his lip, the metallic taste of blood spreading across his tongue as a tinny speaker regurgitated snippets of conversation:

'The weapon isn't at Giza.'

'Why don't I just take you?'

Knight slipped the device inside his coat and retrained his gun on Hunter. 'I assume you can now gauge why I'm a touch upset with you all. My brotherhood isn't really an organisation that responds well to being double-crossed.' He swept a hand toward the window. 'In normal circumstances I'd dispose of you all somewhere out there. The desert is such a reliable substitute for a graveyard.' The priest's eyes narrowed. 'But these are not what any of us would describe as normal circumstances. So here's the deal: take me to the real site and I will overlook your... little indiscretion.'

Hunter's gaze flitted between the terrified faces of his companions. 'What's stopping you from killing us once you have what you want?'

'Nothing. But what other choice do you have?' said Knight, placing his gun against George's head. 'You've got ten seconds before I start erasing your party in the order of least importance. Ten...'

Before he reached nine, the room's windows exploded in a cacophony of broken glass and splintered wood. Hunter threw himself to the floor and pulled the gun from his trousers, simultaneously twisting his body into a roll. 'Everyone hit the deck and find cover.' He shielded his head and pulled the trigger, firing the remains of his clip in the vague direction of Knight and his men.

The last of his 9mm rounds thumped into a wall, and an eerie silence descended on the room. There had been no return fire. Hunter hauled himself behind the nearest sofa. Was everyone dead? What caused the windows to blow? If a round from a sniper rifle, who on earth were the snipers? Could there be a third group with a vested interest in this mess?

On the other side of the room, a low groan morphed into George's recognisable drawl. Hunter risked a look and saw the geologist plucking pieces of glass from his clothing. 'What in the bloodiest pit of hell just happened? And why did that snide A-hole select me as the least important? What about Jack? I've contributed.'

'Get over here, you idiot. Are you hit?' Hunter hissed.

'I'm fine. A few scratches but nothing serious. You can come out by the way. The baddies are in no position to bother us any more.'

Hunter reloaded his pistol and chanced a look around the other side of the sofa. The two guards lay dead in the doorway, their automatic weapons still slung about their necks. Knight was nowhere to be seen. Hunter turned to the decimated window and looked down at the carpet, wary of the sharp fragments of glass lodged in the thick pile. If he stood, might he be risking a bullet in the back?

'And I shouldn't worry about the snipers,' said George, reading his mind. 'I've been in full view of the window this whole time. If we were targets, I'd be lying alongside those two unfortunates in the doorway.'

The logic was sound. Hunter rose to his feet and made a beeline for the guards' weaponry. He frisked the men for spare ammunition and sensed Inma bending over his shoulder.

'Who do you think did this?'

Hunter passed her one of the machine guns. 'Whoever it was, they were professionals. Just look at the entry wounds. Two shots, both clean kills, and both centred on the forehead. Jacob must have turned tail before they shifted aim. Shame.'

'Could it be Hoffmann?' asked George.

Hunter cocked his gun. 'Maybe, although I'm not sure why he'd want to protect us. A couple of hours ago he wanted me dead. He can't be that fickle.' In the periphery of his vision, Hunter saw the bathroom door creak open. He spun on instinct, raising his weapon and ready to open fire.

'Any chance we can get the hell out of here now?' said Jack. 'And please lower the gun. I'm not sure I can take being shot at again today.'

Inma pushed down the barrel of Hunter's gun. 'Jack, for Christ's sake. Rule one, never startle an armed man.'

'He's got a point, though – we need to get out of here,' said George. 'If Jacob hasn't suffered a mortal wound, it won't take him long to round up reinforcements.'

Hunter continued frisking the two guards. He had the green shoots of an idea. 'Bingo.' He stood and threw a set of car keys into the air. 'Jack, pull on the other guard's coat. We need to cover our uniforms. George, grab yourself a gun and let's get the hell out of here.'

Hunter hustled his group into a waiting lift and selected the reception. 'Say as little as possible and follow my lead. George, that means you.'

'Fine – single out the least important member of the group again.'

The doors opened with a ping and Hunter strode to the concierge's desk as if he were a European prince. He clicked his fingers, and a bellhop came running. He threw the guard's keys at him. 'Retrieve my car.'

The boy shrugged and jangled the keys. 'No problem, boss, it'll be out front in two minutes.'

Hunter smiled as the boy rushed off. He followed him outside and called out. 'The quicker you return, the bigger the tip.'

Hunter leant against the doorway and took in a deep breath. Assuming the guard used the hotel lot, they were almost home free. A fruit bat swooped into his eyeline and rose, flapping up into the star-filled sky. The sun was an hour from rising, and the Egyptian nightscape was a spectacle of the purest beauty. It was easy to see why the ancients once revered it as the kingdom of their gods. He tensed as the vulgar sound of screeching brakes and a throaty, over-revved engine replaced the silence. His finger quivered, caressing the hair trigger of the gun hidden under his coat.

'Nice,' said George, raising an eyebrow. 'When these guys choose cars, they seriously choose cars.'

'It's orange,' said Inma.

'Only fair; if the car was black or some other nondescript colour, the bad guys might have problems tracking us,' said Jack. 'In fact, do we have time to find a neon, flashing arrow to stick on the roof?'

'At least it'll be fast,' said Hunter.

The car slid to a stop and the bellhop jumped out, his eyes alive with excitement. 'One Mitsubishi Evolution at your service and, might I add, an excellent choice of motor vehicle, sir.' He held out an expectant hand in Hunter's direction. Hunter patted his pockets, and fished out a few coins as Jack, Inma and George bundled into the powerful Japanese sports car.

The roar of a second engine at the hotel entrance saved his blushes at having to explain the meagre tip. Knight's reinforcements had arrived. He shoved the startled bellhop aside and slid across the Evo's bonnet. Jack shoved open the driver's door and Hunter swung himself inside, slamming it shut behind him.

He pushed the starter button and rammed the car into first, relaxing the clutch and mashing the accelerator into the carpeted floor. The car lurched forward, pinning its occupants against their seats, wheels spinning and billowing smoke as it snaked toward the exit. Time slowed, and then the soft rubber of the racing-spec tyres finally gripped the tarmac. The 350bhp engine kicked in with the finesse of a raging bull. Hunter felt the pull on his cheeks and desperately fought for control, wrenching the wheel left and right as the nimble machine propelled itself into the scant, early-morning traffic like a rocket. The back end slid into a drift as it rounded the hotel gates and moved onto the main road, missing a slow-moving bus by inches. Hunter lined the bonnet up with the potholed tarmac and selected second. They were away.

He glanced in the rear-view mirror, searching for Knight's stooges. 'Where the hell are they? George, can you see anything?' A thunderous explosion answered his question. A plume of fire erupted skyward, illuminating the Pyramids before dissipating somewhere in the hotel grounds.

'Bloody hell,' said George.

'Another notch on the barrel of our friendly neighbourhood sniper,' said Jack. 'John, you best floor it to this "Heliopolis" place of yours. God only knows how many people are keeping tabs on us now.'

Hunter wiped beads of sweat from his forehead and nodded, a look of grim determination etched on his face. He slipped the car into third and focused on the road ahead, choosing to ignore the expressions of surprise as Inma and George processed their destination.

Chapter Forty-Seven

Hoffmann slapped his steering wheel as the bright orange car shot past his hiding place. He shoved the Audi into first and accelerated hard, desperate to keep pace with the fleeing academics. The V8 engine snarled at his touch, spinning the SUV's wheels and propelling the two-tonne machine into the road. He rammed the gearstick into second, beating his fist against the wheel and urging the big car on. He screamed in frustration. The orange blob was already half a mile ahead. His car was quick, but there was no way it could keep pace with whatever vehicle Hunter had commandeered. Hoffmann scowled and eased off the accelerator, his brain whirring as he contemplated other options.

Darren's assigned ringtone blared through the Audi's speakers. He connected the call.

'Mr Hoffmann?' asked Darren.

'Yes, go ahead.'

'The chasing pack is immobilised.'

'Oh well done.' He let the faux compliment hang in the air. 'By the by, this orange car you told me to look out for, any idea of the make and model?'

'I believe it was a Mitsubishi Evolution X, sir.'

'Right... So a car I would need a Ferrari to keep up with.' Hoffmann closed his eyes, taking a moment to compose himself. 'And you didn't think to tell me this, why?' Darren wisely stayed silent. 'Any suggestions where we go from here? At least tell me you know where they're headed?'

'Er no... But on the flip side, the Order can't know either.'

'I disagree,' Hoffmann interrupted. 'They traced our hacker and reappropriated their satellite. Didn't you notice the feed collapse?'

'Shit. I put it down to a fault. I'd finished with it, so didn't flag the issue.'

'If the Order doesn't already have a lock on Hunter, they soon will have.' A surge of adrenaline elevated Hoffmann's heart rate as the answer hit him. 'My god, Darren, that's it. The Order know where they are going. What's going on at the hotel? Any movement?'

'Yes, sir. A group of Order soldiers are readying three Hummers in the courtyard,' said Darren.

Hoffmann drummed his fingers on the steering wheel and smiled. 'At last, a little luck for team Hoff. Okay Darren, it appears we have a convoy to join. Any chance you and your mate can play substitute for two of the Order's goons in the rear vehicle?'

'I'll see what I can do,' said Darren. 'Join us en route. I'll think of a way to cover your appearance.'

Hoffmann grinned. Somehow he'd snatched at least a small victory from the jaws of absolute defeat. 'Darren, remind me you're due a raise when we get home.'

Knight took one last lingering look at the wreckage of the smoking sports car and clenched his teeth, determined to avenge the inconvenient death of his men.

Anderson appeared in his periphery and inexplicably dared to plant his hand in the small of Knight's back. 'I'm sorry, sir, but we need to leave. I've paid off the hotel staff, but it still won't be long before this place is crawling with police and journalists. The explosion would have been visible for miles.'

Knight turned and glared at Anderson, unused to subordinates ordering him around. 'How dare you lay a hand on me. In different circumstances I would have you flogged.' Anderson retracted his arm and retreated. 'Go and make sure whoever you leave behind screams terrorism. Go now before I change my mind,' he hissed. 'And blame al-Qaida if this bombed-out car goes national. Promise them a few more guns or something. They're always willing to trade favours for weaponry, more so since Osama bin Laden's death. Oh and get someone to tell Cleary to wrap up the dig. The old mothball probably still thinks she's about to strike gold.' Anderson nodded and relayed the messages to various underlings, before joining Knight in the lead car.

'Is the satellite back online?' asked Knight, his tongue flicking out to moisten his dry lips.

Anderson tapped the navigation system on the dashboard and nodded. 'Up and running, sir. The hacker they hired squealed like a pig. The boys told me they only removed one fingernail before the boy begged for mercy.'

'Excellent, have him eliminated once his purpose is served.'

The corners of Anderson's mouth curled into a remorseless smirk. 'Way ahead of you, sir.'

The engines of the three Hummers fired, but the convoy remained stationary. 'What's going on?' asked Knight. 'Why aren't we moving?'

Anderson wound down a window and peered outside. 'There appears to be a problem in the rear vehicle.'

Knight turned and noticed two men engaged in a lively argument with the driver of the third car. 'What's going on back there?'

'The driver is saying there isn't enough room to seat the men alongside all the equipment they've got loaded.'

'Do I care? Tell him to let them inside. I don't care if they have to sit on laps. We need all the damn foot soldiers we can carry. If the German is behind tonight's fiasco, the more fingers on triggers, the better.'

Hoffmann glanced at his watch for the umpteenth time. Thirty minutes ticked by, each one only succeeding in adding panic to his already shredded nerves. This was not some ragtag band of money-motivated mercenaries they were dealing with here; what if Darren's plan to infiltrate the convoy failed? What if he was dead? Or worse, captured and singing like a canary? On the verge of his fears escalating into full-blown panic attack, he uttered a joyful yelp as three sets of bright xenon headlights appeared on the horizon.

'Looks like we're in business,' he whispered. The convoy sped past his position. He lifted his foot from the brake and pressed the accelerator, stealthily easing the Audi from its hiding place and into the sparse, pre-dawn traffic.

'Now what?' asked Hoffmann. He flexed his fingers and limbered up his wrists, ready for action. 'Come on, Darren, where are you?' On cue, a series of four short, sharp flashes lit the cabin of the rear car. The door above the vehicle's rear bumper banged open and a body slid to the tarmac. With no time to react and swerve, it thumped under his wheels with a nauseating crunch. Hoffmann cursed and jerked the steering wheel back and forth, doing his best to avoid the three bodies that followed. 'What the hell are you doing man? How is this an incognito approach?' He shook his head, gesturing at Darren as the SUV's headlights picked out his bodyguard's bloodstained face.

The cars slowed to a stop as another red light halted the convoy. Darren jumped from the same door and rushed to the Audi. He wrenched it open and grabbed Hoffmann's arm. 'Sorry, sir, they figured out who we were. Luckily for us they've fitted a blackout screen between the front and rear seats. You need to ditch the car now. And I mean now. If the lights change, we're done for.'

Hoffmann didn't need to be told twice. He snatched up his handgun and slid from his seat, joining Darren in the space behind the convoy. A car turned into the road, illuminating them in its headlights. Hoffmann's eyes widened as dread gripped him. Darren's massive hand gripped him about the neck and shoved him to the tarmac. 'Keep low and calm, sir. Remember if you can see their mirrors, they can see you.'

Hoffmann let Darren take the lead and allowed himself to be half lifted, half thrown into the rear of the Order's Hummer. He lost his footing and planted his hands in a sticky liquid coating the uncarpeted floor.

Theo turned and grinned at him from the driver's seat. 'Nice of you to join us, sir. Please excuse the mess: the previous occupants couldn't be persuaded to leave as quietly as we'd hoped.'

Hoffmann raised his hands. The dim street lighting picked out a thick coat of blood, oozing between his fingertips. A jet of bile raced to his throat and he retched.

'The lights are changing, we're all in. Go, go, go,' yelled Darren, slamming the rear door shut. 'And put the blackout screen back up.' Theo pulled away and kept pace with the lead cars, both of them oblivious to the carnage they were leaving behind.

Chapter Forty-Eight
Heliopolis

Hunter eased his foot off the accelerator as the sports car flashed by a signpost for Heliopolis. The city was ten miles from Giza and, at a hundred-plus miles per hour, the journey was flying. Although there was little to do or see as a tourist, Hunter knew modern Heliopolis was considered one of the nicer areas to live in the vicinity of Egypt's capital. The city's close proximity to the airport meant it was a haven for business executives and sales teams the world over. Recent redevelopment made it a viable alternative to the Cairo hotels and, as an added bonus, there were far fewer of the intrusive street sellers often found milling about Egypt's more famous tourist traps.

Hunter downshifted, slowing to negotiate the tight moonlit streets as they entered the city limits. The change of pace gave him a chance to take in the new surroundings. Little remained of the ancient city. Contemporary apartments, offices and hotels had been erected with little respect for the foundations of the original granite pillars and buildings buried beneath their floors.

'So this is Heliopolis,' said Jack. 'It looks... modern.'

'It is,' said Inma. 'The Egyptians ripped apart the original settlement for its stone to build medieval Cairo. Believe me, at the height of its power this place would have had you weak at the knees. They nicknamed it "Iunu" or "the place of pillars". Think of it like the temple of Karnak, but built to the scale of a city.'

'Heliopolis is where Cleopatra's Needle comes from,' said Hunter.

'Really?' said Jack. 'The thing in London... by the Thames?'

Hunter smiled. 'I would prefer obelisk to thing, but yes. I believe it made its way to the capital around 1877.'

'Look, this history lesson is all fine and dandy,' said George. 'But how are we any closer to finding this Atlantean chamber? Even if you are right about the location, it could be buried anywhere. You yourself said the original city is long gone. What if the chamber is under an office block?' Inma rolled her eyes.

'Come on, Pérez, give him a break. He has a point,' said Hunter. 'I suggest we find an internet café and fast. Who knows how much time we've got before Hoffmann or the Order catch up with us.'

'What do you need an internet café for? I've still got my laptop,' said George. 'I'd have thought my dongle will get a connection here. We aren't far from the city centre.'

'You've got your laptop?' said Hunter. 'George, there are occasions I could kiss you. I won't, but I could.'

'Promises, promises,' said George. 'What do you want me to do?'

'Boot it up and open Google Earth.' Pushing his pelvis toward the steering wheel, Hunter fished in his pockets for the scrap paper he'd written the coordinates on. He teased it from his trousers and passed it backwards. 'Type those numbers into the search engine.'

Inma's brow creased. 'What are they?'

'They represent the point where lines drawn from the pyramid complexes at Giza, Abusir and Saqqara intersect,' said Hunter. 'Just trust me. George, type them in. It's all down to you; tell me where our destiny awaits.'

George snatched the piece of paper and waited for the machine to boot. The computer beeped as it latched onto George's mobile network. 'We have lift off. Entering the coordinates now.' He handed the paper to Inma. 'Double-check for me?' She nodded in agreement and he heard George tap the return key to initiate the search.

Hunter pulled the car over to the pavement and slowed to a crawl. He could see George's screen reflected in the rear window and watched as the program zoomed in on the Earth, diving towards northern Egypt like a missile. The image slowed as the magnification intensified and he recognised the Nile Delta, the Pyramids and Cairo itself before the camera drifted north. It settled on a small piece of parkland in the centre of Heliopolis.

'My god,' said Inma. 'Although it kind of makes sense.'

'Why? What am I looking at?' asked George. 'It's just a park, isn't it? What am I missing?'

'This might make it clearer.' Inma leant over and clicked on Street

View. 'May I present the obelisk of Senusret the first, the second pharaoh of the twelfth dynasty.'

Hunter's eyes glazed as he mulled the revelation. Surely not. Surely they wouldn't have placed it in plain sight? The car mounted the pavement and he cursed, swerving to avoid a telegraph pole. 'Shit, sorry guys. In a world of my own there.'

He noticed Inma looking through the rear window. 'Isn't that the tip of the obelisk behind that building? John, turn around.'

Hunter didn't need to be told twice; he heaved the steering wheel hard left, pulled on the handbrake and accelerated hard. The Evo's back end drifted in an elegant 180° arc. It paused in the centre of the road, white smoke billowing under its chassis. Hunter grinned as the tyres gripped the tarmac and the car thundered forward, speeding back in the direction they'd just come from.

George lifted Inma's head from his lap. 'What are you doing, you idiot? Enough people are trying to kill us without your help.'

'Sorry... but not really. I've always wanted to give that a try.'

Inma slapped the back of Hunter's head. 'Dick.'

Jack massaged his neck. 'Not cool, man, you've given me whiplash. I'll let you off if you tell me why this obelisk is significant.'

'Sorry, George, I should have warned you.' Hunter grinned. 'Totally worth it though.' He glanced up at the tip of the obelisk, illuminated against the night sky. 'As for that, aside from its obvious artistic merits, archaeologically speaking it isn't that important. I only know the textbook basics: four thousand years old, twenty metres tall and carved from something like 120 tonnes of red granite. One of a pair, the other ironically being Cleopatra's London-based needle; they were carved and erected to commemorate the year-thirty Heb Sed Jubilee.' He shrugged his shoulders. 'Anything to add, Dr Pérez?'

'No, you've covered most of it. Although you neglected to mention it's the oldest temple obelisk in Egypt still standing in its original position.'

Hunter's eyes narrowed. 'That's true.' He grinned. 'With so many others plundered for their stone, doesn't that little titbit strike anyone else as a little odd?'

Knight stared at the satellite feed. Hoffmann's hacker was doing a good job. But then again, with little else on the roads at this time of the morning, the heat signature from Hunter's car must be easy to track. 'What are they doing? Are they slowing down?' he asked.

'Looks that way, sir,' replied his driver, a heavyset member of the 135th Egyptian Special Forces Regiment. 'They are in the Al-Matariyyah district near Heliopolis. Would you like me to slow our pursuit until their destination is confirmed?'

Knight drummed his fingers on the passenger window and drew a deep breath. 'Heliopolis? The City of the Sun,' he muttered. 'Where are you taking me, Hunter? What do you know?' He slapped the back of the driver's headrest. 'Give them some space. The last thing I want is for them to jump ship and scatter when we are so close.' He turned to Anderson. 'Do we have any intel regarding the whereabouts of the German?'

'Hoffmann? No, sir. I don't even have confirmation he's landed in the country.'

'Of course he's landed in the bloody country, you idiot. How do you think Hunter got here?'

'Sorry, sir. You're right but our sources have drawn a blank. Maybe he's given up or didn't fly in with the archaeologist.'

'Don't be so naive.' Knight rubbed his eyes and shook his head. 'This is ridiculous: your team receives more money than the rest of our organisation put together, and still this slippery bastard might be strapped to the underside of this car and you'd have no idea.'

Chapter Forty-Nine

Hunter slipped the Evo's gearstick into neutral and engaged the handbrake. 'This is as close as we're going to get in a car. We can walk from here.'

The three academics and the injured police officer stepped onto the deserted pavement. Hunter scanned the street for signs of movement. At least on the face of it, they were alone.

The obelisk dominated the skyline. Lit by four massive floodlights, it stood as a proud monument to the power and influence Heliopolis once commanded. Hunter took the lead and entered the park, signalling for the others to follow. He picked his way through the landscaped gardens, jogging as he closed in on his target. He waved a hand at his companions, urging them to pick up the pace. The sun wasn't far from rising and they couldn't afford to get caught up in the throng of the early-morning foot traffic.

In his periphery he noticed Jack trip and take a heavy tumble on the gravel path. He cried out in agony, gripping his side with both hands. 'Sorry, John, but this isn't happening. I can't carry on. I need to stop or I'll pass out.'

Hunter retraced his steps and pulled Jack to his feet. 'Don't worry about it. No point pushing yourself if it isn't necessary. Go back to the car and rest. I suggest you keep your gun handy, though.' He dropped the car keys into his friend's hand and had an idea. 'As you're going back, can you do me a favour and re-park the car a few streets away? If it is being tracked, moving it might buy us more time. And check the car boot, who knows what delights the previous owner may have squirrelled away. At the very least you might find a bigger gun.'

Jack nodded and turned to leave, clutching his side to stem the bleeding from his torn stitches.

'And then there were three,' said George.

'Can we get a move on? This place is giving me the creeps,' said Inma. 'It's bad enough during the day, but at night it looks like a nuclear wasteland.'

'Not far now. Just be mindful that, however isolated this place looks, there's a good chance we're not alone,' said Hunter, fiddling with the cord of the Atlantean amulet around his neck.

They turned a corner and George darted forward as the base of the obelisk came into view. He knocked Hunter aside and leapt onto the concrete pedestal supporting the obelisk's huge 120-tonne frame. 'Still got it, John boy. I've still got it.' Hunter grinned and watched the panting geologist run his figures over the granite surface. 'It always amazes me how smooth these things are in the flesh,' George continued. 'God only knows how many man-hours went into carving and erecting monuments like this.'

Hunter pulled himself beside George and reached back to assist Inma. Her refusal was predictable, and she scrambled atop the pedestal with a defiant expression on her face. Hunter smiled. 'Please yourself. I was only trying to help.'

Inma's eyes narrowed further. 'Helping degrade an entire gender more like. I bet you wouldn't have considered offering George your hand.'

Hunter winked at her. 'Only because I'm intimidated by his beauty. I mean, look at the legs on it. And as for those moobies… My heart is all of a flutter.'

'Chauvinist.'

'Sorry to break up the courtship guys, but can we get on with this?' interrupted George. 'I don't fancy our chances of avoiding detection during rush hour.'

'Fine by me,' said Inma. 'But now we're here, John, can you please tell us what you expect to find? This site isn't exactly out of the way. If there is something here, what makes you think it hasn't already been removed? Practically speaking, we're not exactly weighed down by digging equipment. Are you proposing we simply push the obelisk over?'

Hunter rubbed his eyes and looked toward the tip of the obelisk. 'Your positivity never fails to amaze, Dr Pérez. And you might be right; someone may have already beaten us to the punch.' He pulled the amulet from his shirt and swung it in front of Inma's startled face. 'Although I'm willing to bet very few people have stood here with the key in the last few centuries.'

'Jesus.' She reached out and cupped the orichalcum artefact in her hands. 'Where the hell did you find this?'

'The cylinder. I guess my subconscious mistrusted Hoffmann from the start.'

Inma's mouth tightened. 'You mean you've held onto this since our first meeting and never thought to tell me?'

'Given your penchant for switching allegiance,' said Hunter, 'I'm pleased I didn't.'

'Well I'm sorry for not having your ability to predict the future. You switched sides as well. We all did what we believed to be right at the time.'

'Shut it, the pair of you,' George hissed. 'Get over here and have a gander at this.' Hunter frowned as he noticed the geologist crouched low against the eastern face of the obelisk and examining a set of hieroglyphs. George pointed a torch at the granite and traced the inscription with its beam. 'Look at the shape,' he whispered. Hunter's heart missed a beat. George tapped the carving. 'Your medallion has been incorporated into this glyph.'

Hunter moved his friend's hand and smiled. 'Hidden within the symbol for the sun god. How very appropriate.'

'The group have split up, sir. Three are heading into the Al-Masalla area and the other has driven off in Mahmood's car. How do you wish us to proceed?'

Knight ran his fingers through his whitening hair and shook his head. 'This has the stench of a diversionary tactic. What do you think, Anderson?'

'I agree.' He cleared his throat. 'But we can't dismiss it. What if the returning driver is Hunter?'

Knight ground his teeth, mulling the dilemma and attempting to put himself in Hunter's shoes. 'True, it could be a double bluff. We have the numbers so let's play it safe. Send a car to investigate. The rest of us will stay with the main party.'

Hunter cursed under his breath. Four thousand years of weathering hadn't done it any favours, and no matter what he tried the amulet refused to bond with the lock.

'Get out the way,' said Inma, shoving him aside. 'This requires a woman's…' At her touch, the worn mechanism clicked and the amulet locked in place. 'Et voilà.'

George rolled his eyes. 'There will be no living with her now.'

Hunter grinned. 'Inma's not one to gloat. Nice work, colleague. Now pray the pass code is still six-one-six.'

'Six-one-six? Is this how you kick-started the Brazilian chamber?' said Inma.

'I'm surprised this is the first time anyone has asked,' said Hunter, talking as he twisted the amulet six rotations to the right. 'Hoffmann even taped the whole thing and still didn't figure it out.'

He sensed George peering over his shoulder. 'Amazing. The lock mechanism must be engineered along the same lines as a modern safe.' The geologist crouched next to him for a closer look. 'Double amazing when you think it took another four thousand years before it was reinvented by Chubb in the 1830s.'

Hunter held his breath. 'This is it, people.' He executed the final rotation. He didn't know what to expect, but hoped for something special; a shower of gold or a few fireworks wouldn't go amiss. The seconds ticked by and nothing happened. The obelisk remained defiant in its silence, as impenetrable as the day of its erection.

'Is it broken?' asked George. Hunter tapped the amulet, willing it to work whatever magic it was designed to weave.

'Maybe the pass code is wrong,' suggested Inma.

'Wait, look there.' George pointed to the base of the obelisk.

Hunter rushed forward, peering over George's shoulder as two lines of blue light broke free of the modern pedestal. They moved at a steady pace, rising up the monument in tandem, about a yard apart. Mesmerised, he watched as, at a height of about three feet, the lines altered their course, each turning ninety degrees and heading on a collision course with the others. The pedestal shuddered as the lines connected.

George grabbed Hunter's arm and fell backwards. 'What the hell is going on?'

'Get off the pedestal,' said Hunter. The academics leapt in unison, their jumps coinciding with the thunderous, rasping sound of tearing rock.

Hunter stumbled and fell, rolling onto his back as a final crack detonated about him. He lifted his head and saw a smattering of startled birds rising from their nests, fleeing the area in terror. 'What the hell was that?'

Inma was the first to get to her feet. 'The modern pedestal must have been built over the entrance. We have to hope the door mechanism is stronger than the pedestal's cement.'

Hunter stared at the deformed pedestal and dusted himself down. The figure of the sun god was no longer visible, replaced instead by a three-foot void of darkness. He shot George a fleeting glance as his stomach turned somersaults and he processed the scene. 'George, if that space is the only way in, you and I both need to start channelling thin thoughts.'

Hunter scrambled to the entrance and offered his hand to Inma. This time she accepted his offer of help and he eased her into the pitch-black corridor beneath the obelisk. George followed with his torch, using it to examine the walls, and patting each of the worked surfaces in turn.

'What are you looking for?' asked Inma, brushing rock dust from her blouse.

'Lights,' said George. 'There's no way a society this advanced overlooked something as basic as light in the dark.'

'The Egyptians used angled mirrors when they worked underground. We may need to wait for sunrise,' said Hunter.

'Mirrors?' scoffed George. 'I'm sure Atlantean technology was way beyond mirrors.'

Hunter turned on his own torch and swept the beam over the smooth ceiling. 'What's that then?' He pointed at a shiny disc-like object wedged into one of the walls.

George rolled his eyes. 'A mirror.'

'What were you expecting, mate? A light switch? At the time the Egyptians built this place, angling mirrors at the sun was the only way to light enclosed spaces.' Hunter paused, frowning as his torch beam illuminated the space. 'The walls are all blank? Weird. Given the time frame, I'd have expected to see images of the gods, animals, battle scenes…'

'Maybe they didn't get round to it,' said Inma. 'They certainly prepared the canvas though. Feel how smooth this plaster is.'

Hunter sniffed the air. It was stale, but breathable. There must be air vents somewhere. He made a mental note to find them, assuming, that is, he ever got the opportunity to excavate. He motioned for the others to follow and stepped into the corridor. After several steps, it became clear the Egyptians had carved a gentle slope into the tunnel. Hunter slowed the pace and made sure to plant each footfall with considered care, mindful of the risk of slipping on the smooth, dust-coated walkway. He locked his eyes on the trail ahead, focusing on the tip of his torch beam, straining for a glimpse of their destination, but to no avail; the bland walls refused to betray any of the secrets they'd been designed to keep.

Hunter staggered. He cried out in pain, his ankle turning on a ridge in the floor. George made a grab for his arm, but too late. He pitched forward, his right foot meeting nothing but thin air. The drop was only a foot, but enough to send him crashing to the floor. He dropped his shoulder, angling his body to protect the torch and the contents of his rucksack. He locked his jaw, sucking up the pain as the smooth flooring gave way to rough granite and tore into his skin, ripping his shirt and staining the sleeve with blood.

'For Christ's sake. I could have done without that.' He rolled over, pushed himself to his knees and brushed the rock dust from his clothing. Why the hell had a random step been carved into the bedrock?

He scrambled to his feet, ready to lash out at George, in part for the lack of help but mostly to cover his own sense of embarrassment. 'I'm fine by the way, thanks for your concern.' George ignored the outburst and walked by, giving him not so much as a glance. 'George, you bast…'

Hunter's anger dissipated. The geologist's focus was elsewhere, his eyes full of wonder and fixed on something over his shoulder. Hunter turned and lifted his torch. The motion was redundant as the hallway lit, the ancient zigzag system of mirrors sparking one after another above his head. The early-morning rays of the risen sun must at last have found their way through the obelisk's entrance. His eyes widened as, little by little, a familiar-looking space emerged from the darkness.

'Christ,' whispered Hunter. 'It's a replica of the chamber in Brazil. Bigger, and there's no sphinx this time.' He darted forward, aware of their limited window with light. It wouldn't be long before the sun rose beyond the tunnel entrance and once again plunged the space into darkness.

'Is this it? There's nothing here,' scoffed George. 'Don't tell me we've come all this way for an empty room? Bloody tomb raiders.'

'It can't be empty,' said Inma, sweeping her hands over the white-plastered walls. 'Otherwise why the light source? The Egyptians only required light when working on inscriptions or artwork. They must have been doing something down here.'

Hunter rubbed his shoulder. 'Look for indentations in the walls or floors. The Brazilian chamber was also blank before I activated it.'

'What do you think I'm doing?' snapped Inma. 'Ordering muffins?'

Hunter watched her and set about patching himself up. He ripped away part of his shirt and tied it about his shoulder to stem the bleeding. George yelled, making him jump. He twisted to meet the danger, grasping for his gun and expecting the worst.

'Put that away, you prize turnip. Why is shooting something always your first thought?' said George. 'Come over here, I've found something.'

Hunter let the gun drop into its holster, joining the stooped geologist in the chamber's centre, and watched as he brushed away dust and debris from a section of the floor. He bent to examine the find, child-like excitement bubbling inside his stomach and masking the pain in his shoulder. 'What is it?'

George moved aside, revealing a shallow hole no bigger than the tip of his finger.

Inma gave up on the walls and joined them. She sucked in a breath and beamed at George. 'Is that what I think it is?'

George returned her grin. 'I hope so, Pérez, me old mucker. Go on,' he urged. 'Try it, it's got to fit.'

Hunter furrowed his brow. 'Am I missing something here?'

Inma smiled. 'It's not nice when people leave you out of the loop is it, Dr Hunter?' She stood and pulled a cord necklace from her cleavage, dangling a bead of orichalcum in Hunter's eyeline. The initial shock gave way to joy. Inma was right. Hell, this time even George was right. The hole was for an orichalcum bead. It simply had to be.

'George,' said Hunter, clamping his hands on his friend's shoulders. 'I think you've just found your light switch.'

Inma wrenched the orichalcum free of its bonds and looked at Hunter, her hand hovering above the vacant opening. She let the bead drop from her fingertips. It bounced, fleetingly lingering on the hole's edge before tumbling inside. The result was instantaneous; the surrounding rock flashed blue five times in quick succession, each flash coinciding with a line of blue light emerging from the bead. Each line diverted left at around two inches, joining the others and arcing to form a perfect circle around the flashing speck of ancient material.

Thirty seconds passed. George cocked his head to one side. 'There must be more to it than a circle with a few lines running through it,' he said. 'You get to see a set of maps, thousands of years in the making and all I get is… whatever this is. John, tell me I haven't risked my life for a bloody circle?'

'Don't be so naive,' said Hunter. 'This is the opening credits. Now we've got to figure out how to kick-start the main feature.' He extended a finger and traced the circle's perimeter. It wobbled at his touch. A smile spread across his face. 'Bingo.'

Hunter gripped the edge with his fingernails and teased it free from the floor. He fell backwards, the granite plug coming away in his hand and popping free with a hiss of trapped air. He scurried forward, bending to examine the perfect four-inch hole left in its wake. Hunter tossed the plug to George and pulled the rucksack from his back.

'It has to be,' he whispered. He fumbled with the zip, his greasy fingers struggling for purchase on the little metal tag. He reached inside and grasped hold of his prize, his hands re-emerging with the Atlantean cylinder.

'Four-inch diameter anyone?' Hunter tapped the circular end in triumph. 'If Inma's bead is the switch, I have a feeling this beauty is the key.'

Chapter Fifty

Obelisk Chamber, Heliopolis

The ground shook, loosening a layer of plaster and coating the three academics in a film of white dust.

Hunter coughed and steadied himself. 'What the bloody hell was that?'

George shook his head and ruffled his hair, sending a second plume of dust into the air. 'Sounded like a bomb. Maybe Jack found something better than a gun in that stupid orange car? I hope he's not done anything daft.'

'Should we assume Jacob et al have worked out where we are?' said Inma, flicking bits of plaster back in George's direction.

Hunter gripped the Atlantean cylinder and collapsed to his knees. 'If they have, I suggest we dispense with ceremony and just get on with it.' He bent forward and aligned the cylinder with the hole, easing the tip inside to test the size. 'It fits,' he whispered. He grasped the heavy artefact in both hands, continuing to slide it into the floor until only his fingertips remained in contact. His forearms quivered as the weight became too much, and he let go. The cylinder dropped the final inch, hitting the base with a satisfying thud. Hunter held his breath, all the while stealing furtive glances at his companions and the chamber walls.

'What happens now?' asked George.

'Perhaps we should try putting the rock plug back on top, like a battery,' suggested Inma.

Hunter eased onto his haunches and stood. 'I guess it's worth a try. George?'

George pulled the round piece of granite from his pocket and lowered it into position, sealing it in place with a tap of his hand. The results were as immediate as they were impressive. The white plaster walls erupted with a sea of colour, inscriptions and pictures appearing almost at will all around the chamber, each of them highlighted and framed by the familiar, pale blue light of Atlantis.

A distant bang sounded way above their heads and the ground shuddered again, this time dislodging a larger section of plaster. It hit the floor with a resounding slap, missing George by mere centimetres. Spooked, the geologist darted for the exit. 'John, we have to get out of here. The earlier explosion must have weakened the integrity of the chamber. We can come back when it's safe. This isn't worth dying for.'

Hunter grasped George's arm, and turned him about. 'George, you know this is once in a lifetime. Leave now and you know we'll never see this chamber again. If Jacob Knight gets his way, we won't even see out the day. We have to make this count now. There is no other choice.'

Inma whistled to get their attention. 'Enough bickering. George, look at the back wall and tell me you still want to leave.'

Hunter followed her gaze. She pointed her torch at an exquisite example of Egyptian artwork, the scene dominated by a carving of the sun god, who stood atop the Earth and was holding a huge land mass above his head. The piece perhaps proved the Atlantean rulers saw themselves as a higher race, but it was no more or less extraordinary than anything covering the other walls.

'What am I looking at?' said George, apparently also confused. 'You can't expect me to risk my life to save a set of drawings.' He turned to leave.

'Wait,' said Inma. 'You need to see it from this angle.'

Hunter looked again, still unsure what Inma was getting at. A shadow obscured some of the inscriptions but other than that... Then it hit him. His body numbed. Flat surfaces don't cast shadows. Something had moved from the wall and out into the chamber. He rushed forward and gasped, hit in the gut by a surge of exaltation. A four-foot section of the chamber wall had edged forward. His jaw tightened, the miracle of engineering verging on the insignificant as his eyes focused upon what lay in its wake. Hunter stared at his two friends, and pointed inside the hole in a state of stunned disbelief. George flicked on his torch and angled its beam into the dark cavity.

A collective hush fell across the chamber as the light raked the shadowy recess, illuminating hundreds of rolls of papyrus; the dry, moisture-free atmosphere was perfect for their preservation.

'Oh my god,' George hissed. 'It's a bloody library.'

'I'll raise your "Oh my god" and go with…' said Hunter.

'Speechless… speechless is better,' said Inma. 'Christ, if we go public, this lot will put finds like the Dead Sea Scrolls in the same category as broken pottery.'

Hunter stood rooted to the spot, his brain unable to comprehend or even process the consequences of what he was seeing. 'I'm not sure how Hoffmann will conquer the world with paper, but from an academic point of view…' He steadied himself on the jutting wall. 'Guys, I think we've just hit the jackpot.'

George looked relieved. 'Maybe we will get through this in one piece after all.'

Hunter forced his leaden legs to move and shuffled around the granite wall plug. He crouched with reverence beside the stash of ancient paperwork. 'Could you lot really be the weapon everyone is searching for?' he whispered. 'Please don't just be another clue.'

He reached inside the recess, trying to determine its depth, and felt his way past tens upon tens of thick papyrus rolls.

'Are they in good nick?' asked George.

Hunter nodded. 'Seem to be. This makeshift safe has done an excellent preservation job.' He eased his fingers underneath one of the topmost rolls and gently inched it free of its ancient hiding place. 'Please don't rip, please don't rip… George, bit of help please?' George rushed to his side, taking the other end of the roll before it dropped. The two men shuffled toward the granite plug and laid the papyrus on top.

'An exact fit,' said George. 'I'm betting that isn't a coincidence. This thing is even the right height for a reading desk.'

Hunter held his breath, barely registering Inma's arm as it snaked about his shoulders. He unfurled the papyrus, his gaze fixating on the hieroglyphic script revealed by each twist of his wrist.

'It's a relatively modern form,' said Inma. 'Although, since you took it from the top, I guess that's not a surprising revelation.'

'You're right,' said Hunter. He pointed to a symbol. 'This one has only been in use for little over two thousand years.'

'Ties in nicely with the date we have for Lindow Man,' said George. 'If the key disappeared on his death, then it stands to reason we're the first visitors since the time of Christ.'

Hunter blew the air from his lungs. 'Funny you should choose to mention him.' He rubbed his face in disbelief. 'Shit, Pérez, are you reading what I'm reading?' Inma glanced at him with watery eyes, a pained and distant expression of shock etched on her face.

'What?' said George. 'I'm not picking up any good vibes here. What does it say?'

Hunter spun around, pulling out more and more rolls of papyrus, anger and fear replacing any concern for their historical value.

'What's going on, John? What are you doing? Have you gone mad? Inma, do something! Can somebody just tell me what's going on?'

Hunter clicked his fingers at George. 'Your notebook and pen, quick.' George handed them over and Hunter swept through the pages in a blur of ink, adding line upon line with each fresh section of papyrus he unfurled. Ten minutes passed before he finally sighed in defeat, sinking to the floor and hanging his head. He ripped the pages from the notepad and passed them to George.

He flicked through them and stared at Hunter, a look of bewilderment in his eyes. 'What do these mean? You've just noted down a few famous figures from history.'

'Religious history,' replied Hunter, his voice hoarse.

'You mean he isn't the only one?' asked Inma.

'He was just the last one.'

George shook his head. 'Come on guys, enough now. Stop talking in code and tell me what's going on.'

Hunter stretched his arms above his head and got back to his feet. 'Two words, my friend. Organised and religion.' George nodded, although it was clear he still didn't understand where Hunter was leading him. 'That is our weapon. It was never a gun, or bomb, or aircraft, or even a ship. The Atlantis weapon is simply a concept.'

'Organised religion?' George repeated.

'Yup,' said Hunter. 'Hindsight is a wonderful thing, but it fits. We were all so concerned with Hoffmann's water-boiling gun, an Order fabrication I expect, we all fell into the trap of approaching the evidence with that bias. As practising academics, we all should have known better.'

'Who was the "last one" you mentioned?' said George, making quotation marks with his fingers.

'Jesus of Nazareth,' said Inma, a bitter tone to her voice. She let the information sink in. 'The passage details an attempt to overhaul Judaism and the polytheism of Roman Europe. The authors intended to create a new religious banner the world could unite under.'

'Is this some kind of bad-taste joke?' asked George.

Hunter shook his head. 'The scribe describes how his Order drugged and impregnated a local woman, confining her to their temple until she showed signs of being with child. Her marriage to an Order member followed, a man tasked with reinforcing and convincing the woman her womb held the seed of God.'

'Bloody hell,' exclaimed George. 'You're talking about the Holy Family.'

'I always wondered why Joseph accepted Mary as his wife,' said Inma. 'Women of the time were usually stoned to death for similar offences.'

'Come on people,' said George. 'I may be a lapsed Catholic, but this is surely blasphemy of the highest order.'

'Interesting choice of words.' Hunter pointed at the notebook. 'Skip to the end. The entry ends with a prophetic statement of support for the child: "We will return to Nazareth when the boy they call Jesus comes of age. We will ensure he unites and brings peace to our world."'

Inma rolled her eyes. 'I'm guessing the violence and bloodshed following Christ's death were never part of the plan.'

He leant forward, collecting the documents scattered about his feet. 'They all follow the same theme, each scroll describing societal manipulation using religion as their so-called "weapon" of choice. The Greek Pantheon. Abraham. Moses. Even Akhenaten's attempt at monotheism in Egypt is documented.'

'The earliest text suggests the original plan was to export and impose Atlantean principles of monotheism on whatever populations they came across. Two deities, the sun ruling the heavens and Sirius, the brightest star, ruling the underworld.'

'The model adopted in Egypt?' said George.

'And even then, only in part,' said Hunter. 'It's clear that once faced with the reality of dealing with actual people, the Atlantean priests were forced by circumstance to adapt their model, tailoring it to the whims and psychology of individual communities.' Hunter gestured at the stash of scrolls to his left. 'And these are the proof. Each sheet of papyrus records a different integration strategy.'

George scuffed his foot, sneezing as another plume of plaster dust rose from the floor. 'Okay, but why would these societies welcome the Atlantean priests at all? Why wouldn't the incumbent leaders just kick them out on their arses?'

'I expect they did from time to time,' said Hunter. 'But it's clear many adopted the doctrines of faith thrust upon them.'

'Yes, but my question is still, why?'

'Ever heard the phrase "you'll always find God in a foxhole"?' said Hunter. The skin on George's forehead creased into a frown.

'What John's trying to say, albeit badly,' Inma interrupted, 'is that religion is often the last haven for the poor, the needy and those near death. You need to take into account how brutal daily life was during the infancy of civilisation. Disease, poverty, crime, murder; all pressing issues in societies where only the strongest survived.' George moistened his lips and nodded. 'Now throw religion into the mix,' she continued. 'Charismatic priests and prophets offering the downtrodden a way out. The concept was simple. Behave in life and be rewarded in death with a first-class ticket into heaven. When life was so hard, who wouldn't take that deal?'

George nodded. 'But what about the guys in charge? They must have felt threatened by this shift in power.'

'Quite the opposite,' said Hunter. 'In fact the implementation of organised religion was tantamount to the creation of law and order. The elite were pleased to incorporate religion into their societies. Religious law was a viable and successful means of suppressing and controlling a growing population. The fear of losing one's place in paradise was enough to subdue even the most desperate of men.'

'He who controls the afterlife, controls life itself,' said Inma.

George stroked his chin. 'If this is true, then why aren't the pair of you jumping for joy? We're sitting on conclusive proof exposing the origins of organised religion and you're acting like someone's died.'

Hunter clicked his tongue against the back of his throat and shook his head. 'If either of us published our findings, what do you suppose might happen?' He clamped his hands on George's shoulders and stared into his eyes. 'Our find flies in the face of the beliefs of millions and millions of Christians, Jews and who knows how many others.' He slapped a hand against a wall in frustration, sidestepping a chunk of plaster as it crashed to the floor. 'And what would we say? Religion is a fraudulent concept.' He turned and pretended to address an audience. 'Oh hello everyone, nice of you to come out. Okay, so the core of everything you believe is rubbish; Jesus was a plant and God a myth designed to keep you in your place and make clever people rich. Now you know, please carry on with your lives.' He gave George a gentle shove. 'Best case we'd get laughed at. Worst case, shot at.'

A slow clap echoed about the chamber. The hair on Hunter's neck stood on end and his limbs stiffened. Knight emerged from the shadow of the corridor, the portly priest dressed to the nines in full Druidic ceremonial regalia.

'Dr Hunter, I see you've uncovered our big, not so secret, secret? I guess a thank you is in order. We might never have rediscovered this archive without you.'

Hunter bit into his lip and drew blood. Knight's scarred bodyguard stepped into the chamber, smirking at him as he flanked his employer. They were joined by another three soldiers, each of them toting machine guns of varying lethality, all aimed in his direction. 'Am I to assume your Order can take credit for the invention of God?'

Knight smiled and smoothed a crease from his robe. 'We didn't invent God, John. We merely manipulated the mechanism for his worship. Whether God, or multiple gods, exists is not for me to say. Only the dead know for sure.' He clicked his fingers, feigning an idea. 'Perhaps you can leave us a sign when you find out for yourself.' He laughed, pleased by his joke, and paused to examine his new surroundings. Hunter watched as the priest's fingers snaked about the mural of a sea creature attacking an Atlantean boat. 'Amazing. Simply amazing.'

He closed his eyes as George piped up from behind him, dreading what the geologist might say. 'Dress it up how you like, but the greed of your predecessors and their lust for power only succeeded in fracturing our society. They did far more harm than good.'

'Ah, Dr Goodheart, my other purveyor of misinformation, nice of you to chip in with your two pennies,' sneered Knight. He nodded at the papyrus documents scattered about Hunter's feet. 'Don't those confirm the original plan was of noble intention however it later morphed? Unification was attempted with Christ and later at the council of Nicaea. It nearly worked until the prophet Mohammed popped up and ruined it all.'

'So instead of unity, the world was left with two huge conflicting armies, both hell-bent on conquering or converting the other,' said Hunter.

Knight's eyes narrowed. 'The soldiers of Christ were given all available resources.'

'What about your story about Zeus and the weapon?' said Inma, finding her voice.

'Our profiling of Dr Hunter suggested he'd believe a tale of that type,' Knight snapped. He turned his back on the academics and examined another inscription, ending the conversation. Hunter inched his arm behind his back. If he could just reach his gun...

He froze as Knight swung the barrel of a silver Colt in his direction. 'Hands where I can see them, John. I'm afraid there'll be no escaping this time. I'm sure you'll understand why.' The priest drew a Zippo lighter from his robes and gestured for Anderson to step forward. Hunter shuddered. He and two of his men each carried a jerrycan. *So this was how they intended to cover their tracks*. Knight waved an arm at the chamber and locked his eyes on Hunter, almost daring him to make a move.

Anderson grinned and emptied a little of the can's flammable contents onto his gloved hand, flicking it into Hunter's face. The stench of petroleum overwhelmed him. He sank to his knees, tears streaming from his burning eyes. 'Just let us go,' he pleaded. 'We won't talk. If you're destroying the evidence, who would believe us anyway?'

'A chance my organisation is unwilling to take,' said Knight.

Hunter watched in dread as the priest spun the Zippo's ignition disc, the cascade of sparks prompting a two-inch jet of fire to rise from the lighter's casing. Knight bent forward, his callous features exaggerated by shadows thrown against the walls by the flickering flame. The light provided by the Atlantean mirrors was fading fast.

A soft tinkling sound breached the silence of the chamber. Knight paused, looking down at Hunter in confusion. The sound disappeared. They can't both have imagined it. Hunter cocked his head to one side and strained his ears. There it was again, louder this time. Something was making its way down the corridor. Knight twisted to face the threat, the flame in his hand accenting an expression of wide-eyed panic.

Hunter anticipated what was coming and shoulder-barged Knight, catching him square in the small of the back. He staggered and lost his balance, cursing Hunter as he fell. Hunter ignored the insult, focused instead on pulling his friends behind the granite desk. He forced their heads to the ground as the sound of a tortured scream from one of Knight's men reverberated about the chamber. 'Grenade, fire in the hole.'

A series of blinding flashes filled the space. Hunter clamped his hands to his head as the resultant trio of blasts rained down death on all sides. Plaster and exposed earth crashed into the chamber, all evidence of the Atlantean inscriptions disappearing and fading back to black. Hunter pulled his feet further into cover as the blast tugged at his exposed feet, debris slicing into his clothes and skin without remorse. The ordeal lasted seconds but death's proximity aged Hunter immeasurably. He wiped a tear from his cheek and poked his head above the protective cover of the wall. The decimated chamber stretched out before him, a series of widening cracks streaking about the walls and threatening collapse.

He picked out the mangled bodies of three men, their limbs twisted in ungodly positions on the chamber floor. Knight was slumped against the wall opposite, coughing blood and grasping at a bloodied stump once comprising his right leg. He'd survived, but for how much longer was anyone's guess. He could see Anderson's jerrycan on its side, protected from the blast by the henchman's body, but now leaking fuel. They needed to get out of here fast; a stray spark would spell the end for them.

Hunter moved from his hiding place and stumbled, tripping on something solid. A military-grade boot wobbled across the floor. Hunter kicked it away, choking back vomit as a protruding bone swung about and knocked against his ankle. He rose, ploughing forward, still dazed, ears ringing but determined the chamber would not become his tomb. The clicking sound of a cocking gun stopped him in his tracks. Hunter reached for his own weapon but his foe was quicker, his hand slapped from his belt as the cold steel of a 9mm barrel bit into the underside of his chin. He looked back to Anderson's body. It was no longer there.

'Tut tut, Hunter. You'll have to do better than that.' The blood-stained face of Knight's number two loomed into view, his trademark smirk spreading across his thin lips. 'I assume those grenades were a present from your friend, Mr Hoffmann?' He spat a mouthful of blood to the floor.

Hunter puffed out his chest and met Anderson's cold eyes, trying his best to conceal the fear in his heart. 'He's no friend of mine. He's as likely to murder me as you are.'

'Liar,' hissed Anderson, jamming the gun still further into Hunter's throat. 'I should have shot you when I had the chance back in that fucking Brazilian prison.'

Hunter started, his blood cooling in his veins. His breathing quickened as repressed memories of torturous sessions with an unknown assailant bubbled to the forefront of his brain. The face never revealing itself, the recollections too painful as they accompanied the unbearable agony of whips tearing flesh from his back, towels pulled taught over his mouth as water filled his lungs and the sound of electrodes sparking before clamping down on exposed skin. A flash of recognition flickered in his subconscious. The scar. His blindfold had slipped and he'd seen the outline of a scar; a scar merged with a smug and never-ending sneer. Anderson was his Brazilian torturer. He screamed and swung an uncontrolled punch born of long-suppressed hate.

Anderson ducked and landed a heavy counter in Hunter's gut. He doubled over, winded and in pain. The underside of a heavy boot connected with his hip, knocking him down and pinning him against the floor. 'So you've finally remembered. I'd have thought it was obvious. What other organisation would have wasted so much time beating an Atlantis archaeologist? I always knew you were hiding something. The soft fool dying in the corner over there saved your life, insisted I let you go. Personally I'd have flayed your skin and fed it to the rats.'

Hunter shook off the blow and kicked out with both feet, aiming for Anderson's kneecap. He saw it coming and parried the blow, using Hunter's momentum to spin him onto his front and lock an arm behind his back.

Anderson holstered his gun and bent to Hunter's ear. He could feel the warmth of his stale breath and the prickle of day-old stubble against his cheek. 'I'm not wasting a bullet on you. You don't deserve it,' he whispered. There was a swish of metal on leather. 'I'm going to cut you nice and slow. By the time I'm done you'll be begging for that bullet.'

'You talk too much.' Hunter twisted his head and, using his only remaining weapon, sank his teeth into the bodyguard's exposed neck. Anderson screamed, his flesh ripping as he wrenched himself free. He clapped a hand against the wound and raised his knife, any plans for a slow death abandoned. Hunter rolled onto his back, and met Anderson's murderous gaze head on. He made a grab for his gun and heard a soft popping sound. The henchman's eyes narrowed in confusion, relaxing into an expression of lifeless indifference. The knife dropped from his hand, embedding upright in a clump of loose plaster. Baffled, he watched Anderson topple forward, blood dribbling from his mouth, dead before he hit the floor.

Hunter scuttled back in horror, snatching Anderson's discarded knife and scanning the chamber for signs of movement. His heart rate peaked as he caught sight of a huge silhouette hunched over Knight's incapacitated body. It could only be Darren. His senses returning, Hunter snatched the papyrus documents lying untouched atop the wall and stuffed them inside his shirt. He turned to face his friends, frowning as George yelled and pointed to his rear. Something heavy smashed against his wrist, the blow knocking the knife from his grasp and sending it skidding across the floor. Someone rammed a blunt instrument into the small of his back. Hunter raised his hands. Lady Luck was definitely not playing fair.

Chapter Fifty-One

Hoffmann slapped Hunter with a rolled section of petroleum-soaked papyrus. It stung, ripping on impact and sticking to his cheek. He peeled it free and flicked it back at the German. Hoffmann dodged left and grabbed Hunter's collar, hauling him to his feet and jamming a gun in his gut.

'Where is it?' he hissed. 'Where's the fucking weapon?'

Hunter met Hoffmann's gaze and snorted, shoving him away and twisting out of the hold. 'Maybe you should ask him,' he whispered, pointing at Knight.

Hoffmann eyed the priest with suspicion. 'Why, what's he done with it?'

Hunter spat a mouthful of bloody phlegm. 'Haven't you worked it out? There never was a weapon. Not in the physical sense anyway.'

The colour drained from the German's face, anger replaced by an expression of dread. 'What do you mean, not in the physical sense?'

'It was religion, Hans. The weapon was organised religion,' said Inma.

The German's right eye twitched and he pushed away from Hunter, rubbing his temples in disbelief.

Hunter gestured at Knight. 'His Order used religion to amalgamate with surviving societies after Atlantis sank.'

Hoffmann wobbled. He looked on the verge of fainting. 'And in so doing Atlantis conquered the armies of the Earth without bearing arms or suffering a single casualty.' Hunter nodded. 'And these papers corroborate this? There is no super gun?'

Hunter shook his head, wondering if the German was capable of processing such a deflationary blow. His mind must be racing. Did he have a back-up plan? Without the physical threat of the Atlantean weapon, his plans to install himself as a European dictator must be crumbling by the second.

Hoffmann paced the chamber and planted himself beside Jacob Knight. He glanced at an open wound, oozing blood from the priest's remaining leg. He tutted and prodded it with the barrel of his gun.

Knight grimaced, sucking air through clenched teeth as he tried to contain the pain.

'So you were just using me to find your lost library?' said Hoffmann. 'I personally find that a little selfish. What do you think Darren?'

Darren shrugged, his gun still trained on Hunter.

Knight turned to stare up into the eyes of his enemy. 'Mr Hoffmann, I presume?' Hoffmann nodded. The faintest of smiles flickered across the priest's chapped lips. 'Good... Then I am sorry to inform you of your loss.'

Hoffmann adopted a look of mock confusion. 'My loss?' He shook his head. 'You must be mistaken, sir. I'm sitting on a cache of documents worth billions, and in the driving seat to expose your pathetic Order for the relic it is.' He tapped Knight on the cheek. 'You, on the other hand, have a gun pointed at your head and no more than thirty seconds to live. So, dearest Jacob, please enlighten me as to why you are sorry for my loss?'

'My death is meaningless,' Knight croaked, coughing yet more blood onto his saturated shirt. 'My successor will never allow you to publicise your finds. Even if you do, who will believe you?' He snorted. 'Blind belief is more powerful a weapon than you'll ever understand.' He scowled. 'Not that I will let you survive long enough to find out...' With an inhuman display of mental strength, Knight raised a shredded arm and opened his fist.

Hoffmann looked at the naked flame and turned to Hunter, his face contorting into an expression of blind panic. Hunter's eyes widened, and he scrambled for cover, joining Inma and George behind the Atlantean desk as the Zippo tumbled through the air and hit the centre of the petrol-soaked floor. Three crisp gunshots and a guttural scream reverberated about the chamber, their origins lost as Anderson's jerrycan exploded and a rush of flames engulfed the chamber.

The fire's initial intensity waned as the fuel burnt away. Hunter risked a quick peek and pulled away in disbelief. Hoffmann must have used Knight as a shield, the latter dead and burning inside his robes. A deathly grin adorned the priest's face; a smoking gun, combined with Hoffmann's pained shrieks, made it apparent why. The German's movement was frantic. He tried in vain to pull himself upright, but slid back to the floor in a bloody heap. Knight's aim had been true, a bullet travelling through the centre of each of his kneecaps.

'Darren?' screamed Hoffmann. 'I need help. Carry me.' Darren looked at his employer. There was no evidence of empathy or pity in his eyes. He glanced at the archaeologists and turned, jogging up the corridor without uttering a word.

Hunter glanced at George and shrugged. 'Serves him right.'

George prodded the dead soldier to their left. 'He was one of Hoffmann's men, wasn't he? Who shot him? Not Darren?'

'He must have done. Unless Jacob fired all three shots.'

'Who the hell cares?' shouted Inma. 'Let's go already. The fire is getting closer. We don't want to be here when the library goes up behind us.'

Hunter nodded and pulled a water bottle from his rucksack, scattering the contents liberally over his arms and legs. 'I suggest you two do the same.'

Inma and George followed his example and doused their bodies in water.

'Now run,' screamed Hunter, thrusting his friends toward the corridor. The pair skipped through the blaze and beat the flames from each other's clothing.

'Everyone okay?'

'I might need a touch of Savlon, but we're alive,' George shouted back. 'Now get your arse over here.'

Hunter didn't need telling twice, vaulting the Atlantean desk as another jerrycan ignited and a second fireball engulfed the library alcove. He darted forward, his feet skipping over the ground as he dodged and weaved the pockets of fire. The brief seconds it took to negotiate the chamber felt like a lifetime before he collapsed, coughing and spluttering alongside George, his lungs struggling for oxygen as smoke filled the space.

Inma tipped the remains of her water over Hunter's burns and pulled him to his feet. 'Come on, John. No time to rest. We've got to get out of here now.'

He rolled onto all fours, ready for the last push, but a pained cry stopped him in his tracks. He yanked on Inma's arm, jolting her to a stop. It was Hoffmann. The German was still alive.

'What are you doing?' said Inma, pulling him toward the exit. 'Leave him. He wouldn't go back for you.'

Hunter wrenched free of her grip, a confusing combination of pity and hate for the dying man welling in his gut. He couldn't leave him. No one deserved to die like this. He ripped a sleeve from his shirt and tied it about his mouth and nose. Inma shook her head and disappeared after George, leaving Hunter to inch his way back inside the chamber. He saw Hoffmann turn his head, his hands clawing the air in panic as Hunter knelt beside him. 'I'm here to help you, fool. Let me take your weight.' He hauled the German to his feet, bracing his legs as he took his weight.

'Thank you,' Hoffmann croaked.

'Don't thank me. Death is too easy an escape for your crimes.' He staggered to the comparative safety of the corridor, reaching the incline as the flames licked at the third and final canister of gasoline. Hunter heard a hiss and a popping sound as the container's lid blew into the air. He closed his eyes and awaited the inevitable.

The orange tsunami of fire caught him in the back like a punch from a heavyweight and knocked him to the floor. Dazed, he writhed on the ground, rolling back and forth to extinguish the flames from his already charred clothing. Hoffmann whimpered somewhere to his right. Hunter reached for him, his fingers finding the collar of the German's jacket. He forced him to his feet and, fighting the pain, focused on planting one foot after another, each step a victory in his head. His will to survive was strong but the pinprick of light at the tunnel's end only seemed to get smaller. He redoubled his efforts, determined today would not be his day to die. Powered by adrenaline alone, he finally fell to his knees, bathing in the slither of golden sunshine atop the sunken entrance. He let Hoffmann drop from his shoulders and eased himself free of the obelisk. Where was George? Where was Inma? He blinked as his eyes adjusted to the bright light and yelled for his friends.

The pair of singed and blackened academics rushed to his aid, propping him up and forcing water into his parched mouth.

'Are you okay?' Inma fretted. 'John, can you hear me? What happened down there?'

Hunter coughed, expelling the last of the smoke from his lungs. 'I'm f…'

A hoarse voice cut through his reply. 'I really wish you hadn't saved me.' The trio turned in unison. Hoffmann had pulled himself clear of the monument like an enormous slug, a trail of blood in his wake. He cocked a small Derringer handgun and waved it at Hunter. 'Conscience-wise, it makes it that little bit harder for me to kill you.'

'I expect you'll muddle through,' said Hunter. 'Where were you hiding that thing?'

'Strapped it to my ankle as a back-up. Lucky I did – I'm sure you'll agree it'd be wrong for me to leave anyone alive to blacken my family name.' Hoffmann squeezed the trigger, his mouth narrowing into a malicious grin.

Hunter jumped as a shot rang out. He patted his body, expecting blood and searing pain, but there was nothing. Had he missed? Surely not from six feet. He looked at the German in confusion. The gun of Himmler's crazed grandson was still aimed in his direction, but something had changed. Hoffmann's eyes glazed and his head toppled forward, hitting the concrete with a resounding thud.

A familiar voice cried out. 'A present from Paul, you sick son of a bitch.'

Hunter twisted to see Jack stagger into the clearing. He was dragging a huge and recently discharged sniper rifle, probably from the Evo. His appearance coincided with a sea of screeching tyres, sirens and flashing blue lights. The chasing pack of police cars had finally caught up with their prey. Jack dropped the rifle and placed both hands on his head. The former police officer smiled and winked at Hunter. He sank to his knees amid a volley of hostile orders from the lead police car.

Hunter waved back and pulled two charred papyrus rolls from his belt. He raised them for Jack to see and glanced at his two friends. Maybe he should have let them burn. Was the world ready for the truth? How would it handle it? Maybe bury its collective head as Knight predicted but, then again, maybe it wouldn't. Surely, however slim the possibility, if he could play a part in releasing the world from the shackles of so many disparate religions, then he should take it. He alone had the power to kick-start the Atlantean dream: unifying the people of Earth under a single banner, creating a world free of prejudice, free of borders and free of war. We all bleed red, regardless of geography, skin colour or faction. It took a catastrophic disaster for Atlantis to acknowledge this fact; what would it take for the modern world to realise the same?

An Egyptian police officer snatched the documents from his hand and forced him to the ground. Hunter smiled as the handcuffs bit into his wrists. Whatever happened next, it would be one hell of a ride.

Epilogue
The Giza Plateau, Cairo

Lucy Donovan stared up into the eyes of the Sphinx, the midday heat creating a haze on the desert floor and a fuzzy halo about the giant sculpture's head. This was so boring. She'd voted for Florida and they'd ended up here, surrounded by flies and litter whipping about her feet. The guide said something about the Sahu region of the sky and Orion. What did she care? She was thirteen and more concerned as to why her boyfriend Saul still hadn't replied to her text.

She yelped as a rat scurried past her foot, disappearing into a tiny hole at the foot of the right paw of the Sphinx. The hole opened up behind it and sand poured through the opening. Intrigued, she glanced at her parents. They were too engrossed in the dull history lesson to notice. Lucy sighed and ambled toward the hole, activating the torch on her phone. She tentatively pointed the device inside, half expecting the rat to dart back out. Her bravery increased as nothing happened and she scraped away at the sand, expanding the opening. She could hear the distinctive sound of falling sand, dropping and hitting something far below.

She forced her arm into the gap, and froze in terror. The ground jolted beneath her, supporting her momentarily before giving way and sucking her under the paw of the Sphinx. She screamed, slipping and sliding further and further from the safety of the daylight. With a sickening crack, she squealed in pain as her flailing left arm smacked against something solid and hung limp at her side. Her phone slid to a stop beside her and Lucy could hear her parents shouting her name. She yelled back and winced as she tried to move her fingers.

'I think I've broken my arm.'

'Stay still, help is on the way,' shouted her dad. 'Don't move.'

Lucy rolled her eyes and lifted the phone. The torch was still switched on and instantly illuminated the space. A huge, cylindrical object dominated the pitch-black room – pitch black with the exception of two rings, each glowing blue and stamped into the cylinder's side, one ring centred inside the other...

Patrons

Shaz B
Guy Banham
Scott Cann
Kate Charles
Jonty Cowan
Jamie Crocker
Rob Crocker
Mark Dance
Renata Dymek
John Elliott
Andrea Goodheart
Neil Grady
Michael Jenkins
Chris Kemp
Jeremy Krause
Ann Manning
Wendy Mullee
Paul Nichols
Michael D. Owens
Lesley Parker
Charlotte Peppard
Kim Reed
Carol Sayles
Thomas Searle
Stuart Shaw
Lesley Sinfield
Henriette B. Stavis
James Sykes
George Daisie Tregunna
Karen Ward
Simon Ware
Charlie Waters